Instrument of Slaughter

By Edward Marston

Instrument of Slaughter

EDWARD MARSTON

Allison & Busby Limited
12 Fitzroy Mews
London W1T 6DW
www.allisonandbusby.com

First published in Great Britain by Allison & Busby in 2012.

A CIP catalogue record for this book is available from
the British Library.

First Edition

ISBN 978-0-7490-0995-3

Typeset in 12/18 pt Adobe Garamond Pro by
Allison & Busby Ltd.

The paper used for this Allison & Busby publication
has been produced from trees that have been legally sourced
from well-managed and credibly certified forests.

Printed and bound by
CPI Group (UK) Ltd, Croydon, CR0 4YY

To our delightful granddaughter,
Seren Rose,
a new star in the family

CHAPTER ONE

January, 1916

The meeting was held in secret. Though they had similar views and shared objectives, they did not want to discuss them in a pub where they were likely to be mocked and vilified. In a time of war, pacifism was a stigma for able-bodied young men. Each one of them had his own collection of white feathers, contemptuous glances and harsh reproaches. Pressure to enlist grew more intense by the day.

'Where's Gordon?' asked Cyril Ablatt, impatiently.

'He swore that he'd be here,' said Mansel Price.

'Then why isn't he?'

'God knows!'

'He can't have forgotten,' said Fred Hambridge. 'It's not like Gordon to be late. Shall I go and look for him?'

'No,' said Ablatt, firmly. 'We'll wait.'

Ablatt was the leader of the group and they'd arranged to meet that evening in the shed at the bottom of his garden. Small and cluttered, it was used as a workshop by Ablatt's father in his spare time. Hambridge, a carpenter by trade, was interested in the various tools on display, not that he could see them all by the light of the candles that provided the only illumination. There was no source of heat and it was bitterly cold. All three of them wore coats, hats, scarves and gloves. They'd been close friends at school and – though they'd gone off in different directions – war had brought them back together again. Ablatt was a tall, slim individual with striking good looks and a confident manner. He worked in the local library where he regularly fielded hostile questions about why he'd so far failed to join the army to fight for King and Country. He always defended his position in a polite but robust manner.

Hambridge was a big, ugly, misshapen, red-haired young man with freckled features and a look of permanent bewilderment. Alone of them, he came from a family of Quakers. Price, by contrast, was shorter, slighter, darker and of middle height. Proud of his Welsh roots, he was at once the most genial and combative member of the group. He worked as a cook for the Great Western Railway, travelling, for the most part, between Paddington and his native country.

'They tried to put me on a military bloody train,' he complained. 'I told my boss it was against my principles to help the war effort in any way. He said that people like me couldn't afford principles. I hate to say it but he had a point. I earn a pittance.'

'Nevertheless,' said Ablatt, 'you must stick to your guns.'

Price grinned. 'I don't believe in guns, Cyril.'

'You know what I mean.'

'I do and I don't. We're different, you and me. While you can get up on your hind legs and spout about pacifism for hours on end, I'm against conscription for a different reason. It's a breach of my liberty, see? That's what I resent. It's the state, taking over my life, telling me what to do, what to wear, when to eat, drink and sleep and who to shoot at. I'm not having that. I've got rights and nobody is going to steal them from me. I don't hold with killing people,' said Price, warming to his theme, 'and never have – simple as that. No government on this earth is going to make me take up arms. In fact—'

He broke off as they heard footsteps approaching along the lane at the back of the house. The garden door creaked open and the steps got closer. Gordon Leach had arrived at last. Ablatt got up to confront him, flinging open the door as his breathless friend was conjured out of the darkness.

'Where the hell have you been?' he asked, accusingly.

Leach raised both hands. 'Sorry – I got held up.'

'This is an important meeting.'

'I know that, Cyril.'

'Then why did you keep us waiting?'

'Let him in and close that bloody door,' said Price. 'It's freezing in here.'

Ablatt stepped back so that the newcomer could enter the shed. Price was sitting on a wooden box and Hambridge was perched on the edge of the workbench. Closing the door, Ablatt took the only chair. Leach had to settle for an upturned bucket. He was a thin, pallid, fair-headed young man with a nervous habit of looking to left and right as he spoke, as if addressing a large and restive audience. After apologising profusely to his friends, he lapsed into silence.

'Right,' said Ablatt, taking charge. 'You all know why we're here. Until this year, recruitment was done on a voluntary basis. The Military Service Act changed all that. Conscription will come in to effect on March 2nd. Any man between the ages of eighteen and forty-one is likely to be called up unless he's married, widowed with children or working in one of the reserved occupations. In other words, all four of us are liable.'

'We simply tell them to bugger off,' asserted Price.

'It's not as simple as that, Mansel,' said Leach, worriedly. 'We'd be breaking the law.'

'There's no law that can make me join the army.'

'There is now.'

'Then we bloody well defy it.'

'That's the point at issue,' resumed Ablatt. 'Are we all prepared to act together as conscientious objectors? Are we all ready to take the consequences?'

'Yes,' said Price, thrusting out his jaw.

'Fred?'

'I've been racking my brains to find a way out,' said Hambridge, seriously. 'I know this may sound daft but why don't we make a run for it? We could head for Scotland and camp out until the war ends.'

'You're right,' said Ablatt with a sneer. 'It sounds daft because it *is* daft.'

'We'd be escaping conscription, Cyril.'

'You won't get me freezing my balls off in the Highlands,' said Price, angrily. 'What are we supposed to live on? Where does the money come from?'

'We have to do *something*,' insisted Hambridge, turning to Leach for support. 'What do you think, Gordon?'

'Running away is not the answer, Fred,' said Leach, clearly appalled by the notion. 'I've got Ruby to think of, remember. We're getting married this year. I can't just run off and leave her.'

'Ruby would understand. It'd only be for a short while.'

'You should try reading the papers,' suggested Ablatt, irritably. 'They all say the same. This war will drag on and on. Why are they bringing in conscription if they think it's all going to be over by Easter? Forget about Scotland.'

'All right,' conceded Hambridge. 'Let's make it Ireland, then.'

'We're not turning tail like frightened rabbits. We're going to stay here and demand our rights as conscientious objectors.'

'Then there could be trouble ahead, Cyril.'

'That's my worry,' admitted Leach. 'How far do we go?'

'All the way,' said Price, pugnaciously.

'We lead by example,' said Ablatt with passion. 'We refuse to fight our fellow men on the grounds of conscience. It's what any good Christian would do. We march under the banner of peace. Let them bring in their tribunals and whatever else they devise to coerce us. We must stand shoulder to shoulder against them.' He rose to his feet and wagged a finger. 'I'm a human being. I will not be turned into an instrument of slaughter wearing a khaki uniform. I will not kill, I will not inflict hideous wounds. I will not turn my back on the teachings of the Bible.' He looked around the faces of his friends. 'I know that Mansel won't let anyone push him around. What about you, Fred? Are you ready to face the music?'

'Yes,' said Hambridge, stirred by his words. 'I think I am.'

'What do you believe in?'

'Peace and universal friendship.'

'Tell that to the tribunal when they haul you up in front of one.' Ablatt's eyes flicked to Leach. 'That leaves you, Gordon.'

Leach licked dry lips. 'I have to consider Ruby,' he said, uneasily.

'The only thing you have to consider is your conscience.'

'But this will affect her, Cyril.'

'No woman wants to marry a coward,' said Price, 'and that's what you'll look like if you don't do what the rest of us are going to do. Ruby won't thank you if you go off to war and finish up dead in some rat-infested trench like my poor dab of a cousin. That's not bravery — it's plain bloody stupidity. Are you going to let someone *dictate* what you've got to do? Well, I'm not — neither is Cyril and neither is Fred.'

'We'll take this to the bitter end,' said Ablatt. 'Join us, Gordon.'

Leach shivered as a blast of cold air blew in under the door. He turned up the collar of his overcoat and pulled his cap down over his forehead. It was easy for the others. They didn't have his responsibilities. Ablatt

11

was a clever young man who'd educated himself and who knew how to put thoughts into words. Price could be bloody-minded whenever he felt that someone was giving him too many orders. Though he belonged to the Society of Friends, Hambridge did not follow Quaker doctrine slavishly but he was nevertheless a born pacifist. He was also strongly influenced by Ablatt and would always fall in behind him. None of the three was prepared to comply with the demands of conscription.

Wishing that he had their unshakable conviction, Leach tried to imagine what would happen in the event of refusal. While he hated the idea of bearing arms as much as any of them, he wondered if they should accept a compromise and help the war effort in a way that did not involve combat. About to suggest it, he saw the warning look in their eyes and realised that it was a waste of time. He was either with them or against them. Since he was too weak-willed to resist the general feeling, he had to accept it and did so with a defeatist nod.

'That's settled then,' said Ablatt, reaching into his pocket to take out a leaflet. 'I've been in touch with the No-Conscription Fellowship. It's full of people who have the same beliefs as us. Take a look at this,' he went on, handing the leaflet to Price. 'The NCF is having a mass meeting here in London early in March and I think all four of us should be there.'

'You can count on me, Cyril,' said Price.

'The same goes for me,' added Hambridge.

'I thought you'd be huddled in a tent up in Scotland.'

'There's no need to be sarcastic, Mansel.'

'It was your idea.' Price read the leaflet. 'This looks good. I like what I've heard about the NCF.'

'It's already got thousands of members,' said Ablatt, 'and many more will swell the ranks. We'll be among them. Is that agreed, Gordon?'

Once again, Leach was the last to pledge himself. He'd already made one momentous decision that evening and it had left him in a state of suspended fear. In the long term, there could be unimaginable horrors. In the short term, there was the problem of explaining to Ruby Cosgrove exactly what he'd agreed to do with his friends. And since they had limited leisure time together, she would not be happy to be told that he preferred to attend a public meeting instead of seeing her. He sought desperately for a way of escaping the commitment but none came to mind. Leach eventually capitulated.

'I'll *try* to come, Cyril,' he bleated.

'You'll be there,' said Ablatt, peremptorily, 'or I'll want to know the reason why.'

Leach's heart sank.

The event was held in Devonshire House, the Quaker headquarters in Bishopsgate, a place that symbolised peace and goodwill. Organisers would later claim that almost two thousand people were crammed inside the building but there was a sizeable crowd outside as well and it was steadily growing. Fuelled by anger at the stance taken by conscientious objectors, hecklers yelled taunts, waved fists and issued wild threats. Soldiers on leave had come to see those they perceived as cowards and shirkers; miserable creatures, in their estimation, who lacked any sense of patriotism. Men who'd lost limbs or eyes in the service of their country added their voices to the hullabaloo. Women were just as ferocious in their denunciation, especially those who'd lost sons or husbands at the front. They couldn't understand why anyone should be allowed to evade their duty so flagrantly when others had made the supreme sacrifice. It seemed unjust.

One truculent old woman, armed with a walking stick in the hope that she might have a chance to belabour someone with it, confided her feelings to all and sundry in a rasping Cockney accent.

'It's cruel, that's what it is,' she said, brandishing the stick. 'Them what's in there ought to be ashamed. I went to visit my husband in prison yesterday. This woman told me they'd locked hers up for being a conchie. I said they ought to throw away the key and leave the swine behind bars for good.' She stuck out her chin with pride. 'My man's in there for thieving. I mean, it's a good, honest, decent crime – not like turning your back on your country.'

There was a surge of agreement from those around her and many other suggestions were made of suitably grim punishments for those who dared to resist conscription. Some boasted of attacks they'd made on conscientious objectors and were clearly expecting a major confrontation with them now. They wanted to hand out much more than a white feather. As the crowd grew ever bigger and more volatile, determination to take revenge hardened. A gang of sailors then joined the throng, emboldened by the beer they'd consumed in a nearby pub and roused to a pitch of fury when they'd heard about the meeting of the No-Conscription Fellowship. They weren't content to shout abuse and hurl dire warnings. They wanted blood.

Uniformed police were on duty but their numbers were totally inadequate and, in any case, their sympathies were largely with the protesters outside the building. War had had a profound effect on them, depleting their resources as many colleagues rushed to enlist, yet widening the scope of their duties. In addition to keeping the peace and arresting criminals, they had to search for foreign spies, prevent sabotage, catch deserters, help to billet troops and perform dozens of other onerous duties unknown in peacetime. Protecting men who refused to bear arms was not an assignment that the majority of them could enjoy. They would show far more enthusiasm when arresting conscientious objectors and hauling them before a tribunal. For the time being, they were content to maintain a presence and rely on the power of their uniforms to keep violent disorder at bay. It was a power that was swiftly diminishing.

* * *

'I didn't know that this was going on for two days,' said Leach, incredulously.

'There's a lot to talk about,' Price reminded him.

'I can't come back tomorrow.'

'You'll have to, Gordon. We've got to see it through to the end.'

'Ruby will kill me. She was really upset when I told her I was going to be here today. She burst into tears. I can't let her down again.'

'Would you rather let *us* down instead?'

'You can tell me what happens.'

'This is history, mun. Don't you want to be part of it?'

'I'm here today, aren't I?'

'It's not enough. Imagine what Cyril will say.'

Leach shuddered. 'I'm too busy thinking what Ruby will say.'

They'd arrived late and been forced to stand at the back of the room. Somewhere in the mass of bodies were Cyril Ablatt and Fred Hambridge, early birds who'd manage to secure seats near the front. Gordon Leach preferred to be on the periphery of an event to which he brought only half-hearted interest. Mansel Price, on the other hand, wished that they were with their two friends, forming a quartet of resistance against the demands of the state. Like his companion, he was surprised by the people who'd converged in such force on Devonshire House.

'I thought they'd all be much the same as us,' he said. 'You know, ordinary lads with a bit of spunk in them. But some of these people look so . . . well, so damned respectable. I heard one man saying he was a bank manager, then there was that chemist we spoke to in the queue. I mean, they've got proper jobs.'

'I've got a proper job as well,' said Leach, tetchily. 'I work in my father's bakery. How is he going to manage if I get dragged off to war?'

'You're asking the wrong question.'

'Am I?'

'How is your father going to manage if you get dragged off to prison?'

Leach blenched. 'Do you think it will come to that?'

'It may do. And you agreed to stand firm with the rest of us.'

'What about Ruby?'

Price sniggered. 'I daresay you always stand firm with her.'

Leach's blush turned his friend's snigger into a guffaw.

The turnout was far larger than either of them had anticipated. Leach found the numbers overwhelming but Price was lifted by the thought that he wasn't just an isolated dissident. He was part of a nationwide movement, albeit one that had a distinctly middle-class feeling to it in his eyes. There was no GWR cook like the Welshman on the platform, neither was there a baker's assistant like Leach or a carpenter like Hambridge. Those about to address the assembly were well-dressed professional men with drooping moustaches and an air of propriety about them. Anyone less like potential lawbreakers was difficult to envisage, yet they were all going to preach the gospel of defiance. There were plenty of fur-collared coats and well-trimmed beards in the audience but there were also workmen in dungarees and skinny individuals in ill-fitting suits frayed at the edges. Lawyers rubbed shoulders with unkempt bricklayers and teachers sat beside those on whom education had had no visible effect. There was more than a smattering of women to offer moral support and gentlemen of the press were there to gloat, scorn, reinforce their prejudices or – in a few cases – treat the occasion with a degree of impartiality.

Leach was still thinking about Ruby Cosgrove when Price nudged him.

'What's a Muggletonian?' he asked.

'What?'

'A Muggletonian. I overheard someone in the queue saying that he was here because he was a Muggletonian. What the hell is that?'

'I haven't a clue, Mansel.'

'Maybe he went to some posh school called Muggleton.'

'Be quiet,' whispered Leach.

'But I'm interested. I want to *know*.'

'We're about to start. Shut up, will you?'

As the chairman rose to speak, the heavy murmur slowly died out. Hambridge waited with something approaching trepidation. It was a paradox. Though he was a Quaker in quintessential Quaker habitat, he was cowed and ill at ease. Hating crowds, he sat hunched up in his seat, profoundly aware of his insignificance. Ablatt, however, was in his element, relaxed and comfortable, already composing in his mind the speech he intended to deliver when he got the opportunity. Nothing would have made the nervous, watchful Hambridge stand up in front of such a huge audience and, by the same token, nothing would deter his friend from doing so.

The chairman was Clifford Allen, a slight, alert, youngish man with a spiritual quality about him and a deep, measured voice that compelled respect.

'Fellow citizens,' he began, 'let me welcome you all to what promises to be a crucial meeting of the No-Conscription Fellowship. You all know the position we take. Conscription is now law in this country of free traditions. Our hard-won liberties have been violated. Conscription means the desecration of principles that we have long held dear; it involves the subordination of civil liberties to military dictation; it imperils the freedom of individual conscience and establishes in our midst that militarism which menaces all social graces and divides the people of all nations.'

He looked around the sea of upturned faces. 'We must offer determined resistance to all that is established by the Act.'

A ripple of applause greeted the declaration of intent. It built and built until it reached the proportions of a tidal wave. The chairman was pleased with the response. The meeting had started on a positive note.

*   *   *

An ovation which delighted those on the platform had a very different effect on those outside. When they heard the sustained clapping, they were enraged. The sound was like a red flag to a herd of bulls. Everyone wanted to break into the building but it was the sailors who acted on their behalf. Pushing their way to the front, they ignored the warnings from the police and clambered over the locked gates, earning cheers of encouragement from the crowd. When stewards tried to persuade them not to interrupt the meeting, they were pushed aside by the drunken sailors. Without quite knowing what they were going to do, the naval boarding party threw open the doors and stormed inside, set on causing some sort of commotion. But it never materialised. The sailors were so surprised with what they found that they came to a halt. The room was filled – it seemed to their blurred eyes – with quiet, pale-faced, mild-mannered men, several of whom were too thin, boyish and puny to offer any kind of fight. Instead of disturbing a group of rabid conchies, it was as if they'd stumbled into a church social. The shock took the wind out of their sails completely.

Nobody came to challenge them and there was no hint of danger. They were instead invited to stay and take part in the meeting. The sailors engaged in some good-humoured badinage and then, shepherded by the stewards, they withdrew in an orderly fashion, ridding themselves of a few valedictory jibes as they did so. Their attack had been effectively stifled. Physical confrontation had been averted.

The chairman was quick to seize on the cause of the interruption.

'It was nice to see such genial visitors,' he observed, dryly, 'but it might be safer if we don't provoke any more disruption. In future, when you approve of something that is said, don't applaud. The crowd outside will hear you. Simply take out a handkerchief and wave it in approval. Do you all agree?'

Hundreds of handkerchiefs fluttered in the air. The suggestion met with unanimous endorsement. Whenever a speech delighted the audience, it was acclaimed in silence. Everyone on the platform said his piece, then it was the turn of people from the floor. Ablatt was among the first. Leaping to his feet, he caught the eye of the chairman and was given permission to speak. He made his way to the aisle so that he could turn to the audience before addressing it. It was as if he'd been waiting for this moment for years and he made the best of it.

'Friends,' he said with a sweeping gesture that took in the entire room, 'I wish to offer my personal testimony. I am a devout Christian. I refuse to act as an instrument of slaughter . . .'

It was his favourite phrase and he'd used it ever since he first saw it in an article. Somehow he'd made the phrase his own. Price, Leach and Hambridge had heard him dozens of times but only in the close confines of a garden shed or a room in one of their houses. They'd never seen him in front of a large audience before and it was a revelation. Ablatt was a natural orator. His voice was clear, his argument coherent and his assurance remarkable. His speech had far more bite and sheer fervour than those of earlier speakers. The spectators were held spellbound by his eloquence. It made his friends proud of him and they lost any vestigial reservations they might have about defying the Military Service Act. While Ablatt was in full flow, Leach even managed to forget about Ruby Cosgrove.

The magic eventually wore off. By the time the meeting came to an end, Leach was full of apprehension again. He not only had to run the gauntlet of protesters outside, he had to face biting criticism from his fiancée and withstand Ablatt's inevitable ire when he told him that he'd be unable to attend on the following day. Price had no such worries. He'd been roused by everything he'd seen and heard. Whatever the consequences, he was ready to withstand the power of the state. As the two of them came out with the rest of the crowd, they were met with jeers and ridicule but there was no longer any sense of menace. They stood aside to let others pass so that they could wait for their friends. In the event, Fred Hambridge came out alone.

'Where's Cyril?' asked Price.

'They asked him to stay behind,' said Hambridge. 'They were so impressed with his speech that they want him on the platform at future meetings.'

'I'm not surprised. He was wonderful. Isn't that right, Gordon?'

'Yes,' replied Leach, one eye on the baying crowd.

'I was going to take my turn,' said the Welshman, 'but I never got the chance. It may be different tomorrow. Not that I'll be anywhere near as good as Cyril, mind you. Talk about the gift of the bloody gab.'

'There's no point in waiting,' said Hambridge. 'He could be a long time. Cyril said we were to go on ahead. He'll join us later at my house. We can talk over what we heard today.'

'Are you sure we should leave him?' asked Leach as the crowd became more vocal. 'I think the four of us should stick together for safety.'

'Cyril can manage on his own, Gordon.'

'What if this crowd turns nasty?'

'That won't worry him.'

'No,' said Price with an affectionate laugh. 'The one thing you can say about Cyril is that he can look after himself.'

The body lay motionless on the ground. Cyril Ablatt would never deliver a speech of any kind again. Someone clearly had none of his qualms about being an instrument of slaughter.

CHAPTER TWO

Detective Superintendent Claude Chatfield was a tall, lean individual in his forties with protruding eyes and thinning hair bisected by a centre parting. He was a man of uncertain temper and could, by turns, be loquacious, withdrawn, peppery, emollient, condescending or passably friendly. As he stood behind the desk in his office at Scotland Yard that morning, he was at his most overbearing, determined to assert his authority over anyone of inferior rank. When Harvey Marmion came into the room, Chatfield welcomed him with a sharp rebuke.

'You're late, Inspector.'

'I came as soon as I could, sir,' said Marmion.

'You should have been here earlier. My message was explicit.'

'I responded to it immediately.'

'If there's anything I hate, it's tardiness. You should know that by now.'

Marmion knew all there was to know about Chatfield and none of it endeared him to the man but, since the latter was higher up in the chain of command, all that the inspector could do was to tolerate his multiple shortcomings and obey him. In fact, Marmion had been quite prompt. Hauled out of bed at five o'clock, he'd thanked the constable who'd brought the message, quickly shaved and dressed, given his wife a farewell kiss, then spurned food in the interests of urgency. When he finally arrived at Scotland Yard, his stomach was rumbling and his eyes were still only half-open.

He was a solid, broad-shouldered man with a full head of hair and the kind of nondescript features that made him invisible in a crowd. Studious by nature, Marmion nevertheless had the physique of a dock labourer. Beside him, Chatfield looked spare and insubstantial. It was one cause of the underlying tension between them. There were several others.

'What seems to be the trouble, Superintendent?' asked Marmion.

'Inefficiency among my detectives,' said Chatfield, meaningfully. 'Anyway, now that you're here, you might as well sit down.' Marmion lowered himself onto an upright chair but the other man remained on his feet so that he held a position of dominance. 'I might as well tell you that you would not be my first choice,' he went on, 'but the commissioner has this strange faith in you and felt that you should take charge of any case that has a degree of sensitivity attached to it, as this one certainly does. You'll need to handle the press with great care.' He sucked his teeth. 'We both suspected that this sort of thing would happen sooner or later.'

Marmion was interested. 'Go on, sir.'

'The body of a young man was found in a dark alley in Shoreditch. He'd been bludgeoned to death. Since he still had his wallet, we can rule out robbery as a motive. The victim's name is Cyril Ablatt. This was in his pocket.'

Picking up a leaflet, he handed it to Marmion who gave it a glance.

'It's that meeting of the No-Conscription Fellowship.'

Chatfield was scathing. 'They're a bunch of lily-livered layabouts.'

'I disagree, sir. Most of them are sincere in their beliefs. Their consciences simply won't allow them to take up arms against their fellow men.'

'Where would we be if *everyone* had that attitude?'

'The vast majority of people don't.'

'Thank heaven for that! We can't fight a war without soldiers. Conchies like this Ablatt fellow are nothing but abject cowards.'

'With respect, sir,' said Marmion, quietly, 'you're making hasty assumptions about the murder victim. Perhaps you should wait until we know more details.'

'The NCF is a hiding place for worthless British citizens too scared to fight.'

'I hope you're not suggesting that Cyril Ablatt *deserved* what happened to him. That would be monstrously unjust.'

'Damn it, man! You're supposed to solve a crime, not take sides.'

'You're the one who's taking sides,' argued Marmion, 'and it's distorting your view of the situation. To begin with, the murder may be wholly unconnected to the fact that the victim may hold pacifist views. It could have been a random attack.'

'It was deliberate and calculated,' insisted Chatfield, smarting at the reproof. 'What could be clearer? That meeting of the NCF stirred up passions. There was a big crowd outside and, at one point, I'm told, it looked as if there'd be a full-scale riot. A gang of drunken sailors actually stormed the building but the attack petered out for some reason. When the conchies eventually left the building, there would have been scuffles. My guess is that Ablatt was trailed by someone who waited for the opportunity to pounce.'

'That's idle speculation, Superintendent.'

'It's an informed opinion.'

'I prefer to keep an open mind. May I ask what action has been taken?'

'I've had the body transferred to the morgue.'

Marmion was disappointed. 'That's a pity,' he said. 'If at all possible, I prefer to see a murder victim at the scene of the crime. It gives me a fuller picture.'

'Are you criticising me?' asked Chatfield, eyes blazing.

'It's not my place to do so, sir.'

'Make sure you remember that in future. As for my decision, I was being practical. If that body had still been there at daylight, there'd be hundreds of ghouls impeding us as they tried to get a look at it. The scene is at present being guarded. You can view it for yourself.'

'I'll do that,' said Marmion. 'The first priority is to inform the family of their son's death. Has someone already done that?'

'No,' replied the other. 'I was leaving that to you.'

'If I can have the address, I'll get over there at once.'

Chatfield gave him the sheet of paper that lay on the desk. 'Luckily, his address was sewn into the lining of his coat. He must have a caring mother. That's all we know about him, I'm afraid.'

'It's a start, sir. And thank you for assigning the case to us,' he added without irony. 'Sergeant Keedy and I are grateful that you've shown confidence in us.'

'The person to thank is the commissioner. It was his idea, not mine.'

'Then I'll be sure to express my gratitude to Sir Edward.'

'The commissioner is like me. He expects results.'

'We won't let him down. If you'll excuse me,' said Marmion, getting up and moving to the door, 'I'll be off to pass on the sad news. And I'll try to arrange for the victim's next of kin to identify the body.'

'That may be difficult.'

'Why is that, sir?'

'From what I hear, the skull has been smashed to a pulp. I don't think anyone will be able to identify what's left of him.' Chatfield drew himself up to his full height. 'The killer must be caught and caught quickly,' he emphasized. 'The public needs to be reassured that a murderer will not be allowed to roam free in the streets of London. However,' he said with a thin-lipped smile, 'there will doubtless be those who have no cause to mourn Ablatt. His death means that there'll be one conchie less to worry about. I can understand that feeling.'

'That's more than I can do,' said Marmion under his breath.

Concealing his disgust, he went out and closed the door firmly behind him.

Since the outbreak of war, Joe Keedy's work days had been longer and his nights under constant threat. Policing the capital was a twenty-four-hour operation. It meant that, while his social life was curtailed, he was amply rewarded with the action on which he thrived. In case he was roused in the small hours, he always had a shave immediately before retiring to bed so that he looked presentable when awakened at short notice and needed simply to put on his suit before being ready to leave. As it happened, when the police car arrived outside his digs, Keedy was already up and dressed. One glance through the window told him that he and Marmion had a new investigation to lead. Chewing a last piece of toast, he swallowed it with a gulp and washed it down with a mouthful of tea. Then he reached for his overcoat and hat before heading for the door.

Standing at over six feet, Keedy was a handsome, wiry man in his thirties who took far more care with his appearance than the average detective. His hat was set at a rakish angle, there was a sharp crease in his trousers and his black shoes gleamed. He bounded down the stairs and let himself out into the cold. A moment later, he climbed into the car beside Marmion.

'Good morning, Harv,' he said.

'You were quick. Were you expecting me?'

'It's a case of intuition.'

'I thought that was something only women are supposed to have.'

Keedy laughed. 'That's what they tell me.'

Marmion was glad to see him. They were good friends as well as colleagues and had developed a mutual understanding that helped to speed things up. As the car made its way through the deserted streets in the direction of Shoreditch, Marmion gave him a succinct report of events.

'It doesn't look as if we have much to go on,' observed Keedy.

'We soon will have, Joe.'

'That meeting of the NCF could be significant.'

'According to our dear superintendent,' said Marmion, 'it explains everything. He's convinced that Ablatt was followed after the meeting, then attacked for daring to oppose the war. It never occurred to him that other factors might be involved.'

'Ah, well, that's old Chat for you. He always jumps to conclusions.'

'It's one of his many charms.'

'I still can't believe he was promoted over you,' said Keedy. 'Everyone knows that you can wipe the floor with Chat when it comes to catching villains. Yet it was that smarmy bastard who was appointed instead of you.'

'He probably did better than me in the interview.'

'He can't do *anything* better than you, Harv.'

'Yes, he can,' said Marmion. 'He can lose his temper much faster than me. He was frothing with anger when I got there and accused me of being late. If it was left to Claude Chatfield, I'd have to sleep in my office.'

'I don't think your wife would like that.'

'She wouldn't, Joe. The house seems empty now that Alice has moved out. If I start bedding down at Scotland Yard, I'm sure that Ellen would want to join me.'

Keedy rolled his eyes. 'That would go down well with the top brass!'

'As for the promotion, be thankful that I didn't get it.'

'But you *deserved* it, Harv.'

'Think of the consequences.'

'What do you mean?'

'If I was Superintendent Marmion, then you'd be travelling in this car with a certain Inspector Chatfield. How would you fancy that?'

Keedy grimaced. 'I wouldn't fancy it at all,' he said. 'I remember the way he used to treat his sergeants. They did the work and he took the credit. No wonder three in a row enlisted in the army to escape him.'

'I hope that *you're* not thinking of doing that, Joe.'

'Of course not – I prefer to do my fighting on the home front.'

'Then I can guarantee you'll have your hands full. Cyril Ablatt is only the latest visitor to the police morgue,' said Marmion, philosophically. 'There'll be plenty of others to keep us occupied and plenty of chances to explode the superintendent's instant theories about each successive murder.'

'Chat is a congenital idiot.'

It was Marmion's turn to laugh. 'And so say all of us!'

The house had a narrow frontage and stood at the end of a terrace in a grimy backstreet. On the side wall of the building, someone had painted patriotic slogans and outright abuse in large white capitals. They were illumined by the gas lamp nearby. Evidently, one of the neighbours objected to Cyril Ablatt's pacifist leanings. Drawn curtains in the front bedrooms testified that most people were still asleep but there was a light downstairs in the Ablatt house as the car drew up outside it. Marmion and Keedy got out and took a deep breath. Passing on grim news always upset them because they had to inflict intense pain. There was no easy way to do it. Marmion used the knocker to give a gentle tap. There was an immediate reaction. Footsteps came scuttling down the passageway, then a bolt was drawn back. When the door swung open, they were confronted by the hunched figure of a bald-headed man in his fifties. In pyjamas, dressing gown and slippers, he had the fatigued look of someone who'd been up all night. Sensing disaster, he let out a deep sigh of resignation.

'It's about Cyril, isn't it?' he asked, biting his lip.

'I'm afraid that it is, sir,' said Marmion. 'Are you his father?'

'Yes, I am.'

'I'm Inspector Marmion and this is Sergeant Keedy. Would it be possible for us to step inside, please? I don't think you'd want to hear this on the doorstep.'

'Of course, of course . . .'

Gerald Ablatt stepped back so that they could step into the dank passageway. Closing the door behind him, he took the detectives into the front room and motioned them to the settee. Removing their hats, they sat down. Ablatt himself was directly opposite, perched on the edge of an armchair. The room was so small that his knees were fairly close to theirs.

'I've been dreading this,' he admitted.

'It's bad news, I'm afraid,' warned Marmion, gently. 'Do you think that your wife ought to hear it with you?'

'My wife died three years ago, Inspector – diphtheria.'

'I'm sorry to hear that, sir.'

'It might be a blessing in disguise. Cyril was our only child. Mary doted on him. I'd hate her to have heard that he's met with some kind of accident.' His eyes widened quizzically. 'That *is* why you're here, isn't it?'

'Yes,' said Marmion, exchanging a glance with Keedy, 'but it was rather more than an accident. A young man was attacked and killed last night. We've reason to believe that he may have been your son.'

For a few moments, Ablatt was stunned and looked as if he was about to fall over. Keedy sat forward in case he needed to catch the man, while Marmion felt guilty at having to administer the hammer blow. With a supreme effort, Ablatt steadied himself and managed to control his emotions. His hands were tightly clasped and his body tensed.

'It must be Cyril,' he said, sorrowfully. 'He always let me know if he was staying the night somewhere. When he didn't come home . . .' He shrugged helplessly. 'I knew that something terrible had happened.'

'The two of you lived alone, then?' asked Keedy.

'Yes, Sergeant, we did. Lots of people complain about sons being a nuisance when they get to a certain age but Cyril wasn't like that. He was no trouble. All he wanted to do was to stay in his room and read his books.' A smile flitted across his face. 'He was a librarian, you know.'

'Then he'd have no shortage of reading matter.'

'You've seen the sort of area this is,' continued Ablatt. 'Most of the lads around here follow their fathers into the same trade. What else is there for them to do? Well,' he said, holding back tears, 'I wanted more for my son. I wasn't having him working as a cobbler like me. It's a good trade because everyone needs to have their shoes soled and heeled, but it's a hard life bent double over a last all day. So I paid for Cyril to go to night school. He was educated, you see.' His face clouded. 'This war changed everything. Until it started, people looked up to Cyril. They admired him. Then the other lads started to join up and everyone began to wonder why my son didn't go with them.' He stood up abruptly. 'I don't agree with what he believed. Let me be honest about that. In his place, I'd have been down at the recruiting office like a shot. But Cyril was entitled to his opinion. He had principles, you see. That's why he went to that meeting yesterday.' He slumped back into the chair. 'Oh, I'm so grateful his mother didn't live to hear this. It would've broken her heart.'

'We'll need someone to identify the body,' said Marmion, softly.

Ablatt stiffened. 'I'll go,' he volunteered. 'He's my son. It's my duty.'

'There's no rush, sir. We'll wait until you're good and ready. Meanwhile, there's something you might do for us. You'll appreciate that we know very little about your son. Anything you can tell us would be valuable. Which library does he work at, for instance? We'll need to speak to his employers. And what about his friends – did he go to that meeting alone or was he with someone else?'

'Oh, all four of them went, Inspector – Gordon, Fred, Mansel and Cyril.'

'Could you give me those names again, please?' asked Keedy, taking out a notebook and pencil. 'We'll need the addresses as well.'

'They all live in Shoreditch.' As Ablatt reeled off the names, Keedy wrote them down. 'Gordon Leach, Fred Hambridge and Mansel Price. Gordon works at the bakery two streets away. Fred is even closer.'

He provided the addresses and explained that the three of them often came to the house. Ablatt had no young lady in his life. Encouraged by the detectives, he then talked about his son with a kind of doomed affection, shuttling between pride in his achievements and despair at his murder. They let him ramble on, garnering an immense amount of information as he did so. The corpse in the police morgue began to take on life and definition. When the recitation finally came to an end, Marmion asked the question that had been on the tip of his tongue since he entered the house.

'Did your son have any enemies, Mr Ablatt?'

The older man blinked. 'No, he didn't,' he answered, resentfully. 'Not the way you mean, Inspector. People didn't like it because he refused to join up and some of them called him names. Then there are those things painted on the side wall. They hurt us at the time but we got used to them. But there were never any real *enemies*. Nobody hated Cyril enough to kill him.' The question had unnerved him somehow and he was trembling. 'I know you want me to come with you but I'll need to get dressed and I'd like a little time to myself first, if that's all right.'

'Take as much time as you like, sir,' said Marmion, sympathetically. 'And thank you for being so helpful. Oh, there is one more thing. We'll need a recent photograph of your son.'

'I'll find one.'

'Thank you. Could the sergeant and I take a look at your son's room, please?'

Ablatt was defensive. 'Why do you want to do that?'

'We're still trying to build up a picture of him.'

'But I've told you all you need to know.'

'His room might be able to add a few salient details.'

'Yes,' said Keedy. 'You told us that he spent a lot of time in it.'

Ablatt gazed upwards. 'He used to read up there – and practise his speeches.'

'You didn't mention any speeches, sir.'

'Didn't I?'

'What sort of speeches were they?'

'The kind he was going to make at the meeting yesterday. Cyril had studied public speaking, you see. It's what gave him his confidence. He could talk the hind leg off a donkey.' He looked suspiciously from one to the other. 'All that you'll find up there is a pile of books.'

'Their titles might tell us something about him,' said Marmion. 'Well?'

It took Gerald Ablatt a long time to reach his decision. Part of him wanted to protect his son's privacy while another part of him was eager to do anything that would help the police. In the end, realism won the battle against family sentiment. Ablatt pointed upstairs.

'It's the room at the back,' he said.

Without another word, he went slowly upstairs, grief visibly weighing him down. In the short time they'd been with him, he seemed to have aged ten years.

'I felt so rotten having to tell him the news,' confessed Marmion. 'It was like sticking a knife into him.'

'He bore up very well – better than most people do.'

'Did you believe everything he told us about his son?'

'Yes,' said Keedy. 'He'd have no reason to lie, would he?'

'Let's go and find out.'

Having given the father time to get to his bedroom, they ascended the stairs. As they did so, they could hear the sound of sobbing coming from behind the first door they reached. They walked along the landing to the room at the rear. Marmion led the way in and put on the light. There was barely enough space for the two of them to get inside. Crammed into the room was a single bed, a bedside table, a wardrobe and a bookcase filled to overflowing. Books also stood on the window sill, the top of the wardrobe and the floor. Many of them were dog-eared and had tattered covers. On the bedside table was a large Bible.

Marmion's eye went to the framed photograph on the wall. It showed Cyril Ablatt and what he assumed was his mother, both smiling at the camera. He knew that it must have been taken at least three years ago when Mrs Ablatt was still alive.

'Nice-looking lad,' he said. 'I wish *I'd* looked like that at his age. It would have made me more popular among the ladies.'

'Yet his father said he didn't have one,' recalled Keedy. 'What does that make him – a mother's boy?'

'I don't know. How would you describe someone who spends most of his time alone in his bedroom?'

'I'd say he was a silly fool. He's missing all the fun.'

'This *was* fun to him, Joe. He loved his books.'

'All work and no play . . .'

'Why did he stay up here when he could have been reading downstairs? It would have been far more comfortable to sit in an armchair. There has to be a reason why he preferred being up here.'

'Tell me what it is.'

'He was secretive,' said Marmion. 'That's what this bedroom says to me. There are things in here that he didn't want anyone else to know.'

'What sort of things?'

They conducted a quick search, opening the wardrobe to check its contents, examining the items on the little mantelpiece and even looking under the bed. Keedy reached out a long arm to retrieve a scrapbook. He flicked it open and saw newspaper cuttings pasted neatly inside it. Most related to the war and to those who campaigned to bring it to an immediate end. Ablatt had also kept photographs of people he admired. One of them showed an old, bearded man in the garb of a Russian peasant.

'Who the devil is this?' wondered Keedy.

'I think it's Tolstoy. He's the man who wrote *War and Peace*.'

'Even I have heard of that. It doesn't make sense, Harv. Why cut out a photo of someone who writes a book about war? Cyril Ablatt was *against* it.'

'So was Tolstoy,' said Marmion. 'In later life, he had a kind of spiritual crisis and developed his own version of Christianity.'

Keedy was impressed. 'How do you know that?'

'Ablatt wasn't the only one who enjoyed reading – not that I get much time for it nowadays. What I do remember is that Tolstoy drew a lot of inspiration from the Sermon on the Mount. He believed in renouncing violence, wealth and sexual pleasure.'

'I agree with him about violence. Our job would be a hell of a lot easier if everyone turned his back on that. But I'm not so sure about wealth. And as for sexual pleasure . . .'

They shared a muted laugh. Marmion then took a closer look at the volumes in the bookcase. There were a few novels and some poetry anthologies but most were related to Christian teaching. There were also two books on public speaking and some political pamphlets. Keedy took down a book from the top of the wardrobe.

'*The Water Babies*,' he noted.

'It's by Charles Kingsley. He was a clergyman.'

'I've never heard of him.'

'We read bits of it to Alice when she was younger. She loved stories. You'd never get her to sleep unless you read something to her.'

Keedy bit back the comment he was about to make and replaced the book on the wardrobe. The room had light-green wallpaper with a floral pattern. He noticed how faded it had become and felt sad that a young man in his twenties had chosen to spend so much of his leisure time locked up in the depressing little room. Keedy's mental scrapbook had much more colourful and exciting illustrations in it than anything found under the bed. In his opinion, Cyril Ablatt had missed so much.

'We still haven't found any real secrets, Harv,' he said.

'But we have a much clearer sense of his personality. There aren't many young men who sleep in the middle of a miniature library.'

'The only book I had in my bedroom at his age was one about embalming. That's what comes of working in the family undertaking business. I was so glad to escape it and join the police force.'

'Yet it's brought you back where you started, Joe – dealing with dead bodies.' He picked up the Bible and turned to the page with the bookmark in it. 'I wonder what he was reading. Ah, it's Matthew, chapter five,' he said with a nod of recognition. 'That's no surprise, is it?'

'Why not?'

'It contains the Beatitudes, Joe. One of them had a special meaning for him – "Blessed are the peacemakers, for they shall be called the children of God." If only that were true! Ablatt was a peacemaker and you can imagine the names he must have been called. War puts poison into some people's mouths.' He was about to put the book down again when a photograph slipped out from between the pages and floated down to the carpet. Marmion picked it up. 'Hello,' he said, 'what do we have here?'

'It's not another picture of Tolstoy, is it?'

'No, it's a photo of a rather striking lady.' After studying it, he showed it to Keedy. 'It's certainly not his mother, so who is it? Someone dear to his heart?'

Keedy snorted. 'She must be fifteen or twenty years older than him.'

'I think you're being unkind, Joe. She's in her thirties, at most – and she's married. You can see her wedding ring. Well,' he continued, 'we may have stumbled on another motive for murder. What if the killer was a jealous husband?'

'She might be a widow.'

'Oh, I don't think so,' said Marmion, turning the photo over so that he could read the writing on the back. 'See for yourself.'

Taking it from him, Keedy read the message.

Until my husband is on night shift again – think of me.

In place of a signature were several kisses.

'You were right,' said Keedy. 'He was a secretive little so-and-so, wasn't he?'

CHAPTER THREE

The day started early for Gordon Leach. While most of Shoreditch was slumbering quietly, he was helping his father to bake the daily assortment of bread. The one saving grace of a job that rousted him out of bed in the small hours was that it kept him warm on a viciously cold day. The pervasive aroma of bread was always pleasing and a world away from the industrial stink that so many Londoners had to endure at their places of work. Leach's father was a big, taciturn man with a walrus moustache who left him to get on with his work in silence. He'd inherited the bakery from his own father and expected his son to take it over in time. Franklin Leach was no pacifist. Indeed, he was a man with few opinions on any subject and was content to live his life in an intellectual vacuum. He simply wanted to keep his trained assistant beside him throughout the war. When they heard a loud knock on the shop door, he looked up and spoke for the first time in an hour.

'Tell them we're closed,' he said.

Leach wiped his flour-covered hands in a cloth and opened the door to the shop. Through the glass, he could see the familiar outline of Mansel Price. On his way to work, his friend had come in search of information rather than bread. Leach unlocked the shop door and opened it so that Price could step inside.

'Is there any news?' asked the Welshman.

'No, there isn't.'

'Something must have happened to him.'

'That's my worry,' admitted Leach. 'I mean, Cyril is always so reliable. If he said he'd be somewhere, he'd never let you down. When I called at the house last thing at night, his father said he wasn't at home.'

'And he still isn't, Gordon.'

'How do you know?'

'Because I've just been there,' said Price. 'Nobody is in. I banged on the door for ages but got no answer. In the end, someone in the house next door opened the bedroom window and told me to clear off.'

They were deeply concerned. Ablatt was not merely their leader. He was their focus, their moral support and their communal voice. The meeting they'd held without him the previous evening had been a shambles. They'd been too busy trying to imagine what Ablatt would have said to formulate any views of their own about what they'd seen and heard. At first, Leach had been grateful when he didn't turn up at Fred Hambridge's house. The young baker was spared the verbal whipping he'd have received from Ablatt for not attending the second session of the No-Conscription Fellowship. As the evening slipped into night, however, Leach became increasingly alarmed. They'd expected Ablatt hours ago. If he'd been unable to come, he would have sent an apology by some means or other.

'There's only one explanation,' decided Leach.

'I can't think of one.'

'They must have talked Cyril into going off with them. After all, he made the best speech by far at the meeting. They'd be mad not to use him again. Yes, that's it,' he went on, vainly trying to reassure himself. 'Cyril's been taken on to the committee or something. They want him on the platform. See it from his point of view, Mansel. He's got what he always wanted – a chance to make a name for himself.'

Price was unconvinced. 'So he forgot all about us. Is that what you think?'

'Yes, it is.'

'That's rubbish and you know it. He'd never forget his friends.'

'It's unlikely, I know.'

'It's bloody impossible, mun.'

'Then where is he and where's his father? Mr Ablatt should have been at home at this time. He doesn't open his shop until nine. Talking of which,' he added, glancing over his shoulder, 'I'd better get back to the oven or Dad will be after me.'

'Yes,' said Price, 'and I've got to feed the travelling public. Not that I can cook them much of a breakfast since they brought in food rationing. They've even watered the beer. There's just no pleasure left in this country.'

Leach gave a half-smile. 'There is if you find yourself a girlfriend.'

'Wish I could, Gordon. But girlfriends cost money I just haven't got. In any case, what girl wants to go out with a conchie? They'd run a mile.'

'Ruby didn't.'

'She's different.' Price saw the clock on the wall. 'Got to go, I'm afraid. Changed your mind about today's meeting?'

'No,' said Leach. 'I promised to see Ruby this evening.'

'But Cyril might turn up there.'

'I hope he does.'

'So do I,' said Price, brightening. 'He's probably the one person who can tell me what a Muggletonian is.'

* * *

39

In spite of the countless times he'd been there, Harvey Marmion had never become sufficiently accustomed to the morgue to feel at ease inside it. He was therefore grateful when Joe Keedy volunteered to take Gerald Ablatt in to identify the body of his son. Marmion remained outside in the corridor. He was not squeamish. Unnatural death created some grotesque corpses and he could look on them without a tremor when they lay at the scene of the crime. Once they were naked on a slab, it was a very different matter. They were dehumanised, robbed of their dignity, at the mercy of the pathologist's sharp and unforgiving instruments. Marmion hated to see someone who was so utterly defenceless.

While he was waiting, he took out the photograph they'd found at the Ablatt house and wondered who the attractive woman was. She wore a pretty dress and her hair was swept up at the back so that her facial features were completely exposed. There was a bewitching dimple in both cheeks. Could she be a lover or simply a close friend? The message on the back suggested the former but the age gap between Cyril Ablatt and her might have been a deterrent. There was also the obstacle posed by what appeared to be his devout Christianity. Acquainted with the Beatitudes, he would also be very much aware of the Ten Commandments. One of them expressly forbade adultery. Yet the telltale photo had been concealed in the Bible rather than in any of the other books. Marmion saw it as a case of the sacred harbouring the profane.

He and Keedy had agreed that they wouldn't show the photograph to the father. Since it was hidden, it was clearly not meant for his eyes. Besides, he had enough to cope with as it was. He was still mourning the violent murder of his son. It would be cruel to introduce proof that his own flesh and blood had kept something from him. The important thing was to identify the woman and that would be fairly straightforward. The name of the photographer was franked into the corner of the photo. They would be able to find out who she was, when the photo was taken and, possibly, where she lived. She would need to be approached with discretion. Marmion didn't want to cause a violent domestic upset with her husband but the woman obviously meant a great deal to Ablatt. She could be an important witness.

When he heard the door open, he quickly put the photo away in his pocket. Keedy emerged with an ashen Gerald Ablatt by his side. The detectives had both been touched to see that the father had taken the trouble to put on his best suit to visit the corpse of his son. The experience had patently had a profound effect on him. His eyes were glazed, his mouth agape and his movements uncertain. Keedy had to help him along with a hand under his elbow. They walked past Marmion in silence, went down the corridor and turned a corner. A minute later, Keedy came back to the inspector.

'Don't tell me,' said Marmion. 'He wanted the nearest lavatory.'

'When he saw the body, he very nearly threw up.'

'Was it that bad?'

'Somebody didn't like Cyril Ablatt. They not only smashed in his skull, they battered his body as well.'

'What about Mr Ablatt?'

'He almost keeled over when the shroud was drawn back.'

'Was he able to identify the body as that of his son?'

'Oh, yes,' said Keedy. 'There was a birthmark on his shoulder and a long scar on his arm that he'd picked up as a boy. Besides, I think he knew in his heart that it had to be his son. We didn't even have to show him the deceased's effects.'

'Poor man!' sighed Marmion. 'He'll need support.'

'His only close relative is a sister. She lives not far away.'

'Then we'll call on her after we've taken him home. We can visit the scene of the crime afterwards.'

'What about the press?'

'The superintendent is going to issue a statement and say that we've been assigned to the case. That means they'll be dogging our heels from now on.'

'A dead conchie won't arouse much compassion, I fear.'

'He's a murder victim, Joe — nothing else matters.'

'It does to the press.'

'Then we may have to educate them.'

They chatted on for several minutes, reviewing the information they'd so far gathered and discussing the form that the investigation would take. Eventually, they saw Cyril Ablatt coming slowly along the corridor towards them with his eyes on the floor. When he reached the detectives, he gazed up at them.

'I'm very sorry about that,' he murmured.

'There's no need to apologise,' Marmion told him with a consoling hand on his arm. 'It's a perfectly natural reaction. Your son's effects belong to you now. When we've collected them, we'll give you a lift home. Then we'll make contact with your sister. At a time like this, you'll need family around you.'

Ablatt looked surprised. 'But I have to open the shop.'

'Nobody will expect you to do that, sir.'

'I hate to let customers down.'

'People will understand,' said Keedy. 'In the circumstances, they'll respect your right to mourn in private.'

'There are so many things to do — funeral arrangements and that.'

'The body won't be released until after the post-mortem.'

Ablatt shuddered. 'They're going to cut him open?' he said, aghast. 'Hasn't Cyril suffered enough already?'

'It's normal procedure in cases like this, sir,' said Marmion. 'A post-mortem might yield some valuable clues — what the murder weapon was likely to be, for instance. We'll let you know as soon as your son's body is ready for collection. And there's something else we'd advise.'

'What's that, Inspector?'

'Don't talk to the press. Newspapers have no right to hound you but that won't stop them trying to do so. If they pester you, we can always put a constable outside your house to keep them at bay.'

'It's not the newspapers that worry me,' said Ablatt, grimly. 'It's them.'

'Who do you mean, sir?'

'I'm talking about the people who painted those things on our wall. When they hear what's happened, they'll be back again.' His face crumpled. 'What kind of cruel things will they say about Cyril this time?'

Of the three friends, Fred Hambridge was the one who relied most heavily on the young librarian. Price had a more independent mind and Leach's main emotional commitment was to Ruby Cosgrove. It was Hambridge who hung on every word that Cyril Ablatt uttered. He was in awe of his friend's superior education and assurance. In their discussions of religion, Ablatt had even made the carpenter look afresh at his Quaker upbringing. Because he wanted to attend the second session of the NCF, Hambridge got to the workshop an hour earlier than usual to compensate for the time he intended to take off in the afternoon. There was plenty to do. He was making a sash window for a customer in Stepney and had a variety of other tasks awaiting his attention. Unlike Price and Leach, he actually enjoyed his job. He'd always been good with his hands and soon learnt the mysteries of working with different woods.

In return for the books that Ablatt had loaned him, Hambridge had made the bookcase that stood in his friend's bedroom. It had been a Christmas present. The carpenter was a slow reader but a quick worker. In the time it took him to read a book from cover to cover, he'd finished, varnished and delivered the gift to a grateful Ablatt. As he worked away at the sash window, he sifted through his memories of the meeting of the NCF. Chief among them was the sense of awe he'd felt when he saw his friend speak with such fire and cogency in front of a room of strangers. Ablatt seemed to grow in stature and importance. The effect on the audience was startling. He had every handkerchief there fluttering madly by way of an ovation. Ablatt's testimony was at once personal and universal, something that came from his inner convictions yet embodying an ideal that all of them shared.

Time sped past in the cluttered workshop. Hambridge was still bent over the bench when his employer finally arrived. Charlie Redfern was a flabby man in his forties with a beard that never managed to come to fruition and, invariably, with a cigarette dangling from the side of his mouth. He had a cheerful disposition and a ready supply of jokes. For once, however, he looked serious.

'Hello, Fred.'

'Good morning, Charlie.'

'You've already started,' said Redfern, noting the window. 'How long have you been here?'

'About an hour or so,' said Hambridge. 'And there's a reason. Will it be all right if I leave earlier this afternoon?'

The request was ignored. 'Which way did you come here?'

'I came the usual way.'

'Then you'll have missed it. There's a crowd up near Drysdale Street. I stopped to see what all the fuss was about – and guess what?'

'Tell me.'

'There's been a murder. Policemen were guarding the place where it happened. The rumour is that someone was beaten to death there.'

Hambridge gulped. 'Did they say who'd been killed?'

'It was a young chap.'

'When did this happen?'

'Sometime last night, I suppose. That's all I know.'

Hambridge's mind was an inferno of doubt and apprehension. On the previous evening, the route to the carpenter's house would have taken Ablatt close to Drysdale Street. Was that the reason he'd failed to arrive? Hambridge was rocked. The thought that his friend and mentor had been killed was horrifying. He couldn't imagine how he and his friends could manage without their leader. There was no proof that the murder victim was Cyril Ablatt but, in his fevered brain, the possibility that it might be swiftly grew into a likelihood before settling into a certainty. He had to know the truth. Reaching for his coat and hat, he put them on as fast as he could.

'I'm sorry, Charlie,' he said, 'I've got to go.'

Redfern was nonplussed. 'But I need you here.'

'I'll explain later.'

Running to the door, Hambridge let himself out.

When they'd driven Gerald Ablatt back home, he told them that his sister was a very nervous woman and that her husband needed to be present when they divulged the terrible news to her. Accordingly, Marmion and Keedy made their way to a forge in Bethnal Green. In central London, the detectives were used to seeing a large number of cars, vans, lorries and buses chugging along. Here, however, horse-drawn vehicles were in the majority and Jack Dalley's livelihood was secure. As Marmion entered the forge, the blacksmith was hammering the last nail into a horseshoe. His customer paid the money owed and led the horse out. Dalley gave Marmion a smile of welcome. He was a brawny man with a gnarled face and dark-green eyes.

'I don't mend cars, sir,' he said, politely.

'Are you Jack Dalley?' asked Marmion.

'That's me, sir – who wants to know?'

Marmion introduced himself and explained, as gently as he could, why he was there. When he heard that his nephew had been murdered, Dalley was shocked and sympathetic. He tore off his leather apron at once and hung it on a nail.

'Perce!' he called to his assistant.

'Yes?' replied the man.

'Take over here. I've got to go.'

'What's the trouble, Jack?'

'I'll tell you later.'

Percy Fry looked mystified. He'd just fitted a rim to a cartwheel and was testing his handiwork. Fry was a sinewy man of middle height with receding hair and wrinkles that made him seem much older than his fifty years. As he watched his employer getting into the police car, he scratched his head.

On the journey to his house, Dalley pressed for details but there was little that the detectives could tell him. The blacksmith had fond memories of the victim.

'Cyril was a good lad,' he said. 'When he was a boy, he loved to hang about the forge and hold horses while I shoed them. There was a time when I thought about taking him on as an apprentice but Gerald was against it. He wanted his son to have a job where he could look smart and not get dirty. But I'd have taught him a *real* trade. Handing out books all day was beneath him.' His lip curled. 'It's the kind of work a woman could do.'

'They've been doing most things since the war started,' said Keedy, 'and doing them as well as men. The inspector's daughter is a case in point. She was a qualified teacher but she gave it up to learn to drive so that she could help with the war effort. And there are thousands like her.'

'I'm not sure I hold with that.'

'It's one of the necessities of war.'

'Yes,' said Marmion, heading off a potential argument, 'but that's not the issue at stake at the moment. What I'd like to hear is what sort of a nephew Cyril Ablatt was. Did you see much of him, Mr Dalley?'

'He called in from time to time,' said the blacksmith, 'and we had tea there on a Sunday every so often.'

'Did he ever mention any enemies he had?'

'No, Inspector, though he was never going to be popular, what with those strange ideas he had. I disagreed with Cyril but I tried not to have a row with him for my wife's sake. Nancy hates family quarrels.'

'His father said that he didn't have a young lady.'

'He always claimed that he didn't have time,' recalled Dalley, 'but I think there was another reason. Cyril talked too much. Girls don't like that. Nora – that's my eldest – went out with him once. She said that she couldn't shut him up. He didn't want female company – just an audience.'

'It seems that he spent all his time reading in his bedroom.'

'That's not right and it's not healthy. If he'd been my son, I'd have burnt those books and told him to act normal. Mind you,' he added, ruefully, 'if I'd been his father, he'd be fighting for his country right now.'

'Would you have forced him against his will?' asked Keedy.

Dalley was blunt. 'I'd have got him into army uniform somehow.'

When they reached the blacksmith's house, they saw a more tender side of him. He asked them to wait outside while he told his wife what had happened. He felt that the blow would be slightly softer if it came from him. The detectives stayed in the car and looked at the small, squat, unpretentious house. Its one feature of note was a wrought-iron gate that gave access to the tiny front garden.

'I reckon that Dalley made that,' said Marmion.

'Why doesn't he live over the forge?' asked Keedy. 'It's a fair old way for him to go every day. It'd be much easier if he lived on the premises. Apart from anything else, he'd be able to keep an eye on the place. There must be some expensive tools and equipment in the forge.'

'There is, Joe. I'm sure he has a reason to live here.'

'I'd be interested to know what it is.'

'Then you'll have to ask him.'

'What did you make of Dalley?'

'He's something of a gentle giant.'

'I don't think he'd be all that gentle if you got on the wrong side of him.'

'We met him at a vulnerable time,' Marmion reminded him. 'His emotions are bound to be a bit raw. He was really shaken when I told him the news.'

'Yes,' said Keedy, reflectively. 'That's the trouble with murder. It wounds so many people. It reaches out to family, then friends, then mere acquaintances. Dalley won't be allowed to forget it. When the story gets into the newspapers, every customer at his forge will want to ask about his nephew.'

'Each time it will be as if someone is twisting the knife anew.'

'Does anyone *ever* get over the violent death of a loved one?'

'I doubt it, Joe.'

The wait was much longer than anticipated. It was light now and there were more people around, setting off to work or coming out to wonder why a car was standing outside the Dalley house. It was half an hour before the couple appeared. The blacksmith was still in his working clothes but his wife, Nancy, was wrapped up in a thick coat with a tippet around her shoulders and a feathered hat. Dalley more or less carried her to the car and it was apparent that she was too grief-stricken to say anything. The detectives expressed their condolences then remained silent during the journey to the Ablatt house. When they got there, their passengers got out, went to the front door and knocked. Gerald Ablatt appeared and his sister flung herself into his arms. He ushered her inside. Dalley came briefly back to the car.

'Thank you,' he said. 'We're grateful for the lift.'

'We'll be in touch, sir,' said Marmion. 'Before we go, however, the sergeant has something to ask you.'

Keedy took his cue. 'I wondered why you didn't live over the forge, sir, that's all. It would save you going to and fro all the time.'

'We used to live there,' explained Dalley, 'but it's not the cleanest place to bring up a family. When my parents died, they left me the house where you took me earlier. We moved into it four or five years ago. As for the forge,' he went on, 'my assistant lives there. Percy and his missus look after the place for me. I take the rent out of his wages.' He pursed his lips. 'He'll have to manage on his own for a long while now. I'm needed here.'

Turning on his heel, he went into the house and shut the door behind him. The car set off and rounded the corner, giving them a clear view of the slogans and taunts painted crudely on the side wall. It was evident that the anonymous artist was burning with hatred for Cyril Ablatt.

'Do you think someone will be back with a paintbrush?' asked Keedy.

'Not as long as Dalley is here,' replied Marmion. 'They wouldn't dare.'

Running the bakery involved the whole family. Gordon Leach's mother worked in the shop with the help of his sister. Having done his stint of baking, Leach had to go off on the first of his delivery rounds. The horse stood patiently between the shafts while he loaded the bread into the back of the cart. Still warm, it was wrapped in tissue paper. When the job was complete, he clambered into the cart and was about to set off. Then he saw the animated figure of Fred Hambridge coming towards him. He climbed out immediately.

'I was hoping to catch you,' said Hambridge, panting for breath.

'What's the problem?'

'You haven't heard, then?'

'Heard what?'

'It was my boss who told me about it. Charlie was coming past Drysdale Street when he saw this crowd. That's how he knew.'

'You're not making much sense, Fred,' said Leach. 'Why don't you get your breath back and tell me what's actually happened?'

'There's been a murder.'

Leach started. 'A murder – where?'

'I've just told you. It was near Drysdale Street.'

'Who was the victim?'

Even as he asked the question, Leach thought of a possible answer and it made his blood congeal. He shook his head in a frenzy of denial.

'No, no,' he protested. 'I don't believe it.'

'I didn't at first,' said Hambridge.

'It can't have been Cyril.'

'It was a young man, according to Charlie. That much is certain.'

'But he had no idea what his name was.'

'None at all,' admitted the other, 'but we have to face facts, Gordon. He was killed last night after dark. And it was near a place that Cyril would have walked past on his way to my house. It all fits. It explains why he never turned up.'

Leach's head was spinning. 'I'm sorry. I just don't believe it.'

'I went to the police station but they wouldn't give me any details. They told me to wait until the newspapers come out this evening. There may be a name in that. When I told them that I was a friend of Cyril, they didn't want to know and told me to stop being a nuisance.'

'There must be some way to find out the truth.'

'We can go to his house and ask his father.'

Leach brought a hand to his throat. 'Oh, no!' he exclaimed. '*That's* why Mr Ablatt wasn't there when Mansel called earlier this morning. He told me that he'd gone to find out if Cyril got back late last night.'

'He didn't get back,' said Hambridge, woefully, 'because he simply couldn't. Someone had battered him to death. What are we going to do, Gordon?'

'We try to find out the truth.'

'We both *know* the truth. Cyril Ablatt is dead. Why argue about it? I was asking a different question. What the hell are we going to do now that we don't have him here to guide us? What would Cyril *want* us to do?'

Leach didn't even hear him. His mind was running on another track altogether. If their friend really was the murder victim, there would be implications. Ablatt had given a brilliant speech at the meeting of the NCF. Had he been killed by way of punishment? Was someone determined to silence conscientious objectors? Leach was overcome by a sense of panic.

'Cyril may just be the first one,' he cried. 'Which one of us is next?'

CHAPTER FOUR

The lane connected two streets in Shoreditch. It was narrow, twisting and unlit at night. When the detectives arrived there by car, policemen were on duty at either end of the little thoroughfare, stopping anyone from using it and trying to move on people who just came to stand and stare. Marmion identified himself to one of the policemen and asked to be taken to the exact spot where the body was found. He and Keedy were escorted to a point near the middle of the lane. The policeman indicated a rickety garden gate set into a recess.

'It was right here, Inspector,' he said.

'Who found him?' asked Keedy.

'I'm told it was a courting couple, sir. You've got to feel sorry for them. They sneak down here for a kiss and a cuddle and they trip over a dead body.'

'That must have cooled their ardour.'

'It was well after midnight – must have been pitch-dark.'

'How did they know it was a corpse?'

'They didn't, sir,' replied the policeman. 'In fact, they thought it might have been a drunk who passed out as he tottered home from the Weavers Arms.'

'That's the pub on the corner, isn't it?'

'Yes. Afraid it might be more serious, they reported it.'

'I'm glad they had the sense to do that.'

'So am I, sir. By all accounts, it was a hideous sight. It's just as well they moved the body away before the public got to see it.'

Marmion was only half-listening. Crouching down, he examined the ground with great care. When he eventually stood up, he stroked his chin meditatively.

'This is not the scene of the crime,' he concluded. 'If it were, there'd be lots of bloodstains and there are hardly any. I think that the victim was killed elsewhere then dumped here. I also think that we're after a local man.'

Keedy was puzzled. 'How can you be so sure?'

'Only someone who knew the area would be aware of this lane. It's a good place to get rid of a dead body – but only after the pub closes and people stop using it to get home. The victim was brought here when there was nobody about.'

'The killer might have needed an accomplice.'

'Why?'

'A dead body is easier to carry if there are two of you.'

'It's possible that someone else was involved, if only as a lookout. The killer was obviously a cautious man. He'd take no chances. Thank you, Constable,' he said to the policeman. 'You can get back on duty now. Keep everyone out of the lane for the time being – especially any press photographers.' As the policeman went off to take up his position, Marmion turned to Keedy. 'What's your immediate reaction?'

'It's someone that Ablatt knows.'

'That was my view.'

'All that we've heard about him so far points to the fact that he's a bright lad. In that photo we saw in his bedroom, he looked young and strong. He wouldn't be easily overpowered unless he was taken unawares.'

'Exactly,' said Marmion. 'If he was approached by an acquaintance, he'd be off guard. The trouble is that he'd have a hell of a lot of acquaintances. Since he worked in a library, he must know any number of people.'

'One of them might be the phantom artist.'

'Who?'

'I'm thinking of the man who painted those things on the side of Ablatt's house. The father had no idea who he was but it must be a neighbour with a malicious streak in him. We need to find out who he is.'

'Or who *she* is,' corrected Marmion. 'A woman can handle a paintbrush as well as a man. I know that Alice can. When I papered her room last year, she insisted on painting the door and the window frame. As soon as we'd done that, of course,' he said, face puckered with regret, 'our daughter decided to move out of the house. We could have saved ourselves all that trouble.'

Keedy was sceptical. 'You surely don't think we're looking for a female killer, do you?'

'We need to consider every option. There's no evidence to suggest that the artist and the killer are one and the same person but it's a possibility we have to bear in mind. As for the murder itself,' Marmion continued, 'it's highly unlikely that a woman committed it because of the brutality involved and the physical strength needed. On the other hand, there could be a female accomplice, someone who incited the crime in the first place. The fairer sex has become a lot more aggressive since the war started. Don't forget that it's women who hand out white feathers.'

'Accusing someone of cowardice is a long way from plotting their death.'

'I accept that.'

'And what sort of man lets a woman talk him into committing a murder?'

'The kind who are naturally inclined that way,' said Marmion, levelly. 'We've met quite a few of them in this job. They just need that final push.'

'No,' said Keedy, 'I disagree with you there, Harv. I don't believe a woman is involved in any way.'

'What about the lady in that photograph we found?'

'I was forgetting her.'

'She could be indirectly culpable. If her husband discovered her friendship with Cyril Ablatt, he might have been enraged enough to kill him.'

'We need to track the woman down.'

'That's what I intend to do – *after* we've interviewed the victim's three friends. I'll start with Gordon Leach. The family bakery is not far from the Ablatt house. I'll find it. You can tackle Fred Hambridge. You've got his address. If you go there first, they might be able to tell you where he works.'

'What about the third friend – Mansel Price?'

'Try his address as well. Find out where he is. If you can't reach him this morning, leave a message to the effect that we'd like to speak to him. By the time he gets it, he'll know why.'

'Yes,' said Keedy. 'This will be on the front page of the evening's paper. Everybody in London will know.' An image of Superintendent Chatfield popped into his mind. 'When he gave his statement to the press, I hope that Chat asked for any witnesses to come forward. *Somebody* may have seen something.'

'It's a long shot but you never know.'

'I take it that you'll have use of the car.'

Marmion grinned. 'It's a privilege of rank.'

'When do I get my own transport?'

'When Sir Edward retires and you succeed him as commissioner.' He slapped Keedy playfully on the arm. 'Come on, I'll give you a lift to Hambridge's house. It's on my way to the bakery. Then I'll see you back at Scotland Yard. The superintendent will want a report on the progress we've made so far.'

Keedy raised an eyebrow. 'I didn't know we'd made any.'

'Then you should remember just how much information we've gathered. Lots of it may be irrelevant but I fancy that we've already made one or two crucial discoveries.' He gave a chuckle. 'The trick is to work out which ones they are.'

When she heard a vehicle drawing up outside the house, Ellen Marmion hoped that it might be her husband, returning for a late breakfast. In fact, it was her daughter who climbed down from the lorry she'd been driving and used her key to let herself into the house. Ellen was delighted to see her.

'Alice!' she cried, embracing her. 'What a lovely surprise!'

'I can't stay long. I came to scrounge a cup of tea.'

'I'll put the kettle on at once.'

Alice followed her into the kitchen and watched her fill the kettle under the tap before setting it on the stove and using a match to ignite the gas. Ellen turned to appraise her daughter with a mixture of pleasure and disapproval.

'I can never get used to you in that uniform,' she said, clicking her tongue. 'Khaki is such an unflattering colour.'

'It cost me two pounds,' said Alice, defensively, 'and I like it.'

'I preferred it when you worked as a teacher and wore your own clothes.'

'There's a war on, Mummy. I'm far more use working for the WEC than I would be keeping a classroom of noisy children in order. Even you must realise that by now.'

'Frankly, I don't but I'm not going to argue about it.'

'Thank you.'

Alice Marmion was a comparatively tall, slim, lithe woman in her early twenties with attractive features and bright eyes. Against her mother's wishes, she'd given up her job at a nearby school in order to join the Women's Emergency Corps, one of the many women's organisations dedicated to helping the war effort. It was interesting work that confronted her with a whole range of problems but it involved long hours and kept her at full stretch. Ellen noticed the signs of fatigue.

'You look tired,' she said, anxiously. 'Are you getting enough sleep?'

'Who cares about sleep when there are so many jobs to do?'

'I do. It's important.'

'So is helping people in dire circumstances.'

'Oh, I *do* wish you still lived at home so that I could take care of you.'

'I can cope perfectly well on my own, Mummy.'

'I worry that you don't get enough food.'

Alice laughed. 'As a matter of fact, I've put on weight.'

'Then you're not getting the right *kind* of food.'

'Stop worrying about me. I've been in the WEC for well over six months now and I've looked after myself all that time. Living on my own gives me the kind of freedom I could never enjoy here.'

Ellen was hurt. 'You make this house sound like a prison.'

'I didn't mean to. I was very happy here –when I was younger, that is. I just felt too old to be living with my parents.'

'We miss you dreadfully. At least,' added Ellen, '*I* certainly do. Your father is hardly ever here so I miss him as well. They got him out of bed around five o'clock this morning for the latest crisis. I probably won't see him again until it's time to turn in.' She pulled a face. 'Who'd marry a policeman?'

'Daddy must have warned you what it would be like.'

'He was just a bobby on the beat in those days. I didn't like him working shifts but at least I knew when I'd see him again.'

'Do you regret that you married him?'

Ellen gasped. 'What a terrible question to ask!'

'Well – do you?'

'Don't be silly. I love your father. I'd just like to see more of him.'

'It may be better when the war's over.'

'That's what I keep telling myself,' said Ellen. 'We live in hope. But I can see why Joe Keedy never married. Working at Scotland Yard is much easier when you don't have a family to worry about.'

'Joe *does* have a family.'

'Yes, but they're up in the Midlands somewhere. He has very little to do with them. He can live a bachelor life and do as he pleases.'

'Not exactly,' said Alice. 'He's in the same boat as Daddy. They're never off duty. The call can come at any time of day or night.'

'Don't remind me.'

The kettle was starting to boil. Ellen turned to reach for the teapot before emptying its contents down the sink and rinsing it out. When steam began to billow out of the kettle, she switched off the gas then poured a little hot water into the pot to warm it up. Spoonfuls of tea followed, then she added the hot water, put the lid back on and slipped the cosy over the pot. When they were side by side, the resemblance between mother and daughter was very clear. The difference was that Ellen was twice Alice's age and had greying hair, a lined face and a spreading midriff. She struggled hard to master her intense concern

59

for her children. Her son had joined the army and was somewhere in France. Her daughter had left home, ostensibly to join the WEC but, in reality, to spread her wings as well. With her husband absent for long periods, Ellen was bound to feel sad and neglected.

'What are you doing today?' she asked.

'I've got to drive to the station to collect another batch of refugees. It's some more Belgians this time. Just as well I've picked up so much French,' said Alice, cheerfully. 'Being in the WEC is a real education. I've learnt how to drive any kind of vehicle and can get by in French and German. More importantly, I've learnt how to look after myself so that I'm not a burden on you and Daddy.'

'What a ridiculous idea!' protested Ellen. 'You never *were* a burden.'

'There were times when I felt that I was.'

'Well, *I* never felt that. As a matter of fact—'

'I'm sorry, Mummy,' interrupted Alice, 'but I'll have to go soon. Could you pour that tea now, please?'

'Yes, yes, of course.'

After putting two teacups on the table, Ellen used a strainer to pour tea into them. They sat either side of the kitchen table, taking it in turns to add milk and sugar to their respective cups before stirring with a teaspoon. Ellen regarded her daughter through troubled eyes.

'Is this what you really want, Alice?'

'Yes, it is. I love working for the WEC.'

'Vera Dowling doesn't. I spoke to her mother yesterday. She said that Vera is finding it too demanding and expects her to give it up soon.'

Alice shook her head. 'Vera would never do that. She has a good moan at times but so does everyone else. We joined the WEC together and we both admire what it's trying to do. Mrs Dowling is wrong, honestly. Vera's like me – she'll see it through to the end.'

Ellen sipped her tea and ventured a smile. 'It's so good to see you again,' she said, 'if only for a short while. Your father will be so annoyed that he missed you.'

'Give him my love,' said Alice, sipping her own tea.

'You haven't seen him since Christmas.'

'We've been so madly busy.'

'We'd hoped that you might at least spend New Year's Eve with us.'

'I told you – I was invited to a party.'

'Well, you're invited to a party here any time you like,' said Ellen, beaming hospitably. 'You can bring Vera Dowling along, if you wish, or any of the new friends you've made in the WEC. I'd like to meet them. And if your father is free, I'll ask him to invite Joe Keedy as well. That would be nice, wouldn't it?'

'Yes,' said Alice, quietly. 'That would be very nice.'

Keedy was in luck. When the police car dropped him off outside Hambridge's house, the carpenter was at home. He was startled when the detective introduced himself and shattered when his worst fears were confirmed. Keedy had to offer a steadying hand. Invited into the house, he saw how spotless and uncluttered it was. There were no paintings on the walls and very few ornaments. The simplicity was striking.

Hambridge slumped onto the settee with his head in his hands. Taking a seat opposite him, Keedy had his notebook and pencil ready. He waited until the younger man recovered enough to be able to meet his gaze.

'I'm sorry,' said Hambridge, semaphoring an apology. 'Cyril was my best friend. I feel so guilty about this.'

'Why should that be?'

'It's because I should have stayed. He sent me on home after the meeting but I should have stayed with him. If I'd done that, he'd still be alive.'

'Not necessarily,' said Keedy. 'We could be investigating *two* deaths.'

Hambridge sat up. 'Do you think I'm in danger, then?'

'I don't know at this stage but it seems doubtful. What I'm hoping to establish is where the murder is likely to have taken place. To do that, I'll need you to describe the precise route that your friend would have taken to get back home.'

'He would have been coming here. This is where we arranged to meet.'

'How would he get back to Shoreditch?'

'The same way as us,' replied Hambridge.

'Would that route take him anywhere near Drysdale Street?'

'Oh, yes. My boss told me that's where the murder took place.'

'It's where the body was found, I grant you, but we've reason to believe that he was set on elsewhere. Let's go back to the meeting,' he suggested. 'Tell me what time you left, when you got back here and when you expected Cyril to join you.'

Hambridge was too disturbed to give an accurate account of his movements. He kept breaking off to wrestle with the horror of what had happened, continuing to blame himself for not being there to offer protection. Keedy had to be patient, teasing out the details one by one until he had a clearer idea of what had occurred on the previous evening. From the way that Hambridge talked about Price and Leach, he gathered that they were close friends who looked to Ablatt for guidance. The bereaved carpenter spread his arms.

'Who could possibly have wanted to kill him?' he asked.

'I was hoping that you might have some ideas on that score.'

'But I don't, Sergeant. I can't think of anyone who hated Cyril. He was so likeable. We've all had difficulties, mind you. There've been people who yelled nasty things because we haven't joined up and an old man spat at us in the street one day, but nobody ever threatened to attack us.'

'What about those slogans painted on the wall of the Ablatt house?'

'Cyril used to shrug those off.'

'Well, his father didn't. They really upset him at first.'

'I know. He told us. But it didn't scare Cyril because he was so brave. He always used to quote that saying. You know – "Sticks and stones will break my bones but names will never hurt me." That was typical of Cyril.'

Keedy was about to point out that someone *had* broken the victim's bones but he decided against it. For all his bulk, Hambridge seemed quite fragile. It was better to steer him away from gory details of the crime. Keedy's pencil was poised.

'How long have you known him?'

'We grew up together.'

'What about Price and Leach?'

'The four of us went to the same school.'

'And you're all conscientious objectors, I gather.'

'I'm a Quaker,' said Hambridge, simply. 'We utterly deny all outward wars and strife. That's what George Fox said and he preached the gospel of peace all his life, even though they put him in prison time and again.'

'What about the others?'

'I'm the only Quaker. Cyril was a true Christian. Mansel refuses to let the state bully him into uniform and Gordon just thinks that war is wrong. It was Cyril who sort of spoke for the rest of us. He made a wonderful speech at the meeting. That's why he was asked to stay behind afterwards. He had a real gift, Sergeant,' said Hambridge, eyes moistening. 'None of us could touch him. Cyril had a way with words. I could listen to him all day.'

Gordon Leach had gone on his delivery round with the furtiveness of a man expecting to be attacked at any moment. Convinced that his friend had been murdered, he felt that his own life was also in jeopardy, even though it was now daylight and the streets were full of people. Customers who came to the door to pay him wondered why he thrust their loaves at them, took the money and fled. It was only towards the end of the round that he slowly regained his confidence and began to control his fears. When he found Inspector Harvey Marmion waiting for him at the bakery, however, his lurking desperation was rekindled. He was given official confirmation that Ablatt was indeed the murder victim and it made him turn the colour of flour.

They were alone in the back room that was still pulsing with warmth.

'I'm sorry to be the bearer of such bad news,' said Marmion.

'I knew it already,' explained Leach. 'Fred – that's Fred Hambridge – came to warn me that he'd heard about someone being beaten to death not far from here. We both guessed it had to be Cyril. He didn't turn up, you see.'

'Turn up where?'

'We agreed to meet at Fred's house after the meeting of the NCF.'

'Why didn't he leave with you?'

Leach told him that Ablatt had been detained by the people who organised the meeting. He also gave details of the route they'd taken back to Shoreditch and an approximate time of their arrival at Hambridge's house. Talking it all through seemed to instil even more trepidation in him. Marmion tried to soothe him.

'I really don't think that you are in imminent danger,' he said, 'and neither are your friends. It was Cyril Ablatt who was singled out. If someone had had designs on any of you, then they'd have lain in wait until they saw a moment to strike. Have you ever felt that you were being watched?'

'No, Inspector, I haven't.'

'What about your friends?'

'They'd have mentioned it if that was the case – and they didn't.'

'Then none of you need be alarmed. For some unknown reason, the killer's target was your friend, Cyril. Do you know what that reason might be?'

'They wanted to silence him.'

'Who did?'

'Someone who knew how good Cyril was at making speeches,' said Leach, blurting out his answer. 'You could never get the better of him in an argument. He'd tie you in knots. And he could hold a big audience as well. He proved that yesterday. They decided to shut him up.'

'And who might "they" be?'

'They're people who demand that we volunteer for the army, so-called patriots who wave the Union Jack and send others off to die on the battlefield. It's got to be one of them, Inspector.'

'I'll reserve my judgement on that.'

'There's so many of them about, you see. I should know. When I deliver the bread, there are three houses I can't go to any more. They say that they won't touch anything baked by a conchie – only their language is not as polite as that.'

'Did Cyril get that kind of response at the library?'

'All the time,' replied Leach, 'but he could always talk himself out of the situation. He even turned the tables on Horrie Waldron.'

'And who might he be?' enquired Marmion.

'He's an old codger me and Cyril knew in the George and Vulture when we used to meet for a drink there. It's in Pitfield Street. Cyril had to pass it on his way home from the library. Anyway,' Leach went on, 'we sometimes saw Horrie in there, sitting drunk in a corner. You could share a joke with him until the war broke out. He turned nasty then. Every time we went in there, he'd have a dig at us for not joining up. It got so bad that we stopped going there altogether.'

'What's this about turning the tables on him?'

'Horrie turned up at the library just before Christmas. He'd obviously been drinking. He tried to cause a scene by telling Cyril he was a coward but he got more than he bargained for. Cyril took him on in argument and made him look stupid. Everyone was laughing at Horrie. According to Cyril,' said Leach, revelling in his friend's triumph, 'he slunk out of there with his tail between his legs.'

'He must have felt humiliated.'

'He was, Inspector – good and proper.'

'And would you say that this Horrie Waldron was a vindictive man?'

'Oh, yes, and he has a foul mouth on him.'

'I wonder why Mr Ablatt didn't mention the incident,' said Marmion. 'When I asked him if his son had any enemies, he denied it.'

'Cyril didn't tell his father everything that happened. In fact, I'm probably the only person who knows about Horrie being turned into a laughing stock at the library. Fred and Mansel have no idea who Horrie Waldron is.' Leach scowled. 'They're lucky. He can be a menace.'

'You described him as an old codger.'

'That's what he looks like, Inspector, but he's probably not *that* old. He just never takes care of himself. Also, he smells. I bumped into him once when I was out with Ruby and she thought he was a tramp.'

'Is Ruby your girlfriend?'

Leach's back straightened. 'She's my fiancée.'

'Congratulations! Have you set a date?'

'It's in July,' said Leach. 'Going back to Horrie, I heard that the landlord at the George and Vulture got fed up with him and threw him out. Last time I saw Horrie, he was going into the Weavers Arms.'

It was not far from where the body of Cyril Ablatt had been found. Marmion made a mental note of the fact. In his opinion, Leach was an interesting character, weak in many respects yet strong enough to hold to his principles in the face of daily hostility. Marmion had seen the way that people could bait conscientious objectors, making their lives a misery by taunting, abusing or sending them poison pen letters. More than one pacifist had been driven to suicide to escape the constant antagonism. Leach seemed unlikely to follow. For all his nervousness, there was a hard inner core that allowed him to withstand the jeers and the innuendo. And since a date for his wedding had been set, he didn't wish to be somewhere in France or Belgium in the summer. Marmion's own son, Paul, was very close in age to Leach and had volunteered readily with his father's approval. Though he didn't condone the stance that the young baker was taking, Marmion nevertheless admired him for his courage in doing so.

He thought about the reported viciousness of the attack on Cyril Ablatt and the problem of getting the body to the location where it was later found.

'Tell me about Waldron,' he said. 'Is he a strong man?'

'He's very strong, Inspector.'

'Does he have a job or has he retired?'

'Horrie will never retire. He'll go on until he drops.'

'What does he do for a living?'

'He's a gravedigger.'

CHAPTER FIVE

Some high-ranking officers at Scotland Yard gave those below them a degree of freedom during the conduct of an investigation. Superintendent Claude Chatfield was not one of them. On the contrary, he insisted on being informed of progress at every stage. As he gave his superior an account of the action taken so far, Marmion provided enough detail to show how thorough he and Keedy had been while deliberately failing to mention the photograph discovered in the victim's Bible. He knew full well that he was courting Chatfield's fury but felt that discretion was paramount. If the lady in the photograph was, even tangentially, connected to the murder, Marmion could reveal the fact of her existence at a later date. If, however, she had no link whatsoever with the crime, he believed that it would be wrong to drag a secret friendship into the light of day, thereby causing pain and recrimination. It was better to let her retreat into anonymity. Chatfield watched him with the intensity of a cat waiting to pounce on its prey. When the inspector finished his report, the other man flashed his claws.

'You're holding something back,' he challenged.

Marmion shrugged. 'Why should I do that, sir?'

'I sense that something is missing.'

'There's a great deal that's missing, sir. Once you let me get on with my work, I'll be able to fill in some of the blank spaces.'

'You've described the interview you had with Gordon Leach. What about the other close friends of the deceased?'

'Sergeant Keedy has yet to return, sir. When he does, I hope that he'll have gleaned something useful from the two young men concerned – Hambridge and Price. They seem to have been part of a close-knit group.'

Chatfield was disdainful. 'Four cowards banded together for safety.'

'That's not the impression I get, sir,' said Marmion.

'I'm not interested in your impressions, Inspector. I want facts. I want firm evidence. The press are already hounding me.'

'I'm sure that you handled them with your usual tact.'

'I told them as little as possible,' said Chatfield with a thin smile, 'but I did ask them to make an appeal on my behalf for any witnesses to come forward. In the course of his journey from that meeting back to Shoreditch, lots of people must have seen Ablatt.' He picked up the photograph supplied by the victim's father. 'I'll release this to the press. The sight of him may jog someone's memory.'

'Will that be all, sir?' asked Marmion, rising hopefully from his chair.

'No, it is not.'

'I think we've covered more or less everything.'

'Sit down again.' Marmion obeyed him. 'What is your next step?'

'To be honest, sir, I was planning to grab a cup of tea and a bite to eat in the canteen. I had no breakfast this morning. After that – or possibly *during* it – I'll liaise with Sergeant Keedy.'

'Let me know what he found out.'

'You'll have a full report before we leave.'

'Where are you going?'

'Back to Shoreditch,' replied Marmion. 'Manpower is severely limited, I know, but I'll deploy the few detectives at my disposal to make house-to-house enquiries in the area where the body was found. I'll then visit the library to speak to some of Cyril Ablatt's colleagues.'

'What about Sergeant Keedy?'

'I'm going to suggest that he works the night shift, sir. When word gets out that Ablatt has been murdered, the person who daubed the wall of his house might be tempted to add to his handiwork. I'd like to apprehend him and find out just how deep his hatred goes. It will mean persuading a neighbour to allow the sergeant to spend the night under their roof so that he can keep the Ablatt house under surveillance.'

Chatfield sniffed. 'That means a claim for overtime.'

'It can be offset against the hours Sergeant Keedy will need to catch up on lost sleep. Our self-appointed artist works by night. No vigil is required in daylight.'

'So you'll be without the services of your right-hand man tomorrow.'

'Only for a short time,' said Marmion. 'The sergeant is very resilient. He manages on far less sleep than the rest of us.'

'I'm still not convinced that it's the best use of his time.'

'It could be, sir.'

'The man may not even show up.'

'That's a possibility we have to allow for.'

'Do you think he's in any way associated with the crime?'

'It remains to be seen, sir. But even if he's not involved in the murder, he's guilty of another crime – libel. What he wrote about Cyril Ablatt is both insulting and untrue.'

'You can't libel the dead, Inspector.'

'The young man was alive when those harsh words were painted.'

Chatfield was dismissive. 'That's immaterial,' he said, flicking a hand. 'Before he acts as a nightwatchman, what will the sergeant be doing?'

'I'm sending him off to the cemetery to speak to Horrie Waldron.'

'Is he that gravedigger?'

'He is indeed, sir.'

'Good,' said Chatfield, rubbing his hands together. 'That's the one positive lead that you've managed to uncover. This fellow fits the picture I envisage of the killer. He knows Ablatt well, he loathes conscientious objectors, he has a record of causing trouble and, I'll venture, he's often sufficiently inebriated to throw off all inhibition. There's no need to send Sergeant Keedy. It's a job for a uniformed constable. He can arrest Waldron and bring him in for questioning.'

'I'd strongly advise against that, sir.'

'Use your eyes, man! He's a prime suspect.'

'He's certainly worthy of investigation,' said Marmion, coolly, 'but we have no evidence to arrest him. Besides, we don't want to alert him to the fact that we harbour suspicions about him or he's likely to be thrown on the defensive. A heavy-handed approach would be a mistake.'

'There's a history of friction between him and Ablatt, leading to that incident at the library. Isn't that what Leach told you?'

'Yes, sir, but he also told me that Waldron spends most of his free time in a pub. How would he even *know* about yesterday's meeting at Devonshire House or be aware of Ablatt's movements after he left Bishopsgate? I'll wager that he's sometimes too drunk to remember what day of the week it is. This murder involved calculation and I don't believe that Waldron is capable of that.'

Chatfield was checked. 'Please yourself,' he said, patently annoyed at the rebuff. 'You're nominally in charge of this investigation. If and when it emerges that this fellow *was* indeed the killer, I hope that you'll have the grace to apologise to me.'

72

'I'll do so on bended knee, Superintendent.'

'Sarcasm ill becomes you.'

'Put it down to lack of food,' said Marmion, getting up again. 'After I've had breakfast, I'm sure that I'll feel much better. As for Waldron,' he added, 'I promise you that – if he *is* guilty – he won't slip through our fingers.'

Abney Park cemetery was much more than a burial ground. It was also an arboretum, a place of architectural interest and a vital green lung in the urban sprawl of Stoke Newington. Horace Waldron never noticed the vast expanse of trees and shrubs. Nor did he pay any heed to the magnificent gates, the Egyptian lodges and the Gothic chapel. His gaze was fixed solely on the earth he had to shift in order to accommodate a new guest. Waldron was a burly man in his late fifties with an unsightly face, pitted with age and reddened by alcohol. His clothes were grimed beyond reclaim and his cap sat precariously on the back of his head. When he arrived for work that morning, he carried a spade over his shoulder. Putting it aside, he first stepped behind a large gravestone so that he could urinate against it with a measure of privacy. After spitting on the ground, he was about to start work when he noticed the dried bloodstains along the edge of his spade. He cleaned them off under the tap beside the shed where he usually kept his implements.

Laughing to himself, he was soon digging his first grave of the day.

When the notion was put to him, Keedy didn't find it at all appealing. Over a cup of tea in the canteen, he explored the idea without enthusiasm.

'What are the chances of him coming tonight?'

'Your guess is as good as mine.'

'That's the trouble, Harv. We're very much in the realm of guesswork. We're guessing that the artist lives nearby and would have an irresistible compulsion to pick up his brush tonight and get back to work.'

'He may wait a few days before doing so,' admitted Marmion.

'He may not even come back at all.'

'Oh, I fancy that he – or she, for that matter – will appear before long.'

'So I have to shiver all through the night in someone's front room for what could be a week or more. Is that what you're saying?'

'No, it isn't, Joe. And if you think the assignment is too onerous, I can always find someone else to shoulder it. You were the one who said we needed to catch him. I was simply giving you the first chance to do that.'

'Yes,' confessed Keedy, 'he certainly needs to be nabbed. It's just that I was hoping for a little free time at the end of the day.'

'Even romance takes second place in a murder case, especially one as problematical as this. You'll have to disappoint her, I'm afraid.'

Keedy made no reply. He thought about the jibes painted on the wall of the Ablatt house. They were cruel and vulgar. Whoever put them there had spent a fair amount of time up a ladder. The artist could have relied on the fact that, even if he'd been discovered at work, nobody was likely to report him to the police. Most people in the area would have condoned what he was doing. A conscientious objector was being punished. Thick white paint was more conspicuous than a frail white feather.

'I'll do it, Harv,' he said at length. 'It could be important.'

'I agree. Before that, however, we've other work to do.'

'What can you tell me about this gravedigger you want me to find?'

'All I know is what I picked up from Gordon Leach.'

He passed on the description given to him of Horrie Waldron then offered his assessment of the baker. Keedy had already told him about the visit to Hambridge's house and how the carpenter was devastated by the news. Unable to make contact with Mansel Price, the sergeant had left a message for him at his digs.

'We can be sure of one thing,' said Marmion. 'All three of his friends relied completely on Ablatt. How will his death affect their resolve? Or, to put it another way, how conscientious will their objections be now that he's gone?'

'Hambridge is a Quaker. It won't change his mind.'

'I'm less certain about Leach. He could waver.'

'Apparently, Price is one of those characters who hates all authority.'

'So do I when it's in the hands of someone like the superintendent.'

Keedy chuckled. 'Did you get another rap over the knuckles from Chat?'

'He wanted Waldron arrested and hauled into Scotland Yard.'

'But we have nothing on him yet.'

'According to Superintendent Chatfield, we do. We have a man with motive and means to kill Ablatt. We simply have to establish that he had the opportunity as well and we can charge him.'

'It's another of Chat's barmy theories.'

'In fairness,' conceded Marmion, 'they're not always so barmy. He made some very significant arrests during his time as an inspector. However, it's an open question as to whether that was luck or judgement. We'll have to give him the benefit of the doubt. Finish your tea,' he went on, standing up. 'We have people to see and answers to get.'

'Right,' said Keedy, swallowing the last of his tea then leaping to his feet. 'I'm ready, Harv. Will you give me a lift to the cemetery?'

'Of course – and we must arrange a place to meet up afterwards.'

'Where do we go then?'

'We need to speak to a certain photographer.'

They left the canteen and walked side by side along the corridor. All that lay ahead of them was the promise of hard work, much of which would be tedious and unrewarding. Yet they felt excited in a way that they always did at the start of a hunt for a killer. Keedy recalled what the inspector had said earlier.

'Why do you think Leach will waver?' he asked.

'I don't doubt the sincerity of his pacifism,' said Marmion, 'and he won't renounce that. But I sensed a weakness. He's engaged to be married. He has to make decisions that involve *two* people. That could make things a lot trickier.'

Leach's head was pounding. So much had happened in the space of a couple of hours that he was confused and fearful. He'd awoken with a sense of dread, then been told what Hambridge had learnt about a gruesome murder during the night. Leach felt certain that it had to be his friend. A Scotland Yard detective had confirmed the name of the victim and questioned him about his contact with Ablatt the previous day. It had left the baker completely jangled. He'd pleaded with his father to be released from his duties at the shop and, since he'd finished his delivery rounds, he was allowed to leave. Leach had arranged to meet Ruby Cosgrove that evening but he couldn't contain himself that long. As a matter of urgency, he needed to speak to her now. She had to be told.

His fiancée had responded to the appeal for help in the war effort by working in a small factory that produced tinned meat to be sent to British soldiers in the trenches. It was boring, repetitive, undemanding labour but it gave her the feeling that she was making a contribution. Ruby worked set hours. Leach knew that during her lunch break she usually popped out of the factory to escape the pandemonium, get some fresh air and enjoy a cigarette.

When he got to the factory, he saw her lurking in a doorway with some of the other female employees. Even though she was wearing an ugly fawn overall and a fawn scarf, the mere sight of Ruby Cosgrove lifted his spirits. Spotting him, the other women nudged Ruby and giggled. One of them whispered something in her ear and she blushed. By the time he got to them, Leach was out of breath.

'What are you doing here, Gordon?' she asked in surprise.

Unable to find the words at first, he gave the other women such a look of desperation that they took pity on him and moved away so that the couple could talk alone. He led Ruby to a low wall and made her sit down.

'I had to come,' he said, lowering himself down beside her.

'Whatever's the matter with you? You're trembling.'

'There's something I must tell you, Ruby.'

'Well, be quick about it,' she said. 'The hooter will go in a minute.'

He looked into her face and realised why he loved her so much. Ruby had an exaggerated prettiness that had captivated him when he first met her and a way of jiggling her head about as she spoke that he found entrancing. He didn't mind that she was rather plump. If anything, it added to her attraction, the large bust swelling under her overall, the generous thighs and wide hips enlarging her contours. He hated having to pass on such tragic news but he could hold it in no longer. Taking her by the shoulders, he inhaled deeply.

'Something terrible has happened,' he said.

She tensed. 'What is it?'

'Cyril is dead.'

'No!' she exclaimed, palms slapping against her chubby cheeks. 'I don't believe it. Tell me it's not true, Gordon. Tell me it's some kind of joke.'

'I swear that it's true – and there's worse to come.'

'What could possibly be worse than that?'

Tears now streamed down his face. 'He was murdered, Ruby. A detective came to the bakery to tell me. While we were all waiting for him at Fred's house, Cyril was battered to death.'

It was all too much for Ruby. She simply couldn't cope with the gravity of the news and its many implications for her fiancé, and for her. While she liked Ablatt, she resented him for taking up so much of Leach's time. All that resentment vanished now, drowned beneath a flood of sympathy. After biting her lip and emitting a laugh of disbelief, she swayed to and fro before fainting into his arms.

When the factory hooter sounded, she never even heard it.

'Are you Horace Waldron?'

'No, I'm not.'

'But I was told that you were.'

'Then you was told lies – my name is Horrie.'

'It's only a diminutive of Horace.'

'What the fuck is that?'

'Never mind, sir.'

'And who are you calling "sir"? What's your game?'

'I need to speak to you.'

'Not when I got work to do.'

'This is important.'

'So is earning my bleeding beer money.'

Joe Keedy could see that he was in for a difficult interview. When he tracked Waldron down in the cemetery, the man was standing in a grave that was three feet deep. Surly and uncooperative, Waldron chewed on a pipe but there was no tobacco in it. He resumed his digging. Squatting down, Keedy put a hand on his shoulder to stop him.

'Let go of me,' snarled Waldron.

'I have to ask you some questions, sir.'

'Bugger off!'

'Or perhaps you'd rather answer them in the nearest police station?'

'That explains the stink round here – you're a copper.'

'I'm Detective Sergeant Keedy from Scotland Yard and I'm involved in a murder inquiry.'

'Then why not leave me alone and get on with it.'

'I *am* getting on with it, sir.'

As the gravedigger tried to carry on with his work, Keedy grabbed the spade and wrenched it from his grasp, throwing it down on the grass. Waldron bunched his fists and issued a string of expletives. After threatening to hit Keedy, he thought better of it. Assaulting a detective had serious consequences. Besides, the sergeant was much younger and looked muscular. Waldron folded his arms and scowled.

'What's this about a murder, then?'

Keedy stood up. 'A man named Cyril Ablatt was brutally killed last night.'

'Really?' asked Waldron, before releasing a guffaw and slapping his knee in celebration. 'Are you telling me that snivelling little coward is dead? That goes to prove it – there *is* a God, after all.'

'I believe that you knew Mr Ablatt.'

'Yes – I knew the cocky bastard and I despised him.'

'Why was that?'

'Cyril always knew best. No matter what the argument was about, he had to have the last bleeding word. Oh, he was clever, I'll give him that. He read lots of books and suchlike. But he looked down on me, Sergeant Whatever-Your-Name-Is.'

'It's Keedy – Sergeant Keedy.'

'Nobody does that to Horrie Waldron. I got my standards, see?' Hauling himself out of the grave, he retrieved his spade and used it as a prop. After looking Keedy up and down, he shifted the pipe to the other side of his mouth. 'Why have you come bothering me, then?'

'Where were you yesterday evening?'

'Where else would I be but in the pub?'

'Would that be the Weavers Arms?'

'Yes – they serve a good pint.'

'Are there witnesses who'd confirm that you were there?'

Waldron eyed him warily. 'Ask the landlord. He'll tell you. Mind you,' he went on, 'I did slip out for an hour or two.'

'Where did you go?'

'That's my business,' said Waldron, belligerently.

'It happens to be my business as well.'

'It's private.'

'There's no such thing as privacy in a murder investigation.'

Waldron was indignant. 'I got nothing to do with that.'

'We'll see,' said Keedy, meeting his gaze without flinching. 'Let me remind you that withholding evidence is a crime. We can also add the charge that you're impeding a police officer in the execution of his duties. If you don't answer my questions properly, we can have this conversation through the bars of a cell in which you'll be locked. Understood?' The gravedigger glowered at him. 'That's better. Now then, let's go back to what I asked. Where did you go last night?'

'I went to see a friend – nothing wrong with that, is there?'

Keedy took out his notebook. 'What's the name of this friend?'

'I'm not saying.'

'In short, there *was* no friend. You invented him.'

'That's not true!' howled Waldron.

'Then why won't you give me his name?'

'It wasn't a man, Sergeant – it was a woman.'

'In that case, give me *her* name.'

'I can't. I got to protect her, haven't I? It's what I promised, see? Nobody else knows about her and me. Nobody else is going to know.'

'And you were with this woman for an hour or two, is that it?'

'Could be longer – I don't have a watch.'

'What did you do afterwards?'

'I went back to the pub – ask, Stan. He's the landlord.'

'I'm more interested in the time when you have nobody who can account for your movements.'

Waldron cackled. 'Oh, she accounted for my movements, I can tell you that!'

As his cackle became a full-throated laugh, he opened his mouth to expose three blackened teeth in the middle of a gaping void. Even from a few yards away, Keedy could smell his foul breath. After his years as a detective, he could usually sense if someone was lying to him but Waldron was difficult to fathom. The woman friend might or might not exist. Looking at the gravedigger, Keedy thought it unlikely because of the man's repulsive appearance, but then, he reminded himself, he'd seen even more hideous faces excite the love and devotion of a woman. Waldron might have hidden charms. His claim had a coarse plausibility.

'You're not helping yourself, sir,' said Keedy.

'What do you mean?'

'If what you say is true, there's someone who can clear your name. Until she does that, you're bound to be viewed as a suspect.'

'I didn't kill Ablatt,' protested the other. 'I didn't even know he was dead.'

'But you're obviously glad that he is.'

Waldron sniggered. 'Best news I've heard in years!'

'Do you have any idea who might have wanted to kill him?'

'I can think of lots of people. I'm one of them.'

Keedy lifted his pencil. 'Can you give me some names?'

'You're the detective – find them.'

'Stop being so obstructive.'

'Ablatt was a conchie,' said Waldron, derisively. 'He was the lowest of the low in my book. Lots of people think the same. The little sod *deserved* to die. None of us would have actually murdered him, maybe, but we'd all like to shake the hand of the man who did.'

Keedy had had enough of his prevarication. 'Put your spade away, sir,' he ordered. 'You're coming with me.'

'I don't finish work until this afternoon.'

'You're leaving right now.'

'Don't be ridiculous!'

'Would you rather that I arrested you first? I'll be happy to do so.'

'Look,' said Waldron, seeing that Keedy was in earnest and trying to sound more reasonable. 'I swear to God that I had nothing to do with any murder. I was in the Weavers most of the night.'

'Mr Ablatt's body was found less than forty yards away.'

'That doesn't mean that I put it there.'

Keedy fixed him with a stare. 'You had the chance to do so during the hour or two you were away from the pub.'

'I told you – I was with someone.'

'Yet she doesn't appear to have a name and address.'

'We got an arrangement, see?'

'Yes, you dredge her out of your imagination whenever you want an alibi.'

'She's *real*,' insisted Waldron. 'She's flesh and blood. I should know.'

'Then tell me who she is,' pressed Keedy. 'And explain why you're so anxious to conceal her name. Is it because she's a married woman?'

'No, she's a widow.'

'Then there's no reason to hide the relationship, is there?'

'Yes, there is,' said Waldron, sourly.

'Why is that, sir?'

Keedy reinforced the question by taking a step nearer to him and looking deep into his eyes. Waldron quailed inwardly. He usually got the better of policemen who tried to question him. Even after he'd been arrested for being involved in a pub brawl, he'd often managed to worm his way out of trouble. There was no escape this time. To get the details he was after, Keedy was prepared to drag him off to the nearest police station and subject him to an interrogation. If he survived that, he'd have to face awkward questions from his boss who'd want to know why he was a suspect in the investigation. Waldron weighed up the situation and capitulated.

'You win,' he admitted, head slumping to his chest.

'Why can't you tell me the woman's name?'

'It's because of Stan at the Weavers.'

'Do you mean the landlord?'

'Yes, Sergeant, and he's got a real temper on him. The woman . . .' He had to force the words out. 'The woman . . . is his mother. If Stan ever found out, you'd have another bleeding murder on your hands.'

CHAPTER SIX

Alice Marmion had never regretted the decision to join the Women's Emergency Corps and to move out of the family home. She was doing work that gave her great satisfaction and she enjoyed the challenge of having to fend for herself. Inevitably, there were drawbacks. While she was happy with the two small rooms she rented in a rambling Victorian house, they came with a landlady who imposed strict rules on her four tenants – all of them young and female – the main one being that no gentlemen were allowed into their respective rooms. Male visitors could only be entertained during specified hours in the drawing room, where they had to sit in one of the uncomfortable single chairs, the settee and the chaise longue having been carefully removed because they might encourage intimacy between couples seated together. It was also inconvenient to share the only bathroom with all the other people in the house, but Alice had circumvented that problem by getting up earlier than anyone else and being the first through the door.

Notwithstanding the house rules, she liked living there and woke up every morning with a sense of control that she'd never felt at home. It was empowering. Never lacking in confidence, Alice now had a greater self-belief and an increased readiness to take on responsibility. It had earned her respect in the WEC. Her friend, Vera Dowling, had marvelled at the changes in her.

'It's amazing, Alice,' she said. 'You can do anything you set your mind to.'

'I never thought I'd drive a lorry, I must admit.'

'You took to it like a duck to water – whereas I was hopeless.'

'That's not true, Vera.'

'As soon as I get behind the driving wheel, I lose my nerve.'

'It's only a question of practice.'

'I tried and tried again but I still made a mess of it. That's why they'll never let me take charge of any vehicle. I start to panic.'

Alice tried to reassure her but it was in vain. The two of them were sitting in the lorry, waiting for the delayed train from Folkestone. On her way to the railway station, Alice had picked up her friend from her digs. Much as she liked Vera, she'd baulked at the idea of actually sharing accommodation with her. It would impose too many constraints. Vera Dowling was a short, shapeless young woman in khaki uniform with a plain, uninteresting face that accentuated Alice's loveliness. Diligent and trustworthy, Vera had thrown herself into her new job with more commitment than skill and, as a result, tended to be given only a supportive role. Unlike Alice, she was not relishing her freedom. Living in digs, she missed the comforts of home and the joy of her mother's cooking. And she'd always had difficulty in making new friends, forcing her to rely even more on the few she already had. As her closest friend, Alice sometimes found that irksome.

'Are you glad you joined the WEC?' she asked.

'You know I am, Alice. As soon as you did, I followed suit.'

'Then why does your mother think that you might give it up?'

'I'd never do that,' said Vera, 'not while you're still in it, anyway.'

'She told Mummy that you were finding it a bit of a trial.'

'Well, that's true – but it doesn't mean that I'm going to pack it in. I just grit my teeth and get on with it. Giving up would be such a selfish thing to do when people depend on me.' She managed a brave smile. 'What are a few aches and pains compared to being driven out of your own home and chased out of your own country? Refugees come first, Alice,' she said. 'They need us.'

'I knew that you felt the same as me.'

'Whatever happens, I'll stay in the WEC until the war is over.'

'That's what I told Mummy.'

She broke off as a fleet of trucks arrived and drew up beside each other. Troops clambered quickly out with their rifles and kit, falling into line when commands were barked at them. In their ill-fitting serge uniforms, they all looked so young and untried. Alice was reminded of her brother, who'd joined the army at the start of the war and whom they'd only seen once since then. He'd gone off with the same alacrity that these new recruits were showing but his letters from the front were hinting at disillusion. She wondered how long it would be before the brave smiles were wiped off the faces of the latest batch of infantry. As they were marched past the lorry in their hobnail boots, some of the men noticed them and waved cheerily. A few whistled in admiration. Alice waved back but Vera was too embarrassed to do so.

'How many of them will come back alive?' she asked, sadly.

Alice hid her pessimism. 'We must pray that they *all* do.'

Vera waited until the last of them had gone past to join the others as they boarded the waiting train. They would soon be on their way to war in a country none of them had ever visited. In the minds of the recruits, there was a whiff of adventure about what they were doing. Having seen so many dead and wounded brought back from the trenches, the friends no longer believed that there was anything adventurous in the conflict. All that they saw were the accelerating losses and the sheer futility.

Vera's question came out of the blue. 'What do you make of Mrs Billington?'

'Why do you ask?'

'I just wondered, that's all.'

'Well,' said Alice, 'I admire her a lot. I know that some people find her too bossy but that's what she has to be to get things done. Hannah is a nice woman and she was one of the very first to join the WEC.'

'There you are,' said Vera, wistfully. 'You call her Hannah because you're on first-name terms with her. She's always Mrs Billington to me. I'd be afraid to call her anything else.'

'She won't bite, Vera.'

'It's the way she stares at me.'

'Hannah does that to everyone,' said Alice. 'When you get to know her better, you'll find out what a warm-hearted person she is.'

Vera frowned. 'I'm not sure that I *want* to know her better.'

'She's the one who really helped me to develop my talents.'

'I don't have any talents to develop.' Vera made an effort to brighten. 'Did you say that you saw your mother this morning?'

'Yes, I called in for a quick cup of tea.'

'Is she still missing you?'

'Mummy would have me back at the drop of a hat.'

'It must be so lonely being there alone.'

'It is, Vera – though she does get out a lot.'

'Did you see your father as well?'

Alice gave a hollow laugh. 'Fat chance of that!'

'Had he already left for work?'

'Daddy went off hours before breakfast. There was an emergency.

That always means another case of murder. Until it's over, all that Mummy will get of him is an occasional glimpse.'

'I'd hate that. I could never marry a policeman.'

'There are compensations,' said Alice, loyally.

'Not enough of them for me.'

'Wait until you meet Mr Right. You won't care what he does for a living.'

'I would if he was a policeman,' said Vera. 'What about you?'

Alice heard the sound of an approaching train and opened her door.

'That'll be them,' she said, getting out of the lorry. 'Come on, Vera – and don't forget to speak in your very best French.'

When it was opened twenty years earlier, the main library in the Metropolitan Borough of Shoreditch had impressed everyone with its Victorian solidity and with the grandeur of its facade. It was less striking now, its novelty gone, its brickwork soiled and the early signs of wear and tear apparent. The first thing that Harvey Marmion noticed was that some slates were missing from the roof. He stood on the pavement opposite for some time, studying the building in which Cyril Ablatt had spent so much of his life. People were streaming in and out, mostly women or older men. The library was obviously popular and well used. Marmion crossed the road and went in through the main entrance. Shelves of books stood everywhere. He could see that it was the ideal habitat for Ablatt.

Having established who was in charge, Marmion introduced himself to Eric Fussell, an exceptionally tall, middle-aged man who kept his back straight and who peered down at people through wire-framed spectacles that seemed to double the size of his eyeballs. Fussell was quick to appreciate the need for privacy. He ushered the inspector into his office and closed the door. As they exchanged niceties, they sat down.

Marmion glanced around the room. It was large, high-ceilinged, lined with books and spectacularly tidy. Everything on the desk was in neat piles, making him feel self-conscious about the clutter in his own office. Fussell exuded intelligence. His manner was polite and confiding.

'What seems to be the problem, Inspector?' he asked.

'I believe that Cyril Ablatt works here.'

'That's correct. He's not here at the moment, alas. If you wish to speak to him, you'll have to go to his home.' His eyelids narrowed. 'Is Cyril in any kind of trouble? Is that the reason he didn't turn up for work this morning?'

'No,' said Marmion, solemnly. 'It's my sad duty to tell you that he won't be turning up at the library ever again. Mr Ablatt's body was discovered during the night. He'd been bludgeoned to death.'

'Good Lord!' exclaimed Fussell. 'That's appalling!' Doubt clouded his eyes. 'Are you quite sure that it was Cyril?'

'No question about it, sir. His father has identified the body.'

'My heart goes out to him. This is dreadful news. Cyril was a fixture here. He used the library regularly for many years before he joined the staff.'

'Mr Ablatt was very proud that his son became a librarian.'

'Technically,' said the other with more than a hint of pedantry, 'he was only a library assistant. I'm the librarian. We're an odd species. Librarians are rather like concert pianists – nobody needs two.'

'I sit corrected, sir. What kind of an assistant was Cyril Ablatt?'

'I couldn't fault him. This was his true *métier*. Large numbers of people go through life either hating their job or regretting the one they failed to get. Cyril wasn't like that. I've never met anyone so happy in his work. It was a labour of love to him.'

'Tell me a bit more about him.'

'What would you like to know, Inspector?'

'Everything you can remember,' said Marmion. 'My mental picture of him is still incomplete. I need more detail.'

'Well, I can certainly give you that.'

As Fussell removed his spectacles, his eyes contracted to a more normal size. Taking out a handkerchief, he blew on the lenses before cleaning them methodically. He kept Marmion waiting a full minute before he spoke.

'Cyril Ablatt is the best library assistant I've ever had the good fortune to have under me,' he began, 'and that includes my dear wife, whom you probably saw at the desk when you first arrived. According to the last census, this borough has a population of over 111,000 inhabitants. Not one of them could hold a candle to Cyril. He was tireless. When someone made a request, nothing was too much trouble for him. He built up a reputation for efficiency and amiability. Then, I fear,' he went on, 'the war broke out and people looked at him differently. His hard-earned reputation slowly began to crumble.'

'How did he react to that?'

'He carried on in the same pleasant and dedicated way – even when some people began to voice their criticism. They couldn't understand why he wouldn't join the army and fight for his country. It reached a point where a few of them refused to let him stamp their books.'

'Did *you* understand his position, sir?'

'I understood it very well. We discussed it at length in this very office.'

'And did you approve of what he did?'

'To be quite candid with you, I didn't,' said Fussell, holding the spectacles up to the light so that he could examine the lenses. 'In times of crisis, pacifism seems quite indefensible. Cyril thought differently, of course, arguing that it was only during a war that pacifism had any real meaning. He could be very persuasive. He'd have made a first-rate public speaker.'

Marmion changed his tack. 'Is the name Horrie Waldron familiar to you?'

'It's eerily familiar.'

'Does he come in here often?'

'Thankfully, he doesn't. You can always tell when he is here by the smell. He never borrows books. He only drops in now and then to read a newspaper.'

'Do you recall an argument he had with Mr Ablatt?'

'I do indeed, Inspector. Waldron was obnoxious. If Cyril hadn't sent him packing, I'd have called the police to remove him.'

'Would you say that he's a dangerous man?'

'When drink is taken, he's a very dangerous man.'

'That confirms what I've heard,' said Marmion. 'By the way, did you know that your assistant went to a meeting of the No-Conscription Fellowship?'

The librarian replaced his spectacles. 'Yes,' he said, adjusting them. 'He showed me their leaflet and sought my opinion. I told him that I thought they were a lot of well-intentioned cranks and that he was better off keeping away from them.'

'What was his reply?'

Fussell quoted it in exact detail. He and his young assistant had evidently had some lively arguments. As the other man talked at length of Ablatt's early days at the library, Marmion wondered why he'd taken a dislike to him. The librarian was astute, well qualified and undeniably in command. Yet he somehow annoyed the inspector. It was partly the way that he shifted between a lordly authority and an ingratiating humility. One minute, he was basking in his importance, the next, he was trying to curry favour. Marmion decided that he wouldn't have liked to work under the man. You never knew what he was thinking.

'Had he lived,' said Marmion, 'we both know what would have happened.'

'Yes, Inspector, he'd have been conscripted.'

'The first stage would be an appearance before a tribunal.'

'Cyril had already worked out what he was going to say.'

'And what about you, sir?'

Fussell was taken aback. 'I don't follow.'

'Surely, you'd speak up before the tribunal on his behalf.'

'I hadn't planned to do so.'

'But you told me that he was your best assistant.'

'He was,' said Fussell, 'I don't dispute that. Unfortunately, libraries do not merit inclusion among reserved occupations. There's nothing that I could say that would be of any help to Cyril.'

'It's not what you could say but what you could *do*, sir.'

'Could you be more explicit?'

'I'm thinking of it from Mr Ablatt's viewpoint,' said Marmion. 'At the very least, you could make a gesture. Your very appearance on his behalf at the tribunal would have raised his morale. Did that never occur to you?'

Fussell's tone was icy. 'In all honesty, it never did.'

'Now that it has, what's your feeling? Had your young assistant requested your help, how would you have responded?'

There was a long pause, then Fussell enunciated the words crisply.

'I'd have been obliged to disappoint him, Inspector.'

'Was that because he could defeat you in argument?' asked Marmion.

He saw the librarian wince.

Maud Crowther was a stout woman in her early sixties with sparkling blue eyes in a face more suited to laughter than sorrow. Age had obliged her to use a walking stick but she'd lost none of her zest. When she opened her front door to him, Keedy guessed that she'd spent much of her life behind a bar counter, serving drinks to all manner of customers with a welcoming smile that had been her trademark. Strangers never disconcerted her. They provided her income. Pleased to see such a good-looking man on her doorstep, she gave him a broad grin.

'What can I do for you, young man?' she asked.

'Are you Mrs Maud Crowther?'

'I am and I have been from the day I married Tom Crowther.'

'I wondered if we might speak in private, Mrs Crowther.'

Keedy introduced himself and told her about the murder investigation. She was horrified to hear the details, all the more so because the body had been found only a few hundred yards from her house. As soon as he mentioned the name of Horrie Waldron, her eyes glinted.

'Don't believe a word that good-for-nothing tells you!'

'You do know him, then?'

'I know *of* him,' she said, carefully choosing her words, 'but I'd hardly call him an acquaintance of mine, still less a friend.'

Keedy could understand why she was trying to distance herself from Waldron and why she was furious that he'd even mentioned his name to a detective. Any relationship between the two of them was meant to be secret. Maud felt betrayed. Inviting her visitor into the house, she hobbled into the front room ahead of him and lowered herself gingerly into an armchair. Keedy sat opposite her. The room was small and crammed with furniture. There was an abiding aroma of lavender.

'Why are you bothering me?' she asked, glaring defiantly.

'I just need to clear up one simple point, Mrs Crowther.'

'Who else knows about this?'

'Nobody,' he replied. 'And I'm talking to you in confidence. Nothing you tell me will become public knowledge. I'm not here to delve into your private life. I simply wish to confirm an alibi.'

She stiffened. '*Alibi* – you surely don't suspect Horrie?'

'I just wish to eliminate him from our enquiries.'

'Why is that, Sergeant? What has he done? What has he said?'

'He knew the deceased,' said Keedy, 'and there was bad blood between them. I interviewed him as a matter of routine. He has a number of witnesses – including your son – who can vouch for his being at the Weavers Arms yesterday, but he admitted that he did slip away for an hour or two. At first, he refused point-blank to say where he'd been.'

'So I should hope,' she said, grimly.

'It was only when I threatened him with arrest that he was forced to disclose your name. My question is simple, Mrs Crowther. Was he or was he not here in the course of yesterday evening?'

Maud Crowther took time to mull things over. As she did so, she looked Keedy up and down. A life spent in the licensing trade had given her the ability to make fairly accurate judgements about the character of any newcomers. Whatever test she applied to Keedy, he seemed to pass it.

'It's not what you think,' she began.

'I make no assumptions, Mrs Crowther.'

'And nobody must *ever* know about it. People wouldn't understand.'

'Can you confirm what Mr Waldron told me?'

'Horrie is not such a bad man, Sergeant,' she said, her voice softening. 'I know he's been in trouble with the police before but never for anything really serious. Whoever killed this poor young man, it couldn't have been Horrie. He just wouldn't do anything like that.'

'Did he call here yesterday or didn't he?'

'So you can stop treating him as a suspect.'

'You haven't answered my question, Mrs Crowther.'

She made him wait. 'He might have done,' she said at length.

'And might he have been here for one hour or two?'

'One hour.' She struggled to her feet. 'I'll show you out.'

Still reeling from the shock of what she'd been told, Ruby Cosgrove was unable to return to work that afternoon. Instead of taking her home where her mother would act as a chaperone, Gordon Leach guided her towards the nearest park. They found a bench and ignored the cold. Ruby was on the verge of tears. Leach slipped an arm around her and they sat there in companionable silence. Instead of being able to enjoy a stolen afternoon of togetherness, they were lost in their respective thoughts. It was Ruby who finally broke the silence.

'What are we going to *do*, Gordon?' she asked.

'I don't know.'

'I can't stop thinking of what happened to Cyril.'

'It's driving me to distraction as well.'

'He never harmed anyone in his life.'

'Cyril was a conchie,' he said, flatly. 'Some people don't like us.'

She grabbed at his coat. 'Are you saying that they may be after you as well?'

'No, Ruby. For some reason, Cyril was picked out. I don't know why.'

'Do the police have any idea who did it?'

'I gave the inspector the name of one person,' he said with a slight surge of importance. 'And the more I think about him, the more convinced I am that it could be him. He hated Cyril.'

'Have the police gone to arrest him?'

'I don't know.'

'But he might do it again.'

'We don't know for certain that he *is* the killer, Ruby.'

'Who is this man? Does he know where you live?'

'Forget about him,' he said, tightening his grip on her shoulder. 'Let the police get on with their job; Inspector Marmion seemed like a shrewd man. He knows what he's doing. All we have to consider is what *we'll* do.'

'There's nothing much that we *can* do,' she said. 'And what about Fred and Mansel – they're in the same position as you. All four of you swore to do the same thing when they tried to force you to join the army. Now that Cyril has gone, the rest of you might feel different.'

'I don't,' he declared, 'and neither will Fred and Mansel.'

'They might be frightened by what happened.'

'That won't change their minds. Conscription is an infringement of our human rights. Nobody can make me put on a uniform and kill people.'

'What if it gets worse?' she asked, dabbing at tears with a handkerchief. 'You saw those awful things they painted on the wall of Cyril's house. Suppose they do that at the bakery? And it's not only you that suffers, Gordon. Because they just don't understand, my parents keep saying that you ought to join up. As for the women at work,' she went on, 'they're already passing remarks about me. I've got some good friends at the factory but there are some nasty ones as well and they keep taunting me for getting engaged to a coward.'

'I'm not a coward!' he protested.

'I know that, Gordon. But lots of people think otherwise.'

'They can think what they damn well like. The only person whose opinion I respect is yours. As long as you support me, Ruby, I can face anything.'

'And so can I!'

In a display of ardour, he pulled her close and kissed her on the lips. Then she huddled into his shoulder and they lapsed into silence again. An old lady with a dog went by, casting a disapproving glance at him.

When an old man shuffled past, he couldn't resist shooting Leach a look of scorn. Instead of sitting on a park bench – he seemed to imply – an able-bodied young man should be abroad with his regiment. The baker had been subjected to so many contemptuous stares that he took no notice of them. Ruby, however, did. The old man's hostility jolted her.

'How can he be so unfair?' she wondered.

'Ignore him, Ruby.'

'I can't stand that look they give you. They don't know what a kind person you really are. You wouldn't dream of hurting any of them, yet they turn on you as if you've done something really horrible.'

'In their eyes, I have. I've stood up for pacifism.'

'But that's a good thing, isn't it?'

'Yes, Ruby – and one day, God willing, people might realise that.'

'I'm so proud of you, standing up for what you believe in.'

'Cyril did that,' he reminded her, 'and he paid with his life. I'll never forget that. He's been my inspiration. It's the same for Fred and Mansel.'

'I'm only interested in *you*,' she said, pulling away to look into his eyes. 'Nobody else matters. You're everything to me, Gordon. That's why I can't wait to become Mrs Leach.'

He looked at her with sudden intensity as an idea whirred away in his brain. The date for their wedding had been set in the summer. If he was compelled to join the army – or imprisoned for refusing to do so – then the marriage might not even take place. Patient years of waiting would come to nothing. Their mutual passion would fall cruelly short of consummation. It would be unbearable.

'I love you, Ruby,' he said, impulsively.

'And I love you.'

'Do you know what we should do?'

'What?'

'We should get married.'

'But it's already been arranged. We've even worked out the guest list.'

'No,' he said, grasping her hands, 'we should get married *now*. There's such a thing as a three-day licence. It's what some soldiers have been doing before they get sent abroad again.'

She was distressed. 'But they don't do it properly in a church.'

'Does that matter?'

'It does to me, Gordon. I've set my heart on a church wedding. Auntie Gwen has already started making my dress.'

'There's nothing to stop you wearing it at the register office.'

'It's not the same.'

He was crestfallen. 'Don't you *want* to marry me?'

'You know that I do. I want it more than anything else in the world.'

'Then we should be man and wife sooner rather than later.'

'Everyone I know has been married in a church.'

'That's the ideal place, I agree,' he said, 'but you have to look at the situation we're in. The law says that I should be called up. One way or another, we may be separated. We must face facts. I may not be able to marry you in the summer. If we have a wedding with this special licence, we can not only be together,' he stressed, 'but I'll be exempt from conscription. Married men are not liable to be called up.'

Ruby looked at him but it was not in the usual adoring way. For the first time in their long courtship, there was doubt in her eyes. While she loved him enough to marry him, she had the strange feeling that she was not only being deprived of the joy of a church wedding; she was being used as an escape route.

CHAPTER SEVEN

Joe Keedy was late arriving at the place where they'd agreed to meet. His diversion to Maud Crowther's house had taken time. When he finally turned up, he found Harvey Marmion waiting for him in the car. On the drive to the photographer's studio, they were able to compare notes. Keedy went first, talking about his encounter with Waldron and of his unexpected discovery that so repellent a man could, inexplicably, arouse romantic interest in a woman. He spoke about her with admiration. Maud had struck him as someone who'd worked hard all her life and retained more than a vestige of her once handsome features as well as her natural buoyancy.

'What did she mean, Joe?' asked Marmion. 'When she told you that it wasn't what you might think – what was she trying to say?'

'I don't know.'

'Perhaps they just play cards together.'

'Oh, I fancy there's more to it than that,' said Keedy with a smile. 'I could tell from her tone of voice. When I first mentioned Waldron's name, she flared up and called him a good-for-nothing. As we went on to talk about him, however, she slowly mellowed and referred to him with real affection.'

'It could still be an innocent friendship.'

'Then why are they both so anxious to keep it secret? Waldron was scared stiff in case Mrs Crowther's son ever found out about it. In the son's place, I certainly wouldn't be happy. I don't mind admitting it. If *my* mother ever got involved with someone as revolting as Waldron, I'd be very upset.'

'It's not a fair comparison,' Marmion pointed out. 'Your father is still alive so your mother is not a widow. If a woman is on her own after years of having a man about the house, she could get very lonely. It may be that Mrs Crowther sees things in Waldron that eluded your sharp eye.'

'It was my sharp nose that turned me off him. He stank to high heaven.'

'Digging graves is not the most salubrious occupation.'

'I can only think that he cleans himself up before he calls on her.'

'That's a matter between the two of them, Joe. The question remains. Do we or don't we treat him as a suspect?'

Keedy pondered. 'We keep his name on the reserve list.'

'Why do you say that?'

'It's because he could have been away from the Weavers Arms long enough to visit his lady friend *and* to commit a murder. Waldron may not be very bright but he has a low animal cunning. It all depends on when Cyril Ablatt was killed.'

'Post-mortems can never be that precise,' said Marmion, sighing. 'The best they can do is to give us an approximate time. I've sent someone to find out when Ablatt actually left Devonshire House yesterday. That will give us a rough time frame in which the murder occurred. However,' he added, thoughtfully, 'from what you've told me about Waldron, I'm not sure that he'll ever get off a notional reserve list of suspects.'

'I still think we should keep probing, Harv.'

'We will, I promise.'

It was Marmion's turn to deliver a report and he recounted details of his visit to the library. Keedy was interested to hear that he'd taken such a dislike to Eric Fussell. As a rule, Marmion was a very tolerant man, able to work effectively with nauseating superiors like Superintendent Chatfield and to give most people the benefit of the doubt. Yet, in the short time they'd been together, he'd obviously taken against the librarian.

'I'm not entirely sure why,' he admitted as he tried to work it out. 'There was just something about him that nettled me. He looked genuinely shocked when he heard about the murder, yet the moment I described Ablatt as a librarian, he pounced on the mistake. Even the death of his assistant couldn't keep his self-importance at bay. Incidentally,' continued Marmion, 'he's had a brush or two with Horrie Waldron. When he's drunk, he reckons, the gravedigger could be very dangerous.'

'I can verify that,' said Keedy. 'I wouldn't like to have an argument with him when he's got a spade in his hands. He's a very strong man.'

'He's obviously capable of bludgeoning someone to death but I don't accept that he'd have the brains to plan the murder. Someone else would have to do that. Waldron might simply be the hired killer, working for another man with a grudge against Ablatt.'

'Do you have any idea who the other man could be, Harv?'

A name trembled instantly on Marmion's tongue and he spat it out.

'It could be someone like Eric Fussell.'

* * *

Having started work early that morning, Mansel Price was due to finish by mid afternoon. Before he'd left the train, he'd cooked himself a meal then wolfed it down in the privacy of the galley kitchen. When he came off duty, he was astonished to see Fred Hambridge waiting for him on the station platform. Though the carpenter knew his friend's shift pattern, he should have been working himself at that time. Price could not understand why he wasn't beavering away in his workshop. Hambridge had a newspaper under his arm. Spotting the Welsh cook, he ran across to him.

'Hello, Mansel,' he said. 'Have you heard?'

Price's face went blank. 'Heard what?'

'About Cyril.'

'What about him?'

'I can't tell you here. Let's go outside.'

They picked their way along the crowded platform towards the exit. Once outside in the street, Hambridge took Price by the elbow and led him to a quiet corner further along the pavement. He opened the newspaper to show him the headline.

'This is the early edition,' he said, giving it to him.

Price saw the front page story in the *Evening News* and gasped in horror.

'Is this *our* Cyril Ablatt?' he asked, incredulously.

'I'm afraid so, Mansel.'

'I just don't believe it.'

'It's true. My boss was the first who told me about it. Then this detective came to my house to ask me all sorts of questions about Cyril. I was too upset to go back to work. It must be years since I cried but I don't mind telling you that I cried my eyes out earlier on.' He pointed to the headline. 'Now we know why he never got to my house last night.'

Price was hypnotised by the newspaper report. It contained few details but the significant one was the name of the victim. He noted that the detective in charge of the case was an Inspector Marmion. Eventually, he thrust the paper back at his friend.

'Does Gordon know about this?'

'He'll know for certain by now because the police will have told him. I warned him earlier on when my boss said there'd been a murder last night but I wasn't a hundred per cent sure that it was Cyril. No doubt about it now.'

'I'll kill the bastard who did this!' vowed Price.

'No, you won't,' said Hambridge, a calming hand aloft. 'You don't believe in killing anybody. That's why you're a pacifist.'

'I'll make an exception for this man.'

'I felt the same at first, Mansel, but it's not our job to get revenge. We must let the police hunt him down.'

'Well,' said Price, venomously, 'at the very least, I'll be dancing outside the prison when they hang the swine. It's awful. Who would *do* such a thing?'

'I wish I knew.'

'Do the police have any idea?'

'Not as yet,' said Hambridge. 'By the way, they want to talk to you. Sergeant Keedy – he's the detective who spoke to me – was going to call at your house and, if you weren't there, leave a message.'

'What can I tell them?'

'Much the same as me and Gordon, I suppose. They want to know everything they can find out about Cyril.'

Price was defensive. 'Well, there's nothing I can add. You knew him better than we did because you used to play in the same darts team as him. I hardly saw anything of Cyril until the war broke out, and Gordon, of course, spent most of his time with Ruby. No,' he said, 'you're the one the police should talk to.'

Hambridge nodded soulfully. 'I've been wondering about his father.'

'What about him?'

'Well, should we go to see him?'

'Oh, I don't know about that. Mr Ablatt's a nice enough man and I feel sorry for him but I'm not sure what we could do – not at this stage, anyway. He'll have family around him and we don't want to be in the way.'

'I suppose not.'

'Let's leave it for a bit, shall we?'

'You're probably right, Mansel.'

'I want to know more details first.'

'So do I. But we mustn't leave it too long,' said Hambridge. 'We owe it to Cyril to show Mr Ablatt what his son meant to us. He must be really upset.'

'*We* may not want to visit the house just yet,' said Price, meaningfully, 'but someone else might.'

'Who do you mean?'

'I'm talking about whoever painted those things on Cyril's wall.'

'Yes,' said Hambridge, 'they were vile.'

'He'll be gloating when he hears the news.'

'Think of those names he called Cyril.'

'I don't know why they were left there. If it was my house, I'd have hidden them beneath a coat or two of whitewash. I'd love to meet the man responsible,' growled Price through gritted teeth. 'He deserves to hang alongside the killer – and I'd like to be the bloody executioner!'

With the newspaper rolled up in his hand, the man walked briskly along the street before turning the corner. He looked up at the wall of the Ablatt house and smiled inwardly. The bold lettering he'd painted there took on a new meaning now and it was one that gave him immense pleasure. Without breaking stride, he held the newspaper up as if it were a weapon and fired an imaginary bullet at the wall. Minutes later, he reached his own home and let himself in. The first thing he did was to go into the garden to check how much paint he still had locked away in his shed. The death of a conscientious objector was something to be celebrated. It was time for some more nocturnal art.

The photographer's studio was in a side street in Finsbury. Several examples of his work were on display in the shop window. Marmion and Keedy looked at three different married couples, standing outside their respective church porches with broad grins and expressions of unassailable hope. Poised over a many-candled iced cake, an elderly couple were marking an anniversary of some kind. There were photographs of young men in uniform and one taken at a children's party. The youngest person in the exhibition was a baby, cradled in the arms of a doting mother while the proud father looked on. Vernon Nethercott catered for all the family.

Entering the shop, the detectives learnt that Nethercott was busy so they were forced to wait. Childish laughter from the next room suggested that the photographer knew how to amuse his customers. The young woman who acted as receptionist had only been with Nethercott for six months and she was unable to identify the woman in the photograph that Marmion showed her. But she boasted that her employer had a remarkable memory and that he'd certainly recall her name. It was some time before Nethercott eventually appeared, shepherding a mother and her two little children out of the shop. All three of them had clearly enjoyed their visit.

Nethercott was taken aback to hear that two detectives had descended upon him. He was a short, slight man with a gleaming bald head and bushy eyebrows.

'Dear me!' he exclaimed. 'I'm not in trouble, am I?'

'No, Mr Nethercott,' said Marmion. 'We simply need your help. Not all that far from here, a murder occurred last night.' The photographer and his receptionist reacted with alarm. 'When we called at the victim's house, we found this.' He handed the photograph to Nethercott. 'Your name and address are franked on it.'

'It's standard practice, Inspector. I do it with all my photographs.'

'Do you recognise the lady?'

'I recognise her very well – though I can't give you an exact date when this was taken. Some months ago – that much is certain. If you want me to be more specific, I'll have to consult my appointments book.'

'That won't be necessary, sir. I just need the lady's name and, if possible, her address. I'm told that you have a wonderful memory.'

'What I remember are faces, Inspector. I treasure people's expressions as they stare at a camera. Each one is unique to a particular individual. Take this lady, for instance,' he said, tapping the photograph. 'When she first came into my studio that day, she was rather uneasy, not to say furtive. The moment I told her to smile, however, she came alive. You can see the delight in her eyes.'

'What was her name?'

'Mrs Skene – Caroline Skene.'

'Does she live locally?'

'No,' said Nethercott, 'that's what surprised me a little. She lives in Lambeth. Why come all the way here when there must be dozens of other photographers nearer to her home? I'm quite well known in Finsbury but I didn't think that my reputation would stretch south of the river.'

'Do you have the lady's address?' asked Keedy.

'I'm afraid not. When she came in to book the appointment, all she told me was that she lived in Lambeth. To be honest, she was a bit secretive.' He gave the photograph back to Marmion. 'I'm sorry that I can't be more helpful.'

'You've pointed me in the right direction, sir,' said Marmion, 'and I'm grateful for that. I'd be even more grateful if you'd tell nobody about our visit.' He turned to the receptionist. 'That goes for you as well, young lady. Mrs Skene is not a suspect in this inquiry. I don't want her name to be spread abroad.'

'We understand, Inspector,' said Nethercott.

Marmion and Keedy left the shop in a flurry of farewells. As they did so, they saw a young couple approaching. The man was in army uniform and the woman was clutching his arm with the desperation of someone holding onto a lifebelt. The detectives stood aside to let them enter the premises.

'I feel sorry for her,' said Keedy. 'She wants something to remember him by in case he doesn't come back from the front.'

'It works both ways, Joe,' said Marmion. 'When he's shipped overseas, I can guarantee that he'll have a photo of that pretty face in his pocket.'

'What did you make of this Mrs Skene?'

'The description of her behaviour fits with what we know. She was furtive because she felt guilty about what she was doing.'

'Why did she choose Nethercott?'

'I believe that Cyril Ablatt might have been involved in that. He told her where she could have a photo discreetly taken. Living where he does, Finsbury is the sort of place you'd expect him to know.'

'So what do we do now – track the lady down?'

'It doesn't take two of us to do that. I'll try to pick up Mrs Skene's trail, starting at the library in Lambeth. The name is not all that common. If it's listed there, I should be able to get the correct address.'

'What about me?'

'I suggest that you call in at the police station in Shoreditch to see if

Mansel Price has made an appearance yet. Hambridge told you that he comes off duty this afternoon. I'll need the car but I'll drop you off on the way to Lambeth.'

'You're assuming that she actually lives there.'

'What's wrong with that?'

'Well,' said Keedy, 'she may have lied about Lambeth and given a false name into the bargain. You could be on a wild goose chase, Harv.'

'I don't think so,' said Marmion, taking out the photograph again. 'What I see here is an honest, self-respecting woman. When she's embarrassed to go into a photographer's studio, she must be troubled by guilt. She's unlikely to be a seasoned liar. Mrs Skene gave her real name. You can bank on that. I'll find her – and it will definitely be somewhere in Lambeth.'

He put the photograph back into his pocket. They walked towards the car.

'How many more of them are there?' asked Keedy.

'I'm not with you, Joe.'

'How many other mystery women will come out of the woodwork?'

Marmion grinned. 'I'd have thought you liked mystery women.'

'Oh, it's not a complaint – just an observation. First, we have Ablatt's secret lady, then up pops Waldron's unlikely friend, Maud Crowther.'

'Men and women are attracted to each other – nothing unusual about that.'

'There is in both these cases,' argued Keedy. 'They're highly dangerous friendships. Ablatt and Waldron had to hide what was going on because they were afraid of the consequences. Ablatt was deceiving Mrs Skene's husband, who may yet turn out to be a suspect. For his part, Waldron was terrified that Maud's son would find out what his mother had been up to.'

'Danger can sometimes add spice to a relationship.'

'Do you speak from experience, Harv?'

Marmion laughed. 'No, I don't and you should know it. Ellen and I already have enough spice in our marriage. Neither of us would ever look outside it.'

'You're an example to us all.'

'Stop teasing.'

'I was being serious – I swear it.'

'Then why are you still single after all these years?'

Keedy's smile was enigmatic. 'That would be telling,' he said.

The discussion on the park bench lasted for over an hour and the issue was never resolved. Leach took Ruby home and left her to explain to her mother why she was back so early. He knew that his suggestion about an almost immediate wedding ceremony would be passed on to Mrs Cosgrove and he feared that she would disapprove. Ruby's own reaction had been ambiguous. She both liked the idea and found it disturbing. Something about it unsettled her and it was not just the fact that she'd be robbed of the joy of coming down the aisle beside him in the dress that her aunt had so patiently made for her. There was an element of suspicion in her manner that Leach had never seen before. It worried him.

On leaving Ruby's house, he walked a couple of blocks to the street where Hambridge lived and was pleased to find the carpenter at home. Over a cup of tea, they bewailed the loss of their friend and speculated on who the killer might be.

'Mansel is going to be as shocked as we are,' said Leach.

'He knows, Gordon. I was there when he found out. I waited for him at the station and showed him the *Evening News*. He was stunned.'

'The three of us must stick together even more closely now.'

Hambridge's brow crinkled. 'Must we?'

'It was a warning, Fred.'

'Was it?'

'What else could it be?' reasoned Leach. 'Because he worked at the library, Cyril was well known in Shoreditch. He made no bones about the fact that he was a conscientious objector. In a sense, he sort of gloried in it.'

'Well, it's nothing to be ashamed about,' said Hambridge.

'Inspector Marmion told me that *we* weren't under threat, but I'm not so sure. I don't *feel* safe. Someone is coming to get us.'

'I'll be ready for him. I hate violence but I'll be carrying a chisel wherever I go. Cyril was killed because he wasn't expecting an attack. I'll be more careful.'

'So will I.'

'But I don't think there's any real danger now,' said Hambridge. 'Not while the police are looking for the killer. He'll lie low until everything blows over – or until he's caught, of course.'

'The inspector said they'd leave no stone unturned.'

'The detective who came here was a Sergeant Keedy. I liked him. He had his wits about him. According to the sergeant, this Inspector Marmion has got a good record for solving murders. He never gives up. He'll be working around the clock to find the person who did this to Cyril.'

'I won't be able to relax until he's behind bars.' Leach finished his tea and put the cup down. 'Can I ask you something, Fred?'

Hambridge gave a silly grin. 'There's nobody else here.'

'What would you think if I got married?'

'I'd be happy for you but you've months to wait.'

'No,' said Leach, 'it could be a lot less than that. There's such a thing as a three-day licence, you see. It's for couples who . . . just can't wait.'

'But you *can* wait – and so can Ruby.'

112

'I want to get married as soon as possible.'

'Oh, I see.'

'The murder has scared me to death. What if someone has got his eye on *me*? I'm a conchie, just like Cyril. I've had my warning. There's only one way out.'

'Sorry – I don't see where marriage comes into it.'

'I'd be safe, Fred. I wouldn't be a conchie, fighting off conscription. I'd be a married man who wasn't liable to be called up. There'd be no need to pick on me. I could carry on as I am.' Hambridge was studying him with mingled curiosity and disgust. 'Do you see what I mean?'

'You're only thinking of yourself, Gordon.'

'No, I'm not. I'm thinking of Ruby as well.'

'She's in no danger.'

'She is, if I get killed. Ruby will lose everything she's ever dreamt about.'

Hambridge was unhappy. 'I don't like the idea.'

'But it will solve a problem.'

'I still don't like it.'

Leach was hurt. 'Why not? I thought I could count on you.'

'You wanted my opinion. You've got it.'

'Things are different now that Cyril is dead.'

'Yes,' said Hambridge with uncharacteristic passion, 'you wouldn't have dared to mention this when he was alive. You'd have done what you pledged to do. You'd have stood beside us, Gordon.'

'It's not as if I'm deserting you.'

The carpenter had said his piece. He sipped his tea morosely, leaving his friend to regret having brought the subject up. His idea had had a lukewarm reception from Ruby and a hostile one from Hambridge. Given the latter's response, he wondered if it would be wise to broach the topic with Price.

'Where's Mansel now?' he asked.

'He's gone to the police station.'

'I'll speak to him later.'

'Well, I wouldn't tell him what you just told me,' warned the other, 'or he'll go mad. Mansel will think you're running out on us.'

The message that Keedy had left for him had asked Price to report to the local police station where he would be told how to get in touch with Scotland Yard. In the event, the Welshman was actually in the building when Keedy was dropped off there by Marmion. Introduced to Price, he borrowed a room where he could interview him in private. As they sat down either side of a table, he noticed the other's expression. Price looked grim and resentful. His muscles were taut.

'There's nothing to be afraid of,' said Keedy.

'I don't like police stations.'

'Is there any particular reason?'

'They're always full of people telling me what to do.'

'I'm not here to tell you anything – except that we need all the help we can get in this investigation. I would have thought you'd be eager to do anything that might lead to an arrest.'

'I am,' said Price, 'but there's nothing I can add to what Fred told you.'

'Mr Hambridge was much more cooperative than you. He tells me that you work on the railway.' Price nodded. 'Do you like your job?'

'It bores me to tears.'

'Then why don't you do something else?'

'It's not easy to find a job if you're my age. Every time I've applied for one, I was told to join the army instead. So I'm stuck with the GWR.'

'That's a reserved occupation, isn't it?'

'Not if you're a cook,' said Price, bitterly. 'We're ten a penny. They

114

can even find women to do my job. Drivers and firemen and so on are different. They're all needed, so they're exempt – what's left of them, anyway. Thousands from the GWR joined up when they had that first recruitment drive.'

'The ones who are left do a vital job,' said Keedy. 'There's no better way to move men and equipment around in large numbers. But let's come back to Cyril Ablatt. Tell me about him.'

Price was hesitant, offering snippets of information between pauses. The longer he went on, however, the more relaxed he became. While he didn't share Hambridge's hero worship of their dead friend, he spoke warmly about Ablatt and added details that Keedy hadn't heard before. The sergeant jotted them down in his notebook. When asked if he could suggest the name of anyone who should be considered a suspect, Price shook his head.

'What about Horrie Waldron?' asked Keedy.

'I don't know him.'

'His name was given to us by Gordon Leach.'

'Gordon may know him but I don't. Who is he?'

'Waldron is a man who crossed swords with your friend, Cyril. Not that that's enough in itself to arouse suspicion. In any case, Waldron seems to have an alibi for the time when Cyril was murdered.'

'Do you have any other suspects?' asked Price.

'We're . . . considering a number of possibilities,' said Keedy, evasively.

'Well, I hope that one of them turns out to be the killer. He needs to be caught and caught soon. You must comb the whole of Shoreditch until you find him.'

'Don't try to tell us how to do our job, Mr Price.'

'I want to make sure that you do it properly.'

'We have procedures, based on long experience.'

'Yes,' said Price with asperity, 'but that's for ordinary victims, isn't it?

Cyril was a conchie. You won't make the same effort for him. I saw the police outside that meeting last night. Some of them looked as if they'd like to tear us to pieces. I thought they were there to keep the crowd back but one big bugger gave me a real shove.'

'I'm sure that it was accidental.'

'Conchies are scum to you.'

'You deserve the full protection of the law in the same way that everyone else does. We make no distinctions based on class, colour, creed or anything else.'

Price was blunt. 'I don't believe you, Sergeant.'

'Then we'll have to *make* you believe us, won't we? Scotland Yard has given this case priority. That's why they put Inspector Marmion in charge. His name is well known in the criminal underworld of London. He's had a long string of successes and they were achieved by a combination of instinct and unremitting hard work. So don't you dare to suggest we're not fully committed to this investigation,' said Keedy with controlled anger. 'We'll do all we can to hunt down the killer and we won't rest until he's hauled up before a judge and jury.'

'Can I go now?' asked Price, cheekily.

'You'll go when I tell you.'

'What did I say? Policemen always have to order you about.'

'Don't you like orders?'

'No, Sergeant, I don't – unless I'm getting paid to obey them, of course.'

'I have to say that Mr Hambridge was much more pleasant to interview.'

'Ah, well,' said Price, smirking, 'Fred is Fred. He's nice to everyone whereas I speak as I find. And I told you at the start – I don't like police stations.'

'That means you've been inside a few,' guessed Keedy. 'I wonder why. Have you been a naughty boy at work – putting poison in the soup or serving ground glass in the omelettes? Do you know what *I'm* beginning to wonder?' he continued, leaning across the table. 'I'm getting a very strong feeling that you might have a criminal record. Am I right, sir?'

The smirk disappeared from Mansel Price's face. All of a sudden, he looked profoundly uncomfortable.

CHAPTER EIGHT

Having spent so much time behind the driving wheel throughout the day, Alice Marmion was glad to return to the depot and park the lorry beside the others. As she and Vera Dowling got out and stretched their legs, they were spotted by their supervisor. Shoes clacking on the tarmac, Hannah Billington strode across to them. She was a striking woman of middle height and indeterminate age, shifting between her mid thirties and late forties, depending on how closely she was scrutinised and in what light. Her husband was a brigadier general, in France with his regiment, and there was a distinctly military air about Hannah as well. Her back was straight, her head erect, her voice crisp and peremptory. But it was the fierce beauty of her face that caught the attention, the high cheekbones thrown into prominence by the way that her hair was severely brushed back. While the other women looked incongruous in their baggy uniforms, Hannah seemed always to have worn a tailored version and it enhanced her sense of authority.

'Did everything go well?' she asked.

'Yes,' replied Alice. 'Apart from one or two problems, that is.'

'Oh – what sort of problems?'

'They were mostly to do with language. Four of the refugees were Walloons who couldn't make head or tail of my French and there was a group of Russian Jews from Antwerp in the group as well. But I think we got through to them in the end, didn't we, Vera?'

'Yes,' said Vera, nervous in the presence of their superior.

'Life would certainly be easier if we all spoke the same language,' said the older woman, briskly. 'It would have to be English, of course. Some of the regional dialects we get from Belgium are real tongue-twisters.'

'How many more will there be?' wondered Alice.

'Oh, they'll continue to dribble out, I suspect. It was far worse when the war first started. We had a quarter of a million Belgian refugees then. It was like an invasion. There was even talk of founding a New Flanders in Britain. Heaven forbid!'

'I don't know where we managed to put them all.'

'Neither do I, Alice, but we did it somehow and we'll have to go on doing it. All the hotels and boarding houses are full up and so are lots of barns, warehouses, pavilions, racecourses, exhibition halls and skating rinks. My husband's golf club has just been commandeered for accommodation.' She brayed happily. 'Not entirely sure that he'd approve of that.'

'The War Refugees Committee is doing a wonderful job,' said Alice.

'And so is the WEC. Don't you agree?'

'Yes, I do.'

'What about you, Vera?'

'Yes, Mrs Billington,' said Vera, meekly.

'Can't you sound a bit more positive?'

'What we do is . . . very important.'

'It's absolutely vital and shows just what women can achieve when we all pull together. Unlike other wars, this one isn't something that's happening in a distant country. It's just across the English Channel and we have to cope with the after-effects. As the refugees flood in, we have to absorb them somehow.'

'I'll have to start learning more languages,' said Alice.

'Your French is really good,' said Vera, 'and far better than mine. When the war is over, you'll be able to teach it.'

'I may not go back to teaching.'

Vera was surprised. 'What else will you do?'

'Wait and see.'

'Yes,' said Hannah. 'It's far too early to make plans for what we'll all do when the war finally comes to an end. Our task is clear. We must concentrate on day-to-day priorities. And while we're on the subject, Vera, I've got some more work lined up for you this evening.'

'Oh, I see,' said Vera, uncomfortably.

'I know that you prefer to be with Alice but she can't always hold your hand. You must learn to be more independent. Alice has already warned me that she wouldn't be available for an evening shift.'

'Actually,' said Alice, 'that's not true.'

'Oh?'

'Things have changed, Hannah.'

'You said that you were doing something with your parents.'

'That was the idea,' said Alice, opening the door of the lorry to reach inside. 'But there's been a slight complication.' She brought out a newspaper and passed it to Hannah. 'We picked this up earlier.' As the other woman read the headline in the *Evening News*, Alice was fatalistic. 'My father has been put in charge of that investigation. Family life just doesn't exist when he's working on a murder case. In other words,' she went on, concealing her disappointment, 'I'm ready to work on into the evening. It may be weeks before I see my father again.'

* * *

121

It was a case of third time lucky for Marmion. A study of the electoral roll told him that there were three families by the name of Skene living in Lambeth. At the first two addresses he drew a blank, but the last one finally introduced him to the woman in the sepia photograph. Caroline Skene was in the front room as the car drew up outside her house. When she saw him get out of the vehicle, she went to the door and opened it. He raised his hat courteously, showed her his warrant card and asked if he might have a private word with her. Though she was mystified, she admitted him and they went into the front room. At his suggestion, she sat down and he took the chair opposite her. The photograph had not done her justice. She was an attractive woman in her mid thirties with pale, delicate skin and she was well dressed, as if expecting to go out somewhere. Marmion sensed that they were alone in the house and he was relieved. In the presence of her husband, it would have been impossible to question her properly.

'What's this all about, Inspector?' she asked, apprehensively.

'I'm afraid that I have some bad news to pass on.'

She sat forward. 'It's not my husband, is it?'

'No, Mrs Skene.'

'There have been so many accidents at his factory. A man had his hand cut off last week. I'm terrified that it will be Wilf's turn next.'

'This is not about your husband,' said Marmion.

'So why have you come?'

'I believe that you know a young man by the name of Cyril Ablatt.'

Her cheeks coloured. 'I think you're mistaken, Inspector.'

'Let me ask you again,' he said, patiently. 'I appreciate why you're so reticent but it's important that you tell the truth.' He looked her in the eye. 'Does the name of Cyril Ablatt mean anything at all to you?'

'No, it doesn't.'

He reached into his pocket for the photograph. 'This is getting a little embarrassing, Mrs Skene. If you've never heard of him, how can you explain the fact that we found this photograph of you in his bedroom?' He held it up for her to see. 'I don't need to read out the message on the back, do I?'

Caroline Skene was dumbstruck. She'd been caught. A friendship that was very precious to her had been discovered by a detective. When kept secret, it was a source of constant pleasure. Now that it had been exposed, however, it suddenly seemed to be morally wrong and faintly ridiculous. There was no point in trying to brazen it out when he held the evidence in his hand. All that she could hope to do was to limit the damage.

'Cyril and I were friends,' she confessed, head down. After a few seconds, she raised her eyes to him imploringly. 'Please don't tell my husband.' she said. 'It would hurt him beyond bearing. It would be cruel. Is that why you came, Inspector? Are you here to speak to Wilf?'

'No, Mrs Skene,' he replied. 'I've no need to see him at all.'

'Thank God for that!'

'What happened between you and Cyril Ablatt is none of my business. The main reason I came is to tell you that . . . a dreadful crime has been committed.'

She shuddered. 'What sort of crime?'

'Mr Ablatt was murdered.'

For a moment, he thought that she was about to collapse. Her mouth fell open and she emitted a strange, muted cry of agony. With an effort, she somehow managed to regain her composure. Taking out the handkerchief tucked under her sleeve, she held it in readiness. Marmion gave her time to adjust to the horror. As a husband with a belief in the sanctity of marriage, he couldn't approve of what she'd apparently done but neither could he condemn it. Caroline Skene was patently a woman in despair. Moral judgements were irrelevant. He just wanted to alleviate her pain. For her part, she was pathetically grateful for his discretion and forbearance. She'd never had dealings with a Scotland Yard detective before and found him unexpectedly considerate. His soothing presence helped her to recover enough to speak.

'What happened?'

'I'll spare you the full details,' he said. 'Suffice it to say that the body of a young man was found in Shoreditch last night. Items found on his person identified him as Cyril Ablatt. His father has confirmed the identification.' A hand shot to her heart. 'I offer you my condolences, Mrs Skene. I suggest that you don't read the newspapers for a while.'

'Is it that bad?'

'The killer used unnecessary violence.'

She shuddered again. 'How did you find that photograph?'

'We had to break the news to his father,' he explained. 'While we were at the house, we asked if we might look at his room so that we might learn a little more about him.' He held up the photo. 'This fell out of the Bible.' He offered it to her. 'Would you like it back?'

'No, no,' she cried, recoiling from it. 'I should never have had it taken.'

'Mr Ablatt clearly treasured it.' He slipped the photo into his pocket. 'Would you like me to destroy it, Mrs Skene?'

She was overwhelmed by his kindness. 'Would you?'

'There's no reason for anyone else to see it.'

'Thank you!'

The problem of discovery might have been solved but the far greater one of her intense grief remained. She could feel it already biting away at her like a greedy animal. Her lips began to tremble and tears formed. Having delivered his message, Marmion felt that he should withdraw quietly but there was an investigation in hand and Caroline Skene had information about the deceased that nobody else could give him.

'When did you last see him?' he asked, softly.

'It was . . . weeks ago.'

'Did you know he was involved with the No-Conscription Fellowship?'

'Yes, Inspector – he mentioned that he might join it.'

'What else did he tell you?'

'He said very little about things like that. We just . . . enjoyed being together.'

'I understand.'

She gave him a shrewd look. 'I don't think that you do.'

'That may be true, Mrs Skene.' He cleared his throat. 'I've no wish to intrude into your privacy but there are some questions I must ask.'

She braced herself. 'Go on.'

'Did your husband harbour any suspicions about the two of you?'

'Oh, no!' she exclaimed.

'How can you be so certain?'

'Wilf is not a suspicious man. If you met him, you'd realise that it would never even cross his mind.'

Marmion glanced at the framed photograph on the mantelpiece. It showed the couple arm-in-arm on their wedding day. At the time, Wilfred Skene had been a tall, angular young man with a neat moustache and dark, wavy hair. His wife seemed as blissfully happy as he did. Though a dozen or more years had passed since the event, she had not aged significantly.

She was adamant. 'He doesn't know and he must never find out.'

'I've no intention of telling him,' said Marmion. 'Let's turn to Cyril Ablatt. Did he ever mention any enemies to you?'

'Cyril had no enemies,' she replied with a sad smile. 'He was a lovely young man and he got on well with everybody.'

'That's hardly borne out by the facts, I fear. Anyone who declares himself to be a conscientious objector is bound to attract criticism. As you may know, someone painted abusive words on the wall of his house.'

'He told me about that. He said he'd simply turn the other cheek.'

'You have to admire his bravery.'

'He was brave and good and honest,' she said, effusively. 'He didn't deserve this. It's wicked, Inspector. Cyril wouldn't hurt a fly.'

'So what reason could there be to kill him?'

Her face was a study in hopelessness. 'I don't know.'

She was still trying to absorb the impact of the devastating news. Marmion felt that it would be harsh to put any more pressure on her. At the same time, however, he sensed that she knew things about Ablatt that might be relevant to the inquiry. This was not the moment to search for them. She needed a breathing space. After dabbing at her eyes, she put the handkerchief away.

He rose to his feet. 'I'll see myself out, Mrs Skene.'

'Thank you,' she said. 'And thank you for being so . . . well, you know.'

'I told you. I didn't come to pry. However,' he went on, 'I believe that you may later think of things that might be of use to the investigation. Anything we can learn about his character and movements will be helpful.' He took out his wallet and extracted a business card. 'This has my number at Scotland Yard,' he said, slipping it into her hand.

'We don't have a telephone,' she bleated.

'There'll be one at your local police station. If you tell them that you wish to contact Inspector Marmion with regard to the inquiry, they'll put you in touch with me. *Anything* – anything at all that you tell me,' he emphasized, 'will be treated in the strictest confidence.'

She didn't seem to have heard him. 'I'd like to be alone.'

'Goodbye, Mrs Skene,' he said, moving to the door. 'I'm sorry to bring such bad tidings but, on reflection, you may find that hearing them from me is preferable to reading them for the first time in the newspaper.'

Leaving the room, he opened the front door and let himself out. On the drive back to Scotland Yard, he found himself wondering about the true nature of the relationship between a mature woman and a young man. How had they first met? What had attracted them to each other? When had they moved on to a degree of intimacy? Was their friendship a pleasant diversion or did they hope for a future together? What had impelled her to take such dangerous risks? Why was nobody else aware of the romance? As the questions multiplied in his mind, there was one that dominated all the others.

What other secrets had Cyril Ablatt kept so carefully hidden?

Joe Keedy's visit to the police station was productive. He not only met and interviewed Mansel Price, he was able to use the duty sergeant's local knowledge to advantage. When he confided that he needed to maintain surveillance on the Ablatt house that night, the sergeant recommended the nearby home of a pair of elderly sisters. They'd been burgled recently and would welcome the presence of a policeman to guard their property during the small hours. The front room of their house, Keedy was assured, would give him a good view of the wall that had been daubed with white paint. He was very grateful. If he'd had to knock on doors in search of a place in which to hold his vigil, there was always the danger that he might alert the artist. Since he (or she) was almost certainly a neighbour of the Ablatt's, it would be ironic if there was a forewarning from the police. Staying with two old ladies obviated the danger of inadvertently coming face to face with the very person he wished to apprehend. It was a piece of good fortune that partially atoned for the evening out that he'd had to sacrifice in the interests of solving a murder

Keedy also learnt that Price was known to the police. He'd been arrested during an affray the previous year but had not been charged. The fractious Welshman had also been involved in two other incidents, one of which – refusing to pay for some groceries – had resulted in a fine. Price detested authority. Each time he'd been brought to the station, it transpired, he'd been awkward under questioning. It helped to explain why he'd been so prickly during his session with Keedy. The carpenter, Fred Hambridge, had been far more amenable and – according to Marmion – so had Gordon Leach. It would be interesting to learn how Price fitted into the quartet that included Cyril Ablatt. Since the latter was the undisputed leader, to what extent had the Welshman accepted to the authority vested in his friend?

Time was rolling on and there were decisions to be made. It would take Keedy far too long to go all the way to and from his digs so he resigned himself to remaining in Shoreditch. He first walked to the recommended house and made the acquaintance of Rose and Martha Haveron, two anxious ladies in their late sixties who confused their recent burglary with an attempt of their long-preserved virginity. Reassured by his status and by his easy charm, they were at the same time appalled to hear about the murder. They had nothing but good to say about Ablatt and his father and had been friendly with his mother until she died some years earlier. Even though it would be the first time that a man had spent a night under their roof, the sisters willingly offered up their front room as an observation post, ready to break with tradition if it would help the police. Indeed, they both revealed a hitherto hidden maternal instinct, offering Keedy food, providing him with blankets and generally trying to make his stay there as comfortable as it could be. He had difficulty escaping their urgent hospitality in order to go shopping.

As he left his two temporary landladies, he looked up at the side of the house on the corner. Nobody was left in any doubt as to who lived there. Amongst other things, Cyril Ablatt was described as a coward, a rat, a rotten conchie and a traitor to his country. The lettering was large but hastily done. Keedy decided that it must have taken the artist a number of visits to complete the work. His sympathy for the dead man welled up. Much kinder words would be etched on Ablatt's gravestone. While the exterior of the house had been defaced, the real damage had been caused inside it. Keedy wondered how the family was coping with it.

* * *

'Shall I make some more tea?' asked Gerald Ablatt, getting to his feet.

He'd done little else from the time that his sister and brother-in-law had arrived. They come to offer him comfort but it was Nancy Dalley who most needed it. Between bouts of tears, she kept dredging up fond memories of her nephew and asking her brother to endorse their accuracy. Ablatt readily agreed with everything that she said, trying to ease her pain as a means of relieving his own. Dalley was forced into the position of an onlooker, watching them suffer and listening to the endless repetition of the same empty phrases.

'I'll do it,' he said, reaching for the tea pot.

Ablatt came out of his reverie. 'You don't know where the tea is, Jack.'

'I'll find it.'

'There are biscuits in the larder.'

'I couldn't touch food,' said Nancy. 'Even a biscuit would make me sick.'

'You haven't eaten anything since we got here, love,' said her husband, solicitously. 'There's no need to starve.'

'All I want is some tea.'

'But we've been here for hours.'

'Tea, Jack – nothing else.'

'I'll get it.'

As soon as Dalley left the room, Ablatt sat beside his sister and they embraced impulsively, letting the tears gush yet again. The murder had completely disoriented them. They'd lost all sense of time, place and purpose. All that they could do was to sit there and offer each other a degree of succour. When the blacksmith returned from the kitchen with the teapot and biscuits, he found them still locked together.

'I'll have to go soon,' he warned. 'It's unfair to leave Perce on his own all day. He'll wonder what's happened.'

'Go when you want to, Jack,' said Ablatt.

'Will you stay here, Nance?'

'Yes,' she murmured.

'I'll come back when I shut up the forge.'

'I'll still be here.'

Dalley put the teapot on the table and opened the biscuit barrel. He helped himself to a digestive them offered the selection to Ablatt who shook his head. His sister had started crying again and he was afraid to leave go of her. The blacksmith munched his biscuit and tempered his sorrow with a light-hearted remark.

'One thing, anyway,' he said. 'Cyril won't ever have to join the army now.'

The moment the words came out of his mouth, he realised how crass and hurtful they could be. However, he was spared any reproach from the others. Neither Ablatt nor Nancy heard what he said. They were miles away, trapped irretrievably in their private misery.

Notwithstanding his shortcomings, Claude Chatfield was an industrious man. By the time Marmion got back to Scotland Yard, the superintendent had immersed himself in the details of the murder, acquired a map of London and its inner suburbs, and set up a press conference. He'd also informed the commissioner about the progress of the investigation. Knowing how finicky Chatfield was about detail, Marmion had taken pains to rehearse what he was about to say. Accordingly, his report was full and lucid. He described his meeting with Eric Fussell and did his best to hide his aversion to the librarian. He went on to talk about Keedy's questioning of Horrie Waldron. It led to the sergeant's subsequent visit to a woman the gravedigger had claimed could supply him with an alibi for the time when he was away from the Weavers Arms the previous evening. Chatfield listened intently.

'Who is this woman?'

'Her name is Maud Crowther.'

'Is that Miss or Mrs?'

'It's Mrs Crowther, sir.'

'So this egregious gravedigger is dallying with a married woman.'

'The lady is a widow, sir,' said Marmion. 'To gain her cooperation, Sergeant Keedy had to promise her that her name would be kept out of any newspaper reports. I think that we should honour that promise.'

'What if she's simply inventing an alibi for Waldron?'

'The sergeant was convinced that Mrs Crowther was honest and reliable, sir. When it comes to women,' he added with a smile, 'I accept his judgements without question. He has an insight into the opposite sex that I lack.'

'This is no time to discuss Keedy's *amours*, Inspector,' said Chatfield with a note of reprimand. 'I know that they are the stuff of canteen gossip but they have no bearing on this case.'

'I disagree, sir.'

'As to this woman, we'll hold her name back for the time being. If, however, she turns out to be an accomplice of sorts, both you and the sergeant will bear the weight of my displeasure.'

'Neither of us wishes to incur that, Superintendent.'

'I don't blame you.' He studied Marmion for a moment. 'Is that all?'

'I believe so.'

'I'd hate to think that you've missed anything out.'

'You've heard everything, sir.'

Marmion's expression gave nothing away. Once again, he'd taken care to make no mention of the woman with whom Cyril Ablatt had enjoyed a secret romance. In addition to everything else, it would have unleashed a torrent of denunciation from the superintendent. Chatfield was a devout Roman Catholic who viewed extra-marital adventures of any kind with revulsion. Caroline Skene's name would have prompted a fiery sermon from him. But that was not the only reason why Marmion kept back details of his meeting with her. He felt sorry for her in her bereavement and was not at all sure that she could endure it. To add public exposure of her friendship with Ablatt would be a crippling blow, leading to dire repercussions with her husband. While Chatfield would think that such punishment was well-deserved, Marmion wanted to protect her.

The danger was that the superintendent might learn that he was being deceived and that would have disastrous results. Official reprimand and demotion were the least that Marmion could expect. A vengeful man like Chatfield would undoubtedly find other means of blighting his career at Scotland Yard. It was a risk that had to be taken. When he gave his word to someone, Marmion strove to keep it. Caroline Skene had been assured of his discretion. He was not going to betray her.

'Right,' said Chatfield, leaning forward and pointing to the map on his desk. 'Based on what we gathered from two of his friends, I've marked the route that Ablatt would have taken from Bishopsgate to the house in Shoreditch where they agreed to meet. Somewhere along that route, he was intercepted and killed.' He looked up. 'How and where did it happen?'

'If only we knew, sir,' said Marmion, bending over the map with interest. 'There seem to be a number of dots here.'

'I've marked the principal locations.' Chatfield used his finger to point them out. 'This is the Ablatt house and this is where Hambridge lives. Over here is the library and – since Waldron is implicated – I've also marked the cemetery.'

Marmion indicated another dot. 'What's this one, sir?'

'It's the pub close to the scene of the crime – the Weavers Arms.'

The Weavers Arms was the haunt of Horrie Waldron, still the only real suspect in the case. When he'd finished his shopping, Keedy decided to pay it a visit. In a large paper bag was the torch he'd just bought along with the razor, shaving brush and shaving soap he needed. The Haveron sisters had given him such a cordial welcome that he felt they deserved more, first thing on the following morning, than the sight of a bleary-eyed detective with dark whiskers. While he was out, Keedy had also availed himself of a snack. A glass of beer was now very tempting. He entered the bar to find that it was relatively empty so early in the evening. Standing behind the counter, the landlord gave him a grin of welcome.

'What can I get you, sir?' he asked.

'I'll have a pint of your best, please.'

'It's on its way.'

Reaching for a tankard, Stan Crowther filled it slowly with practised use of the pump. One mystery was solved for Keedy. When he'd heard Waldron express fear of the landlord, he couldn't understand why such a sturdy man as the gravedigger would be afraid of anyone. The explanation was standing in front of him. Crowther was a beefy man with immense forearms and hands like shovels. But it was his face that gave the game away. Any trace of his mother had been pummelled away in a boxing ring. Crowther had a broken nose, a cauliflower ear and eyebrows that looked to be permanently swollen and misshapen. Hanging on the wall behind the landlord was a framed poster advertising a series of fights. Top of the bill was a heavyweight contest between Stan Crowther and Eli Montgomery.

'In case you're wondering,' said Crowther, putting the full pint in front of him. 'I knocked him out in the fourth round. Old Eli was a good fighter but he had a glass jaw.' He chuckled. 'He went down like a sack of spuds.'

After paying for the beer, Keedy sipped it and gave a nod of approval. There was no need to introduce himself. In the same way that he'd guessed the landlord's former occupation, Crowther had worked out that he must be a detective.

'I was expecting a visit from you sooner or later,' he said.

'Then you'll know why I'm here.'

'It's a bad business, this murder. I mean, we have the odd fight in here and I got nothing against that, provided they don't break the furniture.

133

But murder is out of order – especially when it's almost on our doorstep.' He scratched his cauliflower ear. 'What's the name, sir?'

'I'm Detective Sergeant Keedy.'

'Have you got any suspects yet?'

'These are early days, Mr Crowther.'

'Everyone calls me Stan – except Eli Montgomery, of course. He calls me a black-hearted bastard. Eli always was a bad loser.'

'One man has come to our notice, Stan,' admitted Keedy. 'He's not exactly a suspect but we believe that he and the victim had quarrelled. The man's name is Horrie Waldron.'

Crowther grinned. 'Horrie quarrels with everybody.'

'He'd have more sense than to quarrel with you, I fancy.'

'Even he is not stupid enough to do that, Sergeant.'

'I spoke to him earlier at the cemetery. He tells me that he was in here all evening apart from an hour or two when he popped out.'

'Then he's told the truth for once.'

'You'll vouch for that, Stan?'

'I will,' said Crowther. 'Horrie was in here the moment we opened. For some reason, he was carrying his spade. God knows why. Anyway, he has a pint, looks at the clock and goes out. We didn't see him until a couple of hours later.'

'How did he seem?'

'For once in his life, he looked fairly clean even though he had his working clothes on. He must have sneaked off and had a bath somewhere.'

'What about the spade?'

'Oh, he took that with him but came back without it. The spade is like a fifth limb,' said Crowther. 'I've seen him using it at work. He's amazing. You should see what Horrie can do with it.'

Keedy thought of the corpse on the slab at the police morgue.

CHAPTER NINE

Harvey Marmion understood the importance of being prepared. Before he and the superintendent went off to face the press conference, therefore, they agreed on just how much information about the crime they would release. Because of his reluctance to give them all the available facts, Claude Chatfield had always had a somewhat spiky relationship with reporters. He tended to hoard evidence and, to their utter frustration, hand it out in dribs and drabs. Marmion was more accommodating. He accepted that the press had certain rights and was alive to their needs. Over the years, he'd developed the technique of appearing to tell them everything they wanted to know while cleverly suppressing certain crucial facts. It was the reason why he'd been chosen by the commissioner to head the investigation. Whereas Chatfield was almost hostile to the press, Marmion had built up a rapport with them over the years.

They all knew his story. Marmion's father had been a policeman. Largely because the job entailed shift work and low pay, it never appealed to his son. Marmion instead joined the civil service as a clerk. Fate intervened to change his mind. In the course of his duties, his father was murdered and the killer fled abroad. Maddened by the inability of the Metropolitan Police Force to catch the man, Marmion had taken action himself, launching a fund dedicated to the search for his father's killer. When he had enough cash, he'd crossed the Channel by ferry and begun his own private investigation. With no experience of detection and with all the language difficulties to handicap him, he nevertheless picked up a trail that had eluded British police. Showing the tenacity that was to become his hallmark, Marmion pursued, caught and arrested the killer by force. By selling the story of how he did it, he earned enough from a national newspaper to repay everyone who'd contributed so generously to the fund.

His escapade had a significant result. It turned him into a policeman. After the heady excitement of the chase, he could never return to the tedium of the civil service. Marmion started like his father, walking the beat in uniform in all weathers. By dint of hard work, he earned successive promotions and eventually became a detective inspector at Scotland Yard. There were many people who believed that he should hold a higher rank. One of them was among the clutch of reporters at the press conference. When the police statement containing the basic facts of the case had been read out, it fell to him to put the first question.

'Given your remarkable record of success, Inspector Marmion,' he asked, 'can you explain why you were not appointed to the rank of superintendent recently?'

There was muted laughter at the pained expression on Chatfield's face.

'That question is not relevant to the investigation,' said Marmion, smoothly, 'and, in any case, I believe that the right man got the job.'

Chatfield was mollified. 'Who's next?' he asked, looking round.

They were in the large room reserved for meetings and press conferences. Marmion and Chatfield sat behind a desk and submitted to interrogation. The questions came thick and fast and, for the most part, Marmion was left to answer them. While he named no suspects, he repeated his belief that the killer was a local man who knew both the victim and the area. It was important for press coverage to stress that fact and to ask the inhabitants of Shoreditch if they'd seen anything suspicious on the night in question or if anyone they knew had been behaving strangely in its aftermath. After giving them a description of the life and character of the victim, he asked them to respect the privacy of the Ablatt family and to refrain from harassing them during a time of mourning.

When the questions dried to a trickle, a ginger-haired man with spectacles spoke for the first time. As he learnt more about the murder victim, his sympathy for Cyril Ablatt had waned. There was a note of outrage in his voice.

'This man is a self-declared conchie,' he said with vehemence. 'At a time when police resources are stretched to the limit, why are you devoting so much manpower and effort to a miserable coward who refused to fight for his country?'

'Cyril Ablatt is the victim of a brutal murder,' said Marmion, firmly. 'His death will be investigated with the same vigour as the murder of anybody else.'

'Many people will find that scandalous.'

'They're entitled to their opinion.'

'Wouldn't the time and money spent on this investigation be better used in the fight against crime in the capital?'

'I refute that suggestion,' said Marmion. 'Besides, as a man in your job ought to know, the latest statistics show that adult crime in the capital has actually gone down during the war. It's not difficult to see why. The young men largely responsible for committing it have joined the army in droves. The pattern of crime has changed so dramatically that we have prisons standing half-empty.'

'Then they should be filled with conchies like Cyril Ablatt.'

Marmion's response was tinged with irritation. 'When he became a murder victim,' he said, 'he ceased to be a conscientious objector. I think you should bear that in mind.'

'One last question,' said Chatfield, intervening to bring the proceedings to an end. 'Inspector Marmion and I can't spare you any more time. When we have more information – and when the results of the post-mortem are known – you will be informed.' He saw a hand shoot up. 'Yes?'

'This concerns yesterday's meeting of the NCF,' said a man in a crumpled suit. 'You told us that Ablatt went there with like-minded friends. Who were they?'

When the three of them met in Mansel Price's digs, Leach was unwise enough to reveal his plan for bringing forward the date of his marriage. The Welshman was livid. Leaping up from his chair, he pointed an accusatory finger.

'You're a bloody traitor, Gordon,' he yelled. 'You'd be turning your back on everything you've ever believed in.'

'No, I wouldn't,' said Leach.

'You've lost your nerve completely.'

'I have to consider Ruby.'

'Why? She's not liable to be called up. This is between you and the Military Service Act. Fred and I will defy it. All you're going to do is to dodge it.'

'That's what I told him,' said Hambridge.

Price was shaking with fury. 'Honestly, Gordon, I'm ashamed of you. I thought you were one of us.'

'I still am,' insisted Leach.

'No – you just want to watch from the safety of the sidelines while we take on the government. You've always claimed that you'd rather go to prison than fight in the army. All of a sudden, you've gone soft.'

'It was only an idea, Mansel.'

'Well,' said Hambridge, hotly, 'you know what *we* think of it.'

'I'd never call you my friend ever again,' warned Price.

'Neither would I.'

'Calm down, both of you,' said Leach with a failed attempt at a smile of appeasement. 'Nothing has been decided. If you want to know the truth, Ruby was in two minds about it and I can guarantee that her parents won't like the idea all that much either. At the time when it occurred to me, it seemed like a . . . solution. But,' he added quickly as he saw Price poised for attack, 'I can see now that it wouldn't really solve anything. So why don't we forget all about it? I promise that *I* will.'

'Will you swear to that?' asked Price, standing over him. 'We don't want you sneaking off behind our backs and getting married. I know you're keen to get Ruby into bed but you don't need to be her husband to do that. Anybody else would have pulled her drawers off before now.'

'Maybe he already has,' said Hambridge with a grin.

'I don't think so, Fred. He wouldn't look so desperate if he had.'

'Enough of your sneers, Mansel,' said Leach, angering. 'You're only jealous because you don't have a girlfriend. Let's keep Ruby out of this. The point is that I believe in pacifism as much as any of you. When it's my turn to face a tribunal, I'll nail my colours to the mast.'

'They want you to join the army – not the bloody navy!'

The comment eased the tension at once. They traded a laugh and Price flopped back into his chair. He rented the attic room in an old Victorian house. The minimal warmth from the fire in the grate was countered by a series of draughts that blew in. Hurt that his suggestion had met with such opposition, Leach was consoled by the fact that he'd retained their friendship. Hambridge was pleased that their differences had now been resolved. He hated friction of any sort.

'Think of Cyril,' he advised. 'His death should bring us together, not split us apart. After all, he was the one who showed us what we have in common.'

'I agree,' said Leach.

'We've got to ask ourselves what he would have wanted.'

'There's an easy answer to that,' said Price. 'Cyril would urge us to have the courage of our convictions instead of rushing off to church to get married.'

Leach was upset. 'Don't keep on about it, Mansel,' he complained. 'I've told you that it won't happen. Anyway, it wouldn't have been in a church. It would have been in a register office and that wouldn't have pleased Ruby at all. Instead of thinking about ourselves,' he went on, 'we ought to be thinking about Mr Ablatt. He and Cyril were very close. It must be terrible to lose your only child.'

'Yes,' agreed Hambridge. 'I asked Mansel if we ought to call on him but he thought we should wait a bit until the shock wears off a little.'

'The family will comfort him,' said Price. 'Cyril's aunt and uncle will have been told by now. They'll rally round. The rest of his relatives live outside London.'

'Should we send a card or something?'

'I don't think so, Fred.'

'What about you, Gordon? Should we get in touch?'

'In due course,' decided Leach after consideration. 'Mansel is right. This is a family matter. Let them mourn in private.'

Though he lacked his employer's physique, Percy Fry could work hard for long hours without respite. In the absence of Jack Dalley, he'd done just that at the forge. Lunch had consisted of the gobbled sandwich and the cup of tea that his wife had made for him. He lost count of the customers who came in need of his services and explained Dalley's absence so many times that it was like reciting a favourite passage from a book. As the working day drew to a close, he began to put everything back in its place before closing up the forge. When the blacksmith finally returned to Bethnal Green, he was full of apologies for his abrupt departure. Fry made light of the pressure he'd been under.

'Only too glad to help, Jack,' he said, 'though I'm still not sure what it's all about. When the milkman called in, he said there was something in the paper about a murder in Shoreditch. I hope that was nothing to do with your family.'

'It was, Perce,' said Dalley, grimly. 'The victim was my nephew, Cyril.'

'Blimey! What happened?'

'They're still trying to work that out.'

'Murdered – that's terrible! I remember Cyril well – came in here from time to time. He was a cocky young devil and I liked him for that.'

Dalley told him all he knew about the crime and how his wife and his brother-in-law had reacted to the news. He warned Fry that he might have to take time off again in the course of the next few days.

'Do what needs to be done, Jack,' said Fry. 'I can manage here.'

'You must have been rushed off your feet.'

'Rather be busy than idle.'

'So would I,' said Dalley. 'But what's going to keep me busy from now on is trying to console Nancy. This has shaken her up. She loved Cyril. My brother-in-law is in pieces, as you can imagine, but Nancy is far worse.'

'Anything we can do?'

'Yes – just hold the fort here.'

'Thinking of Nancy,' said Fry. 'Would it help if my wife went to keep her spirits up? Elaine is good at that.'

'Thanks all the same, Perce, but we'll be all right.'

'Offer stays open.'

Dalley gave a nod of gratitude and looked around the forge. He recalled the many occasions when his nephew had visited the place in his younger days. Ablatt had been eager, fresh-faced and uncomplicated. He'd been in awe of his uncle's skills and developed a love of horses. Education had lured him away from the forge and put ideas into his head with which Dalley took issue. On the occasions when they'd been alone together, they'd had some lively arguments. The blacksmith had always enjoyed their exchanges even though they'd shown the wide gap that had opened up between uncle and nephew.

'Who were those men who came here?' asked Fry, washing his hands in a pail of water. 'I didn't catch their names.'

'One of them was Inspector Marmion, who's in charge of the case. The other was Sergeant Keedy.'

'Do they have any idea who killed young Cyril?'

'*They* don't, Perce, but I do.'

'Oh?'

'It was someone who took against him because he was a conchie. To be honest,' confessed Dalley, 'I went off him a bit myself when he started telling me that war was evil and that it was wrong to bear arms. Well, you heard him sounding off in here a couple of times. What are we supposed to do, I asked him – surrender to the Germans and let them take over the country?'

'Yes, I remember what he said.'

'He had a clever answer as usual. Cyril had a clever answer for everything. Even though he was my nephew, there were times when I just wanted to punch him on the nose to bring him to his senses.'

'P'raps you should have done just that.'

'Nancy would never have forgiven me.'

'But it might have saved his life.'

'I don't know about that.'

Fry dried his hands on an old towel. 'How do you feel now?' he asked.

'What do you mean?'

'None of my business, of course, but you don't seem as upset as I'd be if it was my nephew.' Seeing a flash of anger in the blacksmith's eyes, he was immediately repentant. 'Forget I said that, Jack. I take it back.'

Dalley's ire subsided at once and he became pensive. He thought about the moment when he caught his wife and brother-in-law in a tearful embrace. Grief was visibly devouring them. It troubled Dalley that he could not feel their pain to the same degree and that he remained somewhat detached from it all. In spite of their many disagreements, he liked his nephew and should have been shattered by his death. Because he was not, he was assailed by guilt.

'You're right, Perce,' he said, quietly. 'I'd never admit this to Nancy but I can't mourn him the way that she can. It's something to do with his beliefs. Cyril is not the only conchie in the country. There are far too many of the buggers. Women hand out white feathers and you sometimes read stories in the papers about conchies being thrown in a pond or beaten up. It's happening everywhere.'

Fry was terse. 'Got no sympathy for them, Jack.'

'Neither have I – they asked for it.'

'But I'm very sorry about Cyril. I understand people turning on a conchie but there's a limit. Murder is going too far.'

'That's what I think. It's a dreadful crime. You wouldn't want your worst enemy to be battered to death like that.' Dalley was bewildered. 'So why don't I feel like the others? Is there something wrong with me, Perce?' he asked with concern. 'Am I being cruel? Why – God forgive me – am I almost relieved that he's dead?'

* * *

Hannah Billington had committed herself fully to the work of the WEC. She was unfailingly generous with her time and money. At the end of a long day, she was always willing to use her own car as a taxi, driving her colleagues home no matter how far it took her out of her way. It was Alice Marmion and Vera Dowling who were given a lift this time. They were quick to accept the offer. Travelling home after dark could sometimes have unexpected hazards. Relaxed in Hannah's company, Alice was as chatty as ever but her friend was silent for most of the journey. Seated in the back of the vehicle, Vera lacked the confidence to take a full part in the conversation. She was the first to be dropped off. When the car started off again, Hannah turned to her passenger.

'I must say that you make an odd couple,' she observed.

'Really – in what way?'

'You're so forthright and Vera is so reserved. The poor girl wouldn't say boo to a goose, whereas you'd be capable of wringing its neck and roasting it for supper.'

Alice grinned. 'I'm not sure about that, Hannah.'

'But you take my point.'

'I think so.'

'It must be a case of attraction of opposites.'

'Vera is not as shy as she looks. If you want the truth, she was the one who first suggested that we should give up our jobs and join the WEC. It's just that she feels rather cowed by you.'

'Why?' asked Hannah with a laugh. 'Am I that intimidating?'

'You are to Vera.'

'And do I unsettle you as well?'

'Not in the least,' said Alice. 'I admire the way you run things. You've got so much energy and you know how to organise people.'

'I do my best.'

'The WEC is very different from what either of us expected. People kept telling us that it would be full of suffragettes who'd try to convert us, but it's not like that at all. All sorts of people have joined.'

'Yes, that's right – everyone from domestic servants to members of the peerage. Many of us do believe in equal rights for women but we don't ram it down people's throats. Also, of course,' said Hannah, 'the militant suffragettes have suspended their campaign until the war is over. They don't need to break windows in Oxford Street when German bombs will do the job for them.'

'What will happen when the war is over?'

'Who can say? One would like to think that the government will show some appreciation for the work that women have done. We've proved that we can do even the most onerous and dangerous jobs. The least reward that we deserve,' insisted Hannah, taking the car around a sharp bend, 'is a say in the way this country is run.'

'You ought to be a Member of Parliament.'

'Oh, I don't have any ambitions in that direction, Alice.'

'You'd really stir things up there.'

'I'd be bored to tears, spending so much time with all those men.' She peered through the windscreen. 'I've been here before but I can't quite remember how. Am I going the right way?'

'Yes,' said Alice, 'it's the next left then the second on the right. It's so kind of you to give us both a lift home.'

'You worked hard today. You deserve a reward.'

'Thank you.'

Following the directions, Hannah drove on into the street where Alice lived and brought the vehicle to a grinding halt. She looked up at the house.

'Do you like it here?'

'Yes, I do.'

'I would have thought that you'd share with Vera.'

Alice was tactful. 'That would never have worked,' she said. 'We're much better off apart. Vera's just a friend. We're not Siamese twins.'

Hannah laughed and turned to her. Alice had the impression that she wanted to be asked in but it was late and, in any case, her landlady discouraged even female visitors after a certain time. She was about to get out of the vehicle when Hannah put a hand on her arm.

'Have you heard from your brother recently?' she asked.

'No – we haven't had a letter from Paul for weeks.'

'My husband is stationed near the Somme. I get nothing but complaints in his letters. I daren't tell him about his clubhouse.' She released Alice's arm. 'Don't marry a soldier, Alice.'

Alice was amused. 'I'm not thinking of marrying anyone at the moment.'

'With a face like yours, you'll never be short of offers.'

'While the war's on, the WEC comes first.'

'That makes two of us,' said Hannah. 'You go off and get a good night's sleep while I see if I can find my way home. Goodbye, Alice.'

'Goodbye – and thanks again!'

Getting out of the car, Alice waved her off and waited until the car was chugging down the street. Then she ran up the path and used her latchkey to let herself into the house. Any letters that came for the tenants were left on the gatelegged table in the hall. Alice crossed over to it but there was nothing waiting for her.

'Damn!' she exclaimed under her breath.

Ellen Marmion was never sure if she should wait up for her husband or go to bed when she felt tired. In an effort to stay up as long as possible that night, she did some knitting then read a book by the light from the standard lamp. The story failed to hold her attention and she eventually drifted off. When her husband came into the house, he found her slumbering beside a fire that had dwindled to a faint glow. Removing the book from her lap, he set it aside then kissed her gently on the forehead.

'Is that you, Harvey?' she asked, coming slowly awake.

He chuckled. 'Who else were you expecting?'

'What time is it?'

'It's time for bed, Ellen. Come on – I'll help you up.'

She took his hands and let him pull her to her feet. He'd taken off his overcoat and hat and hung them up. She was in her dressing gown and slippers. Before she could stop it, a yawn suddenly escaped.

'Why are you so late?'

'Time stands still when I have another murder case.'

'Where have you been all day?'

'Trudging around Shoreditch and slipping back to Scotland Yard for the dubious pleasure of reporting to the superintendent.'

'*You* should have got that job,' she said with feeling. 'You'd have done it much better than Claude Chatfield.'

'Give the devil his due,' said Marmion. 'He was at his desk an hour before I got there and he was still working when I left. His wife must think she's a nun. We know that's not true,' he added with a laugh. 'She's had five children.'

'How many of them live at home?'

'I'm not sure, Ellen – two at least.'

'Then she won't get lonely. When you go off, I'm entirely on my own. I can't blame Paul for not being here but I do miss Alice. It wouldn't be so bad if she spent the odd night or two here.'

'She values her freedom, love.'

'Well, it's not doing her health any good.'

Marmion was worried. 'How do you know? Have you seen her?'

'Alice called in early this morning,' said Ellen, 'and we had a cup of tea together. She looked so thin and drawn. She claims that she's put on weight but I couldn't see it. There was a sense of fatigue about her.'

'Like father, like daughter!'

'It's not a joke, Harvey.'

'It wasn't meant as one,' he said. 'I was being serious. Alice is like me. When she takes something on, she gives it every last ounce of her energy.' He used a hand to suppress a yawn. 'Up we go. I'm dropping.'

After switching off the light, he put the fireguard in the grate then followed her upstairs. When he'd been to the bathroom and changed into his pyjamas, he clambered into bed beside her.

'What sort of a case is it?' she asked.

'It's a very baffling one at the moment.'

'Do you have any suspects?'

'We might have. It's too early to tell.'

'And is this the sort of time you'll be coming home from now on?'

'Think yourself lucky, Ellen,' he said, snuggling under the bed sheets. 'Your loving husband will actually get some sleep tonight. That wouldn't be the case if you were married to Joe Keedy. He's got to stay awake until dawn.'

When he left the Weavers Arms, Keedy had first walked to the lane where the body had been discovered. The police had gone now, so it was possible to go to the spot where Cyril Ablatt had lain. By the light of his torch, he saw that the blood had been washed away to deter sightseers from finding the exact place. He imagined the shock that the courting couple must have felt when they stumbled on the corpse. It might have had an adverse effect on their romance. Before he returned to his vantage point, he walked around the vicinity to familiarise himself with it. These were the streets that Ablatt and his friends knew by heart. Hiding in one of them, he believed, was the killer. Their job was to root him out.

The Haveron sisters were delighted to see him again and pressed food and drink on to him. They were like a pair of eccentric aunts who'd just encountered a nephew they never knew they had and wanted to make up for lost time.

'Do you do this kind of thing often?' asked Rose.

'As it happens,' said Keedy, 'I don't. This is an exception.'

'Well, it's certainly an exception for us,' Martha chimed in, 'isn't it, Rose? Who'd ever have thought that we'd play host to a detective?'

'It's rather exciting,' said Rose.

'I do hope it's not a waste of time.'

'So do I,' said Keedy, touched by their sweetness. 'But at least I'll be comfortable in your front room. The last time I did this all night, I had to hide in the back of a cattle truck and look through the slats. You can imagine the stench.'

'Oh dear!' said Martha.

'You won't have that problem here,' Rose assured him.

Fortunately, the sisters went to bed early every night and even the presence of a detective did not alter their routine. They wished him well, then withdrew upstairs. When he adjourned to the front room, Keedy could hear one of them walking about in the bedroom above his head. He'd politely declined their offer to light a fire for him. It was evident that Rose and Martha Haveron were ladies of limited means. He didn't wish to make inroads into their coal supply nor did he want to make the room too snug. A warm fire might send him off to sleep. Cold air would keep him awake. Even with the blankets around him, he could feel a bracing chill.

The Ablatt house was diagonally opposite. When he sat beside the window on an upright chair, he could look through a chink in the curtains. It would be impossible to miss anyone who came to add something to the already well-decorated wall. Keedy settled down for what might be a long and fruitless wait. He staved off boredom by going through all the evidence so far gathered. He thought of the conversations he'd had with Hambridge and Price, young men of fundamentally different character who'd been united by a single purpose. He'd liked the carpenter and distrusted the cook on sight. When they came before a tribunal, he suspected, the quiet certainty of the Quaker would be more effective than the Welshman's truculence. The person who really interested him was Horrie Waldron. How on earth had such a reprobate aroused affection in Maud Crowther? Given the size and muscularity of Stan Crowther, both of them were tempting fate. The discovery that Waldron was making secret visits to his mother would enrage the landlord. If he dared to put his head into the pub after that, the gravedigger would need his spade to defend himself.

Hours drifted by and tiredness slackened his muscles. Every so often, his eyes would close for a couple of minutes and he'd have to shake himself awake. Having lost all track of time, Keedy stood up, walked around the room and took off the blankets so that he could feel the piercing cold. It served to galvanise him just in time. From outside the house, there was a loud yell then he heard something thud onto the pavement. Charging across to the window, he pulled back the curtain. A ladder was standing against the wall of the Ablatt house. Beside it was an upturned tin of paint. In the middle of the road, two figures were grappling wildly. Keedy jumped into action. He ran to the front door, let himself out and raced across to the two men. In the course of a fierce struggle, one of them threw the other to the ground and dived on top of him. Keedy grabbed him from behind and pulled him off.

'That's enough!' he shouted.

The man on the ground leapt to his feet, punched Keedy in the face and pushed him against the other man. He then fled off down the street and vanished around the corner. Before the second man could run after him, he was overpowered by Keedy and held in a vice-like grip.

'You silly bastard!' howled Mansel Price. 'You let him get away.'

CHAPTER TEN

Knowing that he wanted to make an early start, Ellen Marmion was up before her husband in order to make sure that he went off to work with a cooked breakfast inside him. When he came down from the bathroom, it was waiting for him on the kitchen table. He gave her a smile of gratitude and sat down.

'How much did you eat yesterday?' she asked.

'I don't remember.'

'Not enough, if I know you.'

'I grabbed something on the hoof,' he said, picking up his knife and fork and attacking a sausage. 'Regular meals are a luxury in my job.'

'You must have food, Harvey.'

'I survive somehow.'

Ellen sat opposite him and clicked her tongue when he began to wolf it down. She poured two cups of tea and added milk and sugar to both before stirring them. Marmion laughed.

'I *can* spare the time to stir my own tea, love.'

'I was only trying to be helpful.'

'Then you can eat my breakfast for me as well.'

'Harvey!'

'There's no need for you to be up this early,' he said. 'It's not six yet.'

'I can't lie in bed when you have to be fed. It's my contribution to this case. I know that it's on your mind. You were talking about it in your sleep.'

He was jolted. 'Was I? What did I say?'

'I couldn't really tell. You just came out with odd words like "gravedigger" and "librarian" and there were some initials – NFC, I think.'

'It must have been the NCF – that's the No-Conscription Fellowship. It's an organisation for people who – for one reason or another – find themselves unable to take part in the war. They come in all shapes and sizes.'

'Are they too afraid?'

'Some of them are, Ellen, but the majority do have a genuine conscientious objection. Look at the murder victim, for instance. Cyril Ablatt was a deeply religious young man with an aversion to taking a human life.'

'I must say that the idea of it worries me as well,' she said. 'I know that Paul had to join the army but it troubles me that our son will have to shoot someone.'

'It's only in self-defence, love. It's a case of kill or be killed.'

She grimaced. 'What a horrible expression!'

'It's an accurate one,' he said, reasonably, 'and you just have to accept it. War turns every soldier into a licensed killer.'

'What happens to them afterwards?'

'When the war is over, you mean?'

'Yes,' she said, frowning. 'What will it have done to them? Will Paul still be the same person when he comes home or will the war leave its mark on him?'

'The experience is bound to have changed him, love.'

'That's my fear.'

'I'll just be glad if he comes back in one piece.'

'Mrs Hooper's son didn't. He lost a leg at Ypres. According to her, he keeps boasting about a German he shot dead. He goes on and on about it. Mrs Hooper is worried stiff about him.' She bit her lip. 'I do hope that Paul doesn't do anything like that.'

'He'll have seen terrible sights,' said Marmion, reaching for his tea. 'It won't be easy to get them out of his mind.'

There was an uncomfortable silence as they ate their breakfast. When she eventually broke it, Ellen found another source of anxiety.

'I'm praying that Alice doesn't go over there as well,' she said.

'There's no danger of that, surely.'

'There might be, Harvey. She mentioned it yesterday. A couple of her friends in the WEC went off to France as dispatch riders. That could be dangerous.'

'They'll be kept well behind the lines, love.'

'I don't want our daughter following Paul over there. Talk to her.'

'Chance would be a fine thing!'

'Alice won't listen to me.'

'Did you listen to *your* mother at that age?'

She smiled. 'If I had, then I probably wouldn't have married you.'

Marmion grinned then forked the last piece of fried egg into his mouth. Glancing up at the clock on the wall, he suddenly accelerated, swallowing his food, draining his cup in a series of gulps and getting to his feet. He went out into the hall and reached for his hat and coat off the peg. As he put them on, he gave a sigh.

'The war has been a disaster for us,' he said. 'We've lost a sizeable

153

number of men to the army and all of our best horses are serving in cavalry regiments. This murder would have been so much easier to solve if I could call on more detectives.'

'They didn't *all* volunteer. Some of them like Joe Keedy have stayed.'

'Oh, I think he was tempted to enlist, Ellen, but he felt that there was important work to do on the home front. Also, of course, endless months in the trenches would play havoc with his social life. Joe is a ladies' man and there aren't many available young ladies in the war zone.'

'You know quite well that that wasn't the main reason he didn't join up.'

'It wasn't,' said Marmion, winking at her. 'He couldn't resist the privilege of working with me. That's why he stayed. Mind you,' he went on, chortling, 'after being forced to spend the whole of last night keeping a brick wall under surveillance, he might be wishing that he was in the army, after all.'

Keedy was annoyed with himself. He'd not only been distracted when the midnight artist had first appeared, he'd accidentally contrived to rescue the man from a beating and to assist his escape. Once he realised what had happened, he and Mansel Price had scoured the streets but there was no sign of the fugitive. It was wrong to blame the Welshman. He deserved credit. While Keedy had had shelter and a degree of comfort in someone's front room, Price had spent hours crouched in a doorway. It enabled him to attack the man before he had time to paint anything else on the wall. The situation was not irretrievable. Keedy had the abandoned ladder and the tin of white paint. On the lid of the tin was a sticker with the name of the shop where it was bought. By first light, he'd sought help from the nearby police station. Two uniformed constables were put at his disposal and a third was waiting to take the paint back to the shop to see if anyone could remember to whom it was sold.

The long trudge began. It reminded Keedy of his days in uniform when he sometimes spent an entire day knocking on doors. Having seen the direction in which the man had run off, he had a measure of guidance. While Keedy carried the ladder, the policemen went down either side of the street at the same time in search of its owner. In the first twenty minutes, they got a negative response on every doorstep. Then they saw a postman coming towards them. Keedy caught his attention and beckoned him over. When he identified himself as a detective, he got instant cooperation.

'Is it to do with this murder?' asked the postman, breathlessly.

'It could be.'

'Then I'll help all I can.'

'We're trying to find the owner of this ladder,' said Keedy.

'It probably belongs to Bill Prosser. He's a window cleaner. You've already come past his house. Did you try there?'

'We've knocked on every door in the street. The window cleaner had an alibi for last night. He's not our man.'

'Then it must belong to someone else,' said the postman, thinking. 'There aren't many people with a ladder that size. In fact, the only other one I can think of round here is Robbie Gill.'

'Where does he live?'

'It's the next street on the left, Sergeant – number thirteen.'

Keedy's hopes rose. 'That could be unlucky for Mr Gill.'

Thanking the postman, he and the two policemen walked to the address given. Since there was no knocker, Keedy used his knuckles to rap on the door. After a delay of a few seconds, he heard someone coming. When the door was unlocked and opened, a stringy man in his forties came into view. There was bruising around his eye and his unshaven cheek was grazed.

'Mr Gill?'

'That's me,' said the man, gruffly.

'I'm Detective Sergeant Keedy and I've come to return your ladder.'

Gill resorted to bluff. 'Oh, you found it, did you? Thank you very much, Sergeant. It was stolen yesterday. I'm so glad to get it back.'

'Why is that, sir? Did you intend to paint slogans on other walls?'

'I don't know what you're talking about.'

'I think you do,' said Keedy. 'Apart from anything else, you assaulted a police officer last night and I take exception to that. You're under arrest, Mr Gill.' He parked the ladder up against the front wall of the house. 'I'll leave this here. You won't need it where you're going.'

Well fed and eager to take up the reins of the investigation once more, Marmion arrived at Scotland Yard and went straight the superintendent's office. Chatfield was poring over the map of Shoreditch.

'Good morning, sir,' said Marmion.

'Ah, you're here at last, are you?' observed the other, making it sound as if the inspector was late rather than an hour earlier than his designated starting time. 'It's going to be another long day. We should have the post-mortem results soon and, with luck, we might get a response to our appeal for witnesses.'

'It hasn't happened so far.'

'That was because the details in the *Evening News* were very sketchy. It's different with this morning's editions. The papers will carry a photograph of the victim and description of the route he would have taken home from that meeting. It will also tell them much more about Cyril Ablatt. And another thing,' he said, folding the map up. 'The killer will read the reports. He'll start to panic.'

'I beg leave to doubt that, Superintendent. I think he's a cold-hearted swine who might enjoy the publicity he's aroused.'

'That's arrant nonsense.'

'Is it?' retorted Marmion. 'He deliberately left the body where it could be found. Doesn't that tell you something about him? Many killers go out of their way to conceal their handiwork in order to delay discovery. Why dump the corpse in a lane when he could have hidden it in the woods or buried it somewhere?' He remembered Horrie Waldron. 'He might have buried it in a cemetery, perhaps. Who would think of looking for it there?'

'You're being fanciful, Inspector.'

'I don't think so, sir. When he put the victim there, the killer was making a statement. He wanted us to *know*.'

'What *I* want to know is how we catch the devil.'

'We stick to procedure, sir. We gather evidence, sift it, follow every lead and maintain relentless pursuit. If we get help from witnesses, all well and good, but we shouldn't rely on anyone coming forward. My men went from house to house in the area yesterday and they didn't pick up a snippet of useful information. Shoreditch was asleep when the corpse was moved. Nobody saw or heard a thing.'

'I remain more sanguine.'

'Then I hope your optimism is justified. Coverage will be extensive. We gave them plenty to bite on at the press conference.'

'Yes,' said Chatfield, offering a rare compliment. 'I thought you handled them very well.' He added a caveat. 'Though there was no need to be quite so friendly towards them.'

'We need the press on our side, sir. We should never antagonise them.'

Chatfield bridled. 'Are you suggesting that that's what I did?'

'Of course not – you've had far too much experience.'

'I certainly have.'

He inflated his chest and pulled himself upright. Marmion waited while the superintendent struck a pose, lost in thought about what he considered to be the triumphs in his career, the latest of which was his promotion to a higher rank. He seemed to have forgotten that anyone else was there. When he finally noticed Marmion, he snapped his fingers.

'I've been remiss,' he confessed. 'Do forgive me. Not long before you came, there was a telephone call for you.'

'Did anyone leave a message?'

'It was Sergeant Keedy.'

'Then he probably yawned down the line at you,' said Marmion.

'On the contrary, Inspector – he sounded almost chirpy. As a result of an incident during the night, he's made an arrest. It's a man who was caught trying to paint something on a wall.'

'Why did you do it?'

'Somebody had to, Sergeant.'

'Did you know Cyril Ablatt?'

'I knew *of* him – that was enough.'

'What do you mean?'

'My wife uses the library. She saw him there lots of times and heard him arguing with people about why he didn't join the army.'

'How did you know where he lived?'

'I followed him one evening.'

'And is that all you did, Mr Gill?'

'You know it isn't. I let everyone know what sort of person he was.'

'Forget your antics with the paintbrush,' said Keedy. 'I'm wondering if you followed him when he came back from a meeting in Bishopsgate. I'm wondering if you decided that calling him names on a brick wall wasn't enough so you killed him out of hatred for his beliefs.'

'No!' exclaimed Gill. 'I never touched him. I swear it.'

'What were you doing on the evening before last?'

'I was at home with my wife and my son. You can ask them.'

'I'll make a point of doing that.'

'I never went anywhere near Ablatt,' said Gill, squirming.

'Did you go out at any stage during the evening?'

'Only for an hour – I went out for a drink.'

'Which pub would that be?'

'The Weavers.'

'That's very close to where the body was found.'

'So?'

'Are you sure that you didn't go into the pub to get some Dutch courage to commit murder?' asked Keedy. 'You don't look like the sort of person who'd have the nerve to do it otherwise.'

Gill was desperate. 'All I did was to have a pint of beer,' he said, shifting uneasily in his chair. 'Talk to Stan Crowther, the landlord at the Weavers. He'll tell you how long I was there. I had a drink, played a game of darts with Horrie Waldron, then left. I was back home by nine. My wife will confirm that.'

Keedy could see that he was telling the truth. Robbie Gill was not the killer. Since the body was dumped in the lane much later than nine o'clock, he could not have put it there. On the other hand, the fact that he knew the gravedigger raised the possibility that he might somehow have been party to the murder. Gill could not be removed entirely from the list of suspects.

They were in a cold, featureless room at Shoreditch police station. Gill sat on the opposite side of the table from Keedy. When he greeted the sergeant at his front door, he was almost pugnacious, but the arrest had sobered him. A plumber by trade, Gill had the shifty look of someone who never expected to be caught. He saw what he was doing as a public duty, exposing a conscientious objector who had the gall to try to justify his position. Every time he heard about Ablatt pontificating at the library, he felt a simmering disgust and felt impelled to strike at him somehow.

159

'What were you going to paint?' asked Keedy.

Gill glared at him. 'Does it matter now?'

'I'd like to know.'

'I was going to add two words – "good riddance".'

'Was that a kind thing to do, Mr Gill?'

'That yellow-bellied conchie deserved it!'

'Did his father deserve it?' asked Keedy. 'He didn't agree with what his son was doing. Did his aunt deserve it? She's not a conscientious objector. Mrs Dalley is simply a heartbroken woman who's lost someone she loved. Then there's Cyril Ablatt's uncle. When we picked him up at his forge yesterday, he told us quite openly that his nephew should have gone into the army. All three of them were in that house yesterday, mourning the death of a murder victim. Did you think it would help them in their bereavement if you taunted them with your jibe?'

'If you're trying to make me feel sorry,' said Gill, recovering something of his confidence, 'then you're wasting your time. I'd do the same thing again.'

'You won't get the chance.'

'Everyone in the Weavers thinks the same as me – conchies are scum.'

'But they don't all sneak out at night and deface someone else's property, do they? That's a criminal offence, Mr Gill.' Keedy sat back and appraised him. 'Do you know what I think?'

'What?'

'I think that I'll send a policeman to your house to check your alibi. We'll find out if you really were there, as you claim, at the time in question. We'll also discover if your wife approves of what you do with a tin of paint in the middle of the night.' He saw the sweat break out on the other man's brow. 'I can't believe that Mrs Gill would be proud of a husband who did what you did.'

'Keep my wife out of this!'

'It was you who wanted to call her as a witness.'

'I acted on my own. Mabel wasn't involved in any way.'

'Indirectly, she was,' noted Keedy. 'It was her visits to the library that drew your attention to Cyril Ablatt. My guess is that you probably asked her to find out as much about him as she could.' Gill's forehead was now glistening. 'To some extent, Mrs Gill aided and abetted you.'

The plumber winced. He had set out during the night to assuage his hatred of a conscientious objector by leaving a taunt in large letters on the side of his house. Gill had not only been violently attacked, he was now under arrest and being accused of murder. The thought that his wife would be questioned by the police when he was not there to control her answers made him quiver.

'Do you know what you should do?' asked Keedy. 'If you have a shred of decency, you should apologise to Mr Ablatt then paint over those words on the wall of his house. But you're not going to do that, are you?'

Gill folded his arms in token defiance. 'No, I'm not.'

'Mr Ablatt will be told about your arrest and he'll see the report about you in the newspaper. If he needs a plumber, I don't think he'll be turning to you somehow.'

Gerald Ablatt had slept only fitfully during the night and was up before dawn. After a breakfast of toast and tea, he went into his son's bedroom and gazed at all the books. They symbolised the education that a caring father had provided by working overtime at his shop. Ablatt had grave misgivings about that education now. Had his son become a blacksmith or even taken up his father's trade, he might well be alive now. He slammed the door shut and went downstairs. Joe Keedy had paid a surprise visit to the house but Ablatt was too preoccupied to take in everything he said. He thanked the detective without quite knowing what he'd achieved. Ablatt brooded on the news after Keedy left. It was still relatively early when Jack Dalley brought his wife. Nancy felt that she had to be with her brother so that they could share their sorrow. As soon as they met, they embraced warmly and she began to weep.

'I'll stay for a while,' offered Dalley, 'but I have to get over to the forge at some point. Perce can't do everything on his own.'

'Go when you need to, Jack,' said Ablatt. 'I'll look after Nancy.'

'The neighbours have been kind,' she said through tears. 'As soon as they found out, they came to see if they could do anything for me. And Jack told me that Percy Fry's wife will come at any time if I need company. In time, I might do. At the moment, I need to be with family.' She hugged her brother again. 'The only place I want to be is here.'

'Nance didn't get a wink of sleep last night,' said Dalley. 'Neither did I.'

Ablatt padded out to the kitchen and they followed him. After filling the kettle, he set it on the stove and lit the gas. He seemed to come out of a daze.

'If you'd got here earlier, you'd have met Sergeant Keedy.'

'What was he doing here?' asked Dalley with interest. 'Have they caught the killer?'

'No, Jack, but they've arrested the man who painted those things on the wall. He tried to have another go last night but Cyril's friend, Mansel, was lying in wait for him. So was the sergeant,' explained Ablatt. 'He was hiding in a house around the corner. The man got away in a scuffle but he was arrested later.'

'Who was he?'

'His name is Robbie Gill and he's a plumber.'

Dalley was roused. 'I know him,' he said, angrily. 'He did some work for us once. In fact, he botched it so I refused to pay him and had to get in someone else.'

'I remember him,' said Nancy.

'Yes, he was a surly beggar.'

'I know his wife,' said Ablatt, dully. 'Mrs Gill brings shoes to be soled and heeled. I doubt if she'll be doing that again in a hurry.'

'I bet you want to give him a good hiding,' said Dalley.

'No, Jack, I don't.'

'*I* would if he'd painted things on the side of my house.'

'What does it matter now? Cyril is dead. It won't bring him back.'

'At the very least, I'd give him a piece of my mind.'

Ablatt was lacklustre. 'There's no point.'

They discussed the matter until the kettle began to boil. Ablatt made the tea and they took it into the front room on a tray with milk, sugar and three cups. He let the teapot stand in its cosy for a couple of minutes before pouring. As they sat in silence, gloom descended on them. Even the blacksmith lacked the will to move. Nobody drank the tea. They just held the saucers in their hands and stared into the cups. When there was a knock on the door, they were startled. It was a rude intrusion into their grief. The shock prompted another bout of tears from Nancy and her husband moved across to comfort her. Ablatt, meanwhile, went off to the front door, making an effort to shake off his torpor.

When he felt ready, he opened the door. A smartly dressed woman lunged forward to put her arms around him. The feather on her hat brushed against his cheek.

'Hello, Gerald,' she said, sobbing. 'I read about it in this morning's paper. I just had to come.'

He stood aside so that Caroline Skene could step into the house.

Marmion was delighted to see Joe Keedy back at Scotland Yard and amazed how bright and breezy he seemed to be. A sleepless night in the front room of the Haveron household didn't appear to have sapped his strength at all. Energised by the arrest he'd made that morning, Keedy gave a full account of what had happened. They were in Marmion's office and the desk was littered with newspapers and correspondence. When he'd heard the report without interruption, Marmion sat back thoughtfully.

'So this Robbie Gill is definitely not the killer.'

'No,' said Keedy. 'He didn't murder Cyril Ablatt.'

'If he's a plumber, he'd obviously have the strength needed. And his tool bag would provide him with a weapon. The post-mortem report came earlier.'

'What did it say?'

'It is full of gory detail,' said Marmion, 'but, in essence, it said that he was battered to death with a blunt instrument that also had a sharp edge. There were gashes all over the body.'

'They could have been put there by the edge of a spade.'

'What about something out of a plumber's tool bag?'

'No – Gill's alibi was sound. Both his wife and his son confirmed that he was at home when the body was – in all probability – moved to that lane.' Keedy read the inspector's mind. 'And before you suggest that he might have murdered Ablatt earlier on and left an accomplice to transfer the corpse to the spot where it was found, let me shoot down that idea. Robbie Gill wouldn't have the guts to do it. At heart, he's a miserable coward. He didn't have the courage to confront Ablatt in person about being a conchie. He could only work in the dark with a paintbrush.'

'Did his wife know what he was doing?'

'She knew,' said Keedy, 'but she certainly didn't approve. That's why he was so jumpy when I said that we'd speak to Mrs Gill. She was ashamed of what he did and horrified that he'd been arrested.'

'What about the link with Waldron?'

'It could be something or nothing, Harv.'

'If they were in cahoots,' said Marmion, 'it's unlikely that he'd produce Waldron's name so readily.'

'I think he was anxious to establish his alibi. He gave me Stan Crowther's name as well in case I wanted to check at the Weavers Arms. By the way,' said Keedy, 'I called at the pub yesterday evening. Crowther is not a man to cross. He used to be a heavyweight boxer and looks as if he still packs a punch.'

'You seem to have had an exciting time, Joe. A boxer, a plumber, a Welsh cook and two nice old ladies who probably fell madly in love with you – that's not a bad haul for one night.'

'What's this about a haul?' asked Chatfield, coming into the office. 'Good morning, Sergeant. I gather there's been a development.'

'Yes, sir,' said Keedy.

'What's this about an arrest?'

'The sergeant had a busy night,' said Marmion.

Keedy took his cue. He gave a carefully attenuated version of events to the superintendent who peppered him with questions throughout. Chatfield criticised him for not catching Gill at the first opportunity but he applauded his enterprise in arresting him at the second attempt. In the presence of their superior, Marmion and Keedy lapsed back into formality. Chatfield loathed over-familiarity between his officers. He felt that it was unprofessional. Nobody got close enough to him to treat him as a friend.

'Well, well, well,' he said. 'So the name of Horrie Waldron crops up again.'

'Only in relation to a game of darts, sir,' said Keedy.

'This fellow Gill may have given himself away.'

'He's not the man we're after, superintendent. I'm certain of that.'

'I question that certainty, Sergeant. Let's keep an eye on him. When

165

it comes to eyes,' he went on with a feeble attempt at humour, 'I daresay that you'd like to close yours and get some much needed sleep.'

'Not at all,' said Keedy. 'I feel as fresh as a daisy. I'll carry on.'

'We don't want you falling asleep on us.'

'Sergeant Keedy is unlikely to do that, sir,' said Marmion. 'He's one of the fittest men at Scotland Yard. If he wishes to press on, I think you should allow him.'

Chatfield gave a nod. 'Very well – you have my blessing, Sergeant.' He handed an envelope to Marmion. 'This has just arrived for you, Inspector. I told you that the newspapers would flush out some witnesses.' He waited until Marmion had opened and read the letter. 'Am I right?'

'Not exactly, sir. It's an anonymous note but it does contain some interesting information.' He passed it back to Chatfield. 'It looks as if I should have another chat with a certain librarian.'

Eric Fussell sat in his office with the door firmly closed. Using a pair of scissors, he cut out an article from a newspaper and read it through with a broad smile. He put the cutting aside and reached for another newspaper. There was a pile of them on his desk. He wanted a complete collection of reports about the murder.

CHAPTER ELEVEN

Charlie Redfern arrived at the workshop to discover his assistant using a plane on the edge of the door he was making. Hambridge broke off immediately and went quickly across to him.

'Morning, Charlie,' he said. 'Sorry about what happened yesterday.'

'No need to explain,' Redfern told him. 'I'd have done the same in your shoes, Fred. When I mentioned a murder, you thought it might be your friend.'

'And it was, unfortunately.'

'I know. I saw it in the paper.'

'But I shouldn't have left you in the lurch like that. It was wrong of me. I'll make up for it by working much longer this evening.'

'Please yourself.'

'Fancy a brew?'

Redfern laughed. 'Ever known me refuse?'

Hambridge filled the kettle. His boss, meanwhile, took off his coat and hat, hung them up, then looked at himself in the cracked mirror on the wall. He smoothed his hair back with a flabby hand and stroked his chin, disappointed that his beard refused to grow beyond a certain point. When he turned back to Hambridge, the latter took an envelope from his pocket and held it out.

'You're not handing in your notice, are you?' joked Redfern.

'I might be, Charlie.'

'I thought you liked working here.'

'I love it.'

'So what's the problem?'

'Read it for yourself and you'll find out.'

Redfern took the envelope from him and extracted a letter. His brow crinkled as he read it. Hambridge was a good carpenter and a loyal employee. Redfern didn't want to lose him. He tried to sound cheerful.

'This may come to nothing, Fred.'

'I'm not so sure.'

'I'll tell them my business will collapse without you.'

'That's what I was going to ask you, Charlie. I need a favour. Will you speak up for me at the tribunal? It might help.'

'Try stopping me.'

Redfern put the letter into the envelope and gave it back to him. It was a summons to appear before a military tribunal. Like thousands of other men of a certain age, Hambridge would have to seek exemption from conscription. If he failed to do so, he would either be forced to join the army or face imprisonment.

'I've heard about these bloody tribunals,' said Redfern, airily. 'They're made up of ordinary men and women so it should be easy to pull the wool over their eyes. You're a skilled worker, Fred. You're needed here.'

'I'm not going to fight,' said Hambridge, reaching for an arresting phrase. 'I refuse to be an instrument of slaughter in khaki uniform. It's morally repugnant to me and an infringement of my individual liberty.'

'Jesus Christ!' exclaimed his boss. 'It's too early in the morning for big words like that. Where the hell did you get them?'

'To be honest, I borrowed them from Cyril.'

Redfern suppressed a smirk. 'Well, they're no use to him now, are they?'

'He taught me another thing to say as well.'

'What was that?'

'I've got to remind the tribunal about William Pitt.'

'Who, in God's name, is he?'

'He was the prime minister donkey's, years ago,' explained Hambridge. 'They called him Pitt the Younger because his father had run the country before him. He was known as Pitt the Elder.'

'You're confusing me already, Fred.'

'Even you must have heard of Napoleon.'

'Oh, yes – what about him?'

'Well, when we were trying to raise an army to fight against him, Pitt said that Quakers were exempt. He respected our beliefs. Thanks to Cyril, I'm going to make that point at the tribunal.'

'What if they still say you've got to go in the army?'

Hambridge stuck out his jaw. 'Then they'll be wasting their breath.'

Harvey Marmion walked into Shoreditch library and doffed his hat. The atmosphere was sombre. All the staff had heard about the murder of their colleague and so had the majority of their readers. They moved about quietly and conversed in subdued voices, and not only because loud noise was forbidden. Marmion had the feeling that one of the assistants had been crying. Her eyes were pools of sorrow and she kept sniffing. Surprised to see him, Eric Fussell hid his displeasure behind a token smile. He invited the inspector into his office and the two of them sat down. Marmion noticed the pile of newspapers in the wastepaper basket and the pair of scissors on the desk but he made no comment.

'I hope that you've brought good news,' said Fussell, hands clasped.

'I'm afraid not, sir.'

'Oh dear – that's disappointing!'

'I'm here to clarify a few details,' said Marmion.

'I've already told you anything that's relevant. There's nothing else that I can add, Inspector.'

'I believe that there is, Mr Fussell.'

'What does it concern?'

'It concerns an application made by Cyril Ablatt. Information has come into my hands suggesting that, when Mr Ablatt considered a job elsewhere, you refused to give him a reference.'

The librarian was indignant. 'That's not true at all.'

'In view of the fulsome way you described him to me, I did find it rather odd. The only reason I could think of you blocking his chance of promotion was that he was too valuable a member of your staff to lose. Is that the case, sir?'

'No, it isn't.'

'So why didn't you support his application?'

'There was no need for a written reference, Inspector,' argued Fussell. 'The job was in Lambeth and I happen to be friends with the librarian there. I made a point of telling him what an excellent choice Cyril would be. I praised him to the skies.'

'Yet somehow he didn't get the post.'

'There was a very strong field, Inspector.'

'Really? That rather contradicts my information.'

Fussell was annoyed. 'May I ask from whom it was obtained?'

'I wish I knew, sir. I received an anonymous letter.'

'Then I should ignore every word in it, Inspector,' said the other, scornfully. 'If someone doesn't even have the courage to sign his name, then he or she can't be taken seriously. It's obviously the work of someone trying to get me into hot water.'

'And why should anyone do that, Mr Fussell?'

'We all make enemies unwittingly – even you, I daresay.'

Marmion laughed. 'I don't have to make enemies unwittingly, sir. I already have them in their thousands. The moment you join the police force, you're hated by every criminal in London. It's an occupational hazard.'

'Yes, I suppose it must be.'

'We're targets for mindless hatred.'

'That must be a constant problem.'

'You learn to ignore it.'

'I'm not sure that I could, Inspector. As for that post in Lambeth,' Fussell continued, 'I fear that Cyril's chances were imperilled by his circumstances. Now that conscription has been brought in, he's more than liable to be called up. That must have been taken into account at the interview. Nobody wants to appoint someone then lose them to the army.'

'But there was no such thing as conscription when he went after that job last year,' Marmion reminded him. 'It was all of eight months ago. Politicians were still fighting over whether or not to bring in compulsory service. This country has never needed it before. It was a huge break with tradition.'

'Regrettably, it was a necessary one.'

'That's immaterial. The point is that it was not a factor in the interview at Lambeth. It shouldn't have tipped the scales against him – whereas the lack of a glowing testimonial from you certainly would.'

'I told you – I gave him strong verbal support.'

'So you preferred to use your influence behind the scenes.'

'Nobody could have done more.'

Marmion had grave doubts about that claim. He made a mental note to seek confirmation from the librarian in Lambeth. He could see why Ablatt had wanted to move from Shoreditch library. According to the anonymous letter, there was a lot of unresolved friction between him and Fussell. At his first encounter with the librarian, Marmion had sensed that that was the case. The primary reason for going to Lambeth, however, had been the fact that Caroline Skene lived there. Ablatt was ready to endure longer journeys to and from work in order to be closer to the woman he loved.

'What did you think of the press coverage of the murder?' asked Marmion.

'I haven't had time to look at it properly.'

'Your staff clearly read some of it. There's a sense of gloom out there.'

'It doesn't stop us from getting on with our jobs, Inspector.'

'That's very commendable.'

'The real headache will come when it's time for the funeral,' said Fussell, composing his features into something faintly resembling grief. 'We all feel duty-bound to go, of course, but someone has to run the library. There's going to be a clash of loyalties.'

'In which way will you be pulled, sir?'

'Oh, I'm the captain of the ship. I have to remain on the bridge.'

The man's pomposity grated on Marmion. Having said on two separate occasions that he revered Ablatt, the librarian couldn't even make the effort to attend his funeral. It was difficult to know if – in staying away – he would be acting out of guilt or indifference.

'You've got plenty of time to arrange cover,' said Marmion. 'The funeral won't be for some time. As yet, we haven't even had the inquest. I would have thought that you had an obligation to be there.'

'I also have obligations to Shoreditch library,' Fussell retaliated.

'It's your decision, naturally.'

'Indeed, it is.'

The emphasis he put on his reply showed that he had no intention whatsoever of paying his respects to a junior colleague he professed to like and admire. It was further indication that the information in the anonymous letter was accurate. Marmion looked down at the wastepaper basket. It had been empty the previous day. It was now filled with newspapers. Yet the librarian had asserted that he'd had no time to study the press coverage of the crime. Marmion was riled by Fussell's amalgam of complacency and spite. He probed more deeply.

'You never really liked Cyril Ablatt, did you?'

'I held him in the highest regard.'

'Then why did you scupper his chances in Lambeth?'

'Pay no attention to that letter. People will say anything to discredit me.'

'I'm giving you the right to defend yourself, sir.'

'I don't need to do that,' said Fussell, disdainfully. 'My record speaks for itself. I've made this place the success that it is.'

'That wasn't what Ablatt thought, was it?'

'He never fully understood library administration.'

'Yet he had a diploma in the subject,' said Marmion, 'and he's learnt a great deal under your tutelage. That being the case,' he went on, measuring his words, 'the critical report he compiled about this library deserves to be taken seriously. My first impression was that you ran this place extremely well. Ablatt didn't think so, did he? You must have been hopping mad when you read it.'

Marmion had touched a raw nerve. Facial muscles tightening, Fussell was visibly wounded. Whoever had sent the letter to Scotland Yard had been well informed about what went on inside Shoreditch library.

* * *

Joe Keedy was still not showing any fatigue after his long night awake. With a new alibi to check, he called at the Weavers Arms when it was still closed and had to be let into the pub by the side door. Stan Crowther wagged a teasing finger.

'I'm sorry, Sergeant,' he said, 'we're not open. I can't even serve a copper.'

'I'm not here for the beer, Mr Crowther.'

'I daresay that my mother could rustle up a cup of tea.'

They went into the bar where Maud Crowther was seated at a table with a ledger opened out in front of her. When she saw Keedy enter she was alarmed, but his face was impassive. He gave no hint of the fact that he'd already met her and offered his hand when her son introduced them.

'Pleased to meet you, Mrs Crowther,' he said.

She shook his hand. 'Hello, Sergeant Keedy.'

'My mother likes to check the books now and then,' said the landlord with a grin. 'She doesn't trust me to get my sums right.'

'Someone has to keep an eye on you, Stanley,' she declared.

'When you ran the pub, I didn't interfere.'

'No, you were too busy losing your good looks in the boxing ring.' She glanced up at Keedy. 'You may not believe this, Sergeant, but Stanley was quite handsome when he was younger. Look at him now.'

Crowther guffawed. 'I don't think he can bear to. I've got the kind of ugly mug that frightens kids and old ladies. Anyway,' he said, leaning against the counter, 'what are you after this time, Sergeant?'

'I want to ask about a customer of yours,' said Keedy.

'What's his name?'

'Robbie Gill – he's a plumber.'

'He *tries* to be, you mean. Robbie doesn't know one end of a pipe from the other. I don't understand how he stays in business.'

'Was he in here on the night that Cyril Ablatt was killed?'

'You don't think that Robbie is a suspect?' asked Maud in amazement. 'Because you're on the wrong track if you do.'

Keedy's gaze flicked to her. 'Why do you say that, Mrs Crowther?'

'I know him, that's why. He hasn't got the courage to kill a mouse.'

'It's true,' agreed Crowther. 'If Mother wasn't here, I'd tell you that Robbie Gill was as soft as sh—'

'That's enough of your bad language, Stanley,' she scolded.

'Have you ever met him, Sergeant?'

'Yes,' replied Keedy. 'I arrested him earlier this morning.'

They were both very surprised at the news. Keedy gave them a highly edited version of events, omitting the fact that he'd failed to catch Gill when first given the chance. Mother and son could rustle up very little sympathy for the plumber. He came to the pub regularly but was not popular there.

'On the night when the murder took place,' said Keedy, 'Mr Gill claimed that he spent an hour or so here. Do you remember seeing him, Mr Crowther?'

'Yes,' returned the landlord. 'He was in at his usual time.'

'He mentioned playing darts with Horrie Waldron.'

'That's possible. I didn't actually see him because the place was crowded but Horrie was definitely here. They could have played darts.'

'In other words, Mr Gill has an alibi.'

'He's not your killer, Sergeant. Look elsewhere.'

'I never thought much of the man,' Maud put in, 'but I think even less of him now that I know what he did. Painting those things on a wall was so sneaky.'

'That's Robbie for you,' said Crowther, moving away. 'If you've finished with me, Sergeant, I need to fetch up some crates of stout from the cellar.'

'Go ahead, sir. Thank you for your help.'

'Mother will make you that cup of tea, if you like.'

'No need,' said Keedy, 'I have to be on my way.'

He waited until Crowther had left the bar and shut the door behind him before turning to Maud. She stood up and kissed him.

'It was so kind of you not to give me away. I can't thank you enough.'

'I told you that you could trust me.'

'My heart stopped beating when you walked in.'

Keedy smiled. 'Yes, I had a bit of a shock myself. However, I won't bother you any longer. I'll be on my way.' He paused at the door as he recalled something. 'Actually, I do have a question for you, Mrs Crowther.'

'Be quick about it. Stanley will be back soon.'

'When a certain person came to see you two nights ago . . .'

'Name no names, Sergeant.'

'Was he carrying a spade at the time?'

Maud was flabbergasted. 'A *spade?*'

'He had one with him when he left here, it seems.'

'Well, he certainly didn't bring it to my house,' she said with a rush of anger. 'If he'd dared to do that, I'd have hit him over the head with it. That certain person came as an admirer – not as a gravedigger.'

Eric Fussell had made the mistake of underestimating his visitor. The librarian thought that he could treat Marmion with the same condescension that he used on his staff. It only served to deepen the inspector's dislike of the man. Marmion was polite but ruthlessly persistent. He kept pecking away at Fussell until he began to see cracks in his well-defended facade. Cyril Ablatt had decided that the library could be run much more efficiently if a series of changes were made. Without telling Fussell, he discussed his ideas with the other assistants and got almost unanimous backing for them. He then stayed behind one evening to type up a report that contained some scathing comments about the librarian's methods. When it was given to him, Fussell had been infuriated.

'He went behind my back,' he snarled. 'That's what I could never forgive.'

'Your wife works here, doesn't she?' remembered Marmion. 'I take it that he never approached her during his research.'

'Cyril wouldn't have *dared* to do that.'

'Yet he did talk to librarians – correction, to library *assistants* – in other parts of the borough. His suggestions seem to have been well received everywhere.'

'They weren't suggestions, Inspector. They were insults aimed at me.'

'I never saw the report,' conceded Marmion, 'so I can't judge, but it's hard to believe that someone as dedicated to his job as Cyril Ablatt didn't come up with some good ideas for improvement.'

'They were stale ideas,' said Fussell, irritably. 'I'd already considered them and rejected them as inappropriate.'

'Yet I'm told that some of them were adopted at Finsbury library and have worked well. The librarian there clearly had more faith in your assistant.'

'He didn't have to work beside him.'

Marmion nodded. 'So there was antagonism between you, after all.'

'It was largely on his side, Inspector. For some unknown reason, Cyril could never accept my authority as readily as he ought to. That's why he drafted that absurd report of his. It was an attempt to undermine me.'

'Then why didn't you sack him?'

'I did,' said Fussell, 'but I was overruled by local government officials.'

'That must have led to a lot of tension between the two of you.'

'I tried to rise above it.'

'How did he react?'

'In fairness, I have to say that he did the same.'

'But you must have nursed some resentment, sir.'

'It was a breach of trust,' said Fussell, 'and that was unforgivable. What the public saw was an obliging young man always ready to advise people what to read. What I saw was – to put it no higher than this – a snake in the grass.'

'So why did you tell me that you liked him?' asked Marmion.

'One should never speak ill of the dead, Inspector.'

'But that's just what you've been doing.'

'It was only because you pressed me about that infernal report.'

'I can see that you must have felt betrayed.'

'Let me be more explicit,' said Fussell, shedding all pretence. 'I loathed Cyril Ablatt for reasons too numerous to list. When I couldn't sack him, I tried to get rid of him another way. I'm sure that a meticulous man like you was going to check my claim that I put in a word for him with the librarian in Lambeth. You can save yourself the trouble, Inspector. It was true. I was so desperate to unload Cyril onto someone else that I traded on a close friendship.'

'Nevertheless, he was turned down for the post.'

'The word had got out about him.'

'What word was that, sir?'

'Cyril Ablatt was a disruptive influence. Nobody wants that.'

The portrait was changing even more. When Marmion took charge of the case, Ablatt was a murder victim with a steadfast belief in the tenets of Christianity and with a job in which he excelled. Darker elements had intruded. He'd not only had an intimate relationship with a married woman, he'd had the gall to challenge the librarian's authority by producing a critique of him. Marmion scratched out the mental note to visit Lambeth. Fussell was being honest for once. He'd tried to shift a burdensome assistant to another library and had failed.

'I can see why you won't be attending the funeral,' said Marmion, 'but, when all is said and done, he did work under you for some while. I daresay that you'll be sending your condolences to his father.'

Fussell was brusque. 'No, Inspector,' he said. 'I'll send no card. I've washed my hands of the entire Ablatt family.'

There was a steady stream of customers at the forge on Bethnal Green and, because Percy Fry was there by himself, they either had to wait in the queue or be turned away. Things had eased by mid morning and Fry was able to snatch a few minutes' rest. He was relieved to see Dalley striding in.

'You're a sight for sore eyes, Jack,' he said.

'I came as soon as I could.'

'No need to come at all. I can cope.'

'If truth be told, I was glad to escape, Perce. All that misery was getting me down. Not that I'm hard-hearted,' said Dalley, keen to correct any misunderstanding. 'I'm very upset at what happened to Cyril, but I'm a practical man. I've a job to do and a forge to run.'

'How's the wife?'

'Nancy is worse than ever this morning.'

'Don't forget that offer we made.'

'Later on – when the worst is over – Nancy might be glad of Elaine's company. But that time may be weeks away.'

'Where is she at the moment?'

'I took her over to her brother's. She can't bear to be apart from him.' He took off his hat and coat and tossed them onto a stool. 'Everyone knows now.'

'What do you mean?'

'It's in all the papers, Perce. The one I saw even had a photo of

Cyril. As we walked to my brother-in-law's house, people were already pointing and whispering. I'm not a blacksmith any more,' complained Dalley. 'I'm the uncle of the lad who was battered to death.'

'That will pass,' said Fry.

'Not for a long while. If he'd been killed in the war, everyone would have showered us with sympathy for a day or two. This is different. Cyril is a murder victim. That makes him a sort of freak. People won't forget that,' said Dalley, sourly. 'As long as the hunt for the killer goes on, the event stays fresh in the mind.'

'They'll catch the bastard eventually.'

'London's got millions of inhabitants. Where do the police start looking?'

'That's up to them, Jack. Let them get on with it, I say. The only thing you need to worry about is Nancy. She's the one who needs help.'

'Too true – she was awake for most of the night again.'

'Might not be so bad when the funeral is over and done with,' said Fry.

'I'm not looking forward to that,' confessed Dalley. 'It'll be harrowing. Nancy and her brother are bad enough now. They both look ten years older. What are they going to be like when they actually bury Cyril?'

From the time that she got there, Caroline Skene had endeavoured to be useful. She made tea, passed round biscuits and offered what solace she could. Her presence was so comforting to Gerald Ablatt and his sister that Dalley had felt able to leave them and return to work. Caroline was in charge. She was tirelessly helpful and full of compassion. When they wept, so did she. Neither of them realised that she had as much cause for anguish as they did.

'It was good of you to come, Caroline,' said Ablatt.

'I felt I might be needed.'

'You are – and we're grateful.'

'Yes,' said Nancy with a woeful smile. 'Thank you.'

'How is Wilf?' asked Ablatt.

'He's fine,' replied Caroline. 'He sends his love.'

'Is he still having that back trouble?'

'Oh, let's not talk about him, Gerald. What are a few back pains compared to what you have to suffer? You can forget Wilf. Think of yourself for once.'

'He can't do that,' said Nancy. 'Gerald always puts other people first. His son has been killed yet he still worries about his customers.'

'I hate to let anyone down,' said Ablatt.

'Do you know what he did last night?'

He was embarrassed. 'There's no need to mention that, Nancy.'

'I think there is. Caroline deserves to know.'

'Know what?' asked Caroline.

'When Jack took me back home last night,' said Nancy, glancing at her brother, 'Gerald should have gone straight to bed. He was as exhausted as we were. Instead of that, he went to the shop and started mending shoes.'

'Never!'

'I simply had to *do* something,' he declared. 'I thought it might take my mind off Cyril. I needed to be occupied. Can't you understand that?'

'Yes,' soothed Caroline, 'I think I can. It seems ridiculous but what you did was right. It fulfilled an urge.' When there was a knock at the door, she got up at once. 'You stay here. I'll see who it is.'

She went to the front door and opened it. The vicar was standing on the doorstep and he asked if he might come in. Caroline would have turned anyone else away but both Cyril and his father had worshipped regularly at the nearby church. She'd heard them speak well of the vicar, an elderly man with a kind face and wisps of white hair curling down from under his hat. In the hope that he might be able to alleviate grief and provide some spiritual sustenance, Caroline stood aside to let him in. When she took him into the front room, Ablatt and his sister looked up with gratitude, pleased to see the old man. Removing his hat, he set it aside and offered a consoling hand to each of them. Caroline put the hat outside on a peg and went into the kitchen to make yet another pot of tea. When she returned, she saw that the vicar had already lifted the morale of the mourners.

It was the chance for which she'd been waiting. After pouring the tea and handing the cups around, she excused herself to go to the bathroom, making sure that she shut the door of the front room behind her. She then scampered upstairs and went straight to Cyril Ablatt's room, opening the door and gazing around with a mixture of sadness and nostalgia. She needed minutes to recover.

Caroline then began a frantic search.

CHAPTER TWELVE

After a hectic morning in the lorry, Alice Marmion drove it back to the depot and brought it to a juddering halt. She looked across at Vera Dowling.

'I don't like the sound of the engine.'

'Neither do I,' said Vera. 'Something is wrong.'

'Let's see if we can find out what it is.'

Alice switched off the engine and got out of the lorry. Vera went to fetch the toolbox in the back of the vehicle. By the time she brought it to her friend, Alice had lifted the bonnet and was peering underneath it.

'Don't touch anything,' warned Vera. 'It will be piping hot.'

'I'm afraid that it could be something serious.'

'We could always go to that garage and ask the mechanic to help us.'

Alice was derisive. 'Ask a man to bail us out?' she said. 'This is the WEC, Vera. We sort out our own problems.'

'Well, don't expect me to do anything. I don't know the first thing about engines – except that they get very hot after a while.' She wiped perspiration from her brow. 'They're a bit like me.'

They'd spent several hours delivering bedding to various emergency accommodation sites. It had meant loading and unloading the lorry a number of times and they were tired. While Alice continued to scrutinise the engine, Vera leant against the side of the vehicle. Hannah Billington emerged from her office and marched across to them.

'What seems to be the trouble?' she asked.

'We don't know, Mrs Billington,' replied Vera.

Alice was more positive. 'We'll soon find out when the engine cools down,' she said, turning to the newcomer. 'It was starting to pull and making a funny noise.'

'It was a bit scary.'

'There was no danger, Vera.'

'You never know. It might have been sabotage.'

'Don't be absurd,' said Hannah. 'Who would sabotage our lorry?'

'I was only thinking of what my friend told me about the Women's Auxiliary Army Corps.'

Hannah was reproachful. 'Oh, come on, *please*. You should have mastered the initials by now. And what did this friend from the WAAC tell you?'

'Well,' said Vera, discomfited by the rebuke, 'when she first started driving a thirty-hundredweight van, the men were very jealous.'

'Why aren't we surprised?' asked Alice, jocularly.

'They did all sorts of things to slow her down. They cut her petrol pipe halfway through, they unscrewed valves, they even changed over the leads on the sparking plugs. What upset her most, however,' she went on, 'was that they emptied the paraffin out of her lamps. When it got dark and she tried to light them, nothing happened. That was a cruel trick.'

'Nobody would *dare* to do that to my drivers,' said Hannah. 'Any vehicles parked here are watched carefully day and night. Luckily, we've got enterprising young women like Alice who can turn their hand to vehicle maintenance as well as to driving. You should follow in her footsteps, Vera.'

'Not me – I'm all fingers and thumbs.'

'Learn from Alice. It's only a question of application.'

'I've tried, Mrs Billington, I really have.'

'You must make more effort, woman,' said Hannah, curtly. She summoned up a smile. 'Anyway, what have the pair of you been up to this morning?'

Alice delivered her report and earned a nod of approval. Vera was too nervous to venture anything more than the occasional word. Hannah looked from one to the other as if weighing something up.

'You've done well,' she said. 'You've done very well, in fact. I trust that the lorry will be ready for action again this afternoon.'

'Yes,' said Alice, confidently. 'I'll have that engine singing like a bird.'

'That's the attitude – every problem can be solved.'

'It certainly can – even if it means oily fingers and a lot of tinkering.'

The older woman gave her braying laugh then promptly changed the subject.

'What do you think of the food here?'

'It's all right, Hannah.'

'Do you agree, Vera?'

'Yes, I do,' said the other. 'It's better than I expected.'

'But it's rather bland and repetitive,' said Hannah. 'We can't blame them for that. We're subject to rationing like everyone else. I just wondered if you'd like a chance to eat something more appetising for once.'

'We'd all like that,' said Alice.

'Then you and Vera must come to tea sometime. Cook makes the most wonderful scones and her chocolate cake is almost sinful.'

'Thank you, Hannah. We'd love to come.'

Vera was less certain. 'Yes . . . thank you for asking us.'

'I'll find a time when we're not so busy and let you know.'

After flashing a smile at them, she turned on her heel and marched off. Vera waited until she was well out of earshot. She could be honest with a friend.

'I don't want to go, Alice.'

'Why do you say that?'

'I wouldn't feel comfortable,' said Vera. 'I've never been to a house with a cook before. Mummy and I make the meals at home. I'd be on tenterhooks. I'll find an excuse not to go. I hope that won't stop you.'

'Oh, no,' said Alice. 'I'd love to go. I'm much nosier than you.'

They met in Marmion's office at Scotland Yard and were able to review what they'd learnt that morning. Marmion talked about his visit to the library and his conviction that Eric Fussell had enough hatred inside him to drive him to murder. Keedy told him about the second encounter with Stan Crowther and how the landlord had confirmed the alibi given by Robbie Gill. Marmion was more interested in the information that Crowther's mother had been there and that she'd hotly denied that Waldron had arrived for a tryst with his spade.

'So where did he leave it?' wondered Marmion.

'Maybe he took it back to his digs before he went to Maud.'

'Why bring it home in the first place? Surely he keeps it at the cemetery. It would have been a bit late to do some gardening.'

'P'raps he used it to bash Ablatt's head in.'

'You've met Waldron. Can you imagine him doing that?'

'Oh, yes,' said Keedy. 'He's mean and dangerous. When he'd had enough beer inside him, I can well imagine him killing someone. What I can't believe is that he'd do that and then go off for a rendezvous with a lady.'

'He could have done it *after* he'd seen Maud Crowther.'

'Her son told me he looked unusually clean when he got back to the Weavers Arms. That doesn't sound like a man involved in a brutal murder. There'd have been specks of blood over his clothing.'

'That's speculation, not evidence.'

'It's all we've got.'

'So where does that leave us, Joe?'

'We're still very much in the dark.'

'There are only two possible suspects so far and, although they were known to each other, they're the most unlikely accomplices. Waldron may have been in the right place at the right time but all he was thinking about, I fancy, was knocking on Mrs Crowther's door.'

'What about the newspapers? Did they bring in any witnesses?'

'They brought in much more than that,' said Marmion. 'I was wading through the messages when you go back here. There were two cranks who claimed that they'd actually done the murder, but then we always get bogus confessions at a time like this. One woman reckons that her husband was the killer because he came home with blood on his face and there was a man who insisted that he witnessed the murder even though he was in Stepney at the time. He must have the most amazing eyesight.'

'We ought to arrest them for wasting police time, Harv.'

'Leave them to their weird fantasies.' He noticed the signs of weariness in his colleague. 'You look as if you're ready to fall asleep, Joe. Take the afternoon off. Get some sleep and start fresh again tomorrow.'

'I don't want to miss any of the fun.'

'What fun?' Marmion's laugh was mirthless. 'If you think it's fun to go to another press conference this evening, you can take over from me and have the superintendent breathing down your neck.'

'No, thanks – keep Chat well away from me.'

'We're going to release a few details about the post-mortem.'

'Not too many of them, I hope. I saw the corpse, remember. We both know the effect it had on Mr Ablatt. When's the inquest, by the way?'

'No date has been set for it yet.'

'The family will want the body as soon as possible.'

'That's always the case,' said Marmion, 'but we have to follow protocol. The inquest must come first.' He picked up the newspaper beside him. 'Have you had the chance to see this?'

'Is that the *Evening News*?'

'They sent over a copy of the early edition.' He handed it to Keedy. 'Just read the first paragraph. The tone has changed completely since yesterday.'

Keedy looked at the front-page feature. 'I see what you mean, Harv.'

'Yesterday, he was a murder victim deserving of sympathy. Then we told them about Cyril Ablatt's background and they latched onto the fact that he was a conscientious objector. Today, he's a different person altogether.'

'The sympathy has dried up almost completely.'

'That's why we have to redouble our efforts. There are far too many people who think that conchies ought to be hanged, drawn and quartered. They'd be quite happy if the killer got away with it. We're going to disappoint them.'

'How do we do that?'

'Something will turn up.'

'I've heard that phrase before.'

'It comes from Mr Micawber in *David Copperfield*.'

'But he wasn't a detective, was he?'

'Oddly enough, he was. It was Micawber who exposed Uriah Heap's villainy and saved the day. He turned out to be a hero in the end.'

'Things don't happen like that in real life.'

'We've had to rely on luck before,' said Marmion. 'Solving a murder is not entirely a matter of logical deduction. Take that anonymous letter I had this very morning. It came out of nowhere.'

'But did it get us any closer to the killer?'

'It might have done, Joe.'

Keedy put the newspaper aside. 'All we've managed to do so far,' he said, disconsolately, 'is to arrest a useless plumber.'

'You did more than that. You stopped him venting his spleen on the wall of the house. Mr Ablatt will be grateful and so will a lot of people in Shoreditch. Most of them are decent folk who'd think what Robbie Gill was going to do was in bad taste.'

As they were speaking, a young woman knocked on the open door and came into the office. She spoke with deference.

'This came for you, Inspector,' she said.

'Thank you,' said the other, taking a piece of paper from her.

The woman walked away. Reading the message, Marmion grinned broadly.

Keedy was curious. 'Well?'

'I told you that something might turn up,' said Marmion. 'This could be it.'

Caroline Skene had never been inside a police station before and she didn't relish the experience. It was so bare and comfortless. When she showed the business card to the duty sergeant, he rang Scotland Yard and asked for Inspector Marmion. He was told to wait while the inspector was found. Caroline, meanwhile, was kept sitting on a high-backed wooden bench. The fact that desperate criminals must have sat on it over the years only deepened her sense of guilt. She had the urge to leave but, since the phone call had been made, she had to stay there. It seemed an age before someone came on at the end of the line. The sergeant spoke to him then offered the receiver to Caroline. She crossed to the desk on unsteady legs and looked at the instrument warily. Unfamiliar with a telephone, she took it gingerly from him.

'Hello,' she said, meekly.

'Is that you, Mrs Skene?' asked Marmion.

She was reassured. 'Yes, Inspector – you told me to contact you.'

'Do you have some information for me?'

'Yes, I do, but I don't want to talk on the telephone.'

'That's fair enough,' he said. 'I was told that you're ringing from Shoreditch police station. Is that correct?'

'It is.'

'Then I'll meet you there. You stay put.'

She looked around. 'I'd rather not talk here, Inspector.'

'I understand. A place like that can be rather intimidating for someone as law-abiding as you. Not to worry,' said Marmion. 'I'll come as soon as I can. Then we'll find somewhere else to have a chat. Is that all right?'

'Yes, Inspector – thank you.'

'Goodbye, Mrs Skene.'

Before she could bid him farewell, the line went dead. Handing the receiver to the sergeant, she went back to the bench and perched on the edge of it. She was not at all sure that she was doing the right thing but the decision had been made now. Still stunned by the death of her young friend, Caroline's grief would only be softened by the arrest of the killer. It was time to be more honest with Marmion.

After finishing work, Mansel Price left the hullabaloo of the railway station and made his way to Fred Hambridge's workshop. The carpenter was stacking a door against a wall when the Welshman arrived. Price was glad to see that his friend was alone.

'Where's the boss?' he asked.

'Charlie went off to price a job,' said Hambridge. 'He won't be back for ages.'

'Good – it means we can talk. I've got news for you, Fred.'

'What's happened?'

'I almost caught the man who painted things on Cyril's wall.'

He described the incident during the night and was enraged that he'd been robbed of the chance to overpower the man. Having lurked in the dark for so long, Price felt that he deserved the kudos of catching him.

'I blame Sergeant Keedy,' he said.

'What was he doing there?'

'The same as me – only he had the sense to stay indoors. He was in the front room of a house nearby. He had a feeling that the man might come back again with his paintbrush. I was mad at him for interfering but the truth is that it was probably just as well. If he hadn't come along, I'd have torn that man to pieces.'

'Then *you'd* have been in trouble with the police as well.'

'The sergeant said that they'd soon find him at daybreak. He left his ladder and his paint. Both could be traced back to him.'

'You did well, Mansel.'

'I got in a couple of good punches, I know that.'

'You should have let me know you were going to stay up all night. I could have waited with you. The two of us could have nabbed him. Anyway,' said Hambridge, crossing to the wall where his coat was hanging, 'I'm glad you called in. I've got something to show you.'

Price grinned wickedly. 'It's not a dirty postcard, is it?'

'No – it's something a bit more serious than that.'

He handed the Welshman the letter. Price took it out of the envelope and read it through, his anger slowly mounting.

'Don't go, Fred,' he urged.

'I have to go. I'd be breaking the law.'

'Burn the letter. Tell them it never arrived.'

'They'd only send another one. You'll be getting one yourself.'

Price was aggressive. 'I don't take orders from on high. If they want me to go before a tribunal, they'll bloody well have to come and fetch me.'

'There's no point in upsetting them, Mansel. It could work against you.'

'I don't care.'

'I'll be seeking exemption on the grounds that I'm a Quaker,' said Hambridge. 'My parents will come to the tribunal and so will Charlie. Having people speak up for you is bound to help. You must have someone on your side.'

'My parents are back home in the Rhondda. They'd never come here.'

'What about your boss?'

'I think he'd be glad to see the back of me. I'll get no help there. Besides,' he went on, grandiloquently, 'I'm ready for a tussle with the tribunal. It'll be a case of no holds barred. I'll tell them just what I think about this stupid idea of enforced military service. It's a form of bloody slavery.'

Hambridge was worried about him. Because of his religion, the carpenter felt that he had a chance of exemption, even though two Quaker friends of his had been conscripted after their appearance before a tribunal. If Price went there with the express purpose of provoking those who sat in judgement on him, he'd be more or less inviting them to deal harshly with him.

'There's no point in deliberately upsetting them,' he argued. 'That's what Cyril taught us. We have to present a reasoned argument.'

'I'll do it my way, Fred – you do it yours.'

Hambridge took the letter back from him and stowed it away in his coat.

'What about Gordon?' he asked.

'He's my big worry, ' said Price, bitterly. 'If he gets married in order to dodge conscription, I'll never speak to the bastard again.'

'I think we talked him out of it, Mansel.'

'I hope so. When I think of all those meetings the three of us had with Cyril, I just can't believe that Gordon would desert us. He was always boasting about the way he'd defy the tribunal. He said he didn't care what they did to him. Then,' he added with utter contempt, 'he tried using Ruby Cosgrove to save him from the army. Thank goodness we changed his mind for him.'

Since he'd last seen his fiancée, Leach had done a lot of thinking. He regretted his suggestion of an early marriage and was still smarting from the comments made by Price and Hambridge. The Welshman, in particular, had been quite vicious with him. They were good friends and he didn't want to lose their respect. Under the guidance of Ablatt, they'd bonded together. If anything, the murder should have tightened that bond and helped them to present a united front against the possibility of conscription. Yet he had threatened to break it apart and couldn't quite understand what had impelled him to do so. Leach was not afraid to go to prison, if necessary. In that eventuality, Ruby had promised to stand by him. Sharing his pacifism, she'd always supported him in his determination to resist fighting.

What did she think of him now? Did she feel the same unquestioning love for him? Leach doubted it. When they'd parted, Ruby had looked at him in an odd and rather unsettling way. It was as if she was discovering an aspect of his character for the first time and was not sure if she liked it. The prospect of an early marriage would have been discussed with her parents. Leach was certain they'd have found the idea unappealing. His own parents had been more amenable. His father was keen to retain his help in the bakery and his mother wanted him saved from the unspeakable horrors at the front. Wounded soldiers were a common sight in the streets, a stark warning to what lay in wait for those sent to the trenches.

Leach loitered outside the factory until the hooter sounded. It was not long before the mass exodus took place, hundreds of bodies streaming out of the building in a rush to get home. Ruby Cosgrove was walking arm in arm with two friends. When she saw Leach, she broke away and trotted across to him.

'I've been dying to see you, Gordon,' she said, accepting a kiss.

'That's good to hear. I thought you were angry with me.'

'Why should I be angry?'

'You didn't like the idea I put to you.'

'That was because I didn't really take it in,' she explained.

It was impossible to have a private conversation in the middle of a crowd so they walked down the road and turned into a quiet side street. Ruby's face was glowing with expectation. He was relieved to see that she'd recovered all of her buoyancy and good humour.

'Mummy and Daddy hated it at first,' she told him, 'but they slowly came to see that there were advantages. In the end, they were in favour of us getting this three-day licence to marry. Daddy said it would save him a lot of money if we didn't have the reception we'd planned. He liked that.'

'Actually,' he said, 'I've had a change of heart.'

Her face clouded. 'You mean that you don't love me any more?'

'Of course I do.'

'Then what are you talking about?'

'It's this three-day licence, Ruby.'

'All the girls at work thought it was so romantic,' she said, dreamily. 'They were very jealous. They all want to be swept off their feet and carried to the altar as quickly as that.'

'But your aunt is making the wedding dress. That will take time.'

'No, it wouldn't, Gordon. I went round to see her last night. Auntie Gwen said she'd only need ten days or so to finish it. She works very fast.'

'What about the church? It's already booked.'

'We simply tell the vicar that we've changed our minds.'

'But that's the thing, Ruby,' he said, awkwardly. 'I haven't.'

She stared at him with surprise tinged with a sense of betrayal. When she left home that morning, it was with the certainty that she could marry him far sooner than planned, with the added bonus of taking him out of reach of conscription. Once they'd thought about it, her parents and her aunt had given their approval and her friends at the factory had all been enthusiastic about the notion. Suddenly, there was a problem. Having made her elated, Leach had just dampened her spirits. Ruby couldn't believe that he would let her down like that.

'I thought it was what you wanted,' she said, lower lip quivering.

'It was, Ruby, but things have changed.'

'What sort of things?'

'I talked it over with Fred and Mansel.'

'I'm marrying *you*, Gordon Leach, and not them.'

'But we came to this agreement, you see,' he said. 'All four of us – Cyril included – vowed that we'd take a stand against conscription together.'

'That was then – this is now.'

'They made me look at it in a different light.'

She flew into a rage. 'In other words, you don't *want* to marry me.'

'There's nothing I want more, Ruby.'

'I hate you for this,' she cried. 'You get my hopes up, then you dash them. Wait till the girls hear about this – they'll have a good laugh at me. You're cruel, Gordon, you really are. What's so special about Fred and Mansel? You always said you put me first. Why let them tell you what to do?'

'Calm down,' he said, trying to put an arm around her.

She pushed him away. 'Leave go of me!'

'There's no need to fly off the handle, Ruby.'

'Is this how it's going to be? Every time we need to make a big decision, will you have to go and take the advice of your friends first?'

'It's not like that at all.'

'Well, that's how it seems, Gordon.'

'I've got . . . obligations.'

'I used to think you had obligations to me.'

'I do,' he said, getting flustered. 'Listen, I can't explain when you're in this sort of state. Why don't we wait until we can talk this over quietly? There's no need for an argument. I love you, Ruby. We're on the same side. Don't you see that?'

'All I see is that you've made me look a fool.'

'That's not true.'

'I've got to go back home to my parents and tell them that it was a joke. You never really wanted to get married to me at short notice, did you?'

'I did!' he protested. 'Part of me still does.'

'Well, I don't want part of you, Gordon Leach. I want all of you. If I can't have that, I'll have nothing at all.'

Pulling out a handkerchief, she turned round and scurried off down the street. He ran after her and grabbed her by the shoulders to bring her to a halt. Ruby was trembling all over.

'Why don't we discuss this another time?' he said, desperately. 'We've obviously got off on the wrong foot.'

'There's nothing to discuss,' she said, laying down her ultimatum. 'It's time you made your choice. Who is more important to you – *me* or your friends? I'm not prepared to share you with them, Gordon. I really mean that.'

Brushing away his hands, she walked off again and he was too dazed to follow. Leach was mortified. Because of his folly, he was in danger of losing her altogether.

Caroline Skene could not be rushed. Marmion could see that. When he got to the police station, she was brooding on the bench. Glad to be rescued from the place, she said nothing as they got into the car. Marmion wondered what she was doing in Shoreditch but did not press her on the subject. When he suggested that they should drive back to Lambeth, she shook her head vigorously. He used his own initiative. Ten minutes after picking her up, they were sitting side by side on a park bench. There was no danger of anyone overhearing them there. Sensing that she wouldn't have got in touch with him unless she had something important to divulge, he was patient and considerate.

'There's no hurry,' he said. 'Take all the time you need, Mrs Skene.'

It was almost over a minute before she finally spoke.

'I owe you an apology, Inspector,' she began.

'Why is that?'

'There's something I should have told you when we first met,' she said, 'but I was too confused by what had happened. The news of Cyril's death shook me to the core. I still haven't got used to it.'

'Tell me about this apology.'

'I'm related to the Ablatt family. Gerald is my cousin.'

'That explains how you met his son.'

197

'We've known each other for years. It was a very long time before we . . . got closer to each other.' She looked up at him. 'Don't be too critical of us.'

'Is that why you were in Shoreditch?'

'Yes, Inspector – I went to offer comfort. If I'm honest, however, I was there for another reason altogether.'

Marmion was ahead of her. 'Did you want to retrieve something, perhaps?'

'Yes, I did,' she admitted. 'I'd sent him letters and given him keepsakes. I didn't want his father finding them. It would have hurt him beyond bearing.'

'And did you find what you were after?'

'I was lucky. The vicar called at the house and that gave me the chance to go upstairs. I searched every nook and cranny. There's nothing left to incriminate us.'

'Falling in love with someone is not a crime, Mrs Skene.'

'It is in this case. It was forbidden love, Inspector. I was married and Cyril was much younger than me. It felt wrong from the start but we couldn't help it.'

'There's something else, isn't there?' he asked. 'I don't think you'd have got in touch with me unless you had important information to give.'

She lowered her head. 'You'll think ill of me when I tell you.'

'I've no reason to do that, Mrs Skene.'

'In a way, it's hampered your investigation. I should have been honest.'

'You were trying to absorb some frightful news,' he said. 'You'd suffered a terrible blow. Anyone would be bewildered in those circumstances.'

'I wasn't that bewildered, Inspector,' she said. 'I knew that I should have spoken up. But it was something that I wanted to keep to myself, a memory that I'll always treasure. It was the newspaper that made me see sense.'

'How did the newspaper do that?'

'It gave details of the murder and showed a diagram of the route that Cyril would have taken on his way home that evening. But that wasn't the way he went at all,' she said, raising her head. 'He didn't go from Bishopsgate to Shoreditch. He came to see me first. Cyril was so excited about what had happened at the meeting that he simply had to tell me about it. I've never seen him so happy.' She inhaled deeply. 'Can you see what I'm trying to tell you?'

'I'm afraid that I can,' said Marmion, letting his annoyance show. 'The murder took place somewhere between Lambeth and Shoreditch. We've been looking in the wrong place.'

CHAPTER THIRTEEN

There were times when Claude Chatfield showed exactly why he'd been promoted to the rank of superintendent. He was a whirlwind of activity, scanning the newspapers, sending his minions here and there, collating all the information he received, reporting to the commissioner, Sir Edward Henry, and organising another press conference. The murder of Cyril Ablatt was only one of the cases for which he was responsible and his grasp of detail in every one of them was impressive. When he and Marmion faced the press again, he even remembered to smile, though his hatchet face was so unused to expressing bonhomie that it came across as a sinister leer. Having filtered the post-mortem report, he gave them enough information to fill a column without descending into ghoulishness. Chatfield also made much of the arrest of Robbie Gill and praised Detective Sergeant Joseph Keedy for tracking the man down. The reporters were familiar with Keedy's name because he'd ably assisted Marmion in the past in some very complex cases.

'I now hand you over to the inspector,' said Chatfield, sitting back.

Marmion took over. 'Thank you, sir.'

He had little to add to what they'd already been told with the exception of the information garnered from Caroline Skene. As a result of what he claimed was an anonymous tip-off, he told them that the police would now widen their search to include Lambeth. The route taken home by Ablatt from Bishopsgate therefore had to be amended.

'How do you know he was in Lambeth, Inspector?' asked someone.

'He was spotted there by a friend.'

'Can you give us the name of that friend?'

'I wish I could,' said Marmion, face motionless. 'But the information is very specific and I've no reason to doubt it.'

'Why didn't this so-called friend reveal who he is?'

'I should imagine that he didn't want to get embroiled in the investigation. As you know, that's all too common. People who have valuable evidence sometimes prefer to pass it on anonymously to avoid any repercussions. In cases of murder, particularly, they fear for their safety.'

'Villains will do anything to scare witnesses,' confirmed the superintendent, 'and I don't need to tell you about jury tampering.'

Marmion invited questions and they were fired at him with the rapidity of bullets from a Gatling gun. He answered them all and set the pencils scribbling into notebooks. Chatfield felt obliged to interject from time to time but it was Marmion they all wanted to grill. He was calm under fire. Though he'd been distressed at the slant some of them had put on their articles, he offered no censure. Nothing he could say would make them view a conscientious objector more dispassionately. When the press conference was over and everyone dispersed, he walked along a corridor with the superintendent beside him.

Chatfield was irked. 'Why didn't you tell me about this tip-off you received regarding Lambeth?'

'I only got the message as I was about to leave my office, sir.'

'You might have mentioned it to me.'

'I was saving it as a surprise.'

'I don't like surprises of that nature, Inspector.'

'I'm sorry.'

'You said you were sure that the information was genuine.'

'I am, sir. My informant used to be a colleague of Ablatt's. If he'd worked alongside him at the library, I think he'd recognise him anywhere.'

Marmion was determined to keep Caroline Skene's name out of the investigation so he'd altered her gender and given her a job at Shoreditch library. Chatfield was suspicious.

'I get the feeling there's something you're not telling me,' he said.

'You know all there is to know, sir.'

'I wonder.'

'I have a high regard for your role in this inquiry so I pass on any information we can glean.'

'Make sure I'm briefed about *everything*.'

'That goes without saying.'

'What are you doing next?'

'There's a mountain of correspondence on my desk,' said Marmion. 'It's been prompted by the press coverage. Much of it is useless – if not downright misleading – but there might be a gold nugget in there somewhere. I didn't have time to go through it all before we met the press.'

'Let me know what you find.'

'I will, sir.'

'Incidentally, what's happened to Sergeant Keedy? When I saw him earlier, he looked as if he was ready to pass out.'

'He finally listened to my advice and went home. The sergeant had been on continuous duty for well over twenty-four hours.'

'That will mean a claim for overtime,' said Chatfield, fussily. 'I'll have to find a way around that. We don't have an unlimited budget.'

'You always did keep a tight hand on the purse strings.'

'It may be the reason I was promoted over you, Inspector.'

Marmion smiled benignly. 'I'm sure that it was, sir.'

When Alice finished work that evening, there was no offer from Hannah Billington of a lift home in her car. She and Vera Dowling had to resort to public transport. The bus journey back to their respective digs turned, predictably, into a discussion about their day in the Women's Emergency Corps.

'I don't know how you did it,' said Vera.

'I *had* to do it, Vera. We needed that lorry.'

'You worked on that engine for ages.'

'I took a leaf out of my father's book,' said Alice. 'When he's involved in a case, he always talks about eliminating the alternatives. That's what I did. I ruled out almost everything that it *could* be, then I was left with what it really was.'

'No wonder you're Mrs Billington's favourite.'

'Oh, I'm not. There are plenty of women much more competent than me. I'm still learning, Vera. That's the beauty of this work. You discover skills that you never realised you had.'

'Speak for yourself,' said her friend, morosely. 'I have no skills at all.'

'That's simply not true. You worked as hard as I did when we delivered that bedding. And, considering that you understood very little of their language, you handled those children very well.'

'My teaching experience came in useful there.'

'Exactly – you *have* got skills. You just don't realise it.'

Vera squeezed her arm. 'Thank you, Alice,' she said. 'You always know how to cheer me up. I'd much rather ride back on a bus with you than have a lift in Mrs Billington's car. When I sat in that, I felt I was trespassing.'

'Don't be ridiculous!'

When the bus reached the next stop, Vera got off. Alice had two more stops to go. It was only now that she was on her own that she became aware of a man sitting at the back of the bus. She could see his reflection in the window. Short, sharp-featured and in his forties, he was staring intently at the back of her head. At first, she tried to ignore him but she remained keenly aware of his attention. Every time she glanced at the reflection, she saw the gleaming eyes and the quiet smirk. Alice was glad when the bus eventually reached her stop but, to her alarm, the man also rose from his seat. Alighting from the vehicle, she set off at a brisk pace. The sound of footsteps told her that she was being followed.

It was only a hundred yards to the safety of her digs but she had to walk down a badly lit road to get there. It was something that Alice had done countless times and there had never been a problem. It was different now. She was being stalked. Every time she quickened her step, the footsteps behind her matched the pace. Indeed, they seemed to be gaining on her. Not daring to look over her shoulder, she broke into a run and quailed as she heard her stalker following her example. She got within fifteen yards of the house before he caught her up. A hand grabbed her shoulder and she was spun round to face the man who had been ogling her on the bus. Alice tried to brush him away but he was too strong and determined. Laughing in triumph, he stifled her scream with a hand over her mouth and used the other to grope her.

His triumph was short-lived. A figure suddenly emerged from the porch of Alice's house and raced towards them. Her attacker was pulled off her and hit with a relay of punches that sent him staggering against a wall. With blood dribbling from his nose, the man took to his heels and sprinted back down the road. Alice turned to her saviour and gave a gasp of recognition.

'Joe!' she cried. 'What are *you* doing here?'

'I was waiting for you to come back to your digs.'

'Thank God for that!'

Keedy grinned. 'Don't I even get a kiss?'

The three friends met at Hambridge's house. Leach was interested to hear that the carpenter had received notification of his appearance before a military tribunal. It was only a matter of time before it was Leach's turn. Price was still bewailing the fact that he'd captured the man who'd been painting words on the side of the Ablatt house, only to lose him when a detective intervened. He now knew that the man had been identified and arrested.

'Even Sergeant Keedy could manage that,' he said with a sneer.

'You can't blame him, Mansel,' said Hambridge. 'When he saw two people fighting in the dark, he wasn't to know which one was you. You should remember that he was actually there. Just like you, Sergeant Keedy had worked out that the man might come back in the night. If you hadn't got in the way, he'd have nabbed him.'

Price was livid. 'I didn't get in the way.'

'You tried to do the police's job for them.'

'How was I to know that the sergeant was there as well?'

'You should have had more trust in him.'

'I wanted to get my hands on that sneaky bastard with the paintbrush,' said Price. 'You never know – he might turn out to be the killer as well.'

'That's unlikely, Mansel,' said Leach. 'If the police thought they'd got the right man, he'd have been charged by now and it would have been all over the *Evening News*. Instead, there was only a mention of that plumber being arrested. I don't think he's anything to do with the murder.'

'I'd have beaten a confession out of him.'

'He can't confess to something he didn't do.'

'You can't solve every problem with your fists, Mansel,' said Hambridge, sternly. 'You've been in trouble with the police before for doing that. When are you going to learn your lesson?'

Price smouldered. 'I can't change the person I am, Fred,' he said. 'At least I was trying to take action. All that Gordon's been doing is looking for a way to get out of being called up.'

'That's not what I was doing at all,' said Leach, vehemently.

'Yes, it was.'

'It was . . . just one option.'

'I never took you for a coward until now.'

'I'm not a coward,' said Leach, jumping to his feet.

'Then why were you trying to hide behind Ruby?'

'Don't keep on about it!'

'What happened to the promise to stick together?'

Leach brandished a fist. 'Shut up, Mansel!'

'If you want a fight, you can have it,' said Price, leaping up.

Hambridge got to his feet and pushed them apart. He stared angrily at each of them in turn until they lapsed back into their chairs. Both of them were sulking.

'That's the last thing we need,' he warned. 'If we fall out with each other, we all stand to lose.' He sat down beside Price. 'It's unfair to keep on at Gordon. He made a mistake and he's owned up to it. He's not going to get married until he can do it properly in a church. Isn't that right, Gordon?'

Leach puffed his cheeks. 'I don't know, Fred.'

'I thought we'd made you change your mind.'

'You did – but I wasn't the only one.'

Price was roused again. 'Are you saying that you are going ahead with that plan to get married as soon as you can?'

'No, Mansel. It's not what I want. I see that now.'

'So what's the problem?'

'It's Ruby. She's decided that she likes the idea, after all.'

'You're not going to let a *woman* tell you what to do, are you?'

'Be quiet,' ordered Hambridge. 'Give him a chance to explain.' Price subsided. 'Go ahead, Gordon. Something's happened, hasn't it?'

'Yes,' said Leach. 'We had a row.'

'You're always having a row with Ruby,' said Price.

'This was a serious one. Her family have ganged up on me. They prefer to have a son-in-law who's at liberty rather than someone who gets locked up in prison. Even though it would be in a register office, Ruby could still wear her bridal dress.'

Price erupted. 'Then you must do the same!' he shouted. 'You can wear sackcloth and ashes as a sign of repentance for doing the dirty on your friends.'

'I didn't agree to go along with it, Mansel.'

'That's a relief, anyway,' said Hambridge.

'I never expected this to happen.'

'You've known the bloody girl for years,' said Price. 'You must have learnt the way Ruby's mind works by now.'

Leach raised his eyes to the ceiling. 'If only I did!'

'It's time you put her in her place, Gordon.'

'You can't use force with Ruby. You have to get your way by reason. In this case, unfortunately, she wasn't ready to listen to it.'

'You did make her the offer,' Hambridge told him.

'I should have kept my big mouth shut.'

'So what will happen now?'

Leach gestured his despair. 'I don't know, Fred,' he admitted. 'I honestly don't know. When I told Ruby that I'd changed my mind, she went mad. At the moment it doesn't look as if we'll have a wedding of *any* kind.'

They went to a nearby café and found a table in a quiet corner. Over a frugal meal, Alice told Keedy about the way that she'd been trailed from the bus stop.

'I doubt very much if he'll bother you again,' he said. 'I think I frightened him off for good. I should have arrested him, but the priority was to comfort you.'

'I was so grateful to see you, Joe.'

'I was hiding in the porch, ready to surprise you.'

'And there was me thinking I'd never see you while you were tied up in this case. How did you manage to get off work? Daddy usually puts in fifteen or sixteen hours a day on a big investigation – sometimes more.'

Keedy told here about his night-time vigil and the subsequent arrest of Robbie Gill. While she admired his tenacity, she was horrified to think that anyone could want to celebrate the murder of a young man by painting some provocative words on the side of his house. He asked her about her own work and she boasted about the way she'd been able to mend an engine. He took her hand between his palms.

'That's not what beautiful hands like these should be doing, Alice.'

'I had no choice. Someone had to get that lorry working.'

'Are you still enjoying the WEC?'

'Yes, Joe,' she replied. 'No two days are the same and I've made a lot of new friends. It's much more exciting than teaching. My one regret is about Mummy, of course. Daddy and I have left her stranded in the house.'

'I don't want to sound harsh but you must think of yourself. Much as

I like Ellen, she was holding you back. You needed space of your own.'

'I realise that now.'

'It means you've been able to do things that were just not possible before.'

Alice laughed. 'That's certainly true.'

'Does your mother suspect anything?' he asked, releasing her hand.

'No, she doesn't.'

'Ellen has always sniffed things out in the past.'

'Not this time, Joe.'

'And you've said nothing to her?'

'Of course not,' she said with a frown of indignation. 'It's what we agreed, isn't it? Besides, what is there to tell? We've only seen each other three or four times.'

'Five – you're not counting this evening.'

'The one thing that Mummy really wanted to know was where I'd spent New Year's Eve. I told her the truth. I went to a party with friends. What I didn't say was that you happened to be one of them.'

Keedy chuckled. 'It was a wonderful night!'

'I remember every second of it.'

They ate their food and drank their cups of tea, content simply to be in each other's company. Alice liked to think that being in the WEC had toughened her and made her able to cope with any contingencies. The incident with the stalker had taught her that she was still vulnerable. All over London there were attractive young women who'd lost their husbands or their boyfriends to the army and who lacked the protection they gave. Alice had been assaulted by one of the predators who roamed the suburbs in search of their perverted pleasure. She'd been lucky. But for Keedy, she could have been in serious trouble.

'Carry a weapon with you next time,' he advised.

'That's illegal, Joe.'

'I'm not talking about knives and guns.'

She giggled. 'So what do you recommend – a knuckleduster?'

'No, Alice. I meant something you probably have in your handbag already. Next time you think you're being followed, take out a pair of scissors or a nail file and hold them ready. One good jab will scare most men off.'

'I'll settle for a sharp kick in the shins. That's what I should have given him this evening. While he was hopping on one leg, I could have reached my front door.'

'Where someone was lying in ambush, remember.'

'Yes, but I wouldn't have had to fight you off.'

They gazed into each other's eyes and had a long, silent conversation. Alice had known him for years but never really seen him in romantic terms.

'What would Ellen say if she knew?' he asked.

'I want to make sure that she doesn't.'

'Would she be for or against it?'

'Oh, I think she'd be very much in favour of it.'

'I've got one parent on my side, then.'

'Daddy would be against you, Joe. If he discovered that you and I had been seeing each other in secret, he'd go berserk.'

'I don't believe that. Harvey never goes berserk. Whatever the crisis, he always stays cool, calm and collected. I sometimes think he has ice in his veins.'

'You wouldn't say that if you'd seen him lose his temper. You only know him as a detective. I've seen him as a father.'

'What has he got against me?'

'Do you really need to ask me that?' she said, nudging his ankle under the table. 'Let's be honest, Joe. Where women are concerned, you have a reputation.'

'I like them.'

'Yes, but you've liked rather a lot of them, Joe.'

'They've always liked me in return,' he countered. 'I'm not a philanderer. I've only ever had one girlfriend at a time.'

'That doesn't matter. To my father, I'd only be the latest in a long line.'

'Come off it, Alice. It's not all that long.'

'All right,' she said. 'Let's just say that I'm not the first.'

'But you might be the last.' He beamed at her. 'That's much better.'

Alice was taken aback by the sudden announcement. Was it some kind of covert proposal? Or had it just popped out? From the expression on his face, she couldn't tell if he was serious or merely joking. Her emotions were in a whirl. She liked Keedy very much and believed that he was extremely fond of her. But her feelings had never been any deeper. The mere hint that he was declaring his love for her made her heartbeat quicken. She had to make a supreme effort to control herself.

'There's another reason why Daddy would be angry,' she said.

'You don't need to tell me what it is, Alice.'

'It would be a real blow to his pride.'

'That's easy to understand,' said Keedy, wrestling with a clash of loyalties. 'Harvey Marmion is one of the best detectives I've ever worked with. Imagine how he'll feel if he discovers what's been going on. It was right there in front of him but he didn't even see it.'

Though evening had long since evanesced into night, Marmion was still at his desk in Scotland Yard, crouched over a map as he tried to plot the possible routes that Ablatt would have taken to get from Lambeth to Shoreditch. The fact that he'd made a detour to Caroline Skene's house in order to tell her about his achievement at the meeting of the NCF showed how important she was to him. Caroline came first. The three friends waiting for him would have been deeply upset to realise that. Keeping the truth from them would be an act of kindness. It would lessen Ablatt in their eyes.

Marmion had even outstayed Claude Chatfield. When the superintendent found him still there, he urged him to go home. They both needed rest. Marmion waved him off, then worked for another twenty minutes before his neck started to ache and his eyelids began to droop. When he struggled to his feet, he felt twinges in his back and his legs. It made him feel grateful that he hadn't stayed up all night in the front room of a house owned by two maiden ladies. Marmion recognised his limits. That sort of duty was for younger detectives. Putting on his coat and hat, he switched off the light and left the building.

Ellen had made a valiant effort to stay awake for him but she kept dozing off. It was the sound of a key in the front door lock that brought her out of her slumber. She sat up and turned on the bedside lamp. Though she strained her ears, she could hear nothing. Marmion had taught himself to move about the house with the stealth of a burglar. Ellen often teased him about it. When he finally put his head around the door, he was sad to see that she was still awake.

'No need to apologise,' she said. 'It's what any wife would do.'

He kissed her gently on the head. 'But you're not *any* wife, Ellen. You're one in a thousand.' He began to undress. 'In any case, you're wrong. When some of my colleagues get home late, there's a torrent of abuse waiting for them. Not every wife has your tolerance.'

'It's not tolerance, Harvey. It's fatigue. I'm too weary to complain.'

'How was your day?'

'It was rather lonely. What about you?'

'Oh, I'm never short of company. I seem to have done a hell of a lot today but I don't have much to show for it. However,' he went on, 'I

213

won't bore you with the details. I'm still trying to make sense of them myself.'

'If you'd got that promotion to superintendent, you'd be home earlier.'

'Don't you believe it,' he said, undoing his laces before kicking off his shoes. 'Claude Chatfield left just before I did. He works all hours.'

'Yes,' she said, 'but he doesn't use as much energy as you. He stays at Scotland Yard all day while you and Joe Keedy have to charge all over the place. Being a superintendent wouldn't have been as dangerous as going to some of the rougher areas of London. There'd be no risks to take.'

'That's exactly why I didn't want the job, Ellen,' he confessed. 'In fact, I made sure that I didn't get it by giving the wrong answers at the interview. With all its headaches and frustrations, I love the job I do. There's nothing to touch the sheer thrill of a hunt for a killer. You're going to have to put up with a mere detective inspector for a little longer, I'm afraid. I hope you won't be disappointed.'

Ellen patted the pillow beside her. 'It suits me fine.'

The man was singing a hymn to himself as he strolled along the road. When he turned down a lane, he had to walk along a dark corridor between the gardens of the houses on either side. Having used the route so often, it never occurred to him that he might be in jeopardy. He was therefore completely off guard when someone leapt out from his hiding place, knocked off the man's hat and clubbed him viciously to the ground. Blood was everywhere but that didn't satisfy the attacker. He was there to kill. He managed to get in a few more heavy blows before he heard someone coming down the lane.

'Hey!' yelled a voice. 'What's going on?'

Abandoning his victim, the attacker ran off at speed into the night.

CHAPTER FOURTEEN

Attempted murder was Marmion's alarm clock. It woke him up early and sent him off to Scotland Yard in the police car dispatched to collect him. It took him the whole journey to come fully awake. He expected the superintendent to be there before him but had not counted on Chatfield being quite so animated at that time of the morning. Almost as soon as he entered the building, Marmion was pounced on.

'He's struck again,' announced Chatfield.

'Who are you talking about, sir?'

'Who do you think?'

'The driver gave me no details.'

'The man who killed Cyril Ablatt has a second victim.'

'How do you know?'

'It's because the *modus operandi* is identical in both cases. He lurks in a dark lane in Shoreditch and uses a blunt instrument to smash someone's head in. Amongst the things found on the victim was a leaflet advertising that fateful meeting of the NCF. In short, he's Ablatt by another name.

My first impulse was right,' said Chatfield with a self-congratulatory smile. 'The man we're after has a grudge against conchies.'

'It seems to me that you're making hasty assumptions,' said Marmion.

'There's too much similarity for it to be a coincidence, Inspector.'

'Perhaps you'd let me make up my own mind about that.'

On the walk to his office, the superintendent gave him the relevant facts. A man in his late twenties was attacked in a dark lane the previous night. Before he could kill his victim, the attacker was interrupted and ran off. Help was summoned and the wounded man was rushed to hospital. He'd sustained serious head injuries and was in a coma but he was still alive. His condition was described as critical. From information in his wallet, he was identified as the Reverend James Howells, a curate at St Leonard's in Shoreditch High Street. A letter from his father, found in his pocket, showed that his family lived in York. Chatfield had rung the police station in the city and asked them to inform Mr and Mrs Howells that their son was in hospital as the result of a murderous attack. The superintendent had also sent word to the vicar of St Leonard's.

'It all fits together,' he said, almost gleefully.

'I don't find a violent attack a subject for celebration, sir.'

'We'll catch him this time. The victim has survived.'

'Yes,' said Marmion, guardedly, 'but we don't know how much he'll remember if and when he recovers consciousness. If there's been excessive brain damage, he may be able to tell us nothing at all. And even if he makes a good recovery, he may have no idea who tried to kill him.'

'He must have. I'm counting on it.'

'Then there's a question of motive, sir. Just because he had that NCF leaflet in his pocket, it doesn't mean that he supports their cause.'

'There's no other conceivable reason why he should have it.'

'I can think of one,' said Marmion. 'He wanted to use it as the basis of a sermon. That's what the vicar of our church did. He stood in the

216

pulpit a couple of Sundays ago and denounced those who refused to take part in what he called a holy crusade against the Germans. The Reverend Howells may be of the same view.'

'That's nonsense.'

'You're resorting to guesswork, Superintendent.'

'The facts speak for themselves.'

'Well, they don't convince me,' said Marmion, as they turned into the office. 'The two incidents could be entirely unrelated.'

'But the second is a mirror image of the first.'

'I dispute that, sir. What we have now is an ambush in a dark lane. Whereas, in the first instance, we had someone killed elsewhere then dumped during the night. That's a critical difference.'

'You may be forced to eat your words, Inspector.'

'Then I'll do so in all humility – but only if I get concrete proof.'

Chatfield was peevish. He hated it when anyone challenged his theories. He had a particular aversion to being contradicted by Marmion. Walking around his desk, he lowered himself into his chair.

'Do you recall the visit you made to Ablatt's father?' he asked.

'I recall it very well, sir.'

'He talked about his son's passion for religion and you saw all those books about Christianity in his room. It was in the first report you gave me.'

'I tried to be as comprehensive as possible.'

'Did you ever ask *which* church Ablatt and his father attended?'

'No, sir, I didn't. Sergeant Keedy and I just let Mr Ablatt talk.'

'Take a look at a map of Shoreditch, Inspector. The most likely church would have been the closest to the house. Do you agree?'

'Yes,' said Marmion. 'That would be logical.'

'Then he was a member of the congregation at St Leonard's,' said Chatfield with the deep satisfaction of someone who'd just made a decisive point in a debate. 'It therefore follows that Ablatt must have known the curate very well. My feeling is that they were birds of a feather.' He bared his teeth at Marmion. 'Do you still think there's no connection between the two crimes?'

Ellen was thrilled to see her daughter for the second time in a week. She liked to think that Alice had come specifically to see her, even though her daughter went straight upstairs to her bedroom to retrieve various items she needed. Alice didn't even have time for a cup of tea. She bundled the things into a bag.

'Have you ever thought about having a lodger?' she asked.

'I feel as if I already have one, Alice – it's your father.'

'I'm serious. We're always looking for accommodation for refugees. Most of them come with families or friends but we do get the occasional person on their own. All they want is a roof over their head.'

Ellen was upset. 'I'd never let anyone have *your* room.'

'But I don't need it any more.'

'You may want it back one day when the war is over.'

'No,' said Alice, firmly. 'I've moved out for good, Mummy. That's no reflection on you and Daddy. I loved it when I lived at home. But everything has changed now and you'll have to get used to it.'

'It's too early to be so certain about that.'

'I don't think so.'

Ellen refused to accept the inevitable. She still nurtured the hope that her daughter would, in time, begin to yearn for the comforts of home and return to live in the family house. She put a maternal hand on Alice's shoulder.

'Let's talk about it properly when you're not in such a rush.'

'There's no point. My mind is made up.'

'Where will you live after the war?'

218

'I don't know. I'll find somewhere. For the moment, I'm happy enough with the place I've got, even though the landlady is very strict. However,' she said with a laugh, 'I'm much better off than Vera. Her landlady is a real dragon.' She gave her mother a peck on the cheek. 'I must be off. Goodbye.'

Ellen eyed her shrewdly. 'Has something happened, Alice?'

'The war has happened. Our lives can never be the same again.'

'I didn't mean that,' said her mother. 'Ever since you've been in the house, you've been smiling to yourself as if you have some sort of secret. It reminds me of the time when you were at school and had your first boyfriend. You came home with a grin on your face but you wouldn't tell us why.'

'That was *years* ago,' said Alice, 'and it never lasted, anyway. I soon lost interest in him. As for boyfriends, the only young men I get to see are terrified refugees from Belgium. I just don't have time for a social life.' Picking up her bag, she went to the front door. 'Give my love to Daddy.'

Ellen went to wave her off. 'Take care, darling. Bye.'

She stood and watched as Alice got into the lorry and drove off. Ellen was both hurt and curious. She wondered why her daughter had just lied to her.

The first person Marmion spoke to at the hospital was the doctor in charge of the case. James Howells had had an emergency operation but was still in a coma. All that the medical staff could do was to wait and watch. The doctor promised that he would get in touch with Scotland Yard the moment that the patient was conscious again, though he warned that Howells might not be able to remember what had happened. In cases of brain damage, it was impossible to predict the outcome. Marmion thanked him and went into the waiting room where the Reverend

Simon Ellway was sitting with his eyes closed as if in prayer. The old man's shoulders sagged wearily. Marmion waited until the vicar's eyes opened before introducing himself. Ellway was distraught.

'Where will it end, Inspector?' he asked in despair. 'Only yesterday, I had to comfort the family of a parishioner of mine, Cyril Ablatt, who was murdered. Last night, someone tried to kill my curate.'

'It's not impossible that the two cases are related,' said Marmion. 'I'm here because I'm in charge of the investigation into the murder as well. Cyril Ablatt worshipped at St Leonard's, then?'

'Oh, yes. He and his father attended services regularly.'

'Tell me a little about your curate.'

The vicar spoke warmly. 'James is a delightful young man. The moment he arrived, he seemed to fit in perfectly. He is indefatigable. Nothing is too much trouble for him. He took a huge load off my back. We had our differences, naturally,' admitted Ellway. 'He didn't entirely share my passion for the Old Testament and, by the same token, I was rather resistant to some of the modern ideas he tried to press upon me. In truth, I suppose, I'm a hopeless traditionalist. But none of our differences get in the way of our friendship. James is like a son to us.'

'Where does he live?'

'We offered him a room at the vicarage but he preferred to be out in the community he served. He has digs within walking distance of the church.' He smiled fondly. 'James is single but I don't think he'll remain a bachelor for long. He's very handsome and sets many a female heart aflutter. My wife used to tease me about it. When James took a service, she said, there are always more young ladies in the congregation than when I'm on duty.'

'Given his popularity, why should anyone wish to attack him?'

'It was more than just an attack, Inspector. It was a case of attempted murder. If someone hadn't, mercifully, come along when he did, James would be dead.'

'Did he ever talk about enemies that he had?'

'No,' replied Ellway, 'because there weren't any. Everyone liked him.'

'People said the same thing about Cyril Ablatt, yet he was murdered.'

'I know. It doesn't make any sense.'

'There is one possible motive.'

'You're talking about him being a conscientious objector, aren't you?'

'Yes – that makes him an object of disgust to some people.'

'You could never be disgusted by Cyril. He was a splendid young fellow.'

'What about your curate?' asked Marmion.

'I don't follow.'

'Did he agree with the stand that Cyril was taking?'

'He did and he didn't,' said the old man. 'He agreed that everyone had the right to take a stand on an issue of moral principle and he admired him for doing so. At the same time, however, James couldn't support him. He felt that the needs of a national emergency should come first. On the subject of war, the Bible is rather ambiguous. They had long theological arguments, quoting bits of the Old and New Testaments at each other.'

'Who won the argument?'

'The issue was unresolved. Cyril tried to persuade James to go to a meeting of something called the No-Conscription Fellowship. My curate showed me the leaflet he'd been given.'

'Did he attend the meeting?'

'No, Inspector. He felt that he'd be there under false pretences.'

Marmion was interested to hear how the leaflet had come into the curate's possession and would take pleasure in passing on the information to Chatfield. It would puncture the superintendent's theory about the second attack being an exact copy of the first. Howells and Ablatt were not interchangeable victims. They were on opposite sides of the argument. The vicar provided a link between the two men.

'You mentioned that you visited Mr Ablatt,' recalled Marmion.

'That's right,' said Ellway with a sigh. 'As you can imagine, I've had rather too much experience of visiting a house of mourning but it's usually because someone has died a natural death. There have also been families here whose sons have been killed during the war, of course, and there have been rather too many of them. What I've never had to do before is to offer consolation to the father of a murder victim.'

'How did Mr Ablatt seem?'

'He seemed totally baffled. He just couldn't understand what was going on. His sister, however, was beyond my reach. She was so consumed by anguish that I don't think she heard a word of what I said. There was another member of the family there,' he went on, 'a Mrs Skene, a cousin of Gerald Ablatt. She struck me as one of those practical women who subdue their own grief in order to help those unable to do so. Yes, Mrs Skene was very capable.'

Marmion did not disclose her ulterior motive in visiting the house. He didn't wish to betray a confidence or to shatter the fond image of Cyril Ablatt that the vicar had. Unlike his young parishioner, Simon Ellway would never have been able to reconcile religious conviction and an intimate relationship with a married woman. After thanking him for his help, Marmion took his leave and headed for the exit. Before he reached it, he saw Keedy coming down the corridor towards him.

'Good morning, Joe.'

'Good morning. The superintendent told me I'd find you here.'

'Did he tell you why?'

'Yes,' said Keedy. 'The killer went after a second victim.'

Marmion took a deep breath. 'That's not quite what happened . . .'

* * *

Against all advice, Gerald Ablatt opened his shop that morning. He felt that he'd been writhing in pain for long enough and he sought the anaesthetic of work. It gave him a sense of purpose and showed him that not everyone in Shoreditch disapproved of the fact that someone hadn't volunteered for military service. Customers were uniformly sympathetic. They made the cobbler feel both proud of his son and comforted in his loss. As a result of his decision to resume work, his sister was forced to stay at home. Promising to come back early, Dalley went off to work. He met the postman on the way and stopped for a chat. When the blacksmith reached the forge, his assistant was dealing with a customer whose horse he'd just shoed. After the bill had been paid, Percy Fry came over to his boss.

'I didn't expect you so soon, Jack.'

'There was a change of plan today. I've had to leave Nancy at home. Her brother went off to open his shop so she couldn't go to the house.'

'Gone back to work, you say? Is that wise?'

'It's my brother-in-law's way of getting through this ordeal.'

'Is anyone sitting with Nancy?'

'No,' said Dalley, 'she's on her own and, to be honest, I'm rather worried about her. Do you think you could ask Elaine to pop over there at some point?'

'Yes, of course – she's been waiting for the call.'

'Thanks, Perce.'

Customers arrived and they were both kept busy for a while, filling the place with the clang of steel and the roar of the fire. It was not until an hour later that the blacksmith had time to pass on a rumour he'd picked up.

'As I was leaving the house,' he said, 'I bumped into the postman. He'd heard something about a second attack in Shoreditch.'

Fry was amazed. 'You mean there was *another* murder?'

'No, it stopped short of that. The killer was interrupted and ran off before he could finish the job. This all took place only two streets away from our house. I daren't tell Nancy about it or she'd be afraid to leave the house.'

'It would scare anybody, Jack. There was nothing like this when we lived in Shoreditch. The place felt safe. Elaine was saying that over breakfast. People used to settle their differences with their fists. They didn't need to kill each other.'

'There was no war on when you lived there, Perce.'

'So?'

'It's changed people for the worst – especially the lads who've fought in it.'

'Well, yes, I'd agree with you there.'

'I reckon that the man who killed Cyril was either a soldier or the father of one who died at the front. He couldn't bear the sight of someone refusing to fight for his country when others have given their lives.'

'We've said it before,' noted Fry. 'Nobody likes conchies.'

'Cyril was the exception. I liked him.'

'So did I – up to a point. What about this second one?'

'What do you mean, Perce?'

'Was he a conchie as well?'

'The postman didn't know any details,' said Dalley, 'but I think it's very likely. In fact, I've got a horrible feeling that he's connected to my nephew in some way. I'd put money on it.' He sucked his teeth. 'When she eventually hears about it, Nancy will be in a terrible state. She's going to start wondering who'll be next.'

One advantage of delivering bread was that Gordon Leach picked up all the local gossip. He was alarmed to hear of the second attack and deviated from his normal round in order to call on Fred Hambridge.

The carpenter and his boss were both at their benches in the workshop. They were horrified by the news of an attempted murder and even more shocked when they realised who the victim actually was. Hambridge knew the name.

'James Howells was a curate at Cyril's church, wasn't he?' he asked.

'Yes,' said Leach. 'He was going to marry me and Ruby.'

'Maybe you've got a jealous rival, Gordon,' suggested Redfern, trying to lighten the atmosphere. 'He tried to bump off the priest to stop you getting hitched.'

'That's not funny, Charlie,' said Hambridge.

'It was only a joke.'

'Well, we're not laughing.'

'We've got nothing to laugh about,' said Leach, anxiously. 'Two people I knew and liked have been attacked in a matter of days. One of them was murdered and the other is in hospital. I'm terrified.'

'You're not in any danger,' said Redfern.

'How do you know?'

'You'd have more sense than to walk down a dark lane at night.'

'The killer could strike anywhere and at any time.'

'The police will get him,' said Hambridge, confidently.

'They haven't got him so far, Fred.'

'They caught that man who painted things on Cyril's wall.'

'So did Mansel. In fact, he got hold of him first.'

'I trust the police.'

'They ought to give us bodyguards.'

'Whatever for?' asked Redfern.

'We need protection,' insisted Leach.

'You're young and strong enough to look after yourselves.'

'Being young and strong didn't help Cyril – or our curate, for that matter. Mansel, Fred or I could be the next on the death list.' He saw

Redfern's smirk. 'That may sound far-fetched to you, Charlie,' he said, raising his voice, 'but it doesn't to me. There's a killer on the loose in Shoreditch. If the police don't catch him soon, my father will need a new assistant at the bakery and you could be looking for a new carpenter. Let's see you laugh at that.'

After leaving the hospital, their first visit was to the scene of the crime. There'd been a considerable loss of blood and James Howells had needed an instant transfusion. Marmion and Keedy then drove on to the local police station and read the statement given by the man who disturbed the attacker. The witness had been returning home when he heard a noise in the lane. He could just make out a figure in silhouette, standing over someone on the ground, hand aloft as if about to strike. His yell had frightened the man off. When he realised how badly beaten the victim was, he ran to the police station to raise the alarm. An ambulance was summoned by telephone. Admitting that he'd never recognise the attacker, the witness said that he was simply glad that he came along in time to prevent a murder.

Since no other witnesses had come forward, Marmion decided that they'd start their investigation by interviewing a suspect for the earlier murder. On the drive to the cemetery, Keedy was curious.

'Do you think the same person is behind both attacks, Harv?'

'On the face of it,' said Marmion, 'it looks quite possible, though I have my doubts. However, we'll proceed on the basis that we're after one culprit.'

'He's someone who hates conchies and doesn't like clergymen.'

'That probably sums up Waldron quite well. He doesn't sound like a regular churchgoer to me. And if he has to listen to dozens of different priests droning on as he's waiting to fill in a grave, I daresay he loathes the whole breed.'

'I'll be interested to see what you make of him,' said Keedy. 'Maybe *you* can explain where his charm lies. I can't see it.'

'Beauty lies in the eyes of the beholder, Joe.'

'You'd have to be as blind as a bat to find Horrie Waldron beautiful.'

'Mrs Crowther's not blind, is she?'

'Quite the opposite, I'd say.'

As the car rolled along at a comfortable speed, it was overtaken by a rasping motorcycle. Marmion was reminded of something that his wife had told him.

'I hope that Alice doesn't go abroad,' he said. 'I encouraged her to move out of the house but I'd be very unhappy if she decided to go to France.'

Keedy was concerned. 'There's no chance of that, is there?'

'It was something she mentioned to Ellen. Apparently, a couple of her friends have gone as dispatch riders. Knowing Alice, I think it would have appealed to her adventurous spirit.'

'For your sake, I hope she doesn't go.'

'We can't stop her, Joe. If she really wants something, she usually gets it.'

'Your daughter takes after you, Harv. She's single-minded.'

'I'd hate to have *both* my children near the war front.'

Keedy was wounded by the information. He couldn't understand why Alice hadn't confided in him. At a time when they were getting closer, she was thinking of going abroad. It was not the best way to let their friendship ripen. As it was, he saw very little of Alice. If she left the country, he'd see nothing at all of her. Keedy was glad that her father could not read his mind.

The car turned in through the gates of the cemetery.

'Where are we likely to find him?' asked Marmion.

'They'll tell us.'

When they reached the reception lodge, Keedy let him do all the talking. He was too busy adjusting to the news about Alice, still wondering why she'd never touched on the subject with him. When Marmion wanted her to remain in England, he was speaking as a father. Keedy had equally strong reasons for not wishing to see her sail off to France. He hoped he'd get the chance to discuss them with her.

It did not take them long to track down Horrie Waldron. Shirt open at the neck and sleeves rolled up, he was leaning against a gravestone as he rolled himself a cigarette. When he saw the detectives coming, he spat on the ground by way of a welcome. Marmion saw how accurate Keedy's description of the man had been. The only difference was that Waldron was not wearing the filthy old clothing on which the sergeant had commented. His shirt, waistcoat and trousers were ragged but they were not stained or impregnated with the stink of the grave. When Marmion introduced himself, he got a scowl of disrespect.

'Do you know the Reverend James Howells?' he asked.

Waldron kept him waiting, lighting his cigarette and puffing on it.

'I might do.'

'Either you do or you don't.'

'I see priest after bleeding priest in here. Never remember their names.'

'This gentleman is the curate at St Leonard's.'

'What's that to me, Inspector?'

'Someone tried to kill him last night.'

Waldron cackled. 'Then he ought to write better sermons,' he said, nastily. 'You wouldn't believe some of the rubbish they come out with. When I first started here, I sometimes used to stand at the back of the chapel to listen to what the priest was saying. It was all I could do not to laugh. Do they get *paid* for spouting all that bleeding nonsense?' His grin vanished as he saw the way that they were looking at him. 'Hey, you don't think that *I* had anything to do with it, did you?'

'Where were you last night just before midnight, Horrie?' asked Keedy.

'I was in my bed.'

'Can anyone vouch for that?'

'I was on my own.'

'What about your landlady?'

'I wouldn't let that old witch anywhere near me,' said Waldron. 'She and her husband sleep upstairs and my room is in the basement. When I let myself in, they can't even hear me.'

'Did you drink at the Weavers Arms?'

'Why are you bothering me with all these questions?'

'We're trying to eliminate you from our enquiries, sir,' said Marmion.

'Well, be quick about it. I got work to do.'

'Were you at the pub?' repeated Keedy. 'We can check, you know.'

'I left there at closing time. Stan will tell you that.'

'And you went straight back to your digs?'

'No,' said Waldron, sarcastically, 'I killed three old ladies and a couple of priests on the way. Why pick on me?' he demanded. 'I've never even heard this Reverend Thingamajig's name before.'

'But you've heard the name of Cyril Ablatt.'

'Oh, yes. I remember that clever bugger. I'll give three cheers at the funeral.'

'That would be very unkind of you, Mr Waldron,' said Marmion. 'I won't ask you why. What I'd like to know is what happened to the spade.'

The gravedigger blinked. 'What spade, Inspector?'

'This one,' said Keedy, touching the implement that stood upright in a mound of fresh earth. 'It was the one you took to the pub on the night Cyril Ablatt was murdered. Mr Crowther confirmed that.'

'It was my spade. I can do what I like with it.'

'Not if you use it as a weapon, sir,' warned Marmion.

'So tell us what happened to it,' said Keedy. 'You took it to the pub and you had it with you when you went out for an hour or so. Why didn't you bring it back with you when you went to the Weavers Arms again?'

Marmion saw him blench. 'Wandering around in the dark with a spade is an odd thing to do, Mr Waldron,' he said. 'Answer the sergeant's question. Where did you leave it when you went back to the pub?'

'And what did you have it for in the first place?' said Keedy, pulling the spade out and holding it up. 'Did you, by any chance, take it home with you yesterday evening as well?'

Waldron's bravado had melted away. Eyes darting, he looked like a cornered animal. He let his cigarette fall to the ground then stamped on it with a brutal heel. After a few moments, he snatched the spade from Keedy's hand.

'Give that here!' he yelled. 'It's mine.'

CHAPTER FIFTEEN

Alice Marmion had said nothing to her friend about her narrow escape from the man who'd followed her. If she'd confided in Vera Dowling, she'd have had to divulge the name of Joe Keedy and that would have let the cat out of the bag. It was important to keep their friendship a secret. Trustworthy in every other respect, Vera was prone to the occasional slip of the tongue. It was safer to keep her ignorant and to be spared her veiled disapproval. She'd never understand why Alice had become involved with a man almost ten years older. If anything, she'd be quietly scandalised and that would have an adverse affect on their friendship. Silence was definitely Alice's best option. Having missed lunch because of the pressure of work, they were having a snack in the canteen that afternoon. As usual, Vera found something to worry about.

'Have you had any more thoughts about Belgium?' she asked.

'Yes,' replied Alice. 'I'm wondering if there's anyone left in the country. We've had so many refugees that the entire population must be here now.'

'I was talking about that idea you had.'

'Ah, yes.'

'Have you made a decision yet?'

'No, Vera. One day, I want to go, and the next day, I've changed my mind. It wouldn't necessarily be in Belgium, of course. I could be driving a motorbike in France.' Her face lit up. 'I might even get close to Paul's regiment. Wouldn't it be wonderful if I could see my brother over there?'

Vera was sad. 'Paul's gain would be my loss.'

'You could always come with me.'

'I could never be a dispatch rider.'

'There are lots of other things you could do over there, Vera.'

'No,' said the other, 'I know my limits and I've already reached them. Besides, I promised Mummy that I'd never go abroad because of the danger. If you desert me, I'll be left on my own.'

'Hardly!' said Alice with a laugh. 'I'm not the only woman in the WEC.'

'You're the only one I get on with.'

'You'll soon find someone else, Vera.'

'Nobody else seems to like me.'

'That's absurd! Lots of people like you.'

'No, Alice, they put up with me because of you and that's very different. Mrs Billington is a case in point. She tolerates me because she admires you.'

It was true and both women knew it. Though she'd had enough courage to leave home, Vera lacked the personality and thrust to mix easily in a group. She always needed someone to lean on. Without Alice beside her, Vera would struggle. She was too shy to make new women friends and too plain to attract male interest. While she sympathised with her friend's plight, however, Alice had to be selfish. In many ways, she recognised, Vera was holding her back. Going abroad would allow Alice to escape from the dependency.

'Look out,' said Vera, tensing as she saw someone approaching their table with a purposeful stride. 'Mrs Billington is on her way.'

'Try to relax. Hannah's one of us.'

'Then why do I always feel so threatened?'

Alice turned to see the older woman coming towards them with a newspaper under her arm. As they exchanged greetings, Hannah sat down beside Alice.

'How would tomorrow afternoon suit you, ladies?' she asked. 'You can come and have a proper tea at my house.'

'Thanks very much, Hannah,' said Alice. 'We'd like that.'

Vera hesitated. 'I'm . . . not sure that I can come, Mrs Billington.'

'Oh dear!' exclaimed Hannah. 'Why is that?'

'I've got . . . something else on.'

'In that case, Alice will have to come on her own. Is that all right?'

'Yes,' said Alice, helping to bail her friend out. 'She did warn me that she'd be too busy to help me all day tomorrow,' she went on, reinforcing the white lie. 'You'll have to come to Hannah's house another time, Vera.'

'I will,' said Vera without enthusiasm.

Hannah took the newspaper from under her arm and unfurled it.

'I take it that neither of you has seen the early edition?' she said, pointing to the front page headline. 'The Shoreditch killer is on the prowl again.'

'Oh, no!' cried Vera.

'Luckily, he was stopped just in time.'

'Let me see,' said Alice, pulling the newspaper closer so that she could read it.

'Your father almost had another murder to solve,' said Hannah, seriously. 'It's clear that the man will stop at nothing. Inspector Marmion needs to catch this devil. Until he does, everyone in London will be looking over their shoulder.'

Alice was dismayed. The new case would not only entail additional work for her father. It would mean that Joe Keedy would be completely preoccupied as well. Given the extended hours he'd now have to work, there was no hope at all of seeing him soon. She would have to survive on memories.

When he read the same newspaper report, Marmion was pulsing with anger. The superintendent had given the press the impression that the inspector agreed with him that the two heinous crimes were the work of the same man. Normally so frugal with the amount of information he fed reporters, Chatfield had said too much too soon and reached a conclusion that – in Marmion's opinion – they'd live to regret. The *Evening News* had turned it into a sensation. All of a sudden, London had a new monster stalking the streets. If he struck again, it was argued, he would be taking on the mantle of Jack the Ripper as an evil phantom who left the police utterly baffled. The article was very unflattering to Marmion, claiming that his hitherto untarnished reputation was slowly crumbling because he'd made no progress with the murder investigation, thereby leaving the killer to choose a second victim with impunity.

'That makes my blood boil!' he said, tossing the newspaper aside.

Keedy picked it up. 'What does it say, Harv?'

'They think we're idiots.'

'If they've been talking to Chat, I'm not surprised. He's the idiot-in-chief.' Keedy read the article. 'This is so unfair,' he said, hotly. 'Anyone would think we've been sitting on our hands for the last few days. It's especially unfair to you. They ought to show more respect.'

'They have newspapers to sell, Joe.'

'That doesn't mean they can print lies.'

'They'd call it "informed opinion".'

'Well, if you want *my* informed opinion,' said Keedy with spirit, 'the man who wrote this drivel ought to be kicked the length of Piccadilly. I'll volunteer to do the kicking and to wear some hobnail boots.'

'Never get into a fight with a reporter. They always have more ink.'

'We can't let him get away with this, Harv.'

'We won't,' Marmion promised him. 'We'll solve both crimes and show him just how maliciously wide of the mark this article is.'

During a morning of ceaseless activity, they paid a visit to Gerald Ablatt's shop where the cobbler had been working quietly away. Aghast at the news of an attack on James Howells, he'd confirmed that his son had been friends with the curate and talked of him visiting the house once or twice. Ablatt was honest. While he appreciated the curate's many fine qualities, he still preferred the vicar's sermons. They offered more comfort and far less challenge. After a series of other calls, the detectives had ended up in the room where Howells had lived. It presented a sharp contrast to Cyril Ablatt's bedroom. Where the latter was small, untidy and filled with books, this one was large, scrupulously organised and devoid of ornament. There was an austere feel to the place. Hidden behind a curtain, a single bed stood in the corner. The furniture comprised a table, a chair and a wardrobe. A neat pile of books stood on the table. Inevitably, the Bible was one of them.

Keedy whistled in surprise. 'This room makes mine look like Aladdin's cave.'

'It is rather bare,' agreed Marmion.

'Where are the paintings, the knick-knacks, the personal items?'

'He didn't need those, Joe.'

'Most of us have *something* to look at.'

'Perhaps he chose to look inwards.'

Marmion sifted through the books on the table. When he picked up the Bible, nothing fell out of it. The Reverend James Howells was patently not a man who spent much money on himself. They opened the wardrobe to find very little inside apart from some shirts, socks, underclothes and a pair of trousers.

'He seems to have lived like a monk,' said Keedy. 'This whole room reeks of self-denial.'

Marmion grinned. 'I'm surprised you know what self-denial is, Joe.'

'I don't.'

'They tell me it's good for the soul.'

'Thanks for the advice.' Keedy drew back the curtain to look at the bed. On a shelf supported by a wall bracket were shaving equipment, a toothbrush and some toothpaste. Getting down onto his knees, he peered underneath the bed then reached for something. 'This might be interesting.'

'What have you found?'

'I'm not sure yet.'

'Can you manage, Joe?'

'I think so.'

Keedy stood up with a small cardboard box in his hands. When he set it on the table, they examined the contents. There were letters from Howells's father and from fellow clergymen with whom he'd studied. There were some family photographs, and a pile of sermons written in a neat hand with various words underlined. Of most interest to Marmion was a small address book. As he leafed through it, he saw that most of the people listed in it lived in Shoreditch and were, presumably, the curate's parishioners. His parents' address was there, as were those of relatives and friends in York. One name jumped out of the address book at Marmion.

'Eric Fussell is in here,' he said, curiosity stirring. 'Yet he doesn't live in Shoreditch, so he's unlikely to attend services at St Leonard's.'

236

Keedy looked over his shoulder. 'I see what you mean. He lives in Lambeth.'

'That raises a question, Joe.'

'Yes – how did your favourite librarian make his way into the book?'

Mansel Price first heard about the attempted murder when he saw it emblazoned across the front of the newspaper stall at the railway station. Too mean to buy a copy, he instead went to a nearby wastepaper bin and retrieved one discarded earlier. He read it on the way to the bakery. Gordon Leach let him in by the side door.

'Have you heard, Mansel?' he asked.

'I've been reading the details on the way here.'

'It's scared me rigid.'

'Well,' said Price, contemptuously, 'it doesn't take much to do that, does it?'

'Aren't you afraid you might be next?'

'No, I'm not.'

'We could be targets.'

'I don't believe that. But just in case anybody does come after me,' said the Welshman, slipping a hand under his coat, 'I'll be ready for him.'

He pulled out a knife and thrust it at Leach, making him jump back.

'Steady on, Mansel! That's dangerous.'

'If anyone attacks me, I'll cut his balls off.'

'Put that thing away before someone gets hurt.'

Price slipped the knife back into its sheath. 'You knew this Father Howells, didn't you?'

'Yes,' replied Leach. 'Some of us go to church.'

'I'm a chapel man myself, though I haven't seen the inside of one since I left Wales. Anyway, I'm usually working on a Sunday. Need the money.'

'James Howells was a nice man. Thank heaven he survived!'

'We don't know that he did,' said Price, realistically. 'The paper says he's still in a coma. He may never recover. That'd be two murders in less than a week.'

Leach was unnerved. 'We need police on patrol at night around here,' he argued. 'It's the only way to make sure there isn't a third victim.'

'If you expect the police to protect you,' said Price with rancour, 'you'll wait till the cows come home. They don't have the men to spare and they couldn't care about us, anyway. Sergeant Keedy couldn't even catch a man about to paint a wall. What chance has he got of arresting a killer?'

'Fred trusts him.'

'Don't listen to Fred. He thinks well of everybody.'

They were interrupted by a knock on the door. When Leach opened it, Ruby Cosgrove threw herself into his arms. After hugging her for a moment, he eased her inside and closed the door.

'What's brought you here, Ruby?' he asked.

'When I heard the news, I just had to come.' Seeing Price for the first time, she broke away from Leach. 'Hello, Mansel.'

'How are you, Rube?'

'I'm terribly upset by what I heard.'

'It wasn't Gordon he banged on the head – it was only Father What's-is-name.'

'We *know* him,' she emphasized. 'Gordon and I saw him in church last Sunday. He was so friendly. Father Howells was going to marry us.'

Price sniggered. 'I thought you were after this three-day licence.'

'No,' said Leach, firmly. 'That's out of the question now. We don't need it any more.'

'You mean that you and Gordon are *not* going to get married, after all?' Price shook his head. 'I wish the pair of you would make up your bleeding minds.'

'Watch your language, Mansel,' warned Leach. 'I won't have you swearing in front of Ruby. As for the wedding,' he continued, shooting Ruby a nervous glance, 'our plans are not definite at the moment.'

'Yes, they are,' she said, decisively.

Leach gaped. 'Are they?'

'That's unless you've changed your mind, Gordon.'

'No, no,' he said, happily. 'I'm dying to get married.'

'Then we leave the date exactly as it was,' she explained. 'We'll have to ask the vicar to take the service, of course, but I'm sure he'll agree to that.'

'Wait a minute, Rube,' said Price, hands on hips, 'there's something you're forgetting. Me and Gordon will be hauled up before a tribunal soon. Fred Hambridge has already had his summons. We're the next in the queue. How can you walk down the aisle with Gordon when he's likely to be locked up in prison with me? We're conchies. Doesn't that mean anything to you?'

'There's no need to be sarcastic with me, Mansel Price.'

'Then don't plan for something that can't possibly happen.'

'But it can,' she insisted. 'My father explained it to me. There's a way for Gordon to stick to his principles without being imprisoned.'

'No, there isn't.'

'He can join a non-combatant corps. They never have to take part in a battle and sometimes they don't even leave this country. You'd be safe, Gordon, and I'm sure we'd get permission from your commanding officer to go ahead with the wedding in the summer.' Squeezing his hands, she smiled lovingly at him. 'Isn't that the perfect solution?'

Leach could sense that Price was simmering with rage. He played for time.

'Let me think it over, Ruby,' he said, tactfully.

* * *

On his third visit to Shoreditch library, Marmion took Joe Keedy with him so that he could get the sergeant's opinion of the librarian. When they arrived, Eric Fussell was in a meeting with his deputy so they had to wait. It gave them the opportunity to scour the shelves. Keedy was fascinated by an illustrated guide to angling.

'It must be years since I got my fishing rod out,' he moaned. 'I used to love sitting in the sun on a riverbank when the fish were nibbling.'

'You go fishing every day in this job,' said Marmion with a grin. 'If you use the right bait and remain patient, you always catch something in the end.'

'The trouble is that it's usually small fry, Harv – petty thieves and so on. I'd rather just toss them back into the water.'

'We're after more than small fry now.'

'Then we need a big hook and a large net.' Keedy replaced the book on the shelf and looked towards the librarian's office. 'I think he's deliberately keeping us waiting. What's he doing in there?'

'He's probably still trying to find out who supplied us with all that information about his feud with Cyril Ablatt. It riled him to think that one of his assistants had dared to betray him.' He saw someone behind the desk. 'It certainly wasn't that lady.'

'How do you know?'

'It's his wife, Mrs Fussell.'

Keedy looked at the portly woman writing something in a pad. She wore spectacles and had her hair pinned up at the back. Putting the pad aside, she reached out some books from under the counter and took them to a shelf nearby. As she stacked them wearily in position, she looked as if she was doing a tedious chore. Clearly, she didn't share her husband's zeal for the working at the library.

Marmion saw the door of the office open. The deputy librarian came out, followed by Fussell who beckoned the detectives over with a lordly crook of the finger. All three of them went into the office. After Keedy

240

had been introduced to the librarian, they took a seat. A copy of the *Evening News* lay on the desk.

'I hope that you've brought me some glad tidings,' said Fussell.

'I'm afraid not, sir,' said Marmion.

'You must have made *some* progress.'

'We're still gathering evidence.'

'That takes time,' said Keedy.

'We have to sort out the wheat from the chaff, you see. The strange thing is that people don't always tell us the truth,' said Marmion. 'Well, you're a good example, sir. You told me what an outstanding assistant Cyril Ablatt was even though you'd done your level best to unload him onto another library.'

'I explained that,' snapped Fussell.

'Indeed, you did – but only when someone had provided me with the facts.'

The librarian was tetchy. 'Why are you bothering me again, Inspector? I would have thought you had plenty to keep you busy.' He indicated the newspaper. 'You have another case on your hands now and someone doesn't like the way you're handling the first one. You and the sergeant are more or less ridiculed in that article.'

'Don't believe everything you read in the papers, sir,' said Keedy.

'The impression given is that you're both floundering.'

'Appearances are deceptive,' said Marmion, easily. 'But let's leave the press to its own peculiar ways. We came here to ask you about Father Howells. I believe that you know him, Mr Fussell.'

'Yes – I've seen him here a number of times.'

'He's also a friend of yours, isn't he?'

'Everyone who comes into the library is a friend of mine. I make a point of fraternising with the readers. It's important to understand their needs and to be aware of their likes and dislikes.'

'You're avoiding the question, sir.'

Fussell looked blank. 'Am I?'

'You knew James Howells as a friend, didn't you?'

'We often had a chat when he came in here, Inspector.'

'And was the friendship no closer than that?'

'Why should it be?' asked Fussell.

'When we visited the house where he lives,' said Marmion, 'we found his address book. Your name was in it.'

'There's nothing unusual in that,' said Fussell, smoothly. 'James – Father Howells, that is – was a regular visitor here. It's not surprising that he kept the address of the library.'

'But that's not what he did,' said Keedy. 'He kept your *home* address.'

The librarian's face was impassive but his eyes flicked to and fro.

'Why did he do that, sir?' asked Marmion, watching him intently. 'Do you worship at St Leonard's, by any chance?'

'No, I do not,' said Fussell, stiffly. 'My wife and I are Roman Catholics.'

'Did you ever meet him socially?'

'What has this got to do with a violent attack in the night?'

'You're avoiding the question again, sir.'

'No,' retorted Fussell, 'I did not meet Father Howells socially. I have, by choice, a very limited social life. After a long day here, all that my wife and I wish to do is to have a quiet evening at home.'

'So you can't explain how your name got into that address book?'

'I don't have the foggiest idea.'

The reply was assertive and bolstered by a defiant glare. Marmion thanked him for his time and rose to his feet. Keedy got up to follow him out. As they strolled towards the door, they walked past Mrs Fussell and saw her avert her gaze from them. When they came out into the fresh air, Marmion turned enquiringly to Keedy.

'You were right,' said the other. 'I disliked him on sight as well.'

'Why did he lie about having his name in that address book?'

'That wasn't the *only* lie he told us, Harv. When we walked out, you must have noticed his wife.'

'Yes, she looked rather bored and unhappy.'

'I don't wish to be unkind,' said Keedy, 'but she's not the most attractive woman. She looks as if she'd be very dull company. For all his arrogance, Fussell has got a real spark in him. Could you really imagine him spending all his spare time at home with a wife like that?'

Maud Crowther placed the flowers in front of the headstone then stood back to gaze down at the inscription. She had made her weekly pilgrimage to the cemetery and was weighed down by sad thoughts of her late husband. After all this time, she missed him as much as ever. They'd been happily married for a long time. Lost in her memories, she stood there in silence for almost twenty minutes. When she finally turned away, she lifted her chin and pulled her shoulders back. Having paid her respects to her husband, she went in search of a friend.

Horrie Waldron was waist-deep in a grave. He was aware that Maud would pay her customary visit to the cemetery but he knew better than to interrupt her. If she wanted to talk, she'd come to him. As a rule, she simply went straight home without even seeing him. Today, it was different. She was anxious to find him. When he saw her walking along the gravel path, he clambered out of the grave and used his arms to semaphore. Maud spotted him and went across the grass.

'Good afternoon, Horrie,' she said.

He gave a sly grin. 'Nice to see you.'

'Have you heard the news?'

'I've done more than that, Maud. I've had the coppers out here after me.'

She was shocked. 'They surely don't think that *you* had something to do with it, do they?'

'They'd pin every crime on me, if they could,' he said, sourly. 'Just because I had a spot of bother with them once or twice, they blame me for every damn thing.'

'Did you mention me this time?'

'No, I didn't.'

'Good – I don't want them sniffing around my house again. It could get back to Stan,' she said, worriedly, 'and you know what would happen then. You'd need someone to dig *your* grave.'

Waldron cackled. 'It'd be worth it, Maud.'

'Don't be stupid. I'd lose my son's respect for ever.'

'Then we make sure Stan never finds out.'

'There's one simple way to do that,' she said, moving closer and clearing her throat. 'Look, Horrie, I've been thinking about this for some time. Maybe we should stop taking all these risks. It's silly at my age. I'm fed up with having to creep round and tell lies to everyone. The game is not worth the candle.'

His hackles rose. 'Are you trying to get rid of me?'

'We'd still be friends.'

'What about my . . . visits?'

'They'll have to stop.'

'But I don't want them to stop, Maud.'

'It's starting to get too dangerous.'

'Thought you liked danger,' he said, looming over her. 'It was all part of the fun.' When she tried to move away, he grabbed her wrist. 'You won't get rid of me as easily as that,' he warned. 'I'll be there at the usual time on the usual day. Is that clear?'

'You're hurting my wrist.'

'Is that clear?' he demanded, tightening his grip.

'I don't want you any more, Horrie,' she said, angrily.

His eyes flashed. 'Got no choice, have you?'

They got back to Scotland Yard to find a pile of putative witness statements awaiting them on Marmion's desk. They related to both crimes. One purported to come from the killer, taunting them with their inability to identify him. A second 'confession' came in the form of a crude cartoon with images of two victims being clubbed from behind. Other people did make a stab at naming the culprit. Among the suspects put forward was a gravedigger from Abney Park cemetery. The information about the second attack seemed more reliable. Three separate people claimed to have seen someone running out of the lane and down the street around the time when the curate had been bludgeoned to the ground. A woman who looked out of her bedroom window caught a glimpse of him as well. All they could see was a tall figure with long strides. He'd vanished into the night.

Marmion and Keedy were still discussing the dubious evidence when the superintendent breezed into the office. Chatfield demanded an instant report on how they'd spent their time. When he'd heard the details of their movements, he was disappointed by their apparent lack of progress.

'This will only give more ammunition to the press,' he grumbled.

'You've given them far too much already, sir,' said Marmion, reproachfully, 'and they fired it straight back at us. Why tell them that we were looking for one man when you had no actual proof of that? You were working entirely on supposition.'

'I was relying on my experience, Inspector.'

'Well, I'd advise more caution in the future. According to you, the curate was Cyril Ablatt by another name yet that's not what the vicar thinks.'

'And he should know,' Keedy interjected.

'The two of them are on opposite sides when it comes to the subject of conscientious objection to military service. That NCF leaflet misled you completely.'

Chatfield was unrepentant. 'I don't accept that.'

'In future,' said Marmion, 'I'd be grateful if you let me handle any press conferences. I am, after all, supposed to be in charge of the two cases. Isn't that why I was given the assignment – because I know how to handle reporters?'

'You were chosen against my wishes,' Chatfield reminded him, spitefully. 'And for the record, I, too, know how to keep the press in its place.'

'Then why did they launch that attack on us in the paper?' asked Keedy. 'It's not helpful when we're mocked like that. Thanks to you, the inspector came in for the heaviest criticism. We expect you to support us, sir, not offer us up as sacrifices.'

'That's enough, Sergeant!'

'Very well,' said the other, backing off, 'but at least you know how we feel.'

'I expect more deference from a junior officer.'

'Then you ought to earn it,' said Marmion under his breath. Aloud, he was placatory. 'There's no point in arguing about it. I'm sure it won't happen again and I'm sorry if the sergeant and I overstepped the mark, sir.'

'So you should be,' said Chatfield. 'What's the next move?'

'I think that we should probe a little deeper into Waldron's private life.'

'How will you do that, Inspector?'

'By taking a look at his digs,' said Marmion. 'To do that, we'll need you to get us a search warrant. I've got a strong feeling that Waldron is hiding something.'

Stroking his chin, the superintendent looked first at Marmion then at Keedy.

'I sometimes get that feeling about you two,' he said, darkly. 'It's bad enough when the public deliberately withholds evidence. When it's my own officers doing it, I resent it bitterly.' He regarded each of them in turn once more. His voice contained an unspecified threat. 'What are the two of you keeping from me?'

'Nothing, sir,' said Marmion, straight-faced.

'Nothing at all,' added Keedy. 'We wouldn't *dare*, Superintendent.'

Horrie Waldron ended his working day by rolling himself a cigarette and locking up his spade in the shed. As he trudged toward the main gate, he reflected on the visit of Maud Crowther. He'd been pleased to see her at first, knowing that she'd taken the trouble to seek him out. But her decision to end his visits to her house had been like a slap in the face. He'd retaliated in the only way that he knew. He regretted doing that now. Maud deserved better of him. She'd taken great risks on his behalf. If the truth came out, he'd escape with a few broken bones, but she'd never be able to look her son in the eye again. That was far worse than a beating. Waldron saw now that his menacing behaviour had been both ill-judged and unfair. A spirited woman like Maud Crowther couldn't be threatened. She had to be wooed and coaxed and stroked like a cat. Waldron needed a change of approach.

On the long walk home, he had plenty to think about. The first thing he had to do was to apologise and he could only do that in person. Barely literate, he'd never trust himself to find the right words for a letter. They'd need to speak but only after a lapse of time. When she walked away from the cemetery, Maud had been puce with anger and indignation. She needed time to calm down. Only then could Waldron even hope to wheedle himself back into her affections. To achieve the best result, the apology should be accompanied by a gift of some sort. That would absorb some of her ill feeling towards him. He spent the rest of the journey trying to choose a gift that would buy back her interest in him. While he accepted that he was only a diversion for her, Maud Crowther meant a great deal to Waldron. Only now that he'd lost her did he realise what she meant to him.

On his way home from work, he habitually called in at the Weavers Arms for the first pint of the evening. Stan Crowther served the beer then appraised him.

'You've spruced up a bit, Horrie,' he said.

'My other working clothes were starting to hoot a bit.'

'I noticed.'

Waldron looked around the empty bar. 'It's very quiet, Stan.'

'We won't see many people in here tonight,' complained the landlord. 'That bugger has scared them off. As long as he goes on cracking heads open, people will be too frightened to leave their houses in the dark.' The gravedigger made no comment. He took a long sip of his beer. 'Had a good day?'

'It was neither good nor bad.'

'My mother was going to the cemetery today to put flowers on Dad's grave. I don't suppose you bumped into her, did you?'

'No, Stan, I never laid eyes on her.'

'I think it's morbid myself – going back to a grave all the time.'

'It helps some people,' said Waldron, absently. 'I got nothing against it.'

'I've only been there once since Dad died.' When another customer came in, Crowther served him before turning back to the gravedigger.

'My mother should have got over it by now. That's what I keep telling her.'

'Women have got minds of their own, Stan.'

The landlord chuckled. 'You can say that again! I've been married for fifteen years now and I still can't guess what my wife is going to do and say. She never does what I expect her to. Is that your experience of women as well?'

'Yes,' said Waldron, ruefully. 'It certainly is.'

After finishing his pint, he put the tankard down and walked off to his digs. For some reason, spending the whole evening at the pub had lost its appeal. He felt the need to be alone. Waldron rented a small, dank, low-ceilinged basement room with a scullery attached to it, enabling him to make fairly basic meals. The scullery was also the place where he did his infrequent washing. He'd rigged up a line from one side of the room to the other. Hanging from it was the shirt, vest and pair of trousers he normally wore at work. Taking the trousers off the line, he held them up close to the light bulb so that he could examine them. Waldron let out a snarl of disappointment.

After a second wash, the bloodstains were still there.

CHAPTER SIXTEEN

London was never allowed to forget that there was a war on. Apart from the fact that uniformed soldiers and sailors were always visible on the streets, there was the accumulated bomb damage. Emergency services were kept at full stretch. They were on duty that evening as a fleet of Zeppelins came up the Thames, cruising at ten thousand feet like a flock of giant eagles in search of prey. Laden with bombs, they'd come to inflict another night of terror on the capital. They had, however, been spotted and aircraft from the Royal Flying Corps were dispatched to intercept them. London was treated to a thrilling exhibition of aerial combat, with the smaller, faster and more manoeuvrable British planes trying to fly above the airships in order to bomb them or to get within machine-gun range. The dark sky was a kaleidoscope of bright flashes and sudden explosions. The sound of bullets and destruction reverberated across the heavens. When a Zeppelin blew up with spectacular effect, it scattered debris over a wide area.

The noise could be heard all over the capital. Percy Fry was holding the reins as the horse pulled the cart through Bethnal Green, reacting nervously to the clamour in the sky. At the end of the working day, he was giving Jack Dalley a lift home. The blacksmith looked upwards.

'Listen to that, Perce,' he said. 'The Huns are back.'

'Those bloody Zeppelins are a menace.'

'They just keep on coming.'

They'd taken the cart because they had to deliver a gate they'd repaired for a customer. Fry intended to pick his wife up at Dalley's house to drive her back to the forge. He listened to the pandemonium with foreboding.

'It sounds as if it's getting closer.'

'Keep the bombs away from us,' said Dalley, staring upwards. 'We already have enough misery to cope with in our family.'

'I hope that Elaine has been able to help.'

'I'm sure she has, Perce. All that Nancy needs is someone to be there with her. To be honest, I'm glad that my brother-in-law went back to work. Having Nancy in his house all day was dragging him down.' He glanced across at Fry. 'It's very kind of your wife to take over, especially when she's not in the best of health.'

'She's bearing up, Jack.'

'What does the doctor say?'

'There's not much he can do, really,' said Fry, resignedly, 'and it's far too expensive for us to keep going back to him and trying new medicine. Elaine never complains. She grits her teeth and gets on with it. Having to help someone else is good for her in a way. It takes her mind off her own troubles.'

'When there's a death in the family, you need all the help you can get.'

'Count on us, Jack.'

'Thanks.'

As they picked their way through the streets, the distant commotion gradually diminished. The air raid seemed to be over and people were left to assess the damage, take the wounded off to hospital and douse any fires caused by incendiary bombs. The Zeppelins had retreated, still hounded by the British aircraft. Everyone knew that they'd soon be back. War now had an immediacy that was unthinkable in the early days of the conflict. Having invaded Belgium and penetrated into France, the enemy was now striking boldly at the very heart of Britain.

'How many more of our soldiers will have to die before it's all over?' asked Fry, pulling the horse to a halt to let traffic go past at a junction. 'It seems as if it could go on for ever.'

'I blame the politicians,' said Dalley, resentfully. 'They didn't put enough soldiers in the field at the very start. They were caught cold. Conscription should have been brought in a year ago. The only way to beat the Germans is with more men.'

'It'd help if we had better weapons and equipment as well.'

'What worries me is this poison gas they use. If it doesn't kill our lads, it blinds them and sets their lungs on fire. What happens if the Germans find a way to drop it in canisters over London?'

Fry pulled a face. 'I'd hate to find out, Jack.'

They continued to discuss the war until they eventually turned into the street where Dalley lived. Bringing the cart to a standstill, Fry got down onto the pavement and followed the blacksmith into the house. When they went into the front room, they saw Nancy Dalley on the settee with Fry's wife beside her, one arm around the stricken woman. Elaine was a pale, gaunt, almost skeletal creature with frizzy grey hair and large, staring eyes. Yet she was putting someone else's needs first. Both women were glad to see their respective husbands. Nancy got up and sought comfort in Dalley's brawny arms. Before he could ask her how she felt, the door opened and Caroline Skene entered with a pot of tea on a tray.

'Oh,' she said, smiling at the newcomers. 'You're back.' She put the tray on the table. 'I went to Gerald's house to see if I could be of any use but he wasn't there. So I came here instead.'

'And you're very welcome, Caroline,' said Dalley, turning to indicate Fry. 'You remember Percy, don't you?'

'Yes, we met at your daughter's wedding. Nancy has been showing me the photos of it.' She gave a nod. 'Hello, Mr Fry.'

'It's nice to see you again, Mrs Skene,' he said with a half-smile. 'And if there's another cup of tea going, I'll be happy to drink it.'

Harvey Marmion took control of the press conference that evening. Though he sat beside the inspector, Claude Chatfield was content to take on the role of an observer. Joe Keedy was seated on the other side of Marmion, always willing to learn from him the art of keeping reporters at bay. The trio of detectives had a lively audience. Hot on the heels of a murder there'd been a vicious attack on a clergyman. Everyone assumed that one man committed two crimes. Marmion disillusioned them.

'It's both foolish and misleading to link the two incidents as a certain newspaper has already done,' he warned, looking around the upturned faces. 'Granted, there are surface similarities. Both victims were young men who suffered bad head injuries, but there the resemblance ends. Cyril Ablatt was killed and mutilated at some unknown spot then brought to the place where his body was later found. In short, gentleman, we are looking for a killer who is both cautious and calculating.'

'And who has so far run rings around you, Inspector,' said a voice.

Marmion smiled. 'Thank you for that vote of confidence.' There was general laughter. 'The second attacker is very different. He takes chances. He struck when other people were still about – one of them actually interrupted him – so he failed in his purpose. That suggests to me that he's impulsive. Unlike Cyril Ablatt's killer, he doesn't plan carefully and bide his time. If you still think that we should be hunting one and the same man, ask yourselves this. If *you* had murdered someone and had the police in full cry after you, would you be reckless enough to commit a second crime in a place, and at a time, when you couldn't guarantee escaping unseen? People who get away with a murder tend to cover their tracks. They don't come back within days to take foolish risks.'

'Why was James Howells the target, Inspector?' asked a reporter.

'I was coming to that. Look closely at the two victims. If they were both the targets of the same man, you'd expect them to have a lot in common, but that's not true at all. They *knew* each other, of course. But they are a world away from being twins. In fact,' said Marmion with emphasis, 'the differences between them are far greater in number and in scope than any similarities.'

He gave a character sketch of both men, comparing the lives they led and the values they held. Keedy watched the reporters, slowly revising their reflex opinions about the second attack and recording the inspector's phrases in their notebooks. Marmion had won them back. He not only convinced them that the first investigation had made some significant advances, he persuaded them that important steps had already been taken to apprehend the man who attacked Howells. In the space of fifteen minutes, he'd ensured that Scotland Yard would have kinder headlines in the morning papers.

Questions came from all sides and they were asked with a degree of respect.

'Is it true that Father Howells is under police guard?'

'It is,' said Marmion. 'His attacker has unfinished business. I can't rule out the possibility that he might strike again.'

'Have any suspects been identified?'

'We have certain people in mind but I'm afraid that I'm unable to release names at this stage. We continue to seek the assistance of the public, however, and ask you to appeal for any information relating to the crimes.'

'What has the hospital said about Father Howells's condition?'

'The patient remains in a coma,' said Marmion. 'The latest bulletin describes his condition as stable. It appears that he's now out of danger. Naturally, I must bow to medical advice. When he recovers, I'll only be allowed to question him if the doctor deems it sensible.'

On the questions went for the best part of half an hour before Marmion called an end to the conference. The reporters rushed off to file their stories, each of them clutching a photograph of James Howells for publication. Marmion was left alone with Chatfield and Keedy.

'That was masterly, Inspector,' said Keedy.

'It's kind of you to say so,' returned Marmion.

'You were like the Pied Piper and they danced to your tune.'

Marmion laughed. 'If you don't mind, Sergeant, I'd rather not be the Pied Piper. If I remember the poem accurately, they refused to pay him.'

'Well done,' said Chatfield, reluctantly.

'Thank you, sir.'

'It was a study in the conjuror's art. You gave them the impression they'd seen something when it wasn't actually there. I can't do that, alas. I'm too fundamentally honest.'

'The inspector was not dishonest, sir,' said Keedy, loyally.

'Maybe not, but he flitted around the edges of it.'

'I'm glad that the reporter from the *Evening News* was rapped over the knuckles. What he wrote in the early edition was both unkind and untrue.'

'We can't control what they write, unfortunately,' said Chatfield. 'When it comes to war reporting, of course, there's strict censorship and some radical papers have been closed down altogether. The *Tribunal* is one of them – a dreadful rag that campaigned against conscription. It's important that the government monitors any information relating to the war so that the public is not misled. I'd like us to have similar powers when it comes to reporting crime.'

'I wouldn't go that far, sir,' said Marmion. 'I just hate press exaggeration, that's all. Newspapers should be reassuring the public, not frightening the living daylights out of them by turning these two cases into a sensation. Instead of vilification, we need their support. I think I rammed that point home.'

Chatfield was officious. 'Forget the press for a while,' he said. 'Let's turn to practicalities. Is your request for a search warrant an urgent one?'

'We'll need it in the morning, please,' said Marmion. 'The best time to go there is when Waldron is at work in the cemetery.'

'I do hope you find enough to justify an arrest.'

'So do we, Superintendent.'

'What of this other suspect?'

'Eric Fussell can be left alone for the moment,' decided Marmion, 'but he must remain under suspicion. While I may have pointed up the differences between the two victims, there are certain links between Ablatt and Howells. One of them is the librarian. We need to find out why.'

When he and his wife got back to their house in Lambeth that evening, Fussell went straight upstairs to the bedroom he used as an office. It was like a small replica of the one at the library, well ordered and stacked with books and magazines. He didn't come downstairs until the meal was on the dinner table. He and his wife sat in a cold silence intermittently broken by an observation about their day at the library. She didn't dare to ask about the visit from the detectives. It was a subject he refused to discuss. When the meal was over, he left her to clear everything away.

'I'm going out,' he said, taking his overcoat from its peg.

She was hurt. 'You're going out *again*, Eric?'

'Yes – and I can't say when I'll be back.'

Gerald Ablatt was pleased when he had an unheralded visitor. Since he'd got back from the shop, all that he'd done was to sit in the kitchen and read the *Evening News*. The report of the latest crime had depressed him. His spirits rose slightly when Caroline Skene called. Inviting her in, he took her into the living room and they sat side by side.

'I didn't expect to see you again,' he said.

'I came earlier but you weren't here. One of your neighbours told me that you'd opened the shop. I couldn't believe it.'

'It's true. I had to get out, Caroline. I just couldn't stay here and brood. It was too painful. I needed to work, and, if I'm truthful,' he confided, 'I needed to get away from Nancy for a while.'

'Then you did the right thing, Gerald.'

'I'm sorry you had a wasted journey.'

'But I didn't,' she said, brightly. 'Since I was in Shoreditch, I thought I'd go and call on Nancy instead. I spent the afternoon there with Mrs Fry.'

He was puzzled. 'Elaine Fry – what was she doing there?'

'She'd come to sit with Nancy to offer consolation. Apparently, it was Jack's idea. He asked if she could go over there.'

'How did she seem?'

'Frankly, she looked ill. The woman is quite haggard.'

'I know,' said Ablatt, deeply sympathetic. 'The last time I saw her was at Nora's wedding last year and she was almost at death's door then. Well, you were there. You must remember how she had to keep sitting down.'

'What I recall is that her husband was very attentive.'

'He needs to be. Percy Fry is a good man. He carries his troubles lightly.'

'Does he?'

'It's not just the sick wife, Caroline. They lost their only child as well.'

She was taken aback. 'When was this?'

'Oh, it was years ago,' he explained. 'The boy was no more than nine or ten at the time. He died of rickets. He just wasted away as his mother seems to be doing. She blamed herself, of course.'

'Most mothers would. They'd think it was because of a deficiency in them.'

'I don't know the full details. According to Jack, they don't like to talk about it and I can understand that. But it makes it all the more remarkable that a woman who nurses a lasting sorrow could find time to comfort my sister.'

'You know her better than I do, Gerald.'

'I knew them both when they lived nearby,' he said. 'Elaine was a customer of mine. I used to sole and heel her shoes but Percy always repaired his boots himself. He's that kind of man – very independent. He's a bit like your husband.'

She raised an eyebrow. 'Oh, I don't know about that.'

'Wilf always liked to do things for himself.'

'That wasn't because he was independent. It was simple, old-fashioned meanness. He gets it from his mother. Wilf would never part with a penny unless he has to,' she said, lips pursed. 'He'd always rather do things himself, whether it's mending shoes or cleaning windows or sweeping the chimney. The trouble is he can't do any of them properly. Still,' she continued, lowering her voice, 'while we have a moment alone, there's something we need to discuss.'

'What's that, Caroline?'

'It's the funeral – have you had any thoughts about it?'

'No,' he replied, a little flustered by the question. 'The body hasn't been released to us yet.'

'What about Nancy?'

'She's in no state to make any decisions.'

'Then you'll have to choose the hymns and the order of service.' Ablatt looked bewildered. 'Unless you'd like some help, that is? I didn't know Cyril that well,' she said, softly, 'but I was very fond of him and I'll do anything I can to help with the arrangements.'

'I see.'

'I'm not trying to interfere, Gerald. If you'd rather do everything yourself, I'll stay out of your way.'

'No, no,' he said, reaching out to take her hand. 'It's kind of you to offer. I need help from someone – thank you, Caroline.'

She sighed with satisfaction. 'That's settled, then.'

'The truth is that I'm all at sea at the moment. I was going to ask the vicar what to do.' He sighed. 'It's strange the way things work out, isn't it?'

'I don't understand.'

'Cyril never expected to die, of course, so he couldn't plan ahead for his own funeral. If he'd done so, my guess is that he'd have wanted Father Howells to take the service rather than the vicar.' He glanced sorrowfully at the newspaper. 'But that's not possible now, is it?'

The Reverend James Howells lay on the bed while a nurse took his blood pressure. Head heavily bandaged, he had various tubes attached to him and was under almost constant supervision. His parents were in the nearby waiting room, hoping for the slightest improvement. The vicar was with them, offering succour, leading them in prayer and telling them time and again what an asset their son was to the parish. Cards and messages of goodwill had come flooding in by hand, showing the anguished parents how popular the curate had been. Only close family members were allowed to visit the single room where the patient was kept, but that didn't stop a stranger from slipping into the hospital and finding out his whereabouts. Wearing a white coat by way of disguise, he lurked in an alcove from which he could keep the room under close observation. When a doctor and nurse emerged before going off in the other direction, he saw his opportunity and moved swiftly forward.

Before he reached the room, however, the door opened and a third person came out. Legs apart and hands behind his back, the uniformed constable was there to prevent any unauthorised visits. The stranger was baulked. As he walked past the policeman, he manufactured a smile.

'Good evening,' he said, pleasantly.

Then he headed for the nearest exit.

Gordon Leach felt as if he were being crushed between two millstones. On one side of him was Mansel Price and on the other was Fred Hambridge. The three friends were in the bakery, discussing the forthcoming marriage. Price was unequivocal. If Leach betrayed his principles and joined a non-combatant corps, the Welshman threatened to assault him. Hambridge took a more reasoned approach but his quiet reprimands were just as wounding as Price's belligerence. The two of them kept on at Leach until the latter could take no more.

'That's enough!' he yelled. 'You've made your point.'

'So what's your decision?' asked Hambridge.

'Gordon has got to tell Ruby that he can't do it,' said Price. 'I don't know why he didn't have the guts to do that when she came up with the idea.'

'It wasn't Ruby's idea,' said Leach. 'It was her father's. Mr Cosgrove was only trying to find a compromise.'

'Remember what Cyril used to say. We never compromise.'

Leach was outnumbered. With Ablatt resurrected, he was up against three of them and his resistance cracked. It had been an article of faith for all four of them that they wouldn't assist the war effort in any way. Joining a non-combatant corps would, in essence, be almost as bad as joining the army. It was easy for Price and Hambridge to maintain their extreme position. They only had to think of themselves. Price's family lived in Wales and took little interest in him. Hambridge's parents supported him in his stance. Leach's situation was more complicated. After apparently being spurned by Ruby, he'd been forgiven in the wake of the attack on the curate. She'd been so concerned for his safety that she came to assure him that she still wanted to marry him and that there was a way to do it that could be reconciled with his pacifist beliefs. What would Ruby say if he rejected the compromise suggested by her father? Would he lose her altogether? What had brought her running to him was a combination of love and fear. If he sided with his friends, Leach might well be sacrificing her love while doing nothing to allay her fear. He was impaled on the horns of a dilemma. All that he could do was to squirm in agony.

Hambridge's softly spoken question was like a stab in the ribs.

'What are you going to do, Gordon?'

'I don't know.'

'You don't *know*,' echoed Price with lip-curling disgust. 'You've spent all this time with Fred, Cyril and me, boasting that you'd never, in a hundred years, join the army, yet you're ready to serve in a non-combatant corps.'

'I didn't say that, Mansel. I'm still thinking it over.'

'What is there to think over?'

'And don't get the wrong idea about a non-combatant corps,' cautioned Hambridge. 'I've got a friend who joined one of those. They sent him off to Belgium as part of an ambulance unit. He spends all his time carrying wounded soldiers on a stretcher. If that's not taking part in the war – then what is?'

'There's another thing, Gordon. Suppose you get sent to the front like that. Do you think the commanding officer will give a monkey's fuck for your wedding plans? He needs every man he's got,' said Price. 'He's not going to release you so that you can get married and have a wonderful honeymoon. You're going to be stuck in some godforsaken place with no chance of even seeing Ruby, let alone jumping into bed with her at long last.'

'Shut up!' howled Leach. 'Let's keep Ruby out of this.'

'But she's the bloody problem.'

'Be quiet, Mansel.'

'Who's going to wear the trousers in the marriage – you or Ruby Cosgrove?'

Leach was on his feet. 'I told you to shut up!'

'Who's going to make me?' demanded Price, getting up.

'I am.'

Leach exploded and grappled with the Welshman. Before they could get in any punches, however, they were each grabbed by the neck and pulled roughly apart by Hambridge. He was seething with fury.

'That's enough!' he bellowed. 'We're *friends*, for heaven's sake! Is this the way to behave? We're supposed to be in this together. Act like it, the pair of you!'

On his way to the hospital, Marmion nursed the faint hope that James Howells might have regained consciousness and been ready to give him some idea who might have been responsible for the attack. In reality, he knew that it rarely happened like that. He'd seen other victims who'd sustained appalling head wounds. Most of them had been unable to remember the moment of attack, let alone speculate on who was behind it. Earlier that year, there'd been the case of a man who was deliberately knocked down by the driver of a motor car. Although he survived, brain damage was so serious that the victim couldn't even speak and was doomed to spend the rest of his life trapped in a private world. Marmion hoped that the curate would escape that fate.

The news at the hospital was not encouraging. The patient was stable but there'd been no marked improvement. He needed more time and continuous care. Marmion spoke to the constable on duty outside the room. The man had just started the night shift. Marmion felt that it was unlikely the attacker would make a second attempt to kill Father Howells but he didn't wish to take any chances. He was pleased to hear that the curate's parents had finally been persuaded to leave. At the invitation of Simon Ellway, they were staying the night at the vicarage. Marmion suspected that Mr and Mrs Howells would be back in the waiting room shortly after breakfast on the following day. Since there was nothing else he could do at the hospital, he was given a lift home in a police car. His wife was still up, delighted at his comparatively early return.

'This is a nice surprise!' said Ellen, giving him a welcoming kiss.

'I'll have to be off again at the crack of dawn, love.'

'At least you're back in time to be fed. And while you're waiting, I've got a treat for you.' She slipped a hand into the pocket of her dressing gown. 'We had a letter from Paul.'

'Wonderful!' he said, taking it from her.

While she made a pot of tea and got out bread and cheese from the pantry, he read the letter avidly, relieved that their son was unharmed. The letter was full of complaints about the privations on the front but it was also reassuring. Absorbing every detail, he read it through three times. Over their supper, he told her a little about the events of the day and was grateful that she hadn't read the barbed criticism of him in the *Evening News*. Ellen was more interested in family matters. She talked about their son's letter and about their daughter's flying visit that morning.

'How was she?' asked Marmion, slicing off some more cheese.

'Alice was in a mad rush as usual.'

'They certainly keep her on her toes in the WEC.'

'She only came to collect a few things from her room.'

'I don't believe that,' said Marmion. 'It was just an excuse to see her mother.'

'Well, she didn't see very much of me, Harvey. She was in and out in a flash – though she did stay long enough to ask if we could take in a Belgian refugee.'

He blinked. 'What? Where the hell would he sleep?'

'Alice said they could have her bedroom,' replied Ellen, sadly. 'It was another way of saying that she's not going to be living here again.'

'She's over twenty-one, love. If that's her decision, we must accept it.'

'I know but you can't blame me for hoping. It was bad enough when Paul left. Now that Alice has gone as well, it's like a morgue in here.'

He laughed. 'I see. So I'm the resident corpse, am I?'

'You know what I mean, Harvey. The place is dead.'

'It's not as if you're here all day, love. You're out doing voluntary work most of the week. I'm very proud of you for helping the war effort. Paul and Alice are doing it in more obvious ways,' he conceded, 'but I don't underestimate what you and women like you are doing on the home front.'

'Thank you,' she said, cheered by the compliment. 'Anyway, there's something else I must tell you about Alice's visit. I could be wrong, of course, but I had this feeling about her.'

'What sort of a feeling?'

'I think that she has a chap.'

'Oh? Did she admit it?'

'No, Harvey. In fact, she denied it strongly but . . . I sort of sensed it.'

'You've had a lot of experience of doing that and you're usually right.'

'I'd love to know who he is.'

'We're not entirely sure that he exists yet,' Marmion reminded her, 'so don't jump the gun. All we have at the moment is your intuition, reliable as it is.'

'Alice was so happy. That's what gave her away.'

'I thought that *I* was supposed to be the detective.'

She smiled confidingly. 'Who do you think it could be?'

'I don't know, love,' he replied, swallowing his food. 'When Alice is good and ready, I'm sure that she'll tell us. Frankly, I hope that she *does* have some kind of social life. She's earned it. And as I said earlier, she's over twenty-one. Our daughter can do whatever she likes.'

Alice Marmion was propped up in bed with a book in her hands. She was trying to read but the romantic novel that Vera Dowling had lent her was failing to hold her attention. Her mind kept wandering to Joe Keedy. The fact that he'd rescued her from an assault had served to strengthen her feelings for him. Alice had travelled home in some trepidation that evening, fearing that the same man might stalk her again. Glad to see that he was not on the bus, she was afraid that he might be lurking near her stop in order to follow her. But there was no sign of him and she was very grateful. Had there been a second attack, Keedy would not have been there to rescue her. At his suggestion, she kept a pair of nail scissors in her pocket but they were not needed.

She'd always been fond of him. When she first met him, she was a callow teenager and he was a young detective constable in his twenties. Her father had seen promise in him and advised him to push for promotion. As the two men began to work together on cases, Alice saw rather more of Keedy and her affection for him slowly intensified. It was matched by her mother's fondness for him and – in spite of the age gap between them – Ellen had hinted that the sergeant and her daughter would be a good match. Because that opinion wasn't shared by Marmion, it was never voiced in his presence. Alice knew he'd disapprove of it on a number of counts.

It had taken her by surprise. From the time that she first met him, Keedy had always had an attractive girlfriend. Some of them lasted for months and one even survived for over a year. Since he appeared to be spoken for, Alice had never seriously entertained the possibility of a relationship with him. They then discovered just how much they liked each other. In the nature of things, their jobs kept them apart but their occasional secret meetings were always more than pleasant and left her with an urge to see him again. Keeping the friendship from Vera Dowling wasn't difficult. She wasn't blessed with sharp instincts. Her mother, however, had had her suspicions aroused and Alice fancied that Hannah Billington was aware that her young protégée might have a man in her life. The maddening thing was that she was unable to tell anyone about Keedy. Until she could do that, the whole thing seemed faintly unreal.

Alice made an effort to dismiss him from her thoughts. On the following day, she was due to go to tea at Hannah's house. That would be a treat, not merely because she liked the woman. She was curious to see where and how someone from a very different class lived. Vera had been shocked to hear that Hannah had released two of her servants to join the army, retaining only a cook-housekeeper. The idea that anyone could have domestic staff was beyond Vera's comprehension. Until she'd joined the WEC, she'd never met a woman in a position to employ them. Now that she had, she was tongue-tied in her presence, whereas Alice found Hannah very engaging. She snatched at the opportunity to get an insight into the older woman's private life. Alice smiled with anticipatory pleasure.

Her reverie was cut short by a sound she could not at first identify. It was a gentle tap but she couldn't work out from where it came. When it happened again, however, she heard it more clearly and realised that something had just tapped on the window of her room. Jumping out of bed, she ran to pull back a curtain. Down below in the garden, Alice could just make out the figure of a man. Her heart began to pound. The only person who would try to contact her at that late hour was Joe Keedy. Leaving the curtain half-drawn to indicate that she knew he was there, she dressed as fast as she could then crept out onto the landing. Alice moved with great stealth. If her landlady realised what one of her tenants was doing, she'd accuse her of breaking one of the cardinal rules of the house. Alice would be lucky to retain the accommodation. She therefore needed to move with an absolute minimum of noise.

When she got to the front door, she paused to make sure that nobody had been roused. Alice then let herself out and walked furtively around to the garden. But Keedy was not there. Had it been a mirage? Or was he teasing her? Either way, she was overwhelmed with disappointment. She was just about to creep back to the front door when a hand shot out to pull her behind some bushes. Before she could speak, a palm was placed over her mouth. When she recognised Keedy in the gloom, her whole body ignited with joy. He moved his hand so that she could speak.

'I didn't dare to hope that you'd be here again,' she said.

He shrugged. 'I just happened to be passing.'

Then he took her in his arms and kissed her.

CHAPTER SEVENTEEN

For a man with crimes to solve and administrative problems to tax him, Claude Chatfield had a strangely contented air that morning. Harvey Marmion soon learnt why. Spread out on the superintendent's desk was an array of national newspapers. Priority on the front pages had been given to the latest developments in the war but there was extensive coverage elsewhere of the murderous attack on the Reverend James Howells. To a man, reporters painted a more favourable picture of the activities of Scotland Yard with regard to the two investigations. Marmion was given credit for the tireless dedication he'd so far shown and the superintendent was also praised. As soon as the inspector walked into his office, Chatfield thrust the newspapers at him. Marmion was pleased to see that, after the censure in the *Evening News* on the previous day, he'd been largely exonerated. He was also amused that the superintendent was commended for putting him in charge of the investigation when Chatfield had, in reality, opposed the appointment.

'What do you think of that?' asked Chatfield, complacently.

'Praise is better than condemnation, sir,' replied Marmion, 'but the fact remains that we haven't actually solved either of the crimes. Only when that's done should we receive any plaudits.'

'It's a question of appearance. This makes us look good.'

'Looking good is not necessarily the same as *being* good.'

'Don't quibble, man.'

'I don't feel that we deserve these plaudits yet, sir.'

'We're in the public eye, Inspector. This kind of window dressing is always to our advantage. With a depleted force having to police a city the size of London, we need all the help we can get from the press.' He took the papers back and put them on his desk. 'When and if you ever rise to the level of superintendent,' he went on, loftily, 'you'll come to appreciate that.'

Marmion ignored the jibe. 'I'm sure you're right, sir.'

'What are your plans for today?'

'I want to start with another visit to the hospital,' said Marmion. 'Father Howells's parents were in too fragile a state to be interviewed yesterday. I'd like to ask them how much they knew about their son's private life. It might yield some clues for us to pursue. After that, I hope, you'll have secured that search warrant for us.'

'It will be ready and waiting, Inspector.'

'Then Sergeant Keedy and I will visit Waldron's house.'

'Let me know if you discover anything of significance.'

After explaining how he intended to spend the rest of the day, Marmion went off to his own office where he found Joe Keedy waiting. The sergeant was studying the map of London that lay on the desk.

'One thing about this job,' he said. 'It certainly gives you plenty of geography lessons. I think I could find my way around Shoreditch blindfold.'

'I'm waiting for the moment when we take the blindfolds *off*, Joe, because I feel that there's something we're simply not seeing as yet.'

'Have you talked to Chat yet?'

'Yes,' said Marmion. 'I left him basking in the praise he's received in the morning papers. He got a pat on the back for assigning us to the case.'

'But we were never his first choice.'

'That doesn't matter. He's probably busy with the scissors right now, cutting out the articles for his scrapbook. He's a walking paradox – a man who hates the press yet who hangs on every kind word they say about him.'

'Well, he won't get any kind words from me,' said Keedy, forcefully. 'I'll never forgive him for getting promotion ahead of you. You're twice the detective he is.'

'That's water under the bridge.'

'I'm not as forgiving as you, Harv.'

As Keedy folded up the map again, he noticed a slip of paper that had been hidden beneath it. He reached out to pick it up.

'Sorry about that,' he said. 'I forgot there was a message for you.'

Marmion took it from him. 'Thank you,' he said, reading the two short lines. 'This could be important.'

'Is it from the hospital?'

'No, Joe, it's from Mrs Skene. She rang from Lambeth police station half an hour ago. If she's that keen to speak to me, it must be urgent.'

'Do you want to go straight there?'

'The hospital and the search come first,' decided Marmion. 'Mrs Skene will have to wait her turn in the queue. Let's go.'

They left the office and walked side by side down the corridor.

'I bet Ellen was pleased to see you home a bit earlier last night,' said Keedy.

'Yes, I got a warm welcome.'

'How is she?'

'I suppose that "long-suffering" is the best way to describe her. But that's true of all police wives. She had one piece of good news for me – a letter from Paul. We hadn't heard from him in ages and Ellen was starting to worry.'

He told Keedy about the contents of the letter and how it could be read in different ways. While his wife had been heartened by its apparently positive tone, Marmion had noticed the hints of despair between the lines. In his judgement, their son was bored, depressed and angered by the futility of war. Of the friends with whom he'd joined up so enthusiastically at the outbreak of hostilities, over half were either dead or wounded. It was a sobering statistic.

'Luckily,' said Marmion, 'Ellen was simply happy that he's alive and well. She was thrilled to hear that Paul was in line for a promotion. Like any other mother, she clings to good news like a limpet.'

Keedy was cynical. 'Is there any good news about the war?'

'That's a fair point.'

'Look how many policemen who joined up have been killed in action. What must their families think of the efforts we're putting in on behalf of a conchie?'

'You know the answer to that,' said Marmion, not wishing to rehearse a familiar argument once more. 'Oh, there was something else that Ellen had been saving up to tell me.'

'What was that?'

'She thinks that Alice has a new chap in her life.'

'Is that surprising? She's an attractive young woman.'

'Yes, but she's always confided in her mother in the past. When she was asked directly about it, Alice denied there was anyone this time.'

'Then perhaps your wife is wrong,' said Keedy.

He already knew about Ellen's suspicions because Alice had told him about the exchange with her mother. Keedy was anxious to guide

Marmion away from the subject because he found the subterfuge difficult. Besides, he still considered himself no more than a good friend of Alice Marmion. Though he'd recently seen her twice in succession, their meetings were too infrequent for anything more serious to develop. That, at least, was what he told himself.

'When it comes to men,' said Marmion with a grin, 'Ellen is never wrong.'

'What makes you say that?'

'She married me, didn't she?'

Maud Crowther was a creature of habit. Having run the Weavers Arms with her husband for so many years, she was accustomed to working long hours in the public gaze. She took pride in her appearance and would never venture outside the house until she'd curled her hair, applied her make-up and put on smart clothing. As she examined herself in the mirror that morning, she could hear the cat crying to be let in but she made him wait until she was satisfied with the way she looked. When she did finally open the front door, the animal darted in through her legs and scurried off to the kitchen to eat the food she'd put in his bowl. Maud, meanwhile, was transfixed. On the doorstep in front of her was a large bunch of flowers. She had no idea who'd left them there or why. Scooping them up, she inhaled their fragrance and smiled. When she took them into the house to put in a vase, she realised that there was a card tucked in among the blooms. On it, in a rough scrawl, was a single word.

Sorry.

'Horrie Waldron!' she said to herself. 'You old rogue.'

News at the hospital was better than expected. The Reverend James Howells had shown the first signs of regaining consciousness. His eyelids had flickered and his lips had started to move as if he was trying to say something. It was still too early for the detectives to talk to him but they were pleased with the improvement in his condition. Marmion asked the doctor in charge of the case to contact Scotland Yard the moment that the patient was able to speak. Though no interlopers had so far been spotted, the policeman was kept on duty outside the room. Marmion always put safety first.

He and Keedy talked to the curate's parents but learnt nothing from them that they hadn't already gleaned from the vicar. Their son kept in regular contact with them by letter but his private life was largely a mystery to them. They, too, were bolstered by the news from the doctor and were eager to be allowed to see the patient again. The detectives left them in the waiting room and drove back to Scotland Yard where Chatfield – true to his word – had a search warrant for them. In the event, it proved unnecessary. When they got to Waldron's address, the landlord admitted them without even asking to see the warrant.

A big, shambling, flat-faced man, he was clearly used to his tenant's uneasy relationship with the police and was prepared to tolerate it. Indeed, he had the look of someone who'd had his own brushes with the law and who therefore took any visits from detectives in his stride. After warning them about the smell they'd encounter, he unlocked the basement door and left them to it. They were met by the stink of leftover food, unwashed dishes and rising damp. Keedy opened a window to let in fresh air, noting that the glass hadn't been cleaned in ages.

'This is more of a lair than anything else,' he complained.

'It's probably all that he can afford, Joe.'

'How can anyone live in conditions like these?'

'Thousands of people do,' said Marmion, 'all over London.'

Their search did not take long because Waldron owned little in the way of clothing and nothing in the way of luxuries. His room contained a low bed, a chest of drawers, an upright chair and a wardrobe with scratches on the doors. Tucked away in a drawer they found a couple of shirts, some detached collars, two pairs of socks in need of darning, threadbare underwear, a pack of cards and some tobacco. The only real surprise was in the wardrobe where a new suit hung beside an old coat and a pair of corduroy trousers, shiny through overuse. Also in there was a pair of black shoes and a lone tie. To their amazement, the shoes had been polished to a high sheen.

'I'll bet he doesn't wear *those* at the cemetery,' opined Keedy.

'No,' agreed Marmion, 'he saves them for a special occasion and I think we both know what it might be.'

Keedy laughed in astonishment. 'He wears that suit when he goes calling on Maud Crowther. That's why it's here.' He felt the material. 'It's good quality.'

'Then the probability is that she bought it for him. Waldron could never pay for a bespoke tailor. The rest of his clothing looks like hand-me-downs.'

They turned their attention to the scullery. The larder was almost bare and the drawer beside the sink had only a few items of cutlery. Unwashed plates lay on the table. Potato peelings and other kitchen waste stood in an enamel bowl. It was the trousers that made their visit worthwhile. Taken down from the line, they were now draped over the back of a chair. When he picked them up, Marmion could feel that they were still damp. He held them up to the window and saw the marks on the knees and the shins.

'What do you think these are, Joe?' he asked.

'Bloodstains.'

'Ask him how they got there.'

The first customer was waiting outside the forge for them. While Jack Dalley unlocked the door and dealt with the man, Percy Fry unharnessed the horse and led him into the stable. He then started work beside his boss. Having driven his wife across to Dalley's house, Fry had brought him back to Bethnal Green on the cart, a journey that took longer than usual because of heavy traffic. They were both kept busy for hours. Since Elaine Fry was not there, they missed the mid-morning cup of tea that she always brought them. Instead, it was Fry himself who had to make it. When he came back downstairs with the tea, the two men took a break.

'It was considerate of Elaine to come again,' said Dalley, 'and I know that Nancy will appreciate it, but I'm not sure that it was wise. Your wife looked as if she ought to have stayed in bed, Perce.'

'Elaine will perk up as the day wears on.'

'We don't want to impose on her.'

'She was keen to go, Jack. She felt that she was able to help yesterday.'

'Oh, she did – no question about that.'

'Don't worry about her,' said Fry. 'Elaine had plenty of rest last night. In fact, she went to bed almost as soon as we got back yesterday. She sleeps like a baby for ten or eleven hours at a stretch.'

Dalley sipped his tea. 'I wish that Nancy could do that,' he said, soulfully. 'She's exhausted. She hasn't had a proper sleep since we heard the news. And that means *I* have to stay awake most of the night with her. It's wearing me out.'

'You could always take another day off.'

'No thanks, Perce. I'm like my brother-in-law. I'm only happy when I'm doing something. If I stay at home, I have to listen to Nancy saying the same thing over and over again. That's why I'm so grateful to your wife.'

'What about that other lady?' asked Fry, before draining his cup with a loud slurping noise. 'Is Mrs Skene going to be there today?'

'I've no idea,' replied Dalley. 'I never expected her to turn up yesterday.

276

Caroline is a good-hearted woman but we haven't seen all that much of her in the past. That's not to say she isn't welcome,' he added, quickly. 'Nancy told me how kind she'd been.'

'Elaine said the same thing about her.'

'Women are so much better at comforting someone in distress. Like most men, I suppose, I just don't know what to do. I always feel as if I'm in the way. My nephew was battered to death yet somehow I couldn't find the right words to say to his father.' He hunched his broad shoulders. 'I felt sort of embarrassed. That's why I prefer to leave the comforting to people like your wife and Nancy's cousin. It seems to come naturally to them.'

Caroline Skene was in need of comfort herself at that moment in time. Pacing up and down the front room, she kept pausing to peer out of the window. Her teeth were clenched, her brow corrugated and her mind ablaze. She couldn't understand why her summons had not been answered. Putting her trust in Marmion, she expected him to respond instantly. Yet it was almost two hours since she made the phone call and he still hadn't appeared. Was he deliberately keeping her waiting? Or could it be that he'd ignored her request altogether? The thought went through her like an electric shock. Marmion was the one person who could help her. If he abandoned her, she would have nobody to whom she could turn.

It was only when she was alone that she was able to mourn properly. In front of her husband, all that she could show was her natural grief over the death of a relative. Marmion was the one person who'd had some insight into the intense pain she felt over the loss of a young lover. He'd been sympathetic and refrained from even the slightest criticism of her adultery. His sole interest was in solving the crime. He was not there to question her behaviour. That had enabled her to confide in him things that she would never divulge to anyone else.

As she was hit by another wave of grief, she sank down onto the settee. A second later, she jumped to her feet as she heard the sound of a car pulling up outside the house. Caroline ran to the window, saw Marmion getting out of the vehicle and went straight to the front door. When she opened it, she didn't even hear his apology for being delayed. She simply burst into tears and went into his arms. Easing her gently back, he closed the door then guided her to the front room. He lowered her onto the settee and sat beside her.

'Thank God you came!' she said, grasping his wrist.

'I wish I could have been here earlier, Mrs Skene,' he said, looking into the frightened eyes. 'Why did you want to see me?'

'It's a long story, Inspector.'

'I've got plenty of time to listen.'

'Something terrible happened yesterday,' she told him. 'I spent some of it with my cousin, Nancy, trying to calm her down. Then I called on Gerald – that's Cyril's father – and stayed a couple of hours with him. I must have left around eight o'clock to make my way back here.'

'Go on, Mrs Skene,' he said.

'I was followed. I didn't notice anything until I got back to Lambeth, but then I had this prickly feeling that someone was watching me. When I got to the corner of the street, I turned round sharply and saw him move behind a lamp post. I lost my nerve completely then,' she admitted, 'and ran all the way here. It was the most awful feeling, Inspector.'

'Was your husband at home?'

'Yes – Wilf was here. He's on early morning shifts this week.'

'Did you tell him what had happened?'

'Of course not,' she said. 'He didn't even notice that I was upset. If I'd told my husband, I'd have had to explain why I was followed.'

'A woman on her own is always at risk of arousing someone's unwanted interest,' said Marmion, disappointed that she had nothing more serious to report to him. 'I'm sorry that you were bothered in that way.'

'You don't understand, Inspector. It's not the first time.'

'What do you mean?'

'It's happened before but . . . I never really noticed it then. When you're with someone you love,' she went on, eyes filming over again, 'you block out everything else. All I could see – and all I *wanted* to see – was Cyril.'

'How do you know that it's happened before?'

'I began to remember odd incidents. For example, there was a time when Cyril and I met in a church. I know you'll think badly of me for doing something like that,' she said, hastily, 'but it was the only place we could be together for a little while. We just sat in a pew at the back and held hands – there was nothing more than that.'

'You don't have to justify it, Mrs Skene. Tell me about being followed.'

'It was as we came out,' she recalled. 'I saw someone on the opposite side of the road who looked vaguely familiar and it crossed my mind briefly that I might have seen him earlier when we first met that evening. But,' she continued, 'I was enjoying the pleasure of being with Cyril so much that I thought no more about it.'

'And you say that there were other instances?'

'I think so, Inspector, but I can't be sure.'

'What about yesterday? Was the person who stalked you the same man you saw when you came out of that church?'

'I couldn't say. On both occasions, I only got a glimpse of him. But there was no doubt about what happened yesterday. I was followed back home. It can only mean one thing,' she concluded. 'Someone *knows* about me and Cyril.'

'Yet you took great care to be discreet.'

'Maybe we weren't discreet enough. Maybe someone saw him coming into this house or leaving it. We were certainly seen together outside that church.'

Marmion pondered. He'd been tempted at first to dismiss her tale as coming from an overheated imagination. The note of hysteria in her voice suggested a woman on the verge of nervous collapse. The more she talked, however, the calmer she sounded and he came to accept that there could well have been recurring instances of surveillance that might have culminated in the murder of Cyril Ablatt. She'd released his wrist now and sat there awaiting his advice.

'I'd like you to do something for me, Mrs Skene,' he said. 'Get paper and pencil then rack your brains. I want you to write down a list of other times when you thought – or had a fleeting suspicion – that the two of you were being watched. If there are enough occasions, we may be able to see a pattern.'

Her face crumpled. 'I'm terrified, Inspector.'

'That's understandable.'

'As soon as my husband left for work this morning, I went to the police station to ring you. When I lost Cyril, I didn't think that anything could be worse. But it looks as if it can. Someone has already killed Cyril,' she said with a shiver, 'and now he's after *me*.'

Keedy had been dropped off at the cemetery. He thought it would be an easy task to locate and arrest Horrie Waldron but he was mistaken. The problem was that the gravedigger saw him first and played hide-and-seek with him. His detailed knowledge of the cemetery allowed him to stay one step ahead of the sergeant. When he realised what was happening, Keedy pretended to give up and walked towards the main entrance. As soon as he reached cover, however, he doubled back in a wide circle. Concealing himself behind a statue, he bided his time until Waldron eventually came back in sight. Keedy gave him a few minutes before sprinting across the turf and grabbing him from behind.

'Don't run off this time, Horrie,' he warned.

'Let go of me.'

'If you try to get away again, I'll handcuff you.' Keedy released him. 'I've come to place you under arrest.'

Waldron was outraged. 'What the hell for?'

'It's no good playing the innocent. We searched that hole you live in.'

'You got no right to do that.'

'It was legal and above board. We had a warrant.'

'You've got a bloody cheek, if you ask me.'

'I'm glad that you mentioned blood,' said Keedy. 'We found the stains you tried to wash off from your trousers.'

'They weren't bloodstains,' said Waldron, wildly. 'I spilt some tomato sauce on them, that's all.'

'You were trying to remove the evidence of your attack on Cyril Ablatt.'

'That's ridiculous!'

'Let's discuss it when we've got you in custody, shall we?'

'You got to believe me, Sergeant. I never laid a finger on Ablatt.'

Keedy was impervious to his protestations. After reading him his rights, he arrested him and invited Waldron to go with him. The gravedigger held his ground as he weighed up the possibilities. In the end, he seemed to give up and let his head fall to his chest. Without warning, he then gave Keedy a firm push and ran off in the opposite direction, darting between the headstones as if the devil was at his heels. Annoyed at the deception, Keedy gave chase, his greater energy and his longer strides eating up the distance between them. Waldron could hear the footsteps getting closer and closer. He put all his strength into an extra burst but it was in vain. Keedy matched it effortlessly and got close enough to dive forward and tackle the fugitive around the thighs.

Waldron came crashing down to the ground and landed head first, dazing himself momentarily in the process. By the time his head cleared, he found that his wrists had been handcuffed behind his back and that Keedy was holding him down. When he tried to wriggle free, Waldron could hardly move. Keedy stood up and took hold of his collar to haul him upright.

'That's another charge, Horrie,' he said. 'You resisted arrest.'

'Piss off!'

'You're determined to make it difficult for yourself, aren't you?'

Waldron was fuming. 'I swear, on the grave of my mother, that I didn't touch Ablatt that night.'

Keedy held him by his lapel. 'So where *did* those bloodstains come from?'

The question took all of the resistance out of Waldron. His face reddened and his whole body sagged. Shifting his feet uneasily, he turned his face away. After a few moments, he found some vestigial defiance.

'I'm saying nothing,' he said.

Caroline Skene took time to go through her memories of times spent with Ablatt. She wrote down a list of incidents, crossing some decisively out then reinstating the odd one after reflection. In the end, she'd remembered six definite occasions when it occurred to her – if only for the briefest of moments – that there might have been someone watching them. She added a seventh, explaining that it referred to a time when Ablatt had arrived at the house and said that he'd had the feeling that he might have been trailed by someone. Since they could see nobody in the street through the window, they dismissed the notion. Caroline now believed they'd been too hasty in doing so. She handed the list to Marmion who read through it.

'There *is* a pattern here, Mrs Skene,' he observed. 'The incidents all took place either during the evening or on a Sunday. If someone is shadowing you, he can only do it outside working hours.'

'The trouble is that I can't be *certain*, Inspector. Did I actually think that something fishy was going on at the time or am I inventing it?'

'Only you can tell me that.'

'I sensed someone might have been there without actually seeing him.'

'Instinct is usually reliable,' he told her. 'It is in the case of my wife, anyway. When she gets the feeling that something is in the air, she rarely makes mistakes.'

'What do we do now?'

'I suggest that you stay indoors of an evening for a while. You're safe enough moving around during the day. If you do need to venture out one evening, keep your eyes peeled. Note the time and place where you get the idea that you may be under observation.'

'I'll be too afraid to leave the house at all now.'

'That's up to you, Mrs Skene.'

'Do you think I'm in danger?'

'I think that you should exercise caution,' he said, choosing his words with care, 'though I don't believe there's any immediate physical danger. If this person has designs on you, he had the opportunity to strike yesterday evening.'

She was reassured. 'Yes, that's true.'

'There's always the possibility that he may just be an admirer.'

'Then it's a strange way to show his admiration,' she yelled, with a sudden flash of temper that she regretted instantly. 'I'm sorry, Inspector. I didn't mean to shout like that. It's rather got on my nerves, I'm afraid.'

'That's not surprising. Answer me this,' said Marmion. 'When the two of you were out together, was there ever a time when one of you recognised anyone that you knew?'

'I never saw anyone I knew but Cyril did.'

'Oh – when was this?'

'It was just before Christmas. Since it was very cold, we had hats, scarves and gloves on. In fact, I had a scarf across my mouth so nobody could possibly have recognised me. But Cyril was afraid that someone might spot him,' she said. 'At one point, he pulled me into a shop doorway and ducked his head. There was someone he knew, walking on the opposite pavement.'

'Did he say who it was?'

'Oh, yes. It was his boss.'

'Eric Fussell?'

'That was the name. Cyril was so anxious not to be seen by him.'

Keedy was soon regretting the fact that he took the prisoner back to Scotland Yard. Hearing that a suspect had been arrested, Chatfield insisted on being present during the interrogation, wrongly believing that his rank would intimidate Waldron. It did nothing of the kind. The gravedigger simply clammed up and refused to answer any questions. While he sat on one side of a table, the detectives sat on the other. Left alone with him, Keedy felt that he could get him talking. But as long as the superintendent was there, threatening impotently, there was no chance.

'You're not helping yourself, Mr Waldron,' said Chatfield. 'Silence is no means of defence. You're our prime suspect. We know that you had reason to hate Cyril Ablatt. We know that you're given to violent behaviour. And we've now found bloodstains on the trousers you wore that night. It appears that you tried in vain to get rid of them.'

Chatfield would like to have confronted him with the trousers but Marmion had promised to bring them back in the car and had not yet returned. Arms folded and eyes on the ceiling, Waldron continued to ignore everything that was said. The superintendent could simply not get through to him. Relief at last came. There was an urgent message from the commissioner and Chatfield had to make a reluctant exit. Keedy had his chance to chisel away at Waldron. It took him five minutes before he got the first few words out of him.

'Do you admit that it was blood on those trousers?'

'It might be.'

'Either it is or it isn't.'

'Can't remember.'

'You remembered spilling tomato sauce on them earlier.'

'Yes, it does look a bit like blood.'

'We didn't find any tomato sauce in your larder, Horrie.'

Waldron stirred. 'Don't you poke around in there!' he demanded.

'There was hardly any food at all,' said Keedy. 'You live on beer, don't you? That's where you get your meals – at the Weavers Arms.'

'Want to go home.'

'You're not going anywhere until we get to the bottom of this.'

'It wasn't me what bashed his head in.'

'Then who was it?'

'Who cares?'

'Everything points to you, Horrie.'

Retreating back into silence, Waldron folded his arms and closed his eyes. Keedy had to fight back the impulse to hit him. Instead, he delivered a verbal blow that had far more effect.

'Maud Crowther is going to be disappointed in you, isn't she?'

'What you on about?' growled Waldron.

'Imagine what she'll think when she hears that you've been arrested,' said Keedy. 'You won't be her blue-eyed boy anymore, will you?'

'Shut your trap!'

Having found his weak spot, Keedy exploited it mercilessly.

'You'd rather forgotten about her, hadn't you? So had we until we went into that skunk's den where you live. We opened your wardrobe and we made an astounding discovery.'

'Keep away from my things, you bastard!'

'We learnt that there are two Horrie Waldrons,' said Keedy. 'One is that drunken gravedigger who can't always be bothered to shave in the morning and who's too quick to throw his weight about. The other one is a man who actually washes and takes pains to look nice for his lady friend, even to the extent of wearing a suit. Is that what you did on the night that Cyril Ablatt died? You went off to see Mrs Crowther in your Sunday best, then you put on your old clothes and committed murder.'

'That's a lie!' howled Waldron, smacking the table.

'How did the bloodstains get on your trousers?'

'I told you to shut up.'

'Perhaps we should ask Stan Crowther. He might have an idea.' Keedy prodded him even harder. 'I daresay he'd be interested to hear that his mother has a secret admirer. What are your chances of getting served in his pub when he knows the truth about the pair of you?'

'I'll kill you!' roared Waldron, diving over the table.

Keedy was knocked to the floor by the force of the impact but he recovered quickly and grappled with his attacker. The sound of commotion brought two uniformed constables to the room. When they came in, they saw that Keedy was now astride his attacker, subduing him with a relay of punches. Turning him over, he snapped the handcuffs back on his wrists then signalled to the newcomers. They hoisted Waldron to his feet and dumped him back in his chair, standing either side of him with a restraining hand on his shoulder. Keedy got up calmly, straightened his coat, picked up his overturned chair and set it down before sitting in it.

He then gave the prisoner his most radiant smile.

'Now that I've loosened your tongue,' he said, 'we'll start again.'

CHAPTER EIGHTEEN

As he delivered bread on his daily round, Gordon Leach contemplated a grim future. Any decision that he made involved substantial loss. There was no escape from it. If he sided with Ruby Cosgrove, he would lose his two closest friends and for ever be despised by them. Yet if he stood shoulder to shoulder with Mansel Price and Fred Hambridge, he risked losing his fiancée. There would also be a loss of liberty. The government's position was unequivocal. Those who defied the call to arms would be sent to prison. It was conceivable that Hambridge's long association with the Quakers might be accepted as a legitimate excuse but it wasn't one that Leach could offer. He would be incarcerated in a military detention centre such as Wandsworth and be subjected to a punitive regime. It was a bleak prospect.

He reminded himself of the reassuring words that Cyril Ablatt had often used. They would not be common criminals. They would be prisoners of conscience, martyrs to a just cause and an inspiration to others. Leach was young, fit and able to withstand the rigours of imprisonment. What he did not know was whether Ruby would be waiting for him when he was released. If she were, he could cope with anything. If not, his time behind bars would be continuous torture. His conscience might be salved but his hopes of a happy marriage would be dashed. A life without Ruby, he felt, was quite meaningless.

Unable to make up his mind, he tried to recall the days when he and his three friends had their regular meetings and committed themselves to an agreed cause of action. It had all seemed so clear then. Though she had misgivings, Ruby had supported his decision. The right path had been chosen. Ablatt's death had introduced an element of panic into the situation. Leach had been convinced that he was also in jeopardy. A second brutal attack had intensified his fears but at least it had brought Ruby back to him. Her love, however, might be conditional on his accepting her father's advice about joining a non-combatant corps. How could he keep her without losing the respect of his two friends?

When he'd had problems in the past, he'd always been able to turn to Ablatt, whose clarity of thought was a godsend to Leach. Since he could no longer rely on him, he decided to call on Ablatt's father instead to see if he could draw strength from another source. After completing his round, therefore, he drove to the cobbler's shop and pulled the horse to a halt outside. He could see Gerald Ablatt through the window, bent over a last as he mended a shoe. Leach let himself into the little shop and was met by a strong aroma of leather and polish.

'Good morning, Mr Ablatt,' he said.

'Oh hello, Gordon,' said the cobbler, looking up.

'I saw that the shop was open when I drove past yesterday.'

'Yes, it's business as usual.'

'How are you?'

Ablatt's head rocked from side to side. 'I'm as well as can be expected,' he said. 'Everybody has been very kind. Cyril's aunt spent a lot of time with me, then my cousin, Mrs Skene, popped in yesterday. I'm never alone.'

'That's good.'

'What about you?'

'Oh,' said Leach, 'I'm all right, I suppose. Well, no,' he corrected, 'to be honest with you, I'm not. I don't really know what to do. Cyril would have guided me in the right direction. Without him, I'm a bit lost.'

'I feel the same,' said Ablatt with a wan smile. 'What's the trouble?'

'I can't bother you with my problems, Mr Ablatt.'

'But I'd like to help. Pretend that I'm Cyril.'

The cobbler was so calm, friendly and steadfast that Leach was persuaded to confide in him. He explained the quandary he was in and how he could see no compromise that would satisfy all parties. Ablatt listened to arguments that his son had put to him many times and he felt a nostalgic glow.

'Well,' he said when Leach had finished his recital, 'we both know what Cyril would have told you. He'd have said you must be true to your conscience. Nothing could be simpler than that.'

'What if I lose Ruby?'

'I think she's more likely to admire you for your principles.'

Leach was unsure about that but he felt oddly comforted by the visit. His difficulties paled beside those of Gerald Ablatt, who, having lost his son in a foul murder, would have to endure an inquest and a family funeral before going back to live alone in an empty house. Leach thought about the slogans there.

'I'm glad they caught the man who painted those words on your wall.'

'Yes – so am I, Gordon.'

'It was a rotten thing to do. At least you know he won't be back.'

'*He* might not be,' said Ablatt, 'but somebody else came in the night with a paintbrush. I couldn't believe my eyes when I saw what he'd done.'

Leach was aghast. 'Was someone else mocking Cyril?'

'Oh, no, it was nothing like that. He did us a favour. The whole wall had been painted white and those cruel words have disappeared. There are some good people here,' said Ablatt, thankfully. 'I'm sorry I had to lose Cyril to find that out.'

Harvey Marmion returned to Scotland Yard to hear about the arrest and questioning of Horrie Waldron. He, in turn, told Joe Keedy about his visit to Lambeth to see Caroline Skene. They were both keenly aware that they possessed information relating to the murder that they hadn't passed on to the superintendent. Chatfield knew nothing of Caroline's existence and the relationship between Waldron and Maud Crowther had also been kept from him. The detectives hoped that they could solve the crime without having to reveal everything to their superior. Should he find out that they'd deceived him, they'd be hauled up before the commissioner.

'It's a chance we have to take,' argued Marmion. 'I gave my word to Mrs Skene that her friendship with Ablatt would not become common knowledge.'

'And I did the same to Mrs Crowther,' said Keedy, seriously. 'Though I'd never break that trust, I did pretend to Waldron that I was going to, if only to provoke him. He went berserk. I charged him with resisting arrest and assaulting a police officer. That gives us enough reason to hold him in custody while we dig deeper.'

'I'd like to have a go at him myself.'

'He's not very cooperative, Harv.'

'The Waldrons of this world never are.' He winked at Keedy. 'I'll appeal to his finer instincts.'

'Horrie doesn't have any.'

'Mrs Crowther obviously thinks that he does. I fancy that another visit to her might pay dividends, Joe. Acquaint her with the plight that her admirer is in.'

'She'll disown the old bugger on the spot.'

'Only if she thinks he's guilty of murder, and the evidence for that is far from conclusive. I've brought the trousers back with me, by the way. There's no doubt in my mind that they're spattered with blood – but did it get there during the murder of Cyril Ablatt?'

'It's possible. Chat, of course, thinks it's highly probable.'

'He's eager to get the case wrapped up so that the press will say more nice things about him. But he's enough of a detective to know that we need more evidence or – praise God that this happens – a confession out of Waldron.'

Keedy chuckled. 'You're more likely to get a volcanic eruption.'

'I'll remember to wear a tin hat.' Marmion seemed to drift off into a world of his own for a few minutes. When he emerged from his daydream, he was surprised that Keedy was there. 'Off you go, then. Talk to Mrs Crowther first, then call at the pub. Her son told you that Waldron had returned there that evening with the same clothes he had on when he left. Ask him if he noticed any bloodstains on the trousers.'

'What will you be doing?'

Marmion adopted a fighting pose. 'I'll be going three rounds with Horrie Waldron,' he said, cheerfully. 'Want to place a bet on the outcome?'

Alice Marmion pointed out that it was not too late to change her mind but Vera Dowling was adamant. She didn't wish to go to tea at Hannah Billington's house that afternoon, though she was looking forward to hearing every last detail about the visit when her friend came back. After loading the lorry, they were having a brief rest. Alice was excited at the thought of the visit to a grand home. It would be a one-sided treat. Alice would never dream of inviting Hannah to tea at her own house and especially not at her digs. She'd be too embarrassed to show the older woman the place where she lived. Hannah had seen it from the outside when she dropped Alice off there but she had no idea how poor the accommodation was. Vera, curiously enough, had a better room in a larger house and she'd pressed her friend to join her there, but it was an offer that Alice had politely turned down. Had she been sharing accommodation with Vera Dowling, there was no way that Keedy would have been able to make contact with her the previous night. Indeed, the evolving friendship with him would have been virtually impossible.

'I told Mummy about your idea,' said Vera.

'What idea?'

'That plan of yours to go abroad.'

'Hey, hold on a minute,' said Alice. 'Nothing's been decided. It was only a possibility that I was considering.'

'I mentioned it in my letter to Mummy. She'd die rather than let me do anything as adventurous as that. And, yes,' she went on, anticipating her friend's comment, 'I know that I'm supposed to be old enough to make up my own mind, but I'd never defy my parents. What about you, Alice?'

'If it meant that much to me, then I'd go – whatever the protests at home.'

'You've made up your mind, haven't you?'

'No, I haven't, Vera. At the moment, there are too many things keeping me here. You're one of them,' said Alice, bringing a smile to her friend's face. 'And there are . . . other reasons why I'm not ready to charge off across the Channel just yet.'

Vera's eyes sparkled with interest. 'What are those other reasons?'

'They're private.'

'Can't you even give me a hint?'

'No,' said Alice, firmly, 'because it would be in your next letter to your mother. That means it would get passed on to *my* mother, who'd be very upset that she had to hear things about me second hand.'

'I never thought of it like that.'

'Please bear it in mind.' She clambered into the lorry and sat behind the driving wheel. Vera got in beside her. 'I'll ask you one more time,' said Alice. 'Are you *sure* you wouldn't like afternoon tea in a mansion?'

'No, no, no,' replied her friend. 'I'd be like a fish out of water.'

Marmion took him by surprise. Because Waldron was used to being interviewed in a room at a police station, the inspector chose to speak to him in the cell where he was being held. It was cramped, cold and austere. To show that he was not afraid of the prisoner, Marmion had the door locked behind him. He studied the gravedigger for some time before speaking.

'I thought we'd have a little chat,' he began.

'I've said all I'm saying to those other two stupid fools.'

'Superintendent Chatfield is not stupid, I can assure you, and neither is Sergeant Keedy. They've had years of experience of questioning suspects, and the kind of mindless abuse that comes out of your mouth just washes off them. For the record, they both believe that you're a guilty man.'

'I done nothing!' wailed Waldron.

'Making a run for it at the cemetery and trying to kill the sergeant – I wouldn't call that nothing.'

'The sergeant deserved it.'

'Yet you came off worst,' said Marmion, looking at the bruises on his face. 'There's not a scratch on him. You picked the wrong man to take on.'

'I didn't murder *anybody*,' insisted Waldron.

'Then how did that blood get on your trousers?'

'Who knows? I pick up all sorts of things in my job.'

'You seemed very anxious to wash those stains off.'

'They're my working trousers.'

'Then why didn't you wear them to work today?'

Waldron refused to answer. Seated on the edge of the narrow bed, he turned his back on his visitor. Marmion took a step forward and tapped him on the shoulder.

'What's his name?' he asked.

'Who are you on about?'

'You're not clever enough to do this on your own, are you? Someone put you up to it. He probably paid you. Who is he, Mr Waldron?'

'I haven't a clue what you're talking about.'

'So you were acting on you own? Is that it?'

Waldron spun round to face him. 'Stop trying to put words into my mouth.'

'Either you have an accomplice or you did it alone.'

'I didn't do anything!'

'Keep your voice down.'

'Then don't accuse me.'

'Where did that blood come from?'

Waldron was contemptuous. 'I couldn't care less.'

'How much were you paid to kill Cyril Ablatt?'

'Nothing.'

'Why did you take your spade home with you that evening?'

Waldron recoiled as if from a blow. Marmion had finally asked a question that shook him. Unable to find an answer, the gravedigger settled for a hurt silence. The inspector changed his tack. His tone was less harsh.

'I'm not sure that I agree with my colleagues,' he said, thoughtfully. 'I don't think that you did kill Cyril Ablatt.'

'Thank God *somebody* believes me!'

'You may have been involved but you didn't actually batter him. To tell you the truth, Mr Waldron, I don't think you'd have the nerve to do that.' Angered by the remark, Waldron was on his feet immediately, glowering at Marmion. 'So what did you do, I wonder? Did you help to transport the body? Did you act as a lookout while someone else dumped it in that lane? Or did you simply tell your accomplice where and how he could find his victim that night?'

'You're making all this up!' sneered Waldron.

'I'm just trying to work out if there's something you're actually capable of, you see; something simple you could be paid to do. No matter how minor it might be, of course, it would make you an accessory and you know what the penalty would be.'

Waldron attempted bravado. 'You don't scare me, Inspector.'

'I'll leave it to the public executioner to do that.'

The gravedigger stumbled slightly as if he'd just been hit by something. His bluster vanished. He was in police custody and they were determined to make him face serious charges. There'd be no fine to pay this time, nor even a short sentence. The shadow of the noose had suddenly fallen upon him.

'I want to be alone,' he said, sitting down again.

'Very well,' said Marmion, 'but I'll be back.'

'Don't hurry. I got thinking to do.'

Maud Crowther went from one extreme to another. When she found the flowers on her doorstep, she was touched. The bouquet was both an apology and a romantic gesture. Having put them in a vase, she kept looking at them every time she came into the living room. She'd decided that she'd been too hard on Waldron. Perhaps he deserved a second chance, after all. Joe Keedy then arrived at the house. Invited in, he told her that the man who had tried to woo her with a bunch of flowers was now in police custody and was suspected of having some involvement in the murder of Cyril Ablatt. In the short term, he was being detained on lesser charges. If she was expecting to see him, she would be disappointed.

Her revived affection for Waldron changed in a flash to hatred. He'd promised her that he'd put his criminal past behind him. Thanks to her, he'd solemnly sworn, he'd turned over a new leaf. For a time, Maud had believed him but Keedy's visit splintered her illusions. When she gazed at the flowers now, it was not with a fond smile. Seen in the cold light of reality, they looked as if they'd been stolen from a grave in the cemetery. They'd be much more appropriate there. Waldron had cheated her. His romantic gesture was nothing more than an act of theft. She grabbed the flowers, yanked them out of the vase and thrust them at Keedy.

'Give these back to him,' she said, tartly, 'and tell him that I never want to lay eyes on that ugly face of his.'

'I need to ask you about some bloodstains on his trousers, Mrs Crowther.'

One glance at her told Keedy that the question was redundant. Horrie Waldron was no longer part of her life and she refused to have anything more to do with him. It was pointless to stay. Keedy thought it unlikely that she'd know anything about the bloodstains. Waldron had been compelled to wear a suit whenever he called on her. She set standards. He lived up to them for a while. But it was all over. Maud Crowther didn't wish to be linked with a criminal in any way. Their romance had crumbled into oblivion. How it had actually begun in the first place, Keedy could only guess. It still seemed bizarre to him. As he left the house, he took away more than a bunch of dripping flowers.

He knew for certain that Horrie Waldron had no claim whatsoever on Maud now. It was something he could use to apply pressure on the prisoner.

From her point of view, Keedy saw, there was an element of relief in the decisive break from Waldron. Their secret meetings would no longer be in danger of discovery. While Maud would regret ever getting involved with him, she would have the satisfaction of knowing that they'd never be caught together now. It prompted Keedy to think of his friendship with Alice Marmion. That, too, was fraught with danger. If it ever came to light, her father would be deeply hurt. It might severely damage Keedy's professional relationship with him. Yet that situation could not continue indefinitely. He and Alice would reach a point where they either decided to go their separate ways or were ready to make a proper commitment to each other. If the latter were the case, they would have to be honest with her parents.

Keedy reflected on his personal problems all the way to the Weavers Arms. It was not yet open for business but Stan Crowther was outside on the pavement, supervising the men who were unloading a delivery of beer from their dray. The landlord gave Keedy a cheerful welcome and took him inside the pub.

'Before you arrest me for selling watered beer,' he said with a grin, 'I'm in the same boat as every other publican. It's a wartime necessity.'

'Yes,' said Keedy, 'it's one more reason to hate the Germans.'

'Have you found out who the killer is yet?'

'No, but we've made an arrest. Horrie Waldron is in custody.'

Crowther gasped. 'You're not charging *him* with the murder, are you?'

'He's being held on lesser charges at the moment. Waldron was arrested because we found bloodstains on his trousers that we believe he was wearing on the night of the murder. In fact,' said Keedy, 'that's what I wanted to ask you about. You told me that Waldron was away for a couple of hours that night and that he came back looking much cleaner than usual.'

'Ha! That wouldn't be difficult.'

'Did you, by any chance, notice any blood on him?'

'The pub was full, Sergeant. I didn't look at Horrie's trousers.'

'But he was wearing the same clothes he had on when he left?'

'Oh, yes,' replied Crowther. 'It's more or less all he has. I don't think he's got a tailor in Savile Row somehow.' His chortle was replaced by a frown. 'But I don't reckon that he's your killer, I really don't.'

'Can you suggest any other way he got that blood on his trousers?'

An innocent question brought a look of guilt into Crowther's eyes. He took a step backwards and licked his lips before mumbling an answer.

'No,' he said, 'I can't.'

Claude Chatfield was interested to hear of the latest interview with Waldron but disappointed that it had yielded no definite result. He was desperate to have some positive news to release to the press. Marmion cautioned against an announcement that they had a murder suspect in custody. They needed much more proof that Waldron was involved in some way. Keedy had been sent off in search of it.

'We need a breakthrough,' said Chatfield, impatiently.

'It's bound to come in due course, Superintendent.'

'I still think there's a connection between the two crimes. I know that you don't believe that, but there's a similarity that can't be ignored.'

'I beg to differ,' said Marmion. 'And even if they *are* linked, Waldron is certainly not a common factor. He may be implicated in the murder but he has no reason to attack Father Howells. I doubt if Waldron's ever been inside St Leonard's church. Besides,' he continued, 'witnesses who saw the attacker run away from that lane say that he was moving at some speed. That rules out our gravedigger. He's not fast enough. When he tried to do with the visit to Hannah Billington's house, she pressed for details. Alice described the house and the delicious tea with mingled awe and gratitude. What she didn't even touch on was the invitation she'd been given in the main bedroom. The euphoria she felt in the wake of her conversation with Joe Keedy had expunged it from her mind. When Hannah came across to them, therefore, Alice was not in the least embarrassed.

'I was just telling Vera what a wonderful time I had yesterday,' she said. 'Thank you once again.'

'It was a pleasure to have you there,' returned Hannah. 'We spend so much of our time in these uniforms that it's good to remind ourselves now and again that we're still very feminine. Don't you agree, Vera?'

'Yes, yes, I do,' replied Vera, nervously.

'We mustn't let this war turn us into honorary men. That will never do.'

She gave them a farewell nod and walked away. Alice was able to relax. It was all over. Whatever had happened between them at the house was forgotten. She wouldn't be invited again and she was happy about that.

Alice banged the side of the lorry. 'Come on, Vera,' she said, making her friend jump in alarm. 'We've got work to do. Let's go.'

Caroline Skene was sorely tempted. When she saw her husband putting on his coat to go off to the social club, she had an urge to beg him to stay in for once so that she wouldn't be left alone. It was an impulse she quickly mastered. To keep him there, she would have had to explain why and she couldn't do that. Accordingly, she let him put on his cap, adjust it slightly in the mirror, then give her his usual peck on the cheek before he left the house. The moment the door closed behind him, the whole place felt cold, undefended and vulnerable. Marmion had promised to come but she sensed that he was not there yet. Caroline ran straight upstairs to the front bedroom and looked out through a chink in the curtains. She was able to watch her husband stroll along the pavement until he was swallowed by the darkness. The street looked completely empty but she was convinced that her stalker was there. Her heart pounded and a film of perspiration appeared on her brow. The man was out there and she was utterly alone.

For several minutes, she was paralysed. She stood there like a statue, unable to move or to think clearly. When she did regain some control over her limbs, she went to the cupboard where she kept a bottle of whisky hidden behind a pile of clothing. There was a small glass in there as well. Pouring herself a tot, she replaced the bottle and sat on the edge of the bed to sip the whisky. Sharp and reviving, it gave her a temporary courage. She told herself that she was not in danger. The front and back doors of the house were locked. If necessary, she could lock herself into the bedroom as well. Nobody could get in. The stalker would surely tire of standing out there in the cold before too long. She simply had to hold her nerve. A second sip of whisky gave her added strength. Caroline felt that she could, after all, cope with the situation.

A loud noise from downstairs shattered her confidence. What had she heard and was it any kind of threat to her? Could it be that her husband had returned? She went out onto the landing and called his name. There was no answer and the house still felt empty. Draining the glass, she left it on the dressing table and was emboldened enough to go downstairs. It was her home. She ought to feel safe. The living room was empty and there was nobody in the front room. Caroline then went into the kitchen and was startled to see that the door had been forced open. As she moved forward, someone who'd been flattened against the wall came up behind her and put an arm around her throat and a hand over her mouth.

'Do as you're told,' warned a voice. 'I don't want to hurt you.'

Caroline almost fainted. He'd come for her at last.

* * *

Harvey Marmion asked the driver to pull up around the corner. He and Joe Keedy then got out and split up so that they could enter from either end of the street where the Skene house was located. Someone was loitering immediately opposite it. When Marmion got closer, he saw that a man had simply been waiting while his dog relieved itself against the wheel of a car. The two of them moved off. Having come into the street at the opposite end, Keedy beckoned the inspector over to look at a horse and cart that stood in the shadows. Marmion let his torch play on the painted board at the rear of the vehicle. He read out the bold lettering.

'Jack Dalley. Blacksmith. Bethnal Green.'

They were in the main bedroom now. Caroline was too terrified either to speak or move. She sat perched on the edge of the bed and his eyes ran hungrily over her.

'I first saw you at Nora's wedding,' he explained. 'You hardly noticed me but I never let you out of my sight. I found out everything I could about you and I started to watch. I know you better than your husband does, Caroline,' he said with a snigger. 'I saw what you did when his back was turned. You let Cyril Ablatt in one night and I watched the light come on in this bedroom. Why *him*?' he cried. 'Why bother with a mere boy when you could have had me? Well, no matter. You're mine at last now. I've lived with a corpse for too long. I need a real woman.'

As he touched her shoulder, she recoiled. 'Leave me alone – *please.*'

'I've earned you,' he said with a grin, 'and you can't refuse me, can you? If you do, I'll tell your husband what you got up to with Ablatt. Then his father will know and so will everyone else in the family. *Everyone* will know what Caroline Skene does when she's on heat like a bitch.' Grabbing her by the hair, he stole a long, guzzled kiss. She turned away in disgust. 'You'll have to get used to that, my love. You'll be seeing a lot

345

of me on your husband's club nights. I followed him there so I know where he goes and how long he's away. That gives us plenty of time.'

He loomed over her and began to take off his coat. She was horrified.

'It was you, wasn't it?' she asked, quailing. 'You killed Cyril.'

'Yes, I did,' he boasted. 'I wasn't having him touching you anymore. It was my turn. I saw you walk to the corner with him that night. You didn't even know I was there, sitting on the cart, did you? I had my chance and I took it. I drove round to the bus stop where he was standing and pretended that I had to take the cart to Jack's house in Shoreditch. Ablatt recognised me from the forge,' he went on. 'When I offered him a lift, he couldn't get on the cart quick enough. All that I had to do was to drive into a dark corner and murder the little bastard.' She let out a scream. 'I hid the body under some sacking and took it to Shoreditch at night.' As she shrank back in disgust, he tried to justify it. 'I did it for *you*, Caroline,' he insisted. 'Don't you understand? I did it for you and me.'

Before she could stop him, he pushed her back on the bed and climbed on top of her. She was pinned down helplessly and his hands were all over her. Because he was thrusting his tongue into her mouth, she couldn't even cry for help. When he lifted her skirt up to her waist, she felt as if she was about to die.

Then came the knock on the door.

Marmion knew that she was in the house and wondered why she didn't answer his knock. When he looked upwards, he saw the curtains in the front bedroom twitch. He knocked for the second time but he could still hear nobody coming. As he looked through the letter box, he was able to see into the kitchen. The sight of the open door galvanised him into action. After signalling to Keedy, he ran down the side entry of the house and reached the kitchen door, pausing only long enough to note that it had been forced open. Rushing into the house, he looked up the stairs.

'Are you up there, Mrs Skene?' he asked.

Though there was no reply, he knew that she was there. Keeping the torch in his hand to use as a weapon, he thundered up the stairs and went into the main bedroom. Caroline was spreadeagled on the bed with her clothes dishevelled. Before he could ask her what had happened, Marmion was hit from behind by a jemmy. He collapsed on to the carpet.

Joe Keedy was waiting by the cart. The front door of the house was flung open and a figure came hurtling out. When he saw someone standing beside the cart, Percy Fry tried to scare him away by brandishing the jemmy but the man held his ground. It was a different encounter this time. Unlike the inspector, Keedy was not distracted by a woman on a bed. Instead of having his back to Fry, he was facing him. He crouched down in readiness to fight. Fry got close enough to recognise him as one of the detectives who'd called at the forge. Keedy couldn't be frightened away. It was Fry who began to wilt. They were only yards apart now. Keedy held out a hand as if to take the weapon. Fry flew into a panic. He hurled the jemmy at Keedy but the latter ducked and it whistled harmlessly over his head.

Fry tried to run away but it was a race he was never going to win. He managed the best part of thirty yards before his legs began to hurt and his lungs seemed on the point of bursting. Every inch of the way, Keedy was gaining on him. As his quarry started to slow down, he put in a spurt that brought him close enough to jump on the man's back. Fry staggered on for a few more yards but the extra burden was too much for him. He crashed to the ground and grazed his forehead in the fall. But he was far from finished. Fry was a strong man. Rolling over, he managed to dislodge Keedy with a fearsome punch. The sergeant replied with punches of his own but they seemed to have little effect. Fry had been toughened by years of working in a forge. When he caught Keedy with a hook, it made his head ring.

Taking advantage of the momentary lull, Fry attempted to get up and run off again but Keedy recovered instantly. He stuck out a leg and tripped his adversary up, diving on top of him and using his weight to pin him face down on the pavement. When Fry continued to buck, squirm, kick and turn the air blue with expletives, Keedy brought the fight to an end, holding the man's head in both hands and banging it on the hard stone until Fry's body lost all resistance. Handcuffs were speedily fixed to the prisoner's wrists, then Keedy stood up and turned him over. Percy Fry lay twitching on the ground.

Marmion was still groggy as he came up behind them. He'd wrapped a towel around his head to stem the flow of blood. In the dark, it looked like a turban.

'Are you going to arrest him, Joe?' he asked. 'Or shall I?'

They'd decided that the announcement had to be made when they were all together. It was therefore several days before their opportunity came. Marmion and Keedy, meanwhile, were praised in the press and Superintendent Chatfield got his share of reflected glory. Two heinous crimes had been solved in less than twenty-four hours. It was finally over. Events in the war returned to dominate the headlines. The inquest into the death of Cyril Ablatt came and went. The funeral took place, organised by Caroline Skene, whose name had been kept out of any of the reports of the case. Now in custody, Percy Fry would never admit that the murder arose out of his obsession for an attractive woman. All that he owned up to was killing someone he hated for being a conscientious objector. That was enough to satisfy the law.

It was over a meal at the Marmion house that Alice and Keedy finally had their chance. Ellen had spotted the signs in her daughter. Alice was vivacious, talkative and laughing too loud at the amiable banter. When there was a natural pause, she felt her mother's hand on her arm.

'I have the feeling that you have something to tell us,' said Ellen.

Alice started. 'Do you, Mummy?'

'Is it that promotion you hinted at or have you decided to go abroad?'

'I hope it's not that job over there as a dispatch rider,' said Marmion. 'There's plenty of valuable work to be done here, Alice.'

'I won't be going abroad, Daddy. I can guarantee that.'

'That's a load off my mind.'

'No,' Alice went on, 'it's nothing to do with the WEC – though that will be affected before too long. The thing is . . .'

As her daughter searched for words, Ellen stepped in excitedly.

'I was right, wasn't I?' she asked.

'Yes, Mummy, you were.'

'So there is someone, after all.'

Alice nodded then glanced across at Keedy. Her parents gave a contrasting response. Ellen was so thrilled that she kissed Alice on the cheek and laughed approvingly. Marmion, on the other hand, turned to stare in dismay at Keedy. He'd been deceived by the person he valued as his closest friend. He realised now why Alice had been unable to spend New Year's Eve with her parents. She'd been with Keedy instead. Fond as he was of the sergeant, Marmion knew only to well of his reputation as a ladies' man. Over the years, he'd seen girlfriends come and go. It distressed him to think that his own daughter would follow in their footsteps.

'How long has this been going on?' he asked, curtly.

'Sound a bit more pleased, Harvey,' said his wife.

'I want to know how long you've both pulled the wool over our eyes.'

'It wasn't like that, Daddy,' argued Alice.

'Then what was it like?'

Keedy spoke up. 'The answer to your question is that it's been going on long enough for Alice and me to make up our minds. I can't blame you for thinking that this is just another case of Joe Keedy having fun with a new girlfriend. It's not like that at all, Harv,' he stressed. 'That life is behind me now and I'm glad. We're serious about this. Alice and I plan to get engaged.' The news produced a whoop of joy from Ellen and a deepening frown from her husband. 'You're the first to know.'

'It's kind of you to let us in on the secret,' said Marmion, dryly.

Ellen nudged him. 'Don't be like that.'

'How am I supposed to be?'

'I think you're forgetting something,' said Alice, smarting at his grumpiness. 'You and Mummy used to meet in secret for the best part of a year before you dared to tell her parents. They didn't like you at all at first.'

'It's true,' said Ellen. 'My father thought he was unworthy of me.'

'There you are, Harv,' said Keedy, brightly. 'You must have felt the way that I'm feeling now. We shared the same uncomfortable experience.'

'I never worked alongside Ellen's father,' said Marmion, pointedly. 'I didn't have to lie to him over a long period.'

'I didn't lie to you. I'm like Father Howells when you first met him. I just didn't tell you the truth. And, yes, there *is* a distinction between the two.'

Ellen was exasperated. 'This is supposed to be a happy occasion,' she complained. 'We've just heard that Joe is going to become one of the family. Isn't that wonderful news, Harvey? He's not threatening to run away with Alice. He wants to marry her.' She nudged him harder. 'Cheer up, will you? What sort of a father-in-law are you going to be?'

'You're right, love,' said Marmion, contriving a half-smile. 'In some ways, it is good news and I wish you both well. I warn you now, Joe, that I'll be a terrible father-in-law.' They all laughed. 'As for what happens between us at work,' he added, 'well, that's a different matter altogether.'

He leant across to kiss his daughter then shook Keedy's hand warmly.

'And there was me,' said Ellen, 'praying that Alice would never make the mistake of marrying a policeman.'

'I'm going to do more than just marry one,' declared Alice, who'd been saving up another surprise for her parents. 'I've decided to leave the WEC in the near future. I'm going to join the Women's Police Service.' She saw the distress on her father's face. 'You'd better get used to the idea, Daddy. We're going to be working together.'